Books by Lisa T. Bergren

THE SUGAR BARON'S DAUGHTERS

Keturah

Verity

Selah

THE RIVER OF TIME

Waterfall

Cascade

Torrent

Bourne & Tributary

Deluge

THE HOMEWARD

Breathe

Sing

Claim

THE GRAND TOUR

Glamorous Illusions

Grave Consequences

Glittering Promises

The Sugar Baron's Daughters · THREE

SELAH

LISA T. BERGREN

BETHANYHOUSE
a division of Baker Publishing Group
Minneapolis, Minnesota

Published by Bethany House Publishers
11400 Hampshire Avenue South
Bloomington, Minnesota 55438
www.bethanyhouse.com

Bethany House Publishers is a division of
Baker Publishing Group, Grand Rapids, Michigan

Printed in the United States of America

Library of Congress Cataloging-in-Publication Data
Names: Bergren, Lisa Tawn, author.
Title: Selah / Lisa T. Bergren.
Description: Minneapolis, Minnesota : Bethany House, a division of Baker
    Publishing Group, [2020] | Series: The sugar baron's daughters ; 3
Identifiers: LCCN 2019040909 | ISBN 9780764230264 (trade paperback) | ISBN
    9780764235528 (cloth) | ISBN 9781493422777 (ebook)
Subjects: GSAFD: Christian fiction. | Love stories.
Classification: LCC PS3552.E71938 S45 2020 | DDC 813/.54—dc23
LC record available at https://lccn.loc.gov/2019040909

Scripture quotations are from the King James Version of the Bible.

This is a work of historical reconstruction; the appearances of certain historical figures are therefore inevitable. All other characters, however, are products of the author's imagination, and any resemblance to actual persons, living or dead, is coincidental.

Cover design by Paul Higdon
Cover photography by Mike Habermann Photography, LLC

Author is represented by The Steve Laube Agency.

20 21 22 23 24 25 26   7 6 5 4 3 2 1

CHAPTER ONE

It was the falcon's piercing cry that first alerted Selah. She shielded her eyes against the bright, tropical morning sun and followed the broad wingspan of the beautiful bird circling above.

"Abraham!" she cried, lifting her skirts and scurrying down the front stairs of the house and toward the stables. "*Abraham!*"

The child appeared in the doorway, eyes wide with alarm.

"Quickly!" she said, shooing him back inward. "Grab your leather gauntlet! 'Tis Brutus above our heads!"

"Brutus?" he said as if not quite understanding. They hadn't seen the bird for months, given that his mistress—Verity—had been away to the American colonies.

"Yes, yes," she hissed, turning his slim shoulders to head deeper into the stables while glancing around to make certain no one else had heard them. "Where is your gauntlet?" she whispered.

"Right here, miss," he said, finally moving to the side wall, where many reins, halters, and other stable tools hung on pegs. He grabbed the glove and then turned to a small barrel of salted fish and took one in his other hand.

"Come quickly!" she said, pulling him outward, half panicked

5

they had taken too long. She knew that Verity had trained Brutus to come to Abraham. Was he still hovering overhead?

With relief, she caught sight of the bird, still circling above them. In the center of the clearing before the house, Abe lifted his arm upward and called to him.

"Selah?" Keturah called from the porch, hoisting her cherubic toddler, Madeleine, to her hip. "What is it?"

"I think 'tis *Brutus*!" she hissed, gesticulating to indicate they needed to keep quiet. She knew her own excited cries for Abraham must have alarmed her sister. Even now, Mitilda followed her mistress out, concerned as well.

The bird, seeming to sense his reward was in hand, swiftly came nearer, his head darting back and forth as he perused the landing field. Seemingly assured, he took one final loop before dropping to Abe's arm, his great wings fluttering until he settled on his human perch.

"It *is* Brutus," Keturah breathed, drawing closer. "From where did he come?" she asked, seeking the waters, probably for signs of her brother-in-law's ship, the *Inverness*. But there were only a couple of ketches—small vessels heading to St. Kitts.

Selah felt her silent disappointment as well as her relief. After so many months apart, both sisters were keen to see Verity but knew if Angus Shubert got wind that Ian McKintrick lingered in nearby waters, Shubert would rouse the British troops to pursue him. Ian's attack on him—justified or not—had resulted in a warrant for his arrest. Only his flight to America had saved him . . . and he had taken Verity with him as his bride.

"Look, Miss Selah," Abe said, gesturing to a scrap of parchment strapped to the falcon's leg with a leather band. Brutus had already swallowed the salt fish whole and nosed about as if hoping Abraham carried another. The boy placated the bird by stroking his chest and cooing lowly to him, much like Verity had often done.

Selah untied the strap and slipped the tiny scroll from his leg. Keturah turned Madeleine in her arms so she could see the falcon, and the pretty, round-faced babe stared in wide-eyed fascination. "What is it? What does it say?"

"Patience, Sissy," Selah said, feeling none of it herself. With trembling fingers, she unwound the band of parchment and whispered the words written in her sister's hand. "We linger in the harbor we discovered a summer past," she read. "Come to us this afternoon if you can. Bring sugar. We have supplies."

Keturah's face became beatific. Not only their sister but supplies as well? With the war in the American colonies gaining momentum, Nevis's supply chain had come to a near halt. Across the island, many plantation owners had significantly cut rations for the slaves. Few slaves had much to lose; already the sisters had seen far too many in Charlestown who had become alarmingly thin. Even the Double T struggled to feed her own.

"You must not tell a soul," Selah said to Abraham and Mitilda. "Take Brutus quickly into the stables, Abe," she said. "Ket and I shall compose a message for him to take back to Verity."

"Yes'm." Abraham immediately turned to do as she bid.

Selah reached out to his mother and squeezed her hand. "She's nearby, Mitilda. We shall see her before the day is out."

"God be praised, Miss Selah!" Mitilda shook her head in wonderment. "God be praised."

Together they hurried into the house to prepare. "Do you think that Gray could take us on the ketch this afternoon?" she asked Ket. "Or would it be best for us to go alone?"

"I think he would be most cross if we went alone. Best to inform him, as well as Philip. We need them to obtain the sugar too."

"What shall be our rationale to be about?" Even though they had built a new pier on the southeast edge of the plantation, there were neighbors who would be sure to see them sail—and not to St. Kitts, which was where they generally voyaged.

"A picnic luncheon, I believe," she said with a sly smile. "As well as a brisk hike to stimulate the blood. Mitilda, would you be so kind as to pack us a basket?"

"Right away, Lady Ket," she said, turning to go, clearly as

excited as they were. The prospect of the sisters' reunion, as well as new supplies, gave them all a resurgence of hope in the midst of a month that had slowly chipped away at any sense of optimism. Two weeks ago, Gray had managed to obtain six barrels of cornmeal and two barrels of salted fish at outlandish prices, and they were perilously close to running out again. Given the Covingtons' poor reputation in town, they were oft the last to be given the opportunity to purchase.

Matthew—their freed black overseer and Mitilda's brother—had persuaded the Covingtons to operate the Double T with a progressively emancipated work force, maintaining that the field workers would toil twice as hard if they labored to better their own futures. Jedediah Reed, the young Methodist preacher who had arrived last summer, had concurred. Within a month, their predictions had proven true. Few of the slaves had ever been truly lazy. But with a measure of promise and hope, every man, woman, and child were working at least 10 percent harder than before, and Gray felt the least they could do was provide a decent food supply . . . which was growing more and more difficult.

To date, Gray and Ket employed twenty-nine freed men and women, and had granted permission to nearly seventy others to work toward their emancipation over the next few years. At that point, they would be given the choice either to work the Double T or go elsewhere. Word spread quickly. Nearly every week, one or two freed people arrived at the Double T, having traveled there from other islands after hearing there was honest work and a living wage—as well as kind bosses—for those who could get to Nevis. Given that America was at war, few wished to leave the West Indies, nor could they afford to return to Africa. For many, the Double T seemed a sanctuary. While Gray had a hard time turning anyone away, Selah found it impossible. Over and over she talked her brother-in-law into "just one more."

Their choices had gradually made the Covingtons and Selah pariahs on-island. Not that they had been popular before—hiring a freed black overseer had already cast them under suspicion. Their latest choices made many plantation owners despise them. Not only were they outproducing every other plantation on-island but they did so with a work force like none had ever seen. And the planters did not abide well by change. They feared it—feared that black men or women, finding new power in their freedom, might attempt to take the island by force. Had not Hispaniola and Jamaica already seen attempts at the same?

But Selah felt more secure among her black friends—and increasingly alongside the lanky young preacher, Jedediah—than she had ever felt as she mingled among the planters at their soirees or in town. It had come as some relief to see the invitations to parties and gatherings slowly dwindle, whether due to a lack of hosting supplies or their dwindling popularity.

In the end, she decided brevity was the best choice for her note, in case Brutus was somehow intercepted. "Watch for our impending arrival," she wrote. Then she scurried out of the house and down to the stables. She strapped the note to the falcon's leg. "Now hurry, Abe," she said. "Send him off before anyone else might spot him."

Angus Shubert was often on the neighboring plantation to their south, Cold Spring, having purchased Chandler's Point as part of his vast holdings and merging it with another plantation farther inland. If he glimpsed Brutus, he would know the falcon was Verity's and come nosing about. "Please, Lord," Selah whispered as she walked with Abe to the center of the clearing, "let him be in Charlestown or at home today." His home was in Gingerland, on the other end of the island. But he delighted in provoking the Covingtons and her anytime he had the opportunity. By marrying the widow of the richest planter on-island, Angus had become wealthy overnight, as well as earned a temporary position on council. Few liked the man, but fewer had the courage to stand against him. It was he who had blackballed Gray in town, ensuring that almost all incoming supplies from England were allocated to other planters before him. Only one lone merchant—the kindly Mr. Kirk—had shown mercy and allowed Gray to purchase those last supplies, and the barrels had to be transported to the Double T under cover of darkness.

Together they walked out into the yard. "Back to Miss Verity, Brutus," Abe whispered to the falcon, lifting his arm. "Back to Miss Verity!" he hissed again as the bird began to climb higher in the sky. They watched as the falcon circled twice—almost as if reluctant to go—then headed toward Saba.

Gideon and Primus entered the yard just as Abraham pulled the long leather glove from his arm. "Was that . . . ?" Primus began, looking to the bird, now small in the distance, then to Selah.

She gave a conspiratorial nod. "Keep it to yourselves, my friends," she whispered. "But Ver is near!"

Both of the black men—servants to the sisters their whole lives— grinned. It was good news that Verity was alive, and even better news that the sisters might soon be reunited. But their guardians well understood the danger. "Take close care, Miss Selah, Lady Ket," Gideon intoned.

"We shall," Keturah promised. She turned to Abe. "Go to the fields, Abraham. Fetch Master Gray and Philip. Tell them they are invited to a luncheon aboard the *Hartwick*."

Selah looked up to the two small sails of the ketch they'd named after their childhood manor, urging the trade winds to propel them faster. She and Keturah held hands, each terribly anxious to get to Verity after so long apart. Gray stood at the wheel while Philip manned the ropes. Given the currents and winds on this side of the island, they had to tack back and forth to get to Saba, but they managed to near the tiny harbor an hour after they had embarked.

"There," Keturah breathed, pointing at the *Inverness*, at anchor in the tiny bay. They could see a couple at her starboard edge, surrounded by sailors. "There she is," she said, tears slipping down her cheeks. Selah and Ket embraced as Philip grinned over at them.

"Oh, do hurry, Gray," Selah said, wringing her hands and looking back to her brother-in-law. Settled around him were twenty small casks of sugar. Primus and Gideon had transferred giant hogsheads into the smaller barrels in order to make it less conspicuous as they carried them to the *Inverness*. Fortunately, the path to the pier, as well as the tiny harbor itself, was largely surrounded by a strip of jungle that delineated the Double T from Cold Spring. And once the diminutive casks were settled into the boat, they were not visible over the edge; therefore any neighbor observing them sail off would only see the luncheon basket sitting on the raised area near the mast—the rest of the boat appearing empty.

While they did not head to St. Kitts, neither did they go to Statia, an island frequented by the British's hated French enemies. There were some plantations on-island, but the Dutch-held Saba was largely uninhabited, the perfect cover for an innocent excursion off-island. Ian McKintrick's men cheered when they came alongside, clearly aware of Verity's excitement over a reunion with her family. Philip brought down the ketch's remaining sail as Gray tossed a rope to Ian, bringing them to a swift stop alongside the big ship. A small boatswain's chair was lowered from a pulley, and Keturah was settled into it first, then hauled upward. Selah could hear the excited squeals of her sisters and could barely wait for the seat to return for her. In minutes that seemed to drag, it soon arrived. "Up you go," Philip said with a grin.

Even as she rose, Gray and Philip took to the rope net on the broad side of the ship, climbing up after the women. Soon enough, they were all embracing, the men gladly shaking hands and gripping shoulders.

"Of all the luncheon guests I might have imagined," Keturah said, "I confess I never thought it would be my dear sister and her husband." She pulled far enough away to examine Verity from top to bottom. "You are well, Sissy? You *look* fine as sunshine."

Verity smiled and nodded. Her brown hair had become bleached in the shipboard sun, taking on golden and rust highlights that Selah thought quite fetching. "And you, Selah," Verity said, hugging her tightly again, "you're even more beautiful than when I left you. You've become quite a lady! Is there a man on-island not in pursuit of you?"

Selah giggled. She was well into her courting years, but there was not a man on-island who would dare to approach her now, given the Double T's reputation. Not that she longed for such attentions. No, she was far too busy tending to the workers on the plantation, as well as their children. And lately she'd done much of it beside the curious young preacher, Jedediah Reed. "Clearly there is much to tell you, Verity. And much for you to tell us!"

"Indeed," Verity said. "Come, let us sit in Ian's cabin. I do so wish you had brought Madeleine. She is well?"

"She is. Fat as a little monkey gorging on mangoes," Keturah said proudly.

"And with the most precious brown curls," Selah put in.

"But we never take her with us when we sail," Ket continued. "Given that we wanted all to appear as normal, we had to leave her behind with Mitilda."

Verity sighed mournfully. "'Tis wise. But I do so hope that Shubert shall drop his claim and this wretched war will end soon. I loathe that it keeps us apart at all!"

Selah took her arm in hers and gestured toward the Union Jack. "You appear to be more in line with the British than you sound."

"Ian flies the flag he needs to pilot any waters we wish, but we are committed to liberty's cause. 'Tis only because of potential British patrols about that we fly Her Majesty's flag." They entered Ian's cabin and settled around a small table. Only the men remained standing.

"So you now work as a rebel privateer?" Gray asked.

Ian turned to him with a pensive but resolute look. "I do," he replied.

"And a smuggler?" Gray pressed.

"When it serves," Ian returned.

"Thank God," Gray said, breaking out into a grin and reaching out to clasp his shoulder. "Brother, Sister," he said, glancing toward Verity, "I must beg your forgiveness. I acted rashly in sending you away when you asked to court Verity, Ian. There have been many a night that I wished I could relive that moment and do things differently."

"Oh, dear Gray. I know you acted on my behalf, attempting to protect me," Verity said. She rose and took his hand in hers.

"A decision I could not argue against in good conscience," Ian said.

"Then I am forgiven?" he asked the two of them.

"Long ago," Verity said.

"Of course," Ian added. "But why the change of heart?"

Together they all sat down, and over the course of an hour, Selah, Gray, and Keturah informed them of all that had transpired at the Double T and on Nevis, as well as learned what had brought the McKintricks to be rebel privateers. They spoke quickly, well aware they could not linger long. The *Inverness* risked much tarrying in these waters.

"You tread on perilous ground yourselves," Verity said, her delicate brow knit in concern as she looked from Keturah to Selah. "There are those on Nevis who would gladly be rid of you."

"We could say the same of you. But what can we do?" Ket asked gently. She turned toward Selah. "To aid the Negroes in this way seems to be the path that God has laid before us. It allows us to operate the plantation but also employ freed men and women."

"If you could only see the hope among them now, Ver," Selah put in. "It has changed the entire feel of the Double T."

"Which is why the majority of our neighbors despise us," Gray said gravely.

"It seems we are on parallel paths, then," Verity said. "Each of us endeavoring to see life, liberty, and the pursuit of happiness for all."

Selah blinked in wonder. "Might you say that again?"

Verity smiled. "'Life, liberty, and the pursuit of happiness.' 'Tis a phrase from the Continental Congress's Declaration of Independence. I have a copy for you. They refer to them as 'unalienable rights,' something that all might assume they have, whether black or white."

"So the rebels intend to set their slaves free?" Selah asked.

"Ah, no," Verity said, sobering. "Many in the north favor abolition, as do an increasing number in Britain, as I understand it. But the demands of the plantations, as well as those who profit upon their labors from across the Atlantic, rally to keep things as they are."

"'Tis a vicious cycle," Gray said. "These plantations require thousands of workers. Those workers produce a high-profit crop, allowing us to purchase more slaves. Islanders purchase more slaves because they want to produce more sugar."

"And yet you are finding a way around that," Ian said. "What with your freed force, as well as those earning their way toward freedom."

"If we are not burned out before that can occur," Gray said, wearily rubbing his face. "I do not know how long I can keep fear at bay with a wife, child, and sister to protect in the midst of it."

"Perhaps you are a forerunner of what is to come," Verity said. "If you can only endure. In ten years, twenty, perhaps much will change."

"Perhaps," Gray said doubtfully. "And what of you and your safety? Now with a rebel captain as your husband?"

Verity cast a stormy look toward Ian. "He intends to establish me on Statia. He says 'tis far too dangerous to continue to sail with him."

"With the war heating up, I cannot blame him. And Statia!" Keturah said, smiling in delight. "That is close enough that we might steal away to you here and there!"

"I do not know if that shall be possible, Ket . . ." Gray began.

"I do," she said resolutely, taking Verity's hand. "If my sister is within a half-day's sail, there shall be nothing to keep us apart."

"It might be best for Verity to come to you," Ian said, lifting a hand to stay Gray's alarm. "After all, there is a warrant for my arrest, but not Verity's. And I intend to keep her in supply with trade goods. Any time you can get her to Nevis, or you there, you shall find supplies like those that fill *Hartwick*'s hold even now."

Gray tapped his lips with a finger. His eyes shifted back and forth as he thought it through. "Perhaps under cover of darkness," he began.

Keturah clapped her hands in glee. "Yes, Gray! We can conjure up a plan. Think of it! Food enough for all on the Double T, as well as a means to sell more of our sugar." Even that had become an issue of late, with many planters rushing to block them from securing space on the limited number of export ships bound for Britain.

"And a way to see our beloved sister," Selah said.

"And perhaps a way for an auntie to someday see her precious Madeleine," Verity said.

Gray peered helplessly over at Ian and Philip. Both men shook their heads and laughed under their breath.

"Once again I am forced to admit that there is no force mightier than the Banning women united," Gray said with mock resignation.

CHAPTER TWO

They feasted at the Double T that night as they had not in months. Ian's men had loaded their boat with dried corn, fish, small barrels of flour and cornmeal, as well as dried beef. It had been so full that the boat had ridden low in the water and the women were forced to gather their legs beneath their skirts, their booted feet perched on mounds of corn. The men of the *Inverness* had not bothered with barrels. They filled every inch of the floor with corn to a depth of two feet, well aware that they could get more in that way. Some became soaked in the wash of the waves that managed to slip into the boat, but that too would be dried out and salvaged in the coming days.

Thanks to the plantation's six dairy cows, they made rich corn chowder for all on the Double T that night, with bits of dried fish in it, alongside fresh biscuits.

His brown eyes wide, Jedediah sat down next to Selah in the meetinghouse. "What sort of bounty has befallen us, Miss Selah?" he asked, lifting his bowl and hungrily spooning a third bite into his mouth.

"The best of bounties," Selah returned.

"A door has opened in the marketplace?" he asked under his breath.

"Of a manner," she allowed.

He gave her a curious look but did not pry further. He was as hungry as the field workers after having toiled with them all day. That had been his way from the start, insisting that he not take a bed or eat a meal inside the main house but rather work and eat alongside the people of the plantation. "If I am to capture their minds as well as their hearts," he had told her one day, "I must live and work beside them. Did Saint Paul not do the same?"

"Saint Paul?" Selah said with a slow blink. "You compare yourself to Saint Paul?"

"Only in that I endeavor to follow his example," Jedediah said. "Most everywhere he went, he was a tentmaker, earning his own keep and getting to know the people of his city. This is my Ephesus," he said, gesturing to the fields. "These are my Ephesians," he added, waving toward the people around them, scraping clean their bowls with bits of hardtack.

His words had both inspired and chafed at Selah. For she had spent countless hours among the people of the Double T, and yet each night she'd returned to the comforts of the main house with her big feather bed and fresh linens. Not that there was an option for her, as a woman. With as much latitude as Gray and Keturah gave her in serving the people of the plantation, she knew Gray would bodily carry her back to the house if she ever attempted to sleep anywhere but in her own room. But it was the fact that she had never considered it before Jedediah arrived that niggled at her. Nor had she given much thought to Saint Paul and how he had conducted his ministry.

His mention of it had inspired Selah to read much of the apostle's works in Scripture, and through them she learned that Paul had suffered shipwreck, starvation, nakedness, beatings, and imprisonment in order to share what he believed. Given that the man was Jedediah's mentor, it alarmed her. What was this strange passion for the Word of God that he would be willing to suffer the same in order to have the opportunity to share his beliefs with others? Surely it was a form of madness.

And yet, as she listened to him preach each evening—even if she

pretended to be preoccupied with tending a sick woman or soothing a teething baby—she gradually came to acknowledge it more
as a God-given passion and not madness. Grudgingly she came to
admit that his passion was infectious. She had simply never met
anyone before who was so invested in and enthusiastic about his
faith. No friend, no family member, no vicar she had ever known.

With the extra measure of food, the meetinghouse became
raucous with singing and laughing that night. And it was into
the midst of this that Angus Shubert strode, flanked by two men.

Selah immediately came to her feet, Jedediah rising beside her.
The Negroes all let their eyes drift to the floorboards, knowing full
well the danger that Shubert embodied. Every person on Nevis was
aware of the treatment slaves received on Shubert's plantations.
There were horrific stories of beatings for minor infractions . . .
a child's hand cut off for stealing a dried apple. Hot oil thrown
on a cook for burning Shubert's supper. Two men forced to work
a field for forty-eight hours straight when they'd edged into the
jungle to drink from a stream. While there were a good number
of freed men and women among them, every one of them knew
that to Shubert, a direct look would be the equivalent of insolence.

"Well now," Angus said, slowly pulling off fine leather riding
gloves one finger at a time as the people about him hushed and
eased away. "Isn't this a sight?" He looked around at the crowd,
bowls in every person's hands, letting his gaze settle on Selah.

Abraham slipped his small hand into Selah's. She half turned
to the boy. "Go, Abe," she whispered. "Fetch Gray and Philip." He
needed no coaxing. The child was out of the building and running
for the main house in seconds.

"Hello," Jedediah said, edging in front of her, cutting off Angus's stare. "I believe we have yet to be properly introduced. I am
Jedediah Reed."

"Reed," Angus grunted, ignoring his outstretched hand. "The
Methodist."

"Indeed," Jedediah said as he slowly dropped his hand to his
side.

18

"I do not shake the hand of Negro-lovers. I hear tell that you eat, sleep, and work with them here." Again his eyes shifted over the crowd about them.

"I do, and gladly," Jedediah said, casting his lopsided grin around the room at his frightened friends. "And if that is how you feel, perhaps we shall never join hands. I confess a sincere love of all people, whether they be black-skinned or white. 'Tis as our Lord would have it."

Angus shook his head in disgust, hands on his hips. "The Lord would have it as it has been since biblical times. Slaves serving their masters and knowing their place. They are little more than cattle. You coddle them needlessly."

"I disagree. Jesus loved all, whether servant or master. Remember that—"

"I am not here to be preached at," Angus said, cutting him off. "We are looking for a runaway. A pretty little thing of about thirteen, named Alice. She was last seen this afternoon in the upper field of Cold Spring. She did not return with the others for supper."

"As you can see," Jedediah said, gesturing around him, "we harbor none but the good people of the Double T."

"*Here*," Angus said, turning toward the door after he had perused each nervous face about him. He ambled over to the giant cast-iron pot and peered inside. Clearly he understood that the Double T's people had eaten well that night and it displeased him. "But we shall search each of the slave cabins to be sure the girl is not hiding with one of them. Given the lax ways of this plantation, I would wager that more than one around here would have a fool notion to harbor a fugitive."

"You have no right to be here," Selah said. She stepped into Shubert's path. "Let alone search the premises."

"I most certainly do," he said, tipping down toward her. "The law says any man searching for a runaway has the right to search any place they might hide, regardless of who owns those places. That girl is my property and I aim to find her."

"Then we shall look for her," Selah insisted. "'Twill be far less of an intrusion for us to search our friends' quarters than you."

"Your *friends*?" Shubert scoffed a laugh under his breath, grinned at his companions, and folded his arms. "Do you mean to say that if you, the biggest Negro-loving woman on-island, found my girl, you would hand her over to me?"

"Of course not," Selah said, folding her own arms and lifting her chin. "I would buy her from you. Because I have no doubt that she fled your plantation due to mistreatment."

"She is not for sale," Shubert hissed, his grin fading. "I will never sell a slave to the Double T while I have a living breath in me. You people threaten to bring us all down with your foolishness." He roughly shoved past her and made his way to the door. Only Jedediah's supportive hand at her lower back kept her from stumbling backward.

Gray and Philip met him at the door. Philip carried a pistol.

"Shubert," Gray spit out. "You know you are not welcome here."

"And rarely do I come, neighbor," Shubert said benignly. "But tonight I have every right to be here."

"Why?"

"Because I am hunting a runaway. And I am certain she has come here, drawn by stories of this Negro-lovin' preacher and the errant ways of your plantation. I have to tell you, Covington, I am not the only one who thinks you risk inciting rebellion across all of Nevis." He picked up an empty bowl from a nearby table. "It has most of us committed to starving you out when you come to the end of your supplies." He tossed the bowl back and it rolled on its side. "Force you to see the error of your ways."

"I am aware of your efforts," Gray said, coming nose to nose with him. "Fortunately I planned ahead. But know this: We harbor no fugitive. So get off my land, Shubert."

"As soon as we search the slaves' cabins," Angus insisted evenly. "You know as well as I that I cannot have a slave running off. It gives the others bad ideas. Every planter here would agree with me."

Gray frowned. Slaves seldom ran away on Nevis. There were

simply too few places for them to go on an island with only thirty-six square miles of land. But some said runaways headed to the top of Nevis Peak. Perhaps two or three a year. Others tried to swim to foreign trading ships, offering their servitude, but few made it. "Some say there are Maroons up there," Gray said, nodding to the towering, jungle-covered volcanic peak. "If the girl truly wished to escape you, would she not begin climbing?"

"Could be," Angus said. "But I aim to make certain she is not *here*, first." He pushed past Gray and headed to the group of cabins up the hill.

Selah rushed down the stairs and placed a hand on Gray's arm. "Can you not stop him?"

"I fear not," he said grimly. "He's right. Slave owners have the right to search any premises they wish when chasing a runaway." Together they followed the men and watched as they began searching the cabins. In one, an old man yelped, surprised by their intrusion. In another, a woman screamed. Gray, Philip, and Jedediah all separated to follow each of the men and make certain nothing untoward happened to their people. Matthew stayed beside Selah.

By the time it was done and the men mounted their horses and rode off, Selah was trembling. Seeing Shubert so near brought back too many bad memories—his manhandling of Keturah, his silent stalking of Verity, his attack on Selah herself that first year on-island. Even though it was three years' distant, for Selah, it was as if it were yesterday.

Jedediah was the first to notice her when the men finally rode off, talking of rounding up a posse to search the peak. "Miss," he said, seeing blood drip from her hand. With long fingers spread in a gesture meant to calm her, he slowly approached her and took the hidden *sgian dubh* from her bloody palm, then pulled a clean handkerchief to gently wind it about the cut. His brow furrowed in concern as he held her small hand in his own. "What is it, Selah?" he asked. "Why do you fear that man so?"

"Because he has threatened her and her sisters more than once," Gray said, turning toward them. "Are you badly injured, Selah?"

"No," she said, willing her voice to steady. "'Tis not deep."

Philip and Matthew drew near too.

"The women of this family have suffered at the hands of that fool," Gray said. "As has Matthew."

Jedediah grimaced and looked from Matthew to Selah. "You too?" His expression was a mix of fury and sorrow.

She nodded slowly, unable to meet his gaze. "The man is a brute," she mumbled.

"I see," he returned.

But Selah knew he did not. He was an innocent, in many ways. Pure of heart, little but the vision of Saint Paul's path before him. The courage to negotiate whatever snares lay before him. But so far he'd encountered little. From his sermons, she'd gathered that he had suffered poverty, hunger, a few nights on the road. Perhaps a bodily push out of town. But he had not suffered risk to his life, of that she was fairly certain.

She had.

She hated how the thought of Angus Shubert being on the Double T sent her to trembling again. How an attack so long ago made her feel weak today.

"Selah," Jedediah said, catching her elbow as she turned to follow Gray and Philip to the main house.

She glanced over her shoulder at him, suddenly wanting nothing more than to be alone, and he dropped his hand.

"I do not know what that man did to you or yours, nor do you need tell me." He paused and rubbed the back of his neck. "But I tell you this. He clearly overstepped. But I want you to know . . . not all men overstep." He stared at her earnestly.

"Of course," she finally said. "I understand that." She gestured to the others, nearing the house below them. "Gray, Philip, Matthew, and others have proven that to me."

"Good, then," he said, looking relieved. Did he worry that she had sworn off all men? Was that a glimpse of yearning in his eyes?

She took a step away from him. "Until tomorrow, Jedediah."

"Until tomorrow." He pulled off his hat and held it to his chest.

Late that night, Selah awoke with a terribly dry throat, even in the midst of air so thick she could feel the sheen of moisture on her forehead. Her gown clung to her. They were apparently in for a few days of damp heat, common during hurricane season.

Thinking a glass of water might aid her in returning to slumber, she reluctantly pulled on a dressing robe and made her way down the stairs and to the kitchen, determined not to wake another soul in the house. Certainly not any of the four British soldiers they quartered. She was in no mood for polite conversation, especially in her dressing gown. So she floated down the stairs, carefully avoiding the fifth and eighth steps that tended to squeak, and moved through the salon, past the dining room and into the kitchen.

In the corner by the door was a pump with a basin beneath. No matter the time of year, one could now pump and produce fresh water from a well that plunged more than sixty feet beneath the surface. It was always sweet and clear. But as she reached for the handle, she heard a muffled feminine sneeze.

She looked over her shoulder in confusion. Mitilda was long abed, as were Sansa and Bessy. There were no other women in the household other than Ket. And Ket had retired long ago.

Selah turned, lifted her sputtering candle, and peered about the room. She was alone.

She decided she had imagined the sound and turned to pump fresh, clean water into the pewter pitcher she would carry to her room. When it was full, she gathered up her candle and pitcher and moved to the door. She was almost through when she again heard a muffled sneeze.

This time it had been directly to her left.

The root cellar.

Selah bit her lip. It was terribly dark and quiet to be lifting the squeaky door. But there was no one but her to do it, and she knew someone was down there. She was sure of it now.

Slowly, she approached the square outline in the floorboards.

She'd been below a few times with Mitilda, but was never fond of the dank odor and found the feel of the earthen walls oppressive. She'd fairly forced herself to descend the second time, and certainly the last. It was there that their cook preserved onions, potatoes, and even a few apples from the American colonies for special occasions.

Selah studied the carved handle in the floorboards, lifting her flickering candle high. What she had heard in the sneeze was light and high-pitched, nothing low or menacing. There was no man or monster below, she told herself. But who? What? Why?

For a brief moment she entertained the idea of turning and going to bed, assuming it had only been her vivid imagination. But Angus Shubert had been on the property not five hours ago, demanding entrance to the slave cabins to search them for his fugitive. Could it be? *Please, God, let it not be*, she thought. They had already invited far too much trouble to the Double T. They did not need a runaway on their hands.

Taking a deep breath, she opened the hatch and let it flop fully open on its rope hinges as she lifted her candle high.

It was the girl's wide brown eyes that caught her first, with tears streaming over her apple cheeks, hands clenched before her. "Please, miss, please don' tell Massa Shubert where I am," she beseeched Selah, over and over again.

Selah was descending the steep stairs before she clearly knew what she was doing. All she had in mind was soothing the poor child. The girl was trembling and beginning to sob in fear and remorse. "Please don' send me back to Cold Spring," she pleaded. "Please, miss, please . . ." The girl sank to her knees and put her forehead and eyes and cheek to Selah's knuckles in supplication. "Please, please, miss. I can' go back. The massa will kill me. And he will make it slow."

Selah swallowed hard against the knot of panic in her throat. As much as she feared Angus Shubert, it was but a tenth of what this girl clearly felt. She knelt before her and drew her close. "Dear girl, upon my life," she whispered, "you are safe with me. I promise."

She felt the slight girl's shoulders shudder and then ease a tiny bit as she held her. After a while she pulled back and whispered, "What is your name?"

The girl hesitated but stilled, as if thinking and comforted by the thought. "My mama called me Akunta," she said. "But i's been a long time since I heard dat name."

"Akunta," Selah said. "'Tis a fine name. I am Miss Selah Banning. But . . . I think Angus Shubert came looking for you. He called you Alice."

The girl was silent for a moment. "Yes. Massa Shubert calls me Alice. Says i's mo' proper than the name my mama gave me."

Selah remained silent.

"He comes to my cabin, Miss Selah. Every night he comes. And he . . . he hurts me. I could'na stay. Not one more night."

Selah considered her words. "Master *Shubert*?"

The girl rubbed her hands on her dirty dress. "Yes'm. Do you think he will come here looking for me again?"

"I do not know," Selah said, swallowing back the rising bile in her throat. Shubert was not the only slave owner to use his female slaves in so vile a manner—the preponderance of mulatto children was testimony enough. Even dear Abraham, her half brother, was a living example of her own father's sinful choices. Yet this girl was but a child. The idea of Shubert forcing himself on her . . .

She swallowed hard again. She had to think and do so quickly. "I need to find you a different hiding place, Akunta. Was it Mitilda who hid you?"

"No, miss. 'Twas little Abe who brought me here."

Selah considered that a moment. *Abraham.* Little more than a child himself. Aiding a runaway? Why, he had never given her any indication that he knew of the girl's whereabouts when she sent him off to fetch Gray. Perhaps he had not discovered her until afterward.

Selah sighed. What was done was done. The question was, what to do next? How was she to get this child away from Shubert's reach? Because Akunta was right. She could not return to Cold Spring. If she did, Angus Shubert would make her an excruciating example of what happened if one dared to try and escape him.

Dear girl, upon my life, you are safe with me, she'd promised. Now . . . how to make good on it?

CHAPTER THREE

She considered waking Ket as she threw on a work dress and pulled on boots. But over the last year, she knew she had pushed them to their limits, gradually persuading them to hire a freed work force and emancipate their slaves. She knew the pressure Gray was under at market; if he was found aiding a runaway, it might be truly over for him—for them all. No, if Ket or Gray knew nothing about this, they could honestly claim they had no knowledge of the girl. But Selah had to get her away from the Double T to somewhere safe. Where? How? And who could help her?

Matthew was her first thought. But no, he would side with Gray. They would hate handing over the girl, but they would be forced to do so, choosing the good of the hundred-some souls of the Double T over one Cold Spring runaway.

There was only one man she could think of who would stand up for the child. *Jedediah.* Perhaps he would aid Selah in finding a solution.

She eased out of the kitchen and took to the path that led to the meetinghouse where the young preacher slept. As she drew closer, she grew nervous about waking the man. It was terribly improper for her to be out at this hour, unescorted. And approaching a bachelor? Her mother would roll over in her grave. But when she arrived, she found him leaning against a porch post, looking up at the sky filled with stars. "Jedediah," she whispered. "You are not sleeping."

"Nor are you. Unless we are both dreaming," he added, a smile in his voice. "I was only talking to God."

She cocked her head, considering his odd words. Praying, he meant?

"What brings you here at this hour?" She heard the subtle note of hope in his voice. Did he think she sought a romantic tryst?

She sat down beside him and looked over her shoulder, into the dark meetinghouse. "Is there anyone else here?"

"Not tonight." He grew more serious. "What is it?"

She bit her lip, taking comfort in the sounds of the night jungle, rife with the hum of cicadas and tree frogs, hiding their quiet conversation. "I found the girl. The one Shubert is after. She is in our kitchen root cellar. Abe hid her there."

Jedediah took a long, deep breath and then rubbed his face. "Well now, that puts us in a pickle. If Shubert were to find out, he'd not only have the right to take back the girl but he'd have the right to haul Abraham to the sheriff."

"He's not going to find out. Because I intend to find a way for the girl to get off this island. She cannot return to Shubert. He has already sorely abused her. Being a runaway . . ." She shook her head. "If he were to get ahold of her again, Jedediah, I fear for the girl's life. Some say a runaway must die, to provide an example. She would not be the first on Nevis to perish for such a reason. And perish in the most painful way possible."

He nodded, clearly well aware. "Then we must come to her aid. Do you have an idea on how we might do so?"

"I-I do not know. I thought . . . well, I thought perhaps you would have an idea."

He stroked his long chin between thumb and forefinger. "Now, I am not a great scholar, Selah, but given the local merchants' reluctance to sell Gray supplies, I assume you obtained the food we ate tonight from a smuggler?"

"Perhaps," she said, looking to the jungle.

"Could that smuggler aid us? Would he be willing to take on the child?"

Selah sucked in her breath. *Verity and Ian.* Why had she not thought of them? They certainly had no love for Shubert. "Perhaps. If we can get to them in time." She glanced to the dark sea, hearing waves crash on the beach below them. "You may not be a scholar, but do you know how to sail?"

"I'm a passable sailor, yes."

"What about at night? Could you get us to Saba tonight?"

"Oh no," he said, shaking his head. "I cannot take you, Selah. But I will take the girl. I shall not put you in such danger."

"The ketch is far too large for one man to manage. And 'twas I who brought you into this," she said, rising. "I shall see it through beside you. Otherwise I must find another partner for my covert work."

He hesitated. "You place me in quite the predicament."

"Yes, well, life is full of difficult choices, is it not?" she said, losing patience. They had no time for this! Now that he had made her see such an obvious course, she was eager to set upon it. "Come now. You must accompany me at once, so we can return before dawn. Or I must find another."

"Aiding this child," he said as he rose, "Selah, it is a capital offense. And given the soured relations the Double T has with the rest of the islanders, there would be few who'd urge clemency."

She stepped toward him. "If *our* Lord and Master was here now, would he not urge us to aid a child suffering unspeakable, daily abuse at the hands of her master? Would he not urge us to be his hands and feet?"

She could see the white of his teeth as a slow smile spread across his face. "Well, yes, I believe he just might."

"Then how can I not do the same?" With that, she turned and set off down the path again, knowing full well that Jedediah would follow. They secreted Akunta out of the main house, hurried down the path to the beach and then on to the pier, then prepared the boat to sail. Selah had watched the men intently that afternoon and endeavored to do what Philip had for Gray.

But as they cast off, she belatedly noticed the winds were stronger than they had been during the day, and once the wind caught in the sails, they nearly capsized.

Selah swallowed a partial scream as Akunta reeled to the lower side of the boat, nearly falling out. Jedediah yelled at Selah to lower the smaller sail, and she prayed that no one onshore heard them over the wind and crashing waves. A minute later, they raced toward the dark outline of Saba, the boat leaning at forty degrees but feeling a bit more secure. With every foot they gained away from Nevis, the easier Selah breathed. But she also recognized how dangerous the crossing might be at this hour. What would happen if a great gust sent them rolling? Might she send Akunta to a watery grave in attempting to save her? *Please, Lord. Aid us. Help us to safely reach Saba and my sister this night, and return without anyone seeing us.*

Jedediah saw Akunta cowering beside the seat, arms pinned between two ribs of the boat's side in terror. "We shall be all right now, Akunta. I am sorry you were so frightened."

The girl did not respond.

"Do you know what the name Akunta means?" he asked. Selah had heard him ask such a question before. He often used it to begin a conversation with someone he had just met. Back in England, his mother had been the one others consulted when seeking the right name for their babe, and over the years he had apparently catalogued each in his mind.

Akunta shook her head.

"I confess I do not know the meaning either. But do you know what Alice means?"

Again she shook her head.

"It means 'nobility,' or one of noble heritage. And you, my friend, strike me as someone of noble heritage. Who else would have dared to do what you did, escaping your tormentor?"

"Alice is just the name Massa Shubert gave me," she said.

"But nothing is happenstance, Akunta. I believe it might have been God who had his hand in that. Reminding you, somehow,

30

that he has bigger plans for you. That you are worthy of so much more than you have received."

His words made Selah tear up. How tender the man was with all those he met. Over and over, his actions surprised her.

"What does Miss Selah's name mean?" the girl asked after a moment.

She could feel Jedediah's gaze turn to her, across the boat. "Well, some say her name as *say-lah*. Others say *se-lah*. I myself like the way Miss Selah and her family say it, *see-lah*. Because it means to pause or to consider. Or to see. Martin Luther thought it a command to pause and reflect on what had just been spoken in the psalms. And Miss Selah . . . well, I have to say she often makes me pause and reflect."

Selah smiled and looked with some embarrassment to the waters, even though she knew he could not see her well in the near dark.

The rest of the voyage to Saba went well, with only a couple of gusts that made Jedediah shout, "Lean! Lean starboard!" The starboard edge lifted perilously both times, but their combined weight kept them from rolling. An hour later, on the leeward side of Saba, the winds abated. "Where?" Jedediah asked. "Where am I to go?"

Selah struggled to see in the dark. The island was a huge black mass, but the white of cresting waves helped her gain a sense of where they might be. "Straight ahead, around that point!" she called. And soon enough they edged into the tiny harbor that still held the giant hulk of the anchored *Inverness*.

She breathed a sigh of relief when she saw it. The McKintricks had talked about potentially weighing anchor that afternoon, but apparently Ian had elected to wait until sunup. "Thank you, Lord," she breathed. "There, Akunta," she said to the child, squeezing her arm. "That is my brother-in-law's ship."

"Will he help us?" the girl asked.

"I hope so." She was reasonably certain he would, especially given his hatred for Angus Shubert. After all, the man had killed poor old Terence and repeatedly threatened Verity.

A shout carried across the water as they tacked back and forth in the gentle breeze, eventually edging near the ship. "Hail, small vessel! Who goes there?" cried a scout.

"'Tis I, Selah Banning!" she called, cupping her hands around her mouth. "I need to speak to the captain and my sister."

Jedediah managed to awkwardly pull them alongside the ship, and Selah dropped the sail. Jedediah caught a sailor's tossed rope and they came to such an abrupt stop, they all nearly fell. Verity appeared over the edge, her hair down about her shoulders, lifting a lamp high. Ian was right behind her. "*Selah?*"

"'Tis I, Verity," Selah said. "All is well. Ian, may we board?"

"Come," Ian said. He turned away, and in a moment the boatswain's seat was lowered for her. Jedediah helped Akunta set the ropes as Selah was lifted aboard for the second time that day. And by the time she stepped onto the deck, more sailors had gathered around in a circle to find out what had brought visitors at such an hour.

"Captain and Mrs. Ian McKintrick, this is my friend, Mr. Jedediah Reed, and Akunta."

Ian frowned at Jedediah even as he shook the man's hand. "May I ask what ye are doing, Mr. Reed? Escorting my wee sister-in-law in the dark of night across treacherous waters? Are ye mad?"

"He did as I bid," Selah interrupted, lifting her chin. She eyed the curious sailors about them. "Please, may we speak in private?"

"Come," Ian said, leading them to his cabin. "Back to your posts, men."

"Aye, aye," they muttered and ambled off in frustrated curiosity.

Once inside their quarters, Verity turned to her, hands on hips. "Well? Out with it, Selah. All of it."

"This is Akunta," she said, wearily sinking to a wooden chair and reaching out to take the girl's hand. "She is known as Alice, a slave of Cold Spring Plantation, and a runaway as of last night. She escaped after suffering in the most vile way at the hands of her master, Angus Shubert."

The man's name brought Verity's head up and stopped Ian's pacing.

"I found her in our root cellar. Abe hid her there. To send her back to Shubert might well mean the girl's death, as well as Abraham's. I saw no other recourse than to help aid her escape."

"Risking your own life, lass," Ian growled, running a hand through his dark hair.

"Are *we* to truly debate risk of one's life for a righteous cause?" Selah asked pointedly. "You, who have pledged your life to serve the Sons of Freedom?"

Ian snorted. "Just as headstrong as your sister, are ye?" he asked, sinking into a chair across from her, legs akimbo.

"Generally, no," Verity put in, with an indulgent smile. "But she has her moments. Especially if one in her care is threatened." She glanced at Akunta, who bit her lip and nervously kneaded her hands, watching them talk. "Is what my sister said true, Akunta?"

The girl nodded.

"Angus Shubert abused you?"

"Every day, ma'am," the girl said, her long-lashed eyes searching the floorboards. "He picks a girl on every plantation. Last month it was Jubie. But then this month it was me. Jubie, well, Jubie could stand it. Me . . ." She shook her head in misery.

Verity grew pale, while Ian rubbed his face and rose again to pace. "Somebody ought to make certain that man never hurts another," he said.

"God's wheel of justice sometimes seems slow to us," Jedediah said. "Angus Shubert will have to give an account to his Maker, and I doubt the Lord will look kindly upon him."

"You are a vicar?" Ian said, slowing to study him.

"An itinerant preacher, currently serving the good people of the Double T."

"The slave folk, you mean," Ian said.

"Any and all who care to listen." Jedediah cast Selah a lopsided grin.

She smiled back at him. He really was so dear . . .

Verity leaned into Selah's line of vision and glanced back and forth between them. "You two are courting?" she whispered.

"What? No!" Selah returned, feeling the heat of a blush rise on her cheeks. "We are . . . friends."

"I see," Verity said, but she gave her sister a sly look that said she saw more than Selah was willing to admit.

Selah frowned in irritation. There was nothing to see between them. Was there? She dared not look Jedediah's way. "Please," she said to Verity, "we need you to take Akunta. Take her away with you. Perhaps she could serve aboard the *Inverness*, Ian? Or you could find her a good home and position in the American colonies when you return? Those who frown on slavery? She cannot stay on Statia or any island where Angus Shubert might gain word of her. He will hunt long and hard for this one. He fears her escape will inspire others among his plantations."

Verity looked to her husband, and after a moment Ian crossed his arms and nodded. "We shall take her."

Verity reached out and put a hand on the girl's shoulder and leaned down. "We shall see you to safety, Akunta. You shall never suffer at the hands of Shubert again. He is our enemy too."

Akunta nodded, tears of gratitude rising in her eyes. "Thank you. Thank you, miss."

Then Verity turned to Selah and Jedediah. "Now, promise me you will not attempt this again, either of you. If Shubert were to find out, he would make sure you both hanged. And given our family's current lack of support on-island . . . *Promise me.*"

They both nodded.

"Then off with you now. You must return to the pier and both be in your beds come sunup, so that no one sees anything amiss."

"Agreed," Jedediah said.

Ian left to get the *Inverness* ready to sail, and Selah breathed a sigh of relief. They would be far away from Saba—and Angus Shubert—before Shubert even gave a thought to Alice potentially making it off Nevis.

The sisters embraced. "Once I am settled on Statia," Verity said, leaning back from her, "I shall come to see you."

"But what of the sheriff—?" Selah began.

"The sheriff would like to find my husband," Verity interjected. "If he asks, I shall truthfully say that my husband sailed off and left me, refusing to tell me where he was headed."

The two shared a fond conspiratorial smile. Clearly Verity had a general idea, if not specific knowledge.

"Warn our brother-in-law that I aim to hold Madeleine every waking hour," Verity said.

"I shall," Selah returned, hugging her. "For you, he might make an exception."

"The men have put two more hogsheads of cornmeal in your ketch," Ian said. "Think the two of you can manage to get them to the house under cover of darkness?"

"I shall see to it," Jedediah said, then shook his hand. "We are most grateful for your aid."

"See my sister-in-law safely home and I shall consider it gratitude enough," Ian said.

"How am I to explain the cornmeal?" Selah asked. "Neither Ket nor Gray know we are here. And if Gray finds out . . ." She glanced at Jedediah worriedly.

"He would send him away as he once did me," Ian said, looking back and forth between them, then to Verity.

"Tell them," Verity said, leading them both to the cabin door and out, "that Saint Nick appears to have arrived early." She gave Selah a wry grin. "Suggest that we McKintricks must have found some way to get additional supplies to the Double T. Which we did, in a way."

"Oh, how I have missed you, Ver," Selah said.

"As have I, you," she said. "But as I said, this time it shan't be long before we are reunited. I will find a way to you. Or you to me."

They embraced once more and then Selah was lowered back into the boat. She and Jedediah untied the rope and lifted the sails. They made it back to Nevis in an hour and came alongside the pier a little faster than Jedediah intended, bumping hard against it before he and Selah could reach out to slow their progress and tie up. She lowered the last sail and secured it, then looked about, trying to remember if they were leaving it exactly as they had found it.

When they were finished, Jedediah lifted the heavy hogsheads to the dock and clambered out. He reached down a hand to aid her. She lifted her skirts in one hand, took his hand with the other, and stepped up onto the dock. After her time atop the waves, the sudden steadiness of wood beneath her feet set her off-balance. She careened to one side, but he held on to her hand and caught her waist with the other.

"Easy, there," he said. "Are you quite all right?"

She blinked and took a deep breath. "I am. Forgive me. A bit too long at sea, I guess."

"Happens to the best of sailors," he said cheerfully. Abruptly he dropped his hands as if belatedly remembering whom he held.

"Jed, I do not know how to thank you."

"There is no need, Selah. You honored me by seeking my aid." He turned to the hogsheads. "Now, I think I shall roll the first of these up to the kitchen, then return for the other."

"I can help. If you would but turn the other on its side, I can roll it behind you."

"I think not, Selah. As Captain McKintrick said, I put you in a fair measure of danger this night already. As a gentleman, it is my duty to see you to the house straightaway. Only the threat of dawn's light forces me to follow with the first of these hogsheads. We cannot let a neighbor spy us with smuggled goods. Though I suspect I am not the first to carry such from the *Hartwick* to the house, am I?"

"Perhaps," she said, swallowing a grin as she flounced past him and down the pier to the beach. She waited there, watching as Jedediah turned the hogshead on its side and began rolling it toward her, his tall form a dark silhouette against a tarnished-nickel sea. He was quick and strong, after toiling in the cane fields, and easily managed the large, heavy barrel up the path, only pausing a couple of times to heave it past bigger obstacles.

They paused outside the kitchen. Selah bent and listened at the door for a moment. Neither Bessy nor Sansa were yet about, ready to stir the oven's coals to bake the morning bread.

"All clear?" Jedediah whispered. "Then, quick, get to your room before you are seen."

"Yes," she said. But she paused, suddenly less than anxious to leave him. She reached out and took his hand. "Jed, I cannot thank you enough for your aid tonight."

After a bit, he covered her hand with his own. "Are you trembling, Selah?"

"I am," she admitted with a nervous laugh. "Our day has held more excitement than the last few weeks combined." But had it been their success in seeing Akunta to freedom or the young minister's brief hold on her waist?

"Indeed. 'Tis not every day you smuggle out a slave and return with smuggled food," he said quietly. "Do you regret it?"

"Not at all. I was awakened by the heat of the night and a parched throat. But could that not have been God's own hand? Tonight . . . Well, tonight I felt as if I was used as his hands and feet as never before."

She could sense Jedediah's smile more than she could see it.

"Would you do it again? Though you promised your sister you would not?" he asked quietly.

Selah thought about it a moment. "What the slaves endure under Shubert's harsh rule . . . I cannot stomach the thought. What about you, Jedediah? Do you regret it?" She frowned and ducked her head. What choice had he? No gentleman turned away a lady, not if he could possibly accommodate her.

He paused and then placed a knuckle under her chin, lifting it gently. "Indeed not," he whispered, then dropped his hand. "Selah, tonight . . . well, I confess I saw much more of you . . . I mean to say I considered you a privileged lady, content to help her people when it suited her. But to think you would endanger your own well-being on behalf of that child . . . " He paused and swallowed audibly. "I find there is much to admire in you beyond your outward beauty and the way you serve our friends."

She smiled. "And I came to see that you are quite brave, Jedediah. Willing to do anything to aid the people you love. Not that I haven't seen that in your work in the fields. But tonight . . . well, it was clearly much more."

They stood there a moment, staring at each other, each trying to make out the other more clearly in the darkness.

Jedediah remembered himself first. "I should get this barrel around the corner so 'tisn't in plain sight."

"Yes, right," she hurriedly agreed. Yet as he turned to the task, she couldn't seem to force herself to leave him. Instead, she followed behind as he rolled it to the small shed around the back of the house.

They turned back, lost in their own thoughts. Selah's scalp tingled. Honestly her whole body seemed to be on alert to Jedediah, tracing her steps with his own. What was this odd new connection? Was it because they had shared a grand adventure?

They were just reaching the kitchen door again when they heard the soldiers around the corner. Selah froze, and Jedediah with her. The men were laughing, clearly somewhat inebriated, and coming in at an unseemly hour. There would be no escape. They would need to account for their presence.

Jedediah turned to her. "Forgive me for this," he breathed, then grabbed hold of her waist and pulled her to him. He had just covered her lips with his when the soldiers spied them.

He was *kissing* her. Selah had never been kissed. Of all the ways she had dreamed it might happen, this was not it. And yet there was something alluring about being in his arms, him smelling of salt and sea . . . so much so that in the moment she forgot why he might have made such a decision.

"Well, what is this?" Lieutenant Angersoll slurred. He lifted his lantern and swayed as he tried to keep his feet.

"Miss Selah?" Lieutenant Cesley said incredulously. "And the *preacher*?"

"Oh my goodness!" Selah said in alarm, stepping away from Jedediah and fanning herself as she blushed. "You seem to have caught us at an inopportune moment."

"Well, we shall not tell on you," Angersoll said, "if you don' tell on us."

"Mum's the word!" slurred Cesley, giving her a slow conspiratorial wink.

"Thank you, gentlemen. I do so appreciate your discretion. Good night, Mr. Reed."

"Miss Banning." He then gave a courtly bow from the waist.

And with that, the men followed her into the house, laughing under their breath.

It was with some relief that she left them in the hallway, entered her room, and leaned against the door. She sank slowly to the floor with relief, even as she silently lamented her damaged reputation with the British soldiers. She could only pray that they would keep her secret as promised. If Gray got wind that she was out at such an ungodly hour with Jedediah—or that they were kissing!—he might well send the preacher packing.

Jed had thought quickly, kissing her like that. The soldiers would be able to testify they had seen them together at the house, not down at the pier. Not that she could ever abide such a story becoming public.

Selah touched her mouth, remembering Jedediah's lips on hers. Her first kiss from a man. And she had to admit that whatever had compelled him to do so, she couldn't find it in her heart to regret it. She remembered his big hands on her waist, the sudden warmth of his body as he pulled her close. The pleasing claim of his lips even as she stood there, frozen and utterly surprised. If he did it again, would she welcome it? Even return his ardor?

Or had it all been entirely a ruse to protect them both?

CHAPTER FOUR

Jedediah lay awake until morning, unable to forget the feel of Selah's slender waist between his broad hands, the pleasing softness of her as he drew close to kiss her. *What have I done, Lord?* he asked in silence. Ever since he had set sail for the Indies, he had considered himself a confirmed bachelor. He had put all thoughts of ever courting a woman, of marrying, on the altar, knowing the itinerant life was best lived alone, answering to no one but his Lord.

But over the last year, Selah had steadily drawn him, becoming his constant thorn in the flesh. He daily confessed his desire for her to God, beseeching him to take it away. Jed knew that even if God did not answer, Gray would. After all, what did he have to offer a Banning bride? With no home and but a few coins in his pocket? He let out a humorless laugh, the sound despondent in the moist morning air.

Most days he managed his wandering heart well, doing his best to give Selah a wide berth. Other days, not so well, his defenses slowly crumbling when he observed her cooing and smiling at a round-faced babe or tenderly caring for the sick. And tonight? Seeing her put her life in danger for Akunta and Abraham?

Well, it had been his undoing.

Again and again his thoughts strayed to her sweet lips, the taste of her, and the longing to have her in his arms again. Soon.

Forgive me, Father. Take away this longing for a woman I cannot have. I know you called me to this place to do your good work, not give in to my base desires. Give me strength, Jesus. Strength to serve you as I have been called. Forsaking all else. Amen and amen and amen . . .

But as Matthew blew his conch shell, summoning the Double T's workers to rise and report, Jed felt no encouragement, no strengthening. Only utter weariness and a frustrating, persistent hope that he would have a reason to see and speak to Miss Selah later that day.

Selah found reasons to be in the kitchen all morning, volunteering to bake bread with Mitilda with their new supplies of flour, as well as hardtack to preserve a great deal of it. Abraham fidgeted and found reasons of his own to be in the kitchen, returning quickly after doing anything his mother asked of him, clearly trying to keep watch over the root cellar. When his mother bent to open the hatch for a jug of vinegar, he hurriedly volunteered to fetch it. He returned up the stairs looking dazed, worried, and without the vinegar.

"Abraham!" Mitilda said, hands on hips. "What has your head in the clouds? You're on fire to help me and then you forget what you were to fetch?"

Hurriedly, he turned and climbed down the steep steps, returned and handed the jug over to her, then moved to the side door. "Need to see to somethin' in the stables, Mama!"

"Fine by me," she muttered. "Maybe you shall be of better use there."

Selah followed him out. The child stood there looking up at Nevis Peak and then down toward the beach as if unsure of where to go next. She approached him and put her arm around his shoulders. "Looking for someone?" she whispered.

"What? No, Miss Selah." Biting his lip, his eyes darted back and forth. "Why?"

"Because you are not off to the stables as you told your mother," she said, crossing her arms.

"I-I . . ."

"You are looking for Alice, are you not?" she whispered, leaning forward to at last relieve his burden.

His golden-brown eyes rounded. "Y-you *know*? Did you find her? Is she safe, Miss Selah?"

"She is." Again she put her arm around his shoulders and walked with him down to the stables to get away from the open kitchen window.

"Where is she now?"

"All you need to know is that she is safe. But you must never, ever do that again, Abraham. They might hang us all if they found out we aided the girl. Do you understand?"

"Yes'm," he said gravely.

"If another runaway ever appears on the Double T, you must come to me or Mr. Jed alone. Do you understand me?"

"Yes'm."

"Most people on Nevis already despise us. We need not give them another reason to suspect us, right?"

"No, ma'am."

"Good. Now get in there and aid Gideon in grooming the horses or mucking out stalls. And forget this ever happened. We must never speak of it again."

He scurried through the dark doorway of the stables, and she heard the older servant greet him. She smiled. She well knew that all the older servants doted on the child.

She turned to look uphill, thinking she would go to the meeting-house or the fields to see how she might help but then thinking better of it. Even the thought of seeing Jedediah again in the light of day made her blush. 'Twould be better to wait until she had her emotions in hand before she faced the man.

Had he really kissed her last night, or had it been naught but a fanciful dream?

No, he had done it. She could still smell the salty tang of his skin, remember the pleasure of his warm lips pressed to hers, the feel of his broad hands at her waist, pulling her to him. And while he had blamed the necessity of an excuse with the soldiers, she sensed it had not entirely been a rash choice. Despite the rapid nature of it, there had been something in the fluid assuredness of his movements that made her think he had been considering it for some time. Perhaps all the way from Saba? Or once he had steadied her on the pier?

Belatedly, she saw Philip and Gray at the washbasin outside the kitchen, scrubbing up for the noon meal. Gray dried his face and neck with a towel and studied her. "Why, Selah, your color is quite high. Is the heat of the day getting to you?"

"What? Truly?" she sputtered, feeling her blush grow deeper. "No, well yes, perhaps it is. Do you think it might let up by tomorrow? I can barely sleep."

"None of us are getting much sleep." Gray fell into step beside her. "In fact, last night I could have sworn I heard voices through my window before sunup."

Selah concentrated on keeping her pace steady and adopted what she hoped was nothing but benign interest in her expression. "There are nights when the jungle itself seems to have voices. The heat keeps the birds and monkeys up too, I think."

He stopped at the kitchen door, resting his hand on the latch, and turned to her. "So you were not up and about last night?"

"Me?" she asked innocently. "Last night I was so weary from the heat that I had one thought only—more water. Perhaps you heard me when I went to fetch some from the kitchen?"

"Perhaps," he said, lifting the latch at last and opening the door partway. When she moved to step past him, he placed a light hand on her arm and whispered, "So you know nothing of the two new hogsheads of cornmeal that arrived in the kitchen shed during the night?"

She turned to him and frowned. "Two *new* hogsheads?" she whispered.

He nodded.

"Another gift from Verity and Ian?" she suggested.

"Would they dare to come here? Truly?"

"They are privateers," Selah replied. "And I think they know what dire straits the Double T is in. You saw for yourself their concern over us." She pulled back her shoulders and dared to look him in the eye. "Food of any sort 'tis a gift these days." Selah opened the door the rest of the way herself, not certain how long she could maintain her charade. "Shall we not simply be grateful?"

"Indeed," he grumbled, following her in. "But why then do I feel like I have yet to thank the right benefactor?"

"Ach, lass," Ian groaned. "I confess this seemed wise to me at the time, but I dinnae ken if I can go through with it." He pulled Verity closer.

She knew what he meant. This impending separation threatened to tear her very heart in two. "We agreed on it," she said softly, laying her head against his chest, just under his chin. "I shall travel with you in time. Only not this time, right?" She lifted her head to look him in the eyes.

"Nay, not this time," he said sorrowfully. She knew his mission, and it was indeed dangerous. He reached up to tuck a strand of brown curl behind her ear. "But I shall miss ye every single day, wife, and count them until I see ye again. Ye shall take close care? Allow George and Trisa to attend ye? There are those who would use ye sorely on this island," he said, casting a suspicious look at the crowd passing their hidden perch in the alley. "Dinnae trust a soul."

"I shan't," she pledged. "Do not concern yourself about me." She straightened the knot of his neckcloth. "Only concern yourself with being clever and staying alive. Dinnae let your temper best ye."

He grinned wryly at her attempt at the Scottish brogue. "I will try me best." With a sigh he leaned forward, kissed her, then took her hand, kissed it too, and led her out to the busy street. They made their way to the harbor and down the dock until they stood before the *Inverness*. For the hundredth time, Verity thought about his mission—to try and commandeer at least three ships from the British or British allies among the West Indies in order to turn them into a small armada of privateering vessels. The war was gaining momentum now, with battles in New York intensifying. And the Continental Navy was having a tough time of it against the vast, powerful Royal Navy. Their thought was that if Ian could draw more attention to the West Indies, fewer of them would be on the American coast to wage war.

Ian was determined to do his small part in turning that particular tide, as well as trade Gray's remaining sugar for some more supplies—for the Double T and beyond. And Verity could not well argue against either cause. She had seen the desperation in her beloved family's faces last week when they had met in Saba's hidden bay. And she had noted they had each lost weight. Their situation was dire, and if she and Ian could ease their pain, it could not happen quickly enough for her.

As if reading her mind, Ian said, "Now, Verity, I dinnae like the idea of ye involving yourself in any smuggling to Nevis directly. I know ye want to make sure your family is kept in good stead, but I fear ye risk yourself. Especially when Angus Shubert will be on the hunt."

"I do not fear him or the sheriff. My only crime is marrying you. But no one has ever been arrested for marrying a wanted man."

"I wouldna put it past him."

She laughed. "He can try. But as much as he wields power on Nevis these days, the people remain subject to the king and his law. And by law there is nothing Shubert can hold against me."

"He is a councilman. He wields more power now. Dinnae tempt him, Verity."

"I will take the utmost care, Ian. Trust me."

He sighed, looked to his ship, then back to her, clearly still fretting.

"Come back to me, Captain, hale and hearty," she said.

"With haste, beloved," he pledged. Then he bent to swiftly kiss her again before hurriedly turning and climbing the gangplank, as if he feared changing his mind.

George, a broad-shouldered, middle-aged house servant, and Trisa, the slim lady's maid who had assisted her in Charlestown, took their places on either side of her. Both were freed slaves— George's master had died and freed him in his will; Trisa had spent twenty years saving to buy her freedom—and both had been sent over to Statia from the Double T. She knew their presence comforted both Ian and her as they parted.

Verity waved at Michael and the other sailors aboard the *Inverness*, then waited as they cast off, drifted away from the pier, and slowly began hauling sail. Her heart pounded as the ship gained speed and grew smaller in the distance. "Dear God," she whispered. "Go with my beloved Ian and his crew. Go before them, beside them, behind them. Protect them and bring them home to me as soon as possible. Amen."

"Amen," George said.

Verity glanced at him in surprise, unaware that her whispers had been loud enough to make out.

He smiled. "Always said a prayer to the good Lord like that when my children went to work in the fields."

Together they began walking down the street. "What became of your children, George? Are they freed now too?"

"Ah, no," he said wistfully, hands behind his back. "My son suffered from the ague and died when he was twelve. My daughter made it to her sixteenth year. Got a cut in the fields that became infected."

"I am so sorry. And your wife?"

"Died, giving birth to my son."

"How terribly sad," Verity said. Though she knew it was not uncommon among slave families. "Do you have any other kin?"

"Only my friends," he said. "And the family of the good Lord. With those who love the Lord, one is never truly alone. That young preacher at the Double T, Mr. Reed, helped me see that."

"Indeed." Verity mulled over his words. Had she ever felt as if her church community were family? There were acquaintances and friends among them for certain. But to call them *family*?

She turned to the woman on her left. "And you, Trisa? How do you feel about leaving the Double T behind again?"

"Truth be told, Miss Verity, I am glad to have some ocean between me and that nasty Mr. Shubert." She had been with Verity the night Terence was murdered.

"As am I," Verity said. "Though this island is full of potential enemies and friends alike. Let us keep our wits about us."

"Yes, miss."

As they walked, Verity thought about George's family, and then Trisa's story. She knew her parents had died when she was little. She was raised in the big house at Red Rocks Plantation. 'Twas an old servant who made her promise to try and sell something in the slaves' market every Sunday and save every shilling to buy her freedom.

"I am so happy to have you both by my side," Verity said, looking back and forth between them. "My heart is eased, as is my husband's. Thank you for being willing to attend me."

"'Tis we who are grateful to you, miss," George said. "The Double T has more than her share of freed people to try and keep fed. You bless us as much as we bless you."

Verity paused to turn at the corner, where the ocean-side street met the one that led to the marketplace. "We have quite a bit of work to do. I must establish my household as well as my business." She handed George a sack of coins and another to Trisa. "George, please go and see if you can purchase some onions and six chickens, as well as some fencing material. I aim to have fresh eggs each day for us. Trisa, please see about finding some soft linens for our bedding. Enough to cover three straw ticks. I must see about meeting with a Mr. Bieulieu regarding future imports. I shall meet you both at the cottage in an hour or two."

The two looked at each other and then frowned at her, hesitating.

"Miss Verity," Trisa said. "Mr. McKintrick . . . well, he done told us if we left you unattended at any hour of the day, we would answer directly to him."

"He . . . what?" Verity asked. "Surely he did not mean *every* hour."

"Oh, yes'm, he did," George said, crossing his arms.

Verity looked to the sea and sighed heavily. She knew Ian had only meant to look after her, but there were places she meant to go that would be all the more difficult to do so covertly if she took company. And yet it was wise to have a companion, especially as a woman. She knew that. Had she not made Ian promise to take care? How then could she not do the same?

CHAPTER FIVE

Selah entered the parlor just as Keturah was handing off little Madeleine to Sansa for a moment to pull on her gloves. "Are you going somewhere?" Selah asked.

"Yes," Ket said, eyeing her over her shoulder as she slipped in her fingers. "To Jeremiah Kirk's store." She reached for her baby, dressed in a freshly pressed white gown and cap, making her look as if she were ready to sit for a portrait.

"Jeremiah Kirk?" Selah said, grabbing hold of her skirts and following her sister out of the house. Kirk was the last merchant in Charlestown who agreed to sell supplies to the Covingtons, and only under cover of darkness. Last night he had refused Gray a hogshead of cornmeal. Her brother-in-law had arrived home at sunset too upset to settle—he had paced for hours. For now, they had a couple weeks' worth of supplies for the plantation, thanks to the McKintricks. But after that? What were they to do?

"Mr. Kirk refused Gray." Keturah set her face beside Madeleine's round cheeks. "But do you believe Mr. Kirk will be able to refuse *us*?"

Selah laughed and put her hands to her own cheeks. The babe was truly adorable. "The man would have to have a heart of lead to look upon the two of you and refuse. Wait a moment. I shall go with you."

"All right. But hurry, Sissy. We have only enough time for an hour in town, and then I must get back before Madeleine becomes fussy for her nap."

Selah rushed to the kitchen, drank a ladleful of water from the pump, then poured more into her cupped hand to wash her face. Mitilda handed her a towel. "Are you off somewhere, Miss Selah?"

"Off to wheedle our way into Mr. Kirk's heart again with Ket," she said, flashing her a grin.

"See that you do." Mitilda gave a light laugh. "Sometimes a woman can take a path no man would dare."

"Indeed." Selah returned to the parlor and grabbed her own pair of gloves from the side table. Keturah and Madeleine were already outside in the fine carriage Gray had purchased from Verity, along with Gideon in the driver's seat and Abraham clinging to the back. Nellie, the young nursemaid, sat on the other side of Madeleine's bassinet. But it was the man facing Keturah that made Selah pause.

Jedediah.

Since their mad quest to help Akunta escape three days past, the man had made himself relatively scarce. He hadn't even been in the meetinghouse last night, saying he was going to call on friends at the Bendley plantation. Yet Selah knew he would be as unwelcome there as they might be. Where had he really gone? Had it only been an excuse to avoid her?

He scrambled out of the carriage to assist Selah up the three small steps, skirt in hand. "Good day, Miss Selah."

"Good day, Jedediah. You are accompanying us to town?"

"Yes, miss." With a duck of his head, he resumed his seat beside her. "I aim to post a letter to my parents, as well as inquire about a Bible Mr. Kirk was attempting to obtain for me."

"A Bible?" Ket said as Gideon urged the pair of horses forward. "Has something happened to yours?"

"No, miss. But I thought I might give one to Matthew."

"Why not give your old one to Matthew and take the new?" she asked.

Jedediah considered that a moment. "Well, ma'am, there are

several reasons. One is that my father gave me mine, and whilst some of the pages have loosed from their binding, it means a great deal to me."

"Is he a minister as well?" Keturah asked.

"Indeed. In Cornwall, at present."

"What did he and your mother think of you setting off for the West Indies?"

Selah dared to glance his way and saw his gentle smile, as well as a far-off look in his eyes as if remembering that day. He tapped his long, gloveless fingers together lightly. "When I explained that God had put it on my heart to come, they said I must go." His smile faded a bit. "Though it pained them greatly to do so. I am their only surviving child."

"I see," Ket said, sorrow etching her face. "Yet it makes their sacrifice all the more valiant."

"If one does not practice what he preaches, he lacks vigor and authenticity when he speaks again."

"Indeed. You had a brother? Or a sister?" Selah dared to ask.

"Two sisters," Jedediah said soberly. "One died when we were but infants. And the other was my dearest companion until she passed at fourteen."

Selah swallowed hard and fought the urge to lay her hand atop his on the seat. "I am so very sorry." What would it have been like to see one of her own sisters die? She could not imagine the heartache.

He forced a small smile. "Her name was Jesenia." He shook his head and looked to the floor of the carriage. "I do not speak of her often."

"You need not now," Selah said.

"It becomes easier with each passing year." He looked at Ket and then to her. "She was a light. So warm and . . . caring." He quickly looked away from her and bit his lip. Was it her imagination or did he edge slightly away from her? "There was not a one in our village who did not know her name," he went on, "nor she, theirs. She oft took food to widows and the ailing. Father kept stores purely for such a purpose, and she delighted in it." He glanced at her again, his eyes lingering on hers as if he held back more that he wished to say.

Selah blushed under his intent gaze and even more so when she knew that Keturah clearly recognized their unspoken bond. She grasped for something that would cool his passionate attention, and yet she inwardly winced when the words left her mouth. "But then she died? How?"

He drew back a bit, blinking. "Y-yes. Six years ago. One of the sick she went to call upon had the pox. Within days she had it too. The rest of my family waited to become ill as well with its catching ways." His tone became dull, distant. "Truth be told, we fairly *wanted* the pox after burying Jesenia. Or at least I did. For a long while, I lost my way. The light was gone. All was darkness."

They rode on in silence for a bit.

"What does her name mean?" Selah asked quietly. "Jesenia?"

His wide lips twitched in a wistful smile. "Saint," he said, tapping his fingers together.

"It is most awful to lose a loved one," Keturah said. "I am gravely sorry that happened to your family."

"As am I," Selah said, fighting the urge to touch his hand again.

He gave them both a sorrowful, lopsided smile and lifted his hands. "Without sorrow, 'tis difficult to know the full threshold of joy."

"I have never stopped to consider that," Keturah said.

"Nor have I," Selah added softly.

Again, they rode in silence.

"What brought back the light for you?" Selah asked impulsively. "What drove away your darkness?"

He smiled a little. The carriage hit a rock in the road, and they all swayed back and forth. "It was rather like that bump we just went over," he said, looking to the sea, remembering. "My father is a prominent preacher. But I think you shall find, Lady Ket, that when little Madeleine grows up, it might be others who speak to her in a way that she can hear. At least for a time."

Keturah nodded and reached in to grab hold of the sleepy baby's hand. "Indeed. Such is the way of children."

"There was a traveling preacher holding meetings in our town. He promised that if we turned to Jesus—turned to him with our whole hearts—the God of light would dispel the darkness in our souls. And so I did," he said with a shrug, his Adam's apple bobbing. "Not that I was a heathen before, as the son of a minister. But there was something more to be done. In that moment, I simply committed my heart to Christ. With all of me. Wholly. No matter the cost. No matter where he led me. I knew then that I could do no other."

The women stared at him. Selah knew that neither of them had ever heard a man speak so boldly and plainly about his faith, nor so . . . intimately.

"And so you have never suffered darkness or despair again?" she asked.

His brows rose and he huffed a laugh. "Ah, no. I would be a liar if I professed any such thing." He glanced at her and cocked his head. "I have been jailed twice. Beaten three times, one time so severely I did not rise for two days. I have had everything stolen from me five times over. Walked my boots to shreds. And wondered more than once if I was on the right road."

It was Selah's turn to gaze at him in surprise. In the sermons she had listened to him preach, he had held back such detail. "And yet you still kept to the road."

"Of course. While the world seemed dark and against me at times," he said, waving about them and then drawing his hand to his chest, "inside I knew the God who was with me and for me. He is the Light that preacher spoke of. The Light that sustains and holds and keeps us, no matter how dark our world becomes. That is the way of Jesus. The way of which Saint Paul spoke. He suffered as well—shipwreck, imprisonment, beatings—but he kept on because he could do no other. As will I."

Keturah cleared her throat, breaking what Selah discovered had become another intense stare between herself and Jedediah. She startled and looked to the jungle out her side of the carriage.

"Where will you go *next*, Reverend?" Ket asked, rather pointedly.

"I know not. All I know is that I am to be here until he calls me elsewhere. And how fortunate am I? To have been led here, to sojourn alongside your family for a time."

"Indeed," Ket said lightly.

Sojourn alongside your family for a time, Selah repeated silently. *He does not intend to stay.*

Their kiss? Well, their kiss had clearly only been a ruse, despite what she thought his eyes had said to her afterward. Simply a ruse to cover their tracks with the soldiers. Nothing more.

And the thought of that brought such an unexpected stab of despair, it unsettled her.

"*Attendez un moment,*" Monsieur Bieulieu said, briefly taking hold of Verity's arm as she turned to leave his shop. He lowered his handkerchief, seemingly remembering himself. He glanced over his shoulder, making sure her servants were out of ear's reach. "You wish to obtain supplies for your kin on Nevis, no?"

"I do."

He crossed his arms. "Consider this, madame. I will introduce you to my contacts on St. Kitts and Martinique and help you establish your mercantile. But we," he added, pushing up his sleeve to reveal the fleur-de-lis tattoo on the inside of his wrist, "shall require some information from Nevis with each shipment. Tell me . . . do your kin have access to any British soldiers?"

"They do," she replied. But instinctively she knew he already was privy to that knowledge.

"Are they of high rank?"

"One is," she said, crossing her own arms. While she was eager to find supplies for the Double T, she was unwilling to put her loved ones in harm's way. Was not one spy in the family enough?

"Do these soldiers suspect you? As the bride of Captain Mc-Kintrick?"

"Yes, I would imagine."

"But what of your brother-in-law? Your sister?"

"Sisters," she corrected, thinking it through. "No, I believe they have the soldiers' implicit trust. They have provided them quarter for over a year now."

Bieulieu let out a sound of disgust and flicked his hand. "Deplorable. A robbery, forcing citizens loyal to the Crown to house and feed her soldiers."

"Agreed," she said.

He drew up stiffly. "Madame, would your kin be able to obtain valuable information for the cause? Perhaps in exchange for supplies?"

"Perhaps," she said slowly, remembering Gray's first, blustering dismissal of Ian due to his confession of smuggling and his desire to support the Sons of Freedom. And yet when they'd met in Saba . . . necessity had seemingly changed his mind. The question was, how far? And were the Covingtons willing to risk the Double T? If they were found out, they could be tarred and feathered and sent adrift on their ketch. Without sails.

"I shall come to call upon you, madame. Or you are welcome to call upon us. I abide with my wife at Hilltop Cottage, at the end of the North Road."

"Until then," Verity said with a curtsy.

"*Jusque là*," he returned and gave a courtly bow.

"Theodore Kirk always favored you," Keturah said. She stepped out of the coach, assisted by Gideon, and looked back at Selah. "That favor could aid us."

Embarrassed, Selah glanced toward Jedediah, whose only reaction was a twitch of his cheek. In agitation? Or amusement?

"Perhaps," Selah hissed, stepping past her. The boy—three years her junior—had followed her everywhere at the very last soiree they'd been invited to, nine months past. Given their diminishing reputation on-island and the wide berth so many of the other guests gave them, his attentions had been all the more obvious.

Only when his father gently urged him away, declaring that he simply must try the delicious rum cake their hosts were serving, had he left her side. Selah waited at the door as Keturah reached for Madeleine from the nursemaid, Nellie, and settled her on her hip. "You would have me use a poor boy's infatuation in order to obtain supplies?" she asked in a whisper as she passed.

Keturah lifted a wry brow and kissed her baby girl's cheek. "If I am not above pretending ignorance to my husband's attempt yesterday, or above using my precious Madeleine's cherubic face, why would I hold you exempt?"

Selah laughed under her breath and followed her sister inside the dark store. She knew Keturah would not be doing this if she had another option and reminded herself that although they had stores of food that would last another two weeks, there was no promise they—or Verity—could obtain more. And with close to a hundred souls to be fed on the Double T, provisions simply had to be obtained, one way or another.

Mr. Kirk's general store had none of the charm Verity's mercantile had once boasted, and in seconds she took in the bare shelves and empty hogsheads underneath signs that showed they'd once held sugar, flour, cornmeal, corn, and sardines. Only the hogshead under *Salt* was halfway filled. Behind the counter stood Theodore, who abruptly stopped cleaning the countertop when he saw who had entered. Remembering himself, he closed his mouth just as his father came in from the back room.

"Why, Mrs. Covington, good day," Mr. Kirk said. "Miss Banning. Reverend Reed," he added. "What brings you three in to see us?" He leaned in with a smile to touch Madeleine's chubby arm. "Forgive me, littlest miss. What brings you *four* in, I should say." Despite his turning away Gray last night, Selah was happy to see that he had not lost his warmth toward her family.

As agreed upon, Jedediah spoke first. "Hearing the ladies were heading to Charlestown, I thought I might see if that Bible arrived."

"It did indeed," Mr. Kirk said, raising a finger as if his memory had just been jostled. "I shall fetch it from the back. It arrived with a number of other volumes from a book trader on St. Kitts. I only need to find that particular crate."

"Very good," Jedediah said, his long face alight. Selah was so distracted for a moment by his joy that she found herself staring.

Theodore cleared his throat. "Miss Selah, it is a pleasure to see you. I have not seen you since we danced at the Brownings' soiree."

Was it her imagination or did Jedediah's excitement dim when he heard those words?

"That was a lovely gathering," she said, turning toward the young man. She set her market basket on the counter and her gloved hands on the top of the handle. Somehow it made them feel closer, despite the counter between them.

Theodore's glance lingered over her gloved hands, and he bit his lip for a moment. She noticed that in the months since their last meeting, Teddy's face had gained the more angular lines of manhood. And his light blue eyes were intent upon hers.

"Sadly, Mr. Shubert's campaign against my family continues unabated," she whispered conspiratorially. Sounds from the back room—grumbling—made her look past Teddy's shoulder. She waved him toward the end of the counter and around it. The young man followed her without hesitation.

The two came face-to-face. He was now a good foot taller than she and broader by half. Probably eighteen, filling out as a man, with the smattering of pimples across his cheeks and forehead easing.

"I so dislike how Councilman Shubert speaks of you," Teddy whispered. "How he has dragged your good name through the mud! 'Tis he who has forced the island to exclude you from our gatherings."

"'Tis no surprise," she said, slowly shaking her head. "I believe him jealous of Gray and Keturah's success at the Double T, in spite of his own grand fortune."

Teddy nodded thoughtfully. "'Tis reprehensible."

They stood there for an awkward moment of silence before Selah rushed on. "You are so kind to take our side in the matter," she said, wrapping a hand through the crook of his arm and gesturing forward, as if she wanted him to lead her on a stroll. She was chastising herself for such a foolish notion—*A stroll about where, Selah? The twenty paces of the store?*—when she caught sight of the beatific look on his face. He clearly still welcomed any excuse to be close to her. Jedediah stood at the counter with his arms folded, turning partially away.

"Listen, Teddy," she said, "I am well aware that your father refused Gray's request to supply us with any provisions last night. If he refuses Keturah today, is there any possible way you can assist us?"

Theodore pulled them to a stop and turned to face her. "What are you asking? To go behind my father's back?"

She felt the heat of a blush rising at her cheeks and shook her head sorrowfully. She laid a hand on his arm. "If there were any other way, I would not ask it of you," she said, meaning every word. "I fear Councilman Shubert means to starve us off the island, and I confess he is doing a good job of it."

Theodore's eyes narrowed. "You mean to say we are the last to refuse you?" he said. "No other still trades with the Double T?"

She shook her head sadly, arching her brows in the middle in what she hoped was a pretty but pleading look.

The boy's face settled into one of decision. "This is unconscionable," he whispered as Mr. Kirk returned to the counter, Jedediah's Bible in hand. "I shall speak to my father."

"And if he refuses you?" she dared.

"Then I shall see what I can do," he said, patting her hand. "I must go," he added, seeing the slight frown on his father's face when he glimpsed them together. Selah moved to the other side of the room, as if she had shared nothing but idle chatter with his son, nor had any deeper interest than one of the twenty garish hats that hung on the hooks. That was the thing, she realized with a start. Kirk's store had no real supplies, but was flush with silver flasks, ceremonial swords, suit coats, and hats. Kid gloves made of the finest leather. Even a set of crystal goblets and another set of China teacups and matching teapot. But not a pound of flour to be found anywhere.

Luxury imports from England and the Continent were clearly still easily obtained. Even Jedediah's Bible. But staples from the Americas? The trade had clearly come to a standstill. The British intended to kowtow the rebels into submission. But were they aware they were starving their own people in the midst of their forceful move? Her hand traced the empty flour bin. For the first time—despite hearing about it from Keturah and Gray and others, despite recognizing how welcome the smuggled supplies had been—the knowledge of how the *entire* island was in danger became abundantly clear. Fear sent shivers up and down her neck. Fear for their servants and slaves trying to earn their emancipation. Would they even survive to see their freedom papers? How could Ket, Gray, and she keep them alive if merchants did not even have anything to trade should they be willing?

And yet Theodore's whispered promise made her think that Mr. Kirk must have something more, back in the storeroom. Or that they might be expecting another shipment any day. But was that only innocent hope or based on something likely to occur?

She returned to Keturah's side. Madeleine was fussing, and her sister patted her back and pulled off her hat. It was stiflingly hot in the store.

"Mr. Kirk," Ket began, "I know my husband came to see you last night. And I know you are under some duress not to sell supplies to us. But I wanted to remind you that we have a little child to feed. Little Madeleine here." She lifted the baby higher. "And she is but one of many children on the Double T. Can you not spare even one hogshead of corn? Or meal? Perhaps a crate of dried beef?"

The door opened behind them, setting the bell to ringing. Selah looked back, and against the bright backdrop of sea and sky, Angus Shubert's form made her sigh in frustration. Had he been watching them? Or the store? The door slammed behind him. As usual he had two men in company.

Selah prayed a quick prayer for courage and clenched her hands. She knew Shubert wouldn't dare to attack her or Ket here in the store, not with witnesses present. Still, her heart didn't seem to remember that. In spite of how it raced, she adopted a demure, calm expression, as her elder sister did before her. They would not give him the satisfaction of seeing fear on their faces. Rage, perhaps. Derision, certainly. But never fear.

The men moved to flank them. Jedediah edged closer to her and Keturah in a protective stance. Shubert leaned against the counter, his back to the Kirks, and folded his arms. "Kirk told me just this morning that he declined to sell anything to your husband," he said to Ket. He glanced over his shoulder at the merchants. "Which was a very wise decision given your lack of support on-island."

He reached out to touch Madeleine, but Keturah pulled her away. Shubert's mouth soured. "You wouldn't be here attempting to use your feminine wiles to change Kirk's mind, would you?" His eyes slid to Selah and then back to Ket.

"We are appealing to common compassion," Keturah said. "Something that you seem to be convincing everyone on-island, including the more gracious like Mr. Kirk, to ignore."

Shubert shrugged. "This is easily solved, Mrs. Covington." He waved at Selah and Jedediah. "Rein in these two. Rescind your plan to set your remaining slaves free. And send those freed already on the next ship to wherever they wish to go." He snapped his fingers. "Just like that, all your problems go away."

"Not all our problems, Mr. Shubert," she said, staring unflinchingly into his eyes. "There is still the issue of your seat on the council. Those who care about the future of Nevis do not believe that seat should remain yours."

Shubert laughed, looked to his companions, who joined him, then back to her. "Your errant choices at the Double T have only strengthened my position on the council. Most Nevisians realize we must have an iron hand on the Negroes or the rebellion in America is liable to spread down here to us."

"Most Negroes I know do not wish to rebel," Selah said, daring to take a half step forward. "They only wish to be treated fairly. If you were in chains, forced to work another man's fields, would you not wish for the same? Decent food? Pay for your work? Freedom to make your own choices?"

Shubert pulled back, a wry expression on his face, shook his head and gestured to her. "See what I mean, gentlemen?" he said to the others. "They speak nonsense! Did this come from you?" he asked, turning to face Jedediah and poking him on the chest.

Jedediah clenched his teeth. "I do not know if the Covingtons and Miss Banning have found me influential at all. I speak only to their people, rarely to them."

Shubert leaned forward. "And what do you tell them? Do you fill those African heads with rebellious ideas?"

"I endeavor to fill them with hope. With the understanding that they are treasured souls in the eyes of God."

"In the eyes of God? Does not the Bible say that slaves should serve their master?"

"Indeed it does. But Colossians tells us that masters should also provide slaves with what is right and fair, because masters know they are subservient to the Master in heaven."

Shubert's eyes narrowed. He darkened a church door a tenth as often as he darkened his own tavern's. "Listen, boy, I could tar and feather you with a snap of my fingers and no one would come to your defense."

"I would," Selah said, taking his arm.

"As would I," said Keturah on his other side.

Shubert huffed a laugh. "Two women coming to your aid? Lady Ket has some fight to her, but this little bit?" He leered down at Selah and cocked his head, leaving the rest unsaid.

Selah felt Jedediah's arm muscles tighten, and in turn she tightened her own grip. "Pay him no heed, Jedediah. He is more bluster than bite."

This made Shubert laugh outright. "Now, pretty Miss Selah, don't be coy! You and your sister *know* that is not true. I've had both of you in my arms, one way or another," he whispered. He reached out to touch her cheek, and she slapped his hand away.

"Stay away from her," Jedediah said, stepping between them.

Angus eyed him. While the two men stood at about the same height, Shubert had a good seventy pounds on Jedediah. Selah was caught between admiration and terror for him. Shubert grabbed hold of his jacket lapels and pulled him closer. "Listen to me, preacher boy. You need to move on from Nevis. We don't want you here. Some think that you help calm the Negroes. I think you rile them up."

"That is not up to you," Jedediah said, wrenching away from his grip. "I only go where God sends me."

"Where God sends you?" scoffed Shubert.

"Where God sends me," he affirmed. "He brought me here. He will give me a sign when 'tis time to leave."

Shubert nodded as if taking that in. "Consider this your sign, boy." Then he rammed a fist against Jedediah's cheek with such force that Jed spun away from Selah and went crashing into the empty flour bin behind him, breaking it with his weight.

He did not rise.

"Angus!" Keturah shouted. "What have you done?"

Selah ran over to the fallen man. "Jedediah!" she cried. "*Jedediah!*"

CHAPTER SIX

Jedediah was unconscious, lying halfway in the empty flour bin and half out. Shubert eased out of the store, followed by his men, acting as if nothing more had transpired than a normal business transaction. Theodore and Mr. Kirk lifted Jedediah out of the decimated flour bin and laid him flat on the floor. Selah didn't know she was crying until Teddy handed her a handkerchief. "He will be all right, Selah," he said, daring to touch her shoulder as she knelt beside him. She could feel the conflict inside him, torn between sorrow, anger, and jealousy for her care over Jedediah.

But all she could really see was Jedediah.

Ket handed the baby to Mr. Kirk and leaned down to listen at Jedediah's nose and mouth. "He breathes," she said, reaching out to touch Selah's hands. "Calm yourself. He is not dead, only unconscious."

"Yes, yes," she said. She trembled all over, and she knew it was partially due to the wake of Shubert's latest attack and memories of what he had done to her and Keturah. She shook her head. To so brazenly reference it, and in front of others! Her cheeks burned. What must Teddy and Mr. Kirk think? And yet, even as the thought raced through her head, she realized that such stories had long been shared and whispered about repeatedly since the day it happened. Such was the way of island gossip.

Keturah squeezed her trembling hand, forcing her to look her in the eye. "'Tis all right, Selah. The lout is gone. You are no longer in danger."

"So 'tis true. Shubert tried to hurt you, Selah?" Teddy asked, crouching beside her and offering a tin cup of water. Mr. Kirk brought a damp cloth for Jedediah's cheek, which Keturah gently laid against it.

"Once, yes, he tried," she said. "If Verity had not had a dagger from Captain McKintrick . . ."

"Which we should have had today," Ket said grimly.

Selah nodded. In her haste to accompany Ket to town, she had forgotten hers in her room. Clearly, Ket had too.

"He needs to be stopped," Mr. Kirk said. "But I do not know who has the power to do it."

Jedediah moaned, coming to, and said something, but none of them could understand it.

"What did you say, Jedediah?" Selah asked, leaning closer to him.

"I said he is strong," he muttered, clearly in pain as he blinked slowly, "but he is not invincible." After a moment, he lifted a hand to gingerly touch what had to be a throbbing cheek. Carefully, he sat up, moving his jaw back and forth as if to see if it still was in working order. "We must pray, my friends. Pray for direction on how to rid the island of this Mr. Shubert."

Verity threw blade after blade against the trunk of the tree, getting ever closer to the center but never quite hitting it. The sgian dubh threw more true, but if she ever had to throw the dagger, she would need another to draw. Perhaps Monsieur Bieulieu would help her obtain others. She smiled in satisfaction. When Ian returned to her, he would be quite impressed with her progress.

Brutus screeched overhead, and she looked up to see Akunta running toward her. In the end, Ian had thought it best not to take the girl with him into probable battle, and Verity was still trying to find the girl the right position on another island. Behind her, she could see dust from the road rising. Someone was approaching, and both girl and bird sought to warn her. Ian had rented this cottage with the views in mind—as well as a clear visibility of the sea—and dubbed it "Eagle View." From here she could monitor the comings and goings of ships near St. Kitts, which she marked down in a journal. Given its proximity, Statia was a burr under the saddle of the loyalists of St. Kitts, given their propensity to trade with anyone and everyone. They knew that Statia was likely supplying their enemies, the French and Spanish that held other islands in the Indies among them. And they were forces the American rebels lobbied to come to their aid.

Akunta reached her, panting from her effort. "Who is it, Akunta?" She shielded her eyes to try to see the coach.

"George thinks 'tis Monsieur Bieulieu," she answered.

"Very well. Let us get to the cottage. Is Trisa preparing some refreshments?"

"Yes'm."

"Wonderful. Be sure to help George take care of his horse and carriage straightaway. Bring him the step stool, then be sure his driver can find some shade and water for his horse." The girl nodded, and Verity knew she was telling her to do things she would do anyway, eagerly taking on every task she could to prove herself useful. Still, it settled Verity's nerves to chatter on. Bieulieu approached. What was her answer? Would she assist him in obtaining information from Nevis in exchange for supplies? What would Ian think of that? Her sisters?

They reached the cottage just as Bieulieu's driver pulled around the front and drew his smart stallion to a halt. Verity hadn't seen this horse when she was at his shop and stopped to pat the stallion's neck and croon over him. "He is lovely," she said, admiring his forelock and glistening coat.

"Indeed, but not as fine as the pair you are rumored to have on Nevis."

"True," she said with a smile. She felt a pang of guilt—not her first—that Ket and Gray had to feed her horses in the midst of their struggle. She knew she should tell them to sell the team and carriage to anyone who would give them a fair price or exchange them for supplies. She simply could not make herself do it yet. The pair had been a gift from Ian. And also from Duncan, in a way. To think of them in another's hands, to be given anything less than wonderful care or feed . . . she could not bear the thought.

"Welcome to Eagle View Cottage," she said as the man bowed over her hand.

"*Merci beaucoup*," he said, straightening. "'Tis aptly named." From under the brim of his hat he took in the sweeping views and then offered his arm. They climbed the steps and settled on veranda chairs just as Trisa set a tray with teapot, cups, and biscuits on the table between them. She immediately poured a cup of the steaming liquid for each of them.

Bieulieu lifted his teacup and savored a sip. "A fine brew. From where did you obtain it? I have had a terrible time importing tea of late. I fear our American friends will soon have to resort to their dreadful dandelion tea more often than not. The British have a solid hold on the Indian trade."

"'Tis my last tin that I brought from New York," she admitted. "My cousin—a spy for the Sons of Freedom—made certain I had squirreled it away in my trunk before we made our escape."

"And your cousin is?"

"Albert Harrington. Once an alderman in New York, now presumably with the Continental Congress in Philadelphia."

"I see." Bieulieu tucked his chin thoughtfully. "Do you have any other cousins who might be of such use?"

She offered him a biscuit. "I fear not. All that remain are back in England."

"So our best use of your connections is your family on Nevis. Given that they quarter a high-ranking soldier?"

"Perhaps. Major Woodget is rather tight-lipped."

"Does he keep papers in his room? Letters from his commander and the like?"

Verity swallowed before nodding. Was he suggesting she go into the man's room and rifle through them? She shook her head. "I do not believe my brother-in-law would sanction such action. As host to those men, 'tis his duty to protect their property and privacy."

"Then do not let him know, and he can honestly profess ignorance," he said easily. "Is your sister as dedicated?"

"Less so, but she will stand behind her husband's decision." She nervously twisted her handkerchief. "There are many on Nevis who are wise to Ian's connections to the rebels. I shall be suspected too."

"What is to suspect?" he asked, raising his hands. "You are but a woman in need of a visit with her beloved sisters, no? You might say your husband has abandoned you." His lips twitched in a sly smile. "You need not inform them for how long."

"That is plausible," she admitted.

"What of your other sister? Might she aid us?"

"Selah?" The name emerged from her mouth, laced with doubt. But had it not been Selah and the young preacher who had dared to bring Akunta to them on Saba? Obviously her little sister was no longer a child; she was capable of making daring decisions. Verity settled back in her chair, considering, and looked to the sea. No, Selah was no longer a young girl. She was a young woman, coming into her own. And she owed Verity, in a way, for saving Akunta.

"I can see you thinking," Bieulieu said. "What is it that drives your Selah? Might she be a friend to our cause?"

"Perhaps." Verity nodded. "But 'tis the well-being of the plantation's workers that most captivates her mind and heart. She would do much to keep them fed. And if we were to aid others in danger to escape"—she cocked a brow—"she might be willing to do a great deal."

"*Bon*," he said, patting his thigh. *Good*. "I believe you should sail frequently to Nevis. Arrive with nothing but a small trunk. Stay a night or two—make it appear as nothing more than a weekly reunion between sisters."

She hesitated, resorting to wringing her handkerchief again. 'Twas one thing to become a spy herself, yet quite another to lure her sister into doing so.

"We shall load a ketch with supplies that they can off-load at night. You can do a bit of reconnaissance. Have a conversation with Miss Selah and perhaps venture into the major's room to see what is readily visible." The words tumbled off his tongue as if she prepared to do little more than propose a game of whist.

But the desire to see her sisters—to hold little Madeleine—was what ultimately made her agree. At least to determine if there was a way to review the major's correspondence. "I shall go. Day after tomorrow? You shall make the arrangements?"

"Indeed."

She rose with him, and again he bowed over her extended hand. "You are a fine woman, Mrs. McKintrick. An asset to our cause."

"We shall see about that. I might not be able to obtain anything valuable at all," she warned. "I am reluctant to endanger my loved ones."

He shrugged his round shoulders. "These are perilous times, madame, regardless of which side of the line you find yourself. Do what you can on Nevis. Something is always better than nothing." He walked down the steps and turned back to her as he placed his tricorn atop his head. "Remember that any information gained shall benefit your husband as well, yes? The more we aid the cause, the sooner this war—and your separation—shall end."

Keturah insisted that Jedediah spend the night in the big house, where they could keep watch over him. Given that his head was throbbing so much he could barely tolerate keeping his eyes open, he could not summon the strength to dissuade her. Only Lieutenant Cesley, who had to temporarily move in with Lieutenant Angersoll, seemed to take issue with it. As the younger soldiers assisted the man up to his room, Major Woodget turned to Selah. "So Councilman Shubert struck the lad for no reason?"

"Indeed," Selah said. "They had a disagreement, but Jedediah was nothing but polite in his retort. It was Angus Shubert who resorted to violence. Will you carry my complaint to the sheriff?

He was not in his office when we stopped by, and I wished only to get Jedediah back to the Double T to rest."

"Of course," the major said.

Gray and Philip had been listening in. Philip paced while Gray leaned against a wall, arms crossed. "Tell us exactly how it transpired, Selah."

She glanced nervously at Ket. Situations like this—especially when they involved Angus Shubert—made Gray fiercely angry. But she had no choice other than to tell her brother-in-law everything.

The muscles in Gray's jaw twitched as he slowly turned toward his wife. "You should not have been there at all, Ket," he said quietly. "You knew I had already been to see Kirk about supplies and been refused."

Keturah sighed as she sat down. "I hoped he would not be able to refuse me and your fetching daughter."

"I could have told you Shubert would be keeping watch on his mercantile. He knows Kirk still has a soft spot for us. And given his intent to try and starve us out, he needs to close that supply chain."

"He truly is reprehensible, is he not?" asked Major Woodget.

"Reprehensible is too kind a word for him," Gray said.

"I will speak to the sheriff myself," the major promised. "Just as soon as you pen your report, Miss Selah. You should sign it as well, Lady Ket."

"Thank you, Major," Selah said, and Keturah nodded. "Is there . . . is there nothing you can do about the supply issue?"

The older man gave her a sorrowful look. "Believe me, I have tried. But as despicable as we believe Shubert to be, there are many on-island who owe him in one way or another. And unfortunately there is nothing illegal in persuading merchants not to trade with the Double T. However, striking Reverend Reed is something the sheriff would have just cause to pursue."

He shifted his tricorn in his hands. "I am keenly aware that it is a struggle to feed all on the Double T, including those of us you have been asked to quarter. I have gained word that a supply ship is due any day, and you can be certain I will see to it you are compensated for the supplies you have expended on us and, with a bit of luck, still more beyond that."

"Thank you, Major," Gray said. "We would be most grateful."

Selah rose to meet Ket at Gray's writing desk. The sooner they could send off their report on what had transpired, the happier she would be. She withdrew a piece of vellum from the shallow drawer and uncorked the ink before glancing up at her sister as she handed Madeleine to her eager father. Together they pieced together what they wished to say, and Selah swiftly wrote it out. Once complete, she read it over, sanded it, then handed the report to the major.

"We shall see to it the sheriff receives this right away," he said, glancing at Captain Howard. They left the house, Gray and Philip following them out.

Keturah went to the kitchen to consult about supper plans, and Selah found herself suddenly alone. She laid a hand on the carved post at the bottom of the staircase, looking upward. She wanted to go look in on Jedediah but knew Mitilda had been up there not fifteen minutes before. And if Ket found her in his bedchamber, she would be most displeased.

No, for tonight, all that could be done had been done. She longed for nothing more than a dip in the pool up the hill or one in the ocean. After enduring the oppressive heat over the last few days and the drama in town, she needed the kind of escape only a swim could afford. Selah was about to go and ask Keturah when Abe came running in. "Miss Selah! Your sister! She just arrived at the pier!"

"Verity?" Selah squealed. "Tell Ket!" She picked up her skirts and raced out the door, down the steps, and took to the beach path. Halfway down, surrounded by the dense angel's trumpet shrubs covered in peach flowers that lent a heady scent to the air, she came across her sister. "Verity!"

"Selah," Ver said with a smiling sigh of satisfaction, opening her arms.

"Oh, I am so glad to see you," Selah said, sinking into her embrace. "More than I can say, actually."

"Because of the supplies I bring," Verity asked under her breath, turning to take her arm, "or because you needed me?"

"Well, primarily because I am so glad to see you," Selah said. "But I cannot deny that supplies are always welcome. Only this morning, Mr. Kirk refused me and Keturah."

"Try not to fear that too much, dear one. I have a plan that might ease such tension. At least for a while."

"A plan? Perhaps we may speak of it whilst we take a dip in the jungle pool?"

"Oh, that sounds divine!" Verity said, squeezing her arm. "'Tis been so hot on Statia that I thought I might melt like a pool of beeswax in the flames."

"Here as well."

Keturah discovered them on the path then, and all three embraced. For the first time all day, Selah felt she could take a deep breath. *If only we three could always be together*, she thought. In their combined presence, she felt settled. Whole.

Selah knew that was no longer possible—to always be together. Already they were merely fortunate to have Verity within reach for a time. And who knew whom Selah would marry herself, and where her husband would wish to go? As Verity scurried up the stairs, anxious to get her hands on the baby, Selah paused and looked back toward the turquoise sea. They had come together across the broad Atlantic. Verity had traveled even farther, to the American Colonies and back. Would the sea take Selah away at some point too?

She wrapped her arms around a veranda post and continued to scan the windswept waves between Nevis and St. Kitts. There had not been a potential suitor in some time. Teddy Kirk was dear, but she could no more imagine kissing him than Abe's monkey Biri. And thoughts of kisses only reminded her of Jedediah. Of how it had felt to be in his arms. Of how he had moved to protect her, best as he could, in the store. What would it be like to have him court her? What would it be like to marry a preacher, intent on going anywhere in the world God directed him?

Selah shook her head. *No.* As much as the man intrigued and delighted her with his fine heart and mind, her place was here, as close to her sisters as she could be. Even if she remained a spinster to the end of her days.

CHAPTER SEVEN

That evening, after Verity held the cherubic Madeleine for hours, entertaining her with little presents she had pulled from her satchel—a new silver rattle from Spain, a ball from Germany, and a jack-in-the-box from France—the sisters finally made their escape to the pool.

When Verity sank into the blessedly cool water, she moaned with pleasure. "I simply must find something like this on Statia. I would be entirely less cross in the heat if I knew this was awaiting me at the end of the day."

Selah smiled. "Or you could simply move back in with us," she said. "Return to the Double T until Ian returns for you?"

Verity gave her a tender look. "I shall be here as often as I can to see you all. But 'tis good that I might smuggle in some goods here and there, yes?"

"Indeed," Ket said, leaning back against the mossy rocks. "But how long can you afford to do so? I can only assume that supplies on Statia are as costly as they are on Nevis."

"To some extent," Verity said, settling beside her, "but the French have a steadier supply of grain and corn than the British do. They have already supplanted their American supplies with those from Africa and are running fairly effective blockades against British vessels attempting to do the same."

"Even though they have not formally signed on to support the Patriots?" Keturah asked.

"Oh, they are in support of the Patriots," Verity said. "They simply prefer to keep that support covert for as long as possible. 'Tis far less expensive to operate via espionage and smuggling in weapons and supplies than 'tis to commit soldiers to the cause."

"If they did, perhaps it would end this madness faster," Keturah said.

Verity moved out in the water to better see both of them. "Would you like that? To see this budding war end before it fully flowers?"

Keturah blinked wearily and rubbed her wet face. "Would not *everyone* like that? A war that lingers will only further wound us all. Men shall be lost on both sides. Women and children, without adequate supplies, shall perish. War brings pestilence with it. How many will die of dysentery? Exposure to either sun or snow? Yes, of course I would like to see it end sooner than later."

Verity lifted a hand cupped with water and watched it drip to the surface. "Would you be willing to do something to aid our cause, Ket?" she whispered, glancing around at the dense jungle around them. "Or you, Selah? Something that would help the Sons of Freedom forward? After all, the sooner we convince the British to relinquish their hold on the colonies, the faster this all ends."

Selah frowned. "Of what do you speak?"

"I think you know of what I speak," Verity whispered, steadily staring into her eyes before facing Ket. "You quarter four soldiers, one of whom likely has important papers in his desk. Information that would be advantageous for the rebels' cause to know about, sooner rather than later."

"You have chosen a life of espionage, Verity," Ket said quietly, "and I understand your rationale for doing so. Indeed, I have thought about it more than once, given my irritation with Britain's ignorance of how they harm her own. But our position on this island is already perilous. Our association with you, the wife of a known rebel captain, brings us additional scrutiny. We cannot do more."

"Even if it meant that I could keep the Double T in constant supply of food, clothing, and more in return for your sugar?"

Ket's eyes narrowed. "I have Madeleine to consider, Verity. Selah here as well."

"I too am considering them both," Verity said.

"Are you?" Keturah bit out, moving to exit the pool. "I think not. I think you are only considering ways to further *your* cause."

"I am considering that as well," Verity said calmly, refusing to chase after her. "But also how to keep my beloved family and the people of the Double T from slowly starving to death. You spoke of the perils of war. Without access to proper food, how much more vulnerable shall you all be to the next round of the pox? Or malaria?"

Keturah sighed as she pulled her loose dress over her head and ran her fingers through wet hair. "I will consider what you've said, Sissy. But you know I would have to discuss it with Gray."

"Of course," Verity said.

Clearly unsettled by their discussion, Ket lifted her hands and looked up to the sky, gauging the sun. "Are you two coming? Supper will be on the table in an hour."

"We shall follow you in a few minutes." Selah knew as well as Verity did that when Ket grew agitated, the best remedy was to give her some time and space to think through what was bothering her. In time, she would settle, regardless of what she decided about Verity's proposal.

"Very well," Keturah sniffed, turning to descend down the path.

Verity leaned against the bank with Selah again, and the two stared up toward the swaying palms filtering the early evening sun. Both were chilled, but it was better to be shivering for once rather than having sweat trickling down their backs.

"Verity," Selah ventured, "if Keturah refuses you, I might not. To keep the people of the Double T alive . . . I think I would consider it worth the sacrifice of loyalty to the Crown."

Verity said nothing for some time. "Your love for them goes deep, Sissy."

"More and more each day, it seems."

"And what of the young preacher who accompanied you that night with Akunta? 'Twas he who rose to your defense in town?"

"'Twas," Selah admitted.

"Has he opened your heart further to the people?"

Selah considered that. "He has made me think of what I am willing to give up to aid them. Never did I believe a white man might come and work with our people, sacrificing every comfort to do so. Never did I believe a white man would toil in the fields beside them, expecting no pay other than food and a roof over his head. All so that they might see his love for them and open their hearts to the Word of God. 'Tis alone what fuels him."

"Are you certain 'tis that alone? Does he not have an eye for you?"

"Oh! I do not know."

Verity moved away from the rock wall and faced her. "Come now, Sissy. Out with it. This is the pool where all three of us have had very frank conversations about the men in our lives. Is this Jedediah Reed a man you would like to court you?"

Selah sighed. "I am uncertain." She ran her hand through the water, watching as tiny waves circled outward and away. "With Ian, you were well aware of the dangers you would face. Becoming a rebel's bride, joining him in his work to aid the freedom fighters. But Jedediah . . . do you know what he said to Angus Shubert before he hit him?"

Verity shook her head.

"He said he would leave this island only when God gave him a sign to do so. I have never known anyone who received a sign from God. Nor anyone who spoke of it as if it were a common occurrence. Have you?"

Again, Verity shook her head but this time gave a small smile. "And yet it sounds like that intrigues you. Yes?"

Selah nodded. "Yes, he *does* intrigue me. I have never met anyone like him."

"You admire him."

"In ways, yes. He is so purely focused, Ver. So passionate. If you could hear him preach . . ."

"May I? Does he preach every night?"

"Most nights, but tonight he shall be abed. Recovering from his injury."

"Ah, yes," Verity said. "Would your Reverend Reed declare me bound for hell if I said I wished Angus Shubert would catch the pox and die?"

Selah giggled and lifted her brows in surprise. "Perhaps. But I think even Jed would like to see Shubert shanghaied and hauled off to the Orient."

Verity moved to exit the pool, shivering as her wet skin met the shadows of the trees about them. Reluctantly, Selah followed. "Then perhaps there will be another opportunity for me to hear him when I visit next."

"Perhaps," Selah said, drying off and reaching for her dress. And in that moment, her intense desire to have Verity listen to Jed surprised her. Was it because she wanted affirmation of her admiration for him?

Verity had slept with Selah, but come morning her elder sister had claimed more than three-quarters of the bed. Giving up on further slumber, Selah hurriedly dressed, brushed her hair into a loose braid, then eased out of the room and tiptoed down the hall to the room Jedediah temporarily inhabited. The door was firmly shut, and there were no sounds within.

There was no way she could check on him unaccompanied. So she moved to the stairs and down to the kitchen, intent on helping Mitilda put together a tray that might entice the young man to break his fast, even if his headache persisted. She sliced fresh mango and cooked two eggs that Verity had brought. Mitilda placed a fresh biscuit on the tray and poured steaming tea into a cup. Selah leaned over it and inhaled deeply. They hadn't had tea in weeks, and she knew Verity likely had sacrificed her own stash in order to share.

This morning—at least for one day—the household would have a breakfast like they had not enjoyed in a long time. Sansa lifted the tray. "Shall I take it to Mr. Reed now, miss?"

"Oh . . . would you mind if I accompany you? I'd very much like to see for myself how he fares."

"Only to know how he fares, is it?" Mitilda asked pointedly, casting her a sly grin.

"Well, yes," Selah insisted, feeling the heat of a blush at her cheeks. "The man came to my defense yesterday. I owe him a measure of care."

"I think that man had a measure of your care even before yesterday."

"Mitilda! You truly are speaking out of turn," she said, leaning closer in order to whisper.

"Am I?" Mitilda whispered back, lifting a brow. "Forgive me then, miss," she said as she straightened. But there was no apology in her pretty eyes, only triumph. "See to it you stay in the room with Miss Selah, Sansa. I will not have her reputation compromised by someone discovering them alone."

"Yes'm," Sansa said, then followed Selah out the door.

It was good that Mitilda did not know about the kiss Jedediah stole, Selah thought. Or had she heard something about it from the soldiers? The cook always knew far more about everyone on the Double T than anyone else and seemed to take a certain pride in it.

Together, she and Sansa climbed the stairs, and after a brief knock, Selah opened the door for Sansa.

Jedediah was sitting up in bed, his rumpled hair and wan complexion somehow pulling at her affections, along with the spreading bruise on his lower cheek. "How do you fare this morning, Jedediah?" she asked as Sansa settled the tray of food on the table beside him.

He gave her his loose grin, winced, and rubbed his jaw on the bruised side. He shrugged slightly before running a hand through his hair. "Better with your fine company, Selah. As well as dear Sansa's," he added easily. "And with food such as this? Did my throbbing head keep me from seeing a supply ship drop precious cargo at the Double T?"

"Something like that," Selah said with a small smile. "How *is* your head?"

"Better than yesterday and through the night. But still a trouble." He closed his eyes and gingerly touched his cheek. "Does it look as terrible as it feels?"

Sansa came to the other side of his bed. "I can get you a new poultice, Mr. Reed. Did it help las' night?"

"Yes, I believe it did. As did your tincture for the headache. Do you have any more of that?"

"I do." She moved to go and fetch it but then paused at the door, as if remembering Mitilda's stern warning.

Selah stifled a sigh and turned to go with her. "See that you eat all that fine food, Jedediah. It shall be an aid to your headache, I believe, by easing your empty stomach."

"Yes, ma'am," he said with a smile. But it was followed by another wince. "And then perhaps a bit more of a nap. After that, I shall rise and relinquish this room back to its rightful master."

"Do not rush," Selah said. "Rest and rest well. You can stay another night if necessary. I am certain Lieutenant Cesley shall not mind, now that he's settled next door."

"Thank you, Selah," he said as she closed the door behind her. She stood there a moment, thinking about the sound of her name on his lips, as well as Verity's questions about him the night before. And then she reluctantly followed Sansa downstairs to wait for him to rise.

By early afternoon, Selah wondered if she should concoct a reason to check on him again. She had utilized any excuse she had to linger about, waiting on him. She'd completed hours of embroidery. Watched Verity walk Madeleine back and forth across

the veranda, cooing and smiling and continuing on even as the
babe slept. She finally turned to the harpsichord and shuffled the
music to a minuet by Bach, her favorite whenever she was feeling
unsettled. Her fingers felt stiff, and she realized it had been quite
some time since she had played. Still, she soldiered on, easing into
the chorus, losing her place, starting again and then losing her
place again. When she'd finished, she began again, and while it
was imperfect it went much more smoothly. She searched a leather
folder of sheet music and brought out another favorite.

When she looked up, she discovered Jedediah was standing at the
end of the harpsichord, flashing her his lopsided grin. "Jedediah!"
she cried. "What are you doing up out of bed?"

"Sansa's tincture brought further aid to my throbbing head.
And then I could not help but hear you down here playing."

"I disturbed your rest. Forgive me."

"No, no. I found it . . . intriguing. Here I had come to believe
that you had no imperfections, and then I heard how you were
abusing this fine musical instrument." He sidled a teasing grin at
her as he ran his hands across the beautiful mahogany.

"A-*abusing* it!" she said, standing up, hands on hips. She was
half infuriated by his uncharacteristic affront, half amused by
his daring. "I suppose you can do better? The harpsichord is an
awkward partner for most musicians."

"Ahh, but I am not like most musicians," he said, lifting a cocky
brow.

She stiffly gestured to the bench. "Well then. Prove yourself."

"It has been some time, though, since—"

"Ah, no," she said, waggling a finger at him with a grin. "One
cannot so sorely offend his hostess and then not show her why he
believes he has due cause."

"Due cause?" He stifled another teasing grin. "Can you honestly
not hear yourself, dear lady? You are as kind as you are beautiful,
Miss Selah. But you really should not be trusted alone with an
innocent musical instrument."

She laughed in shock. Over the fact that he had called her *dear lady*, but also that he thought her beautiful. But that he would say such a thing so plainly! Had Shubert's punch robbed him of any sense of decorum? Or had it been Sansa's tincture, ingested with a heady portion of rum?

Surely her sisters had teased her over the years for her lack of prowess on the keys. But neither of them had even tried to play since they came to Nevis. There was something to be admired in the attempt, wasn't there?

She bit her lip and pointed again to the bench. "Play, Reverend Reed. Play with such beauty that I can do nothing but accept your teasing criticism." She folded her arms.

"As you wish," he said, sliding onto the bench with practiced ease. He glanced up at her, and she could see that the bruise on his cheek had darkened to an ugly purple. "I do not wish to add injury to insult," he said. "Shall I play something other than what you were attempting?"

She huffed out a shocked laugh and folded her arms. "Next you shall tell me you compose your own pieces?"

"I have, but I confess it has been some time since I attempted to recall them."

"Uh-uh," she said, waving a finger. "No excuses. Grace me with one of those, Reverend Reed." She moved to perch on the edge of the settee. Perhaps a challenge such as this would knock him down a peg or two.

His long fingers moved over the keys, and his face became intent. From the moment he closed his eyes and leaned in, playing a tune that spoke of yearning and hope, Selah was utterly captivated. As the song built to a crescendo, Ket, Mitilda, and Sansa emerged from the kitchen to listen, as did Gray and Verity from the veranda. And when he finished, she had no choice but to applaud along with everyone else.

Afterward, Gray made formal introductions between Jedediah and Verity, unaware the two had met before. Both managed to behave rather naturally.

"Jedediah," Selah said, eager to move past their awkward

exchange, "that was possibly the most beautiful thing I have ever heard."

"I concur," Gray said, clapping him on the shoulder. "Where did you learn to play like that, man?"

"There was a time my parents intended me to become a church organist. I have played ever since I was a small child."

"As have I," Selah said. "But as you have witnessed, my lessons never seemed to stick as they have with you."

"It goes beyond lessons," Gray said. "You have a gift, Jedediah."

"It must have sorely grieved your parents when you did not pursue a position in a grand church," Selah said.

Jedediah shook his head and gave her a small smile. "They were saddened, primarily because they would not have the opportunity to hear me play. We never had the means to purchase our own instrument. I could only play at my tutor's home or in the church."

"Well, feel free to play ours anytime you wish," Keturah said. "I would love to hear more."

"As would I," Selah said.

"You know," Gray said, "that has given me a thought." He paced to the window, hands clasped behind his back, then turned toward them. "What if we invited a portion of our neighbors for an evening of music? Hearing Jedediah play might keep them from agreeing to Shubert's attempt to cast him as nothing but a rabble-rouser among the slaves. And 'twould give us opportunity to break down a portion of the walls he has built around us."

"Oh no, sir. 'Tis been years since I played before an audience," Jedediah began.

"And time away has obviously not hindered you," he retorted. "That was as finely played as any I enjoyed in England's concert halls."

"But, Gray," Keturah said, "how would we provide refreshments for such a gathering?"

"I wager Verity could assist us with some delicacies," he said, lifting an arched brow in her direction. She nodded eagerly in return. "And there is always plenty of rum punch to be shared. We shall invite them for an after-dinner event. They shall understand. Many face similar challenges in supplies."

"Do you believe any would attend?" Keturah asked. "After all, 'tis been a long while since we were invited to another's home."

"Nevisians grow weary of the constant strain of our times. The promise of music and some levity shall prove impossible for most to decline, even from us. I shall begin with the Brownings. If they agree to come, others will surely follow."

Keturah nodded. "And let us include the Kirks. Perhaps if some of our neighbors heard of Shubert's transgressions from someone other than those of the Double T, they would look more leniently upon us."

Gray clapped his hands together. "Good, then. 'Tis agreed. We shall gather in four days' time for a proper soiree on the Double T."

"Four days?" Keturah choked out. "How can we possibly be ready in four days?"

"Verity," he said, moving toward her, "can it be done? Might you find some delicacies to offer our guests?"

"I believe so, yes."

"The rest is at hand, correct?" He gestured around the house, then to Jed. "I do not want Jedediah's bruise to fade before those who once were our friends hear him play. I want them forced to consider who Shubert truly is."

Keturah stared at him, slowly crossed her arms, and then tapped her lip before pointing at him. "You, my love, are beginning a campaign to oust our greatest threat from his councilman's seat."

Gray barely hid a smile as he lifted a brow. "It may have crossed my mind."

"'Tis brilliant," she said.

"Let us hope so." Gray put a hand on Jed's shoulder again. "And you, my friend, must show them that you lead our people not toward unrest but peace. Preach of that in the coming days, will you? We need our visitors to see the bounty of the Double T—be it our contented people or the verdant cane fields. Are you so willing?"

Jedediah nodded, looking a bit dazed. "If you truly believe it will assist you, sir, I am willing."

"Good man." With a firm pat to his shoulder, he led Keturah to the veranda to further discuss their plans. Mitilda and Sansa returned to the kitchen, Verity behind them, and once again Jedediah and Selah were alone.

"You shall play a piece or two yourself?" he asked her.

"Ah, no. As you have heard, I play primarily for my own amusement. I shall not give others reason to tease me as you have."

Jedediah chuckled and shook his head as Selah walked to the harpsichord and leaned against it. "What is it?" she asked.

"My Lord," he said.

"Your Lord?"

"Yes. Only our Lord would find such a way to put me back in my place." He fingered two keys, thinking. "I confess I only wanted to show off a bit," he said, meeting her gaze.

"Oh?" Selah felt the heat of a blush return to her cheeks.

"Yes. I was teasing you, and in so doing I used a bit of bravado. And now the Lord has made certain I shall do nothing but practice for days so that I shall not embarrass you or your kin."

She grinned. "See that you do not abuse this poor instrument," she said, running her fingers across the wood as she left him. "Or I shall have my opportunity to tease *you* mercilessly about it," she cast over her shoulder.

CHAPTER EIGHT

The mood was high on the Double T a couple of days later, even among those in the meetinghouse. Gray had succeeded in securing the Brownings' agreement to attend their gathering later in the week, and the rest of the family knew that with them in attendance, families such as the Welands, Hudsons, and Carlsons would attend too. After that, they were uncertain. There could be many others who came out of curiosity, or many who refused out of fear of repercussions from other Nevisians. The Covingtons prepared for nearly a hundred, yet they feared there might be as few as twenty.

"Whatever will be, will be," Jedediah said to Selah after she had professed her concern.

Now that she'd engaged in Gray's vision of beginning to whittle away at Angus Shubert's foundation, she could think of little else. "I recognize that," she said, rising to pace. "But I can wish for the very best."

"Or we can pray for it."

Matthew looked up at them from his Bible reading. "Do you believe that the Lord cares about things such as island parties?"

"I do," Jedediah said. A child of about five climbed onto his lap, reaching up to touch his injured cheek, and Jed crossed his eyes at him, making him laugh. "The Lord cares about parties because he cares for his people." He gave the boy a gentle hug and then set him to the side. "And justice," he went on, rising to face Selah, Matthew, and the others who were coming closer. "And power as well—he is concerned about power. By both those who wield it and those who find themselves oppressed. But no matter where we find ourselves, 'tis he who holds ultimate power."

Still others drew nearer to listen. More poured in from the porch outside. This was how it transpired every evening. After supper, casual conversation turned into an opportunity for him to teach.

"So if God on High cares for us and cares for those things that concern us, and if he holds ultimate power—which he certainly does—then we are best served by trusting him for what will be rather than fearing what might not." He cast Selah a tender smile before moving on.

She nodded and smiled in return. It struck her then. Since Jedediah Reed had arrived on the Double T, her understanding about God and faith had expanded and deepened in ways she hadn't anticipated. In fact, she hadn't even known she *wanted* to grow in such ways. But it excited her to press into such matters.

"So if we are to put our lives in our faithful Father's hands, we relinquish fretting and fear. We trust what comes as his will, knowing that he remains with us through it all," Jed said, moving about the meetinghouse. "And in time, *in time*, even if 'tis not until the day we leave this earth and enter eternity, 'twill all be made right. With that in mind, we can rest in what is today."

Selah took a long, deep breath. His words made sense to her. But could she really be at peace with Angus Shubert, even if he held on to his councilman's seat? Even if he continued to use every opportunity to taunt and harass her and her family? Even if she continued to learn of further abuse of his people?

She spoke before she thought. "How are we to forgive those who have abused us?" she asked. "To live in peace with our tormentors?"

All eyes shifted to Jedediah, who looked gravely back at her. "The world is full of evil. Truth be told, we are full of evil. I sin. You sin. We make poor choices. Some give in to temptations that impact us. So it helps me, at least, to feel compassion for those who oppress or abuse me, knowing that only the grace of God keeps me from similar transgressions."

"Compassion for them!" exclaimed an older man.

"Yes, compassion for them," Jedediah said. "For when I can summon compassion for my enemy, then I can also summon grace."

"Some souls don' deserve grace," groused an older woman.

"It certainly appears that way, does it not?" he said, nodding in agreement. "Thankfully, Christ is merciful. No one who believes in Christ lives beyond grace. To judge another is to sit on our Savior's throne. And not a one of us—be they white or black—has that power."

Selah rose and went to the door. She did not want to think of Angus Shubert receiving God's mercy. She wanted Angus Shubert to suffer as he had made others suffer. When Jed's back was turned, she slipped outside, breathing in great draughts of the cooling evening air. She had not even realized she had been holding her breath.

Grabbing hold of her lantern, she scurried down the steps and along the path to the big house. She was almost there when Jedediah caught up with her. She heard the rushing steps of his boots in the gravel and turned, knowing it was him before she did so.

"Selah," he said, panting. He straightened and ran a hand through his hair. "You left. Why? Did I offend you?"

"No," she said, shaking her head. "Well, yes."

"What? What did I say?"

She lifted her gaze and studied him. "You were preaching about Angus Shubert. A man who hit you. A man who tried to hurt me and my sisters. A man who has hurt many others."

"Yes," he said softly.

She swallowed hard. "You are apparently more adept with turning the other cheek than I, Jedediah. My heart heard your words. But my mind desires to find a way to make Shubert pay for all the evil he has done."

He nodded and bit his lip. "I understand."

"But you," she said, reaching up to lightly trace his bruised cheek, "have already forgiven him?"

They stared into each other's eyes until he gave her a rueful smile. "I am working on forgiving him. Angus Shubert is not the first or last man who has hurt me. Nor will he be the last to hurt you, Selah." He rubbed the back of his neck. "Which reminds me . . . I must beg your forgiveness. Belatedly."

"Forgiveness?"

"For stealing a kiss from you that night we . . ." His words faded away as he glanced around, obviously worried someone might overhear them speaking of Akunta.

She lifted her chin, considering him. "The kiss was merely a means to cover our tracks with the soldiers, yes?" She could feel the slow burn of a blush climbing her neck.

"Well yes, but—"

"It was rather quick of you, to think of it," she said. She dared to look up into his eyes again, finding her heart was pounding. She wanted him to deny it. To confess that he had kissed her for reasons beyond explaining why they were out together at such an hour. But she could only make out sorrow in his eyes. Regret.

"Selah, I am not free to pursue you. Nor am I worthy of a lady of your stature. Do you not see how your sister objects to our idle flirtation? And for that I must beg your forgiveness too." He drew in a deep breath. "You are a fine woman, winsome in many ways. But my heart is already claimed by this ministry, this calling. I hope you can understand."

"Oh, of course," she said, lifting a hand, forcing a light smile. "Of course!"

"'Tis not any shortcoming I find in you, Selah. 'Tis only that—"

"There is no further explanation necessary, Jed. We are friends. As you said, there has been nothing but idle flirtation between us. I shall see that curtailed at once. Shall you?"

He nodded once, looking most unhappy. "I must confess—"

"No, Jed." She shook her head. "I believe you have confessed enough. Good eve," she said with a brief curtsy, then turned to go without another word.

But as she slipped through the kitchen door and dropped the

latch, she leaned her back against it, imagining Jedediah reluctantly returning to the meetinghouse. And it was only then that she wished she had allowed him to say what else he'd wished.

Because now her mind would be full of *I-wonder-if*s all night long.

Idle flirtation, he'd said, and she repeated it. The words roiled about in Jedediah's mind as he trudged back up the hill. There had been a part of him that wanted her to object to him calling it that. Show him that she cared for him. Yet what right did he have to wish for that when he was not willing to do the same? Truth be told, he had long thought of kissing her before it happened, but that had not made it right. A gentlewoman should be warned, asked. Not simply pressed upon.

He hoped she would not avoid him or the meetinghouse now. He definitely sensed interest in her about the faith. She seemed to linger when he preached; he had assumed she was hungry to learn and grow. But tonight, it seemed only to repel her. What was it he had said? He tried to recall every word, each nuance that might have led to such a poor outcome.

Had it been the fact that he was obviously referring to Shubert? Or that he had apologized for his kiss? He had half a mind to tell her that he had thought of little else since, despite his earnest prayers for relief from his Lord. But it was good that she had cut him off. 'Twas best if he allowed what germinated between them to wither.

But why did it not feel right?

This was the reason Paul remained single, he thought. It was impossible to put on the mind of Christ when one was besotted. The task was dizzying.

He climbed the steps to the meetinghouse. So absorbed was he in his thoughts that he did not see Matthew waiting on him. The young overseer leaned against the wall of the meetinghouse, arms crossed.

"Our Miss Selah," he began, bringing Jed's head up, "she has a mind of her own."

"Wh-what? Oh, yes," Jed said. "Of course."

"She been through her share of trials and tribulations," he continued on.

Jedediah considered him, trying to make out his expression in the dark. What was he trying to say? "I have gathered that," he said at last.

"I've been here to witness most of it," Matthew said. "Almost from the start. Miss Selah is young, but I have seen her stand up to face down a giant, like David and Goliath. I have seen her nurse the sick through the night, forsaking her own need. I have it on good authority that she has hidden away her own rations of food when supplies are lean, and given them to the young and old among us."

Jedediah turned to face him, hands on his hips. "Matthew, why are you telling me this?"

Matthew shoved off the wall, strode to the edge of the porch, and stared out to the sea, the wash of her waves a constant, soothing rhythm. He glanced back, and Jed could make out the fine lines of his nose and cheek, strikingly similar to his sister Mitilda's, in the dancing light of the lantern.

"I am telling you she has a good heart."

Jed frowned. "You think I am unaware of that?"

"Are you?"

"Yes."

"I've seen you, Jedediah, looking after her. She is a mighty fine-looking woman."

"Yes, she is. Perhaps the most comely woman I have ever met."

"So if it is not her heart or beauty that holds you back from pursuing her, why are you dragging your feet?"

Jed looked away, embarrassed to be so easily discovered. "It is because I am uncertain. I have always thought I would remain single. This ministry is full of hardships, hardships no lady should be asked to endure. 'Twould be unfair of me."

Matthew stared at him. "You were preaching on God's will this night. Trusting him for what is, not fearing what might be."

"I was," Jed said slowly.

"You mean to say that the God who brought you here, the God who brought Miss Selah here, the God that set two white folks on such a similar path did not intend for you to be together?"

After a moment, Matthew left Jed standing there. Something he had never done before. Something no black man, freed or not, did in the presence of a white man. Despite Jed's efforts to show every single soul on the Double T that he was no better than they, it stung a bit. And he took the sting as a rebuke from his Lord. *Such pride, Father,* he confessed. *Such sin yet in my heart.*

Jed closed his eyes and leaned against the porch post. God had brought him far over the years since he had been called, and yet he clearly had much to learn still. He opened his eyes and stared at the stars in the inky black sky, listening to the waves below, the hum of the jungle beside, and the gentle laughter and conversation of the Double T's people behind him. But his mind was on one person—Selah. His head swung toward the big house, imagining her upstairs, preparing for bed.

Who was this woman who had so thoroughly woven her path with his? Was she but a temptation? Or was she, as Matthew intimated, partly why he had been led to Nevis in the first place?

Keturah and Gray finished their morning meal and prepared to head out on a ride. They were to meet Matthew in the middle field in an hour's time. Ket paused at the door, taking note of Selah, idling at the window.

"Selah? Would you care to ride with us?"

"Oh, I do not wish to intrude."

"You are no intrusion," Ket said. "Come. You look as if you need a bracing island wind to chase away whatever's troubling you."

"If only an island wind could always do so," she said, following her sister out the door.

"It never fails to at least aid me." Ket turned back to look her in the eye. "Especially after all this heat we have endured."

"True," Selah responded. She took a deep breath as they left the house, glad to feel the breeze lift her hair. Ket was right. Some time away from the house would do her good. Gideon, seeing her in company with Gray and Ket, disappeared into the stables, obviously set on saddling her mare before they arrived. Whilst she had little of the prowess Verity had with horses, Selah enjoyed climbing up the steep slope of Nevis Peak to look out and beyond.

They had to wait a few minutes for Gideon to complete his task, but she was soon into her sidesaddle, her thigh around the hook and her skirts back in place to protect her modesty. It grated on her to have to ride sidesaddle, given that the sisters had spent weeks if not months in breeches, working the fields—how much easier would it be to ride astride too?—but she followed Keturah's lead. She knew the goal was to behave as the islanders wished them to, as genteel plantation ladies. After all, if they were to come across any friends or neighbors besides Shubert, they hoped to convince them to come to their upcoming gathering, not grant them a reason to turn them down.

Selah gave in to the rocking gait of her tawny mare, following Gray and Keturah up the road, then on to the narrow path that led to the fields. Vervet monkeys chattered at them from the sprawling branches of a purple-flowered jacaranda tree, seeming to complain about the horses' sudden appearance in their midst. A bird swooped overhead, crying out with his particular singsong call as if to make sure they admired his green, red, and gold breast. The wind rushed in gusts through the ferns and palms on either side of them. Selah closed her eyes and inhaled deeply, taking comfort in the sounds and sights of the island that had become her home.

Was it only her particular mood or did the island seem more alive this morning? Selah knew not, but she was glad for it. Ruminations over Jedediah had unsettled her. This was exactly what she needed. A chance to reconnect to the island and her kin, not think about the newest arrival in their midst.

They skirted the lower field, where the field hands toiled this day. Matthew, spotting them, moved to speak to Cyrus, the man he frequently left in charge when he was not present, then untied his horse, mounted, and came after them. Selah knew that Jedediah was likely among the workers in the field and did her best not to look for him. But curiosity won out and there he was, lifting a hoe and ramming it into the ground in tandem with three others, working as a team to widen a furrow for new cane. They had cleared a stand of cane that had died—from disease or rot—and were clearly intent on replanting by day's end.

He did not lift his head and look in their direction, even though she saw two others take note of their presence. She had spent some time in the fields with these people herself; she knew they likely shared word that the master and the mistresses were about. Still, Jedediah did not turn his head. Perhaps he was no more eager to see her than she was to see him.

It was with some relief that they left the lower field and entered the path to the middle field. Matthew caught up to her minutes later, pushing his mare to a trot. "Good morning, Miss Selah. Lady Ket, Master Gray."

"And good morning to you, Matthew," Selah said. "How do our people fare this day?"

"They are well, by and large. Only two sick today and resting in their cabins."

"Good, good," Selah said. Gray had established that there would be leniency for those who fell ill, as opposed to other plantations where slaves were expected to work unless they could not rise from their beds. "What plagues them?"

"Emanuel is nursing his gouty foot. And Oriana has a fever."

"I see," Selah said. "Did you have Sansa fetch you some nettle tea for Emanuel's foot?"

"I did. Before sunrise."

"And what of Oriana's fever? Is this the first day she suffers it?"

"The second, miss."

"Hmm. And she has plenty of water within reach? Something to eat?"

"She does. Bessy said she would look in on her in an hour or two."

"Good. I shall look in on them too when we return."

"They would welcome a visit from you, miss."

They arrived at the broad expanse of the middle field, where one side had been buried in a mudslide three years past and now swayed with fat, healthy cane. But here on the lower corner, the cane ailed, the normally green stalks spotted and brown, some black.

"Is it the rot?" Gray asked, turning his gelding in a circle. He reached out to grab hold of a stalk and pull it closer. "This is what you wished me to see?"

"Indeed," Matthew said. "I misjudged the flow of the hill. The way the furrows run, they are holding far too much water."

"So you wish to cut them down and replant, after we re-plow the furrows?" Gray returned, only mildly dismayed by his overseer's admission.

"I do." Matthew urged his mount to draw closer to Gray. "But I suggest we do not replant sugar."

Ket stared at him, a look of confusion on her face. "What?"

"I suggest we bring the furrows vertical so there is far more run-off. But I wish to plant corn and squash and pumpkin, not cane."

Gray considered Matthew's words, his gaze level and contemplative. "Your mind is on food, not sugar."

"Yessir. If the food is becoming as expensive to import as what we gain in selling sugar—which has become more difficult of late—then would it not be wise to consider it?"

Gray rubbed his chin and looked out at the fields. "'Tis a good plan, Matthew. And something I had not thought about until now."

"'Tis not what most planters would ever do," Ket put in. "Many already thought us mad for dedicating five acres to planting crops that might sustain us. And for keeping our dairy cows."

"But now they do not, I'd wager," Selah said. Every day, they were able to supplement what the workers grew themselves in tiny plots around their cabins. "What if we planted more than corn and squash to sustain us? What if we dedicated a portion we allowed to go to seed? Then we'd have another thing to bring to market. Perhaps something even more enticing than sugar at this point in time? Something our neighbors may wish to purchase?"

Gray's face moved from surprise to wonderment. "You brilliant girl. I think you are dead right, Selah. Ket? Matthew? Do you agree?"

Both nodded, smiling in shared excitement.

"If the promised concert tomorrow night does not bring our old friends back to us," Ket said, "perhaps the idea of raising a saving crop of their own might do so."

"It shall further my campaign to take Shubert's seat," Gray said.

Selah blinked. "You . . . *you* endeavor to be a councilman?"

"I do. If I cannot rid us of Shubert, the next best thing is to wrest control from him, yes?"

"Yes," Selah said slowly. Her heart picked up its pace at the thought. Could he possibly do it? Gray would be such a better councilman than Angus, leading Nevis forward rather than backward.

"I like this plan," Gray said. "Let us begin on the morrow, Matthew. Bring the field hands here to raze this cane, clear it, and begin re-plowing. If the weather holds, we might have the new corn and squash in by next week."

"I shall do so, sir."

"'Tis an audacious plan," Gray said, clapping his hands together.

"We rarely do things as others would on Nevis," Keturah said. "Why stop now?"

CHAPTER NINE

Verity entered the cool, shadowed alley and on the next block began making her way down a serpentine cobblestone road. Ian would not like that she was doing this . . . attempting a bit of espionage on her own. But if she could assist, would it not help bring this war to a swifter end and therefore see her reunited with him? Besides, being a woman kept her from immediate suspicion. It was a small comfort, at least. She was not so naïve that she didn't realize she still had to take the utmost care. While Statia was full of Britain's enemies, she did not doubt that they had spies of their own here as well. 'Twas why Bieulieu sent her to another today. He did not know for certain what the Sons of Freedom wished to obtain. *A layer of protection,* she thought.

Around the corner she spied the white walls and bougainvillea that ran alongside François's house. Glancing back and forth along the narrow road and seeing no one, she opened a new wrought-iron gate and closed it behind her. She paused before the wooden door, suddenly afraid and wishing Ian were at her side as he had been before. Was she a fool to enter alone? And yet, what else could she do? She bit her lip and looked over her shoulder again, wondering if she should scurry home to the shop.

But as she looked over her shoulder, the door opened, and a

man grabbed hold of her wrist and yanked her inward, making her yelp in surprise.

The man slammed the door shut and pulled her against his chest. She almost bit her tongue when she felt the cold, round end of a pistol barrel press against her neck. "*Qui es-tu? Que fais-tu ici?*" whispered the man. *Who are you? What are you doing here?*

"I am Verity McKintrick. Captain Ian McKintrick's wife," she whispered back, resisting the urge to reach for her dirk. She didn't sense true threat in this man, only suspicion. She needed to assuage his fears. "Where is François? I have come to see him."

"Who sent you?" the man growled, pressing the pistol barrel a bit harder into her neck. "How did you know François lives here?"

"I have been here before, with my husband," she said calmly. "And it was Bieulieu who sent me this morning. He did not tell you?"

"We have not spoken for two days," he said, releasing her. She turned to face him, and he bowed slightly. "'Tis been too dangerous. Forgive me for manhandling you, madame, but there are British spies about. Why is your husband not here?"

"My husband is at sea, privateering on behalf of the Continental Congress. Please, I wish to speak to François," she said, settling her features in what she hoped was a calm expression, despite her pounding heart.

He folded his beefy arms. "You are unarmed?"

"I am. Aside from this." She slid the dirk out from her waistband. "And if I had meant you harm, you would have found it buried in your gut whilst you still held me."

He grunted as he took the dirk from her, but the tension in him seemed to ease. "François!" he barked, moving to the stairs. "Come at once! You have a visitor."

She heard a door open upstairs, followed by the heavy clomp of boots across the wooden floor. Soon enough, the man descended, a towel in his hands and his hair wet and slicked back, as if he had recently concluded a bath.

She curtsied and he bowed. "Ah, Mrs. McKintrick. I had gained word that you were on-island. Our newest tradeswoman?"

"That is my intent," she said. Clearly there were few secrets here, even on an island that was rumored to specialize in them. "I am primarily trading sugar for staples for my kin on Nevis."

"I see." He gestured for her to take a seat on a nearby settee.

She did so while the first man resumed his position by the door, peering out a small curtained window, his eyes on the street.

"Monsieur Bieulieu indicated there is a supply ship arriving tomorrow or the next, and that I might be in line for some of the supplies she carries. But in turn—"

"In turn you must do something for us, yes," he said, leaning forward. He tapped the fingers of his left hand against his right. "Does your husband know you are here, madame?"

She lifted her chin. "I married a rebel sea captain and assisted him in obtaining some valuable information that was brought back to you. Whilst he is away seeing to his privateering duties for the Continentals, I thought I might be of some use to the cause here."

"Indeed." He leaned back in his chair, upholstered in a dilapidated brocade, and crossed his leg over his knee. "I will go to great lengths to see my goals met, Madame McKintrick. But your husband is a formidable man with a reputation for hotheadedness. When he returns to our harbor, shall I expect him to arrive at my house here and beat me for utilizing his wife's—" he paused to cough delicately—"services?" He gave her a sly look.

"So long as those services are utilized in a genteel manner and I remain unharmed," she returned evenly, "Ian shall have no issue with you."

"And what if you are caught and hanged?" The words slipped off his tongue in so idle a fashion that it gave her pause.

"I must not," she said after a breath. "For then my Ian shall *certainly* be raging about."

François slowly rubbed his scruffy cheek, considering her.

"And yet we are still conversing because I suspect I may have access to something you need," she went on. "Something the good major with the Nevisian garrison might have in hand?"

She was guessing, but it only made sense, given what Bieulieu had mentioned already. And the narrowing of the man's eyes, the lifting of his chin, told her she had guessed correctly.

He uncrossed his leg and leaned toward her again. "Major Woodget has undoubtedly received a missive that other garrisons have received as well, but we have been unable to verify. There are several ships en route to the Americas, and they are expected to stop for water and repairs on Nevis, as they oft do, in a few weeks' time. What we need to ascertain is what they carry. We suspect they shall be laden with weapons and staples to provision the troops stationed in New York and beyond. They are as hungry for the essentials as the islanders are these days. Whilst the Patriots lack weapons and ships to equal the British might, they continue to eat meat and vegetables and fruit. Aside from some smuggling, thus far they have managed to keep much from Britain's reach."

He rose and began to pace the room, hands clasped behind his back. "We can surmise what the Brits' ships carry. But if we knew the specifics, Madame McKintrick, we could then formulate a plan on how best to rob the British of their weapons or a good portion of their supplies, whichever is more viable."

"I see."

"Surely Major Woodget keeps his correspondence in a locked box, even in the relative sanctuary of your sister's home?"

She nodded. She had seen it herself, walking down the hall. A broad, shallow box sitting on the desk.

"Might you steal said box?"

She considered that. Even in the folds of her skirts, she would not be able to conceal the entire box. Could she? And it would take only seconds for the major to see that someone had absconded with the box and sound the alarm. She shook her head. "'Tis quite wide. The risk of discovery is too great."

He sighed. "Then you must find a way to steal his key."

"Or," she said, tapping her chin, "make a copy of it."

He raised a brow. "That would take some time and expose you on at least two occasions. Once to make a wax imprint, and another to steal into his room and unlock the box."

"But 'tis not an exposure to take the key from his person, for he carries it in his coat pocket." She thought back to numerous occasions when she'd seen the older man with his hand in that pocket, as if rubbing the key like one might a worry stone. "I shall prepare to do either, whichever presents itself first. How long do we have?"

He cocked his head. "Two, perhaps three weeks. Clearly, the earlier we obtain the information, the better we shall be prepared to take advantage of it."

"Clearly."

"Good, then. You shall do it?"

"I shall," she said, the words leaving her mouth before she had time to fear the repercussions. She tried to swallow but found her tongue dry. "And in turn, Monsieur Bieulieu shall find me a place in line for the supply ship tomorrow?"

"There shall be no line for you, madame. We shall obtain the supplies for you in exchange for the sugar already in your small store. Half will be yours immediately, and half when you succeed at this mission. The supplies shall be double the value of your brother-in-law's sugar. You may choose to trade them in your store or smuggle them to Nevis. It matters not to me."

Verity thought that through. Truly, the agreement was better than she had hoped. *Double the value of sugar?* There was no other way to gain so much for the Double T.

She need only steal into the major's room, discover what she must, and return to Statia without the entire Nevisian garrison chasing her down . . .

Would she be able to do it? There was not a soul on Nevis who did not suspect her.

But they would not suspect Selah, she thought. And in order to care for the people of the Double T, she knew firsthand how far her sister was willing to go. She had discovered as much the night she arrived with Akunta.

Jedediah would be back with the field workers any minute. They had spent an exhausting afternoon beginning to clear the half-dead cane in the middle field, cutting it down with machetes, bundling it, then handing it off to women to separate diseased from healthy stalks. They burned the diseased and left the rest to rot. Later, they would use the rotting cane as mulch in other portions of the field. Tomorrow they would return to the middle field to rip out the rest of the cane and plow up the roots, clearing it for the proposed new crop of corn and squash.

Selah had heard all of this from the woman who had returned to the meetinghouse an hour prior with a deep cut on her hand. She left as the men emerged on the road, still unsure of all she was feeling about Jedediah, and unwilling to confront it. She tried not to look his way as she descended the stairs, but with a swift glance she glimpsed his tanned face and chest among his black-skinned brethren. She was hurriedly turning toward the house when a man called her name.

Selah reluctantly turned and spotted a visitor on horseback coming down the drive behind the field workers, the men parting before him.

Teddy Kirk tipped his hat to her and grinned, then turned to greet Jed as he passed him. "I see you have made a full recovery, Reverend Reed," he said, slowing his horse to walk beside him for a bit.

"God be praised," Jedediah said.

"God be praised, indeed," Teddy said. But then he searched for Selah again and said a curt "Good day, sir."

"Good day, Mr. Kirk," Jed said gently. Yet she noticed the narrowing of his eyes as they shifted between the young man and Selah.

"Miss Selah! Just whom I hoped to meet." Teddy gave her a broad smile. He truly had fine white teeth; had she not noticed that before? He swung off his saddle and walked beside her, leading his horse.

"What brings you to the Double T this eve, Teddy?" she asked as he offered her his arm. She took it, feeling a curious little thrill in thinking this might make Jedediah a bit jealous.

"A gift," he said, gesturing to the horse's back. "My father allowed me to bring twenty pounds of flour. We thought it might be a boon for your party tomorrow eve."

"Oh, Teddy," she enthused, spying it. "That is wonderful. We can make some fine cakes in the morning with such riches!"

"And more," he said conspiratorially. "It shall feed hungry mouths here too, yes?"

"Of course. You will take some sugar back as payment?"

"No," he said as they neared the kitchen. "Father does not wish to receive any payment, Selah. That way he can honestly tell Angus Shubert that he did not trade with you."

She smiled. "That is quite clever of him. And most generous. Please thank him. From all of us. It means more than you could know." She paused. "Is there nothing we can do, though, to repay your family?"

He cocked his head and cast her a small smile. "Only save me a dance on the morrow and you can consider your debt paid in full."

"Such a flirt, Teddy!" she said with a grin, playfully pushing against his arm. Was Jedediah watching them, even now?

You do not wish to be with Jed, and yet you want him to yearn to be with you? So shallow, Selah! You are a deeper river than this. She clasped her hands together and gave him a more demure nod. "I shall save you a dance."

"Perhaps I should have asked for a kiss too," he whispered in her ear as he set his hat atop his head.

Her eyes flew wide. "When did you become such a scoundrel?" she whispered back, fingers hovering in front of her lips.

"I am no longer a besotted pup following you about," he returned, "but a man now, fully prepared to court a bride. My father aims to leave the mercantile in my hands and return to England. He is determined to obtain and outfit a ship of his own so that he might secure supplies purely for Nevis, regardless of what comes of this war."

Selah's brows lifted. "Well, that would be a wise course of action. He would dominate the trade on-island if he succeeds."

"Indeed. And with that power in hand, he need not refuse any customers, particularly those he considers friends. Nor could certain councilmen press him to do so." A spark of triumph lit up his eyes. "In fact," he said, reaching for her hand, "he may well be able to demand certain councilmen do as he demanded instead."

She nodded in wonder. "He decided all this over the last few days?"

"We did, together."

She looked upon him with new respect, and he colored, reminding her that despite his newly mature bravado, there was a bit of the pup yet in him.

"Until tomorrow, Miss Selah." He lifted her hand to gently kiss it.

"Until tomorrow," she said. But as she watched him set the bag of flour by the kitchen door and mount up, giving her one last hopeful smile, her eyes traveled past him, up the road.

And there was curious disappointment in her heart when she saw that Jedediah was no longer in view.

Chapter Ten

"Miss Selah! Miss Selah!" Abe cried, tearing into the kitchen.

"Abraham, how many times have I told you to mind yourself in the house?" Mitilda asked, hands on hips.

"Sorry, ma'am," the boy said, tucking his chin and forcing himself to stand straight and still. "Miss Selah, 'tis your sister! Miss Verity is back!"

"Already?" Selah asked, taking off her apron. She had joined Mitilda and Sansa to help them prepare for the party that night. "Why, she must have left Statia before the sun was up!"

"She must have smelled your mango tarts from over there," Abe said and edged closer to the table. He reached for one but a warning clap from his mother stopped him.

"Oh, Mitilda, might he have but one?" Selah asked. "He picked most of the mangoes himself." There were already dozens and dozens complete. Selah's hope was that they could make enough for not only every guest that night but also every one of the Double T's workers.

"All right, son, but leave the rest for tonight, you hear me?"

"Yes'm." He gleefully grabbed hold of a tart and bit into it while tugging Selah out the door. He was clearly as excited to see Verity as she was.

"I do so love that Verity is nearer at hand," she said as they took to the path.

"'Twould be even better if she was back in Charlestown," he said.

"Do you think she managed to smuggle in more supplies?" she whispered.

"Knowing Miss Ver, yes!"

As if in answer, she saw George, Verity's footman, rolling a barrel up the path. "Good morning, Miss Selah," he said.

"Good morning!"

Right around the bend came Trisa, carrying a cask of her own. They exchanged pleasantries too. "Where is your mistress?" Selah asked over her shoulder.

"Down by the ketch. Keeping guard!" Trisa returned.

Selah laughed as Abe excitedly pulled her along. "Go on, Abe. Run ahead." She couldn't keep up with him, given her skirts, and the boy was now plainly itching to get to the beach.

"Miss Ver! Miss Ver!" Abe called, racing around a clump of coco plum bushes. "We have mango tarts!"

"Mango tarts!" Selah heard Verity say. "And here I thought you were needing my supplies in order to be ready for the party tonight." She finally reached the beach and spied her sister, giving Abraham a hug. Selah bent, took off her slippers, and rushed to be next.

"Welcome home, Sissy," she said, holding her for a moment longer. Then, spying the boat filled with supplies, she dropped her arms. "My goodness! What have you brought?" She stared in amazement at the ketch, lying low in the water due to all she carried.

"Abraham, fetch Gideon and Primus, would you?" Verity asked. "We shall need assistance unloading all of this."

"Assistance?" Selah said, walking down the pier and glancing over her shoulder. "We shall need ten men!" She shielded her eyes and nervously scanned the nearby ridge. "What if Angus Shubert sees us?"

"What if he does?" Verity asked with a sigh. "I would say there is not a man on Nevis—including the four soldiers you are forced to quarter—who would deny that Gray has little recourse. If Shubert is blocking him from trade in Charlestown, what is he to do in order to keep you all alive?"

"Be that as it may, Verity, I would assume Gray would like to keep it a secret for as long as possible."

"Agreed. So let us do our part to get the boat unloaded, yes? If mercy does not make our friends ignore your ongoing resources, surely that champagne shall." She reached out and touched Selah's arm. "But whilst we are yet alone . . ."

"Yes?" Selah asked, turning back to her.

Verity stepped closer. "When we were swimming, I asked you if you might consider aiding me and the Patriots' cause."

Selah's breath caught. She knew, of course, what Verity was asking. She'd thought about it time and again since. But now . . . today? Tonight? "What is it you seek?"

"The key to the major's correspondence box," she said.

"His . . . *key*? But, Verity, he keeps that in his pocket!"

Verity nodded and took her arm, heading up the path. "We shall simply have to find the means to separate the major from his coat."

Selah shook her head. "You know as well as I that a proper soldier rarely is parted from his red coat."

"Unless said soldier is overheated after dancing?"

Selah put a hand to her cheek. "What is it that you are after?"

"A missive. Sent to all island garrisons, alerting them of an approaching group of supply ships from Britain. They carry weapons and food. We hope to find out what each ship carries."

"In order to . . ." She drew her to a stop.

"'Tis best if you not know that. But it will aid the cause in a significant way, Selah," she said, reaching out to take her hand. "And if we are able to obtain this information, we will be rewarded with as many supplies for the Double T as I have brought this day. 'Twould keep the people of the Double T fed for a good month or more . . ."

Which would get us closer to our garden crops, Selah mused, looking to the sea, then up to the circling Brutus. Did she have it in her to do this? If it meant helping her beloved people and family?

Verity leaned closer. "So you will aid me tonight?"

"I shall consider it," Selah said.

"Consider quickly, Sissy," Verity hissed under her breath as Gideon and Primus arrived around the curve of the path, followed by Abe, George, and Trisa. "Or I must come up with another plan."

Eight servants were dressed in livery and held lanterns along the road, ready to greet guests as they arrived that evening. The plantation fairly hummed with excitement. Selah, dressed in her least worn gold gown, paced from one end of the veranda to the next. She hadn't been in her finery for months. It felt a bit foreign as Dolly, a new maidservant, laced up her stays and then helped her put on the dress. Her drab day dresses were much softer and far more comfortable, but it felt special to have earrings at her lobes, a pearl choker around her neck, and gloves on her hands.

Jedediah appeared around the corner and slowed, taking her in as she did him. He was dressed in polished boots, tan breeches, a crisp white shirt, and long blue jacket, all borrowed from Gray. She had prepared herself to exchange social niceties with him that eve; 'twas the least she could do, given that it was his music that had opened the door with their neighbors again.

"Miss Selah, you look most lovely," he said, leaning over her hand in a brief bow.

"And you appear every bit the fine gentleman," she returned.

"Due to your brother-in-law's generosity."

"He was happy to assist." She considered taking her leave then, but curiosity won out. She cocked her head. "You appear much more at ease in your finery than I imagined. Did you oft wear such clothing in England?"

"Much of the time," he said. "Given that I made my living as a musician before God called me to serve him among the islands."

She considered that as they moved to stand side by side at the rail. She had imagined him as a student as he played in the church, not as a paid performer. But something else intrigued her more. "I have read of missionaries saying such things. What does a calling from God sound like? Do you mean he spoke to you in words?"

He glanced at her, considering. Perhaps he was reluctant to linger, given their last awkward exchange. "God oft speaks to me," he began carefully, "as he does to you, Selah. It only takes a listening ear and a welcoming heart to learn how to hear him. For me, he often draws my attention to an idea. He captures my imagination, and then if it is truly of him, he will affirm that word to me. Friends or family might mention something of the same. Or I might come across a passage in a book that relates to it."

"So how did you receive the calling to come to the Indies?"

"Ahh." He looked to the sea, his eyes growing distant, as if remembering the moment. "I was strolling along the quay and observing the sugar ships unloading whilst others were provisioning to head out again. I thought I would like to see the West Indies one day. But given that I was a musician, not a planter, I knew that would only be possible as a tourist." He gave her a small smile. "And, frankly, I did not have the means to travel simply for pleasure."

"And then?"

He crossed his arms, his eyes taking on a faraway look. "And then that night I was invited to a meeting held by Quakers. The speaker was a freed slave who had spent most of his years in the West Indies. He spoke of horrible abuse, Selah, even showed us the scars on his back—evidence of years of whippings. He said there were many days that he wished to die, but then one thing changed."

"And that was . . . ?"

Jed turned to lean on the rail and look at her. "The man was sold to another planter, a good and godly man. That man taught every one of his slaves to read and write. He gave each one a Bible when they could read. And then he gave them their freedom after seven years of service."

Selah lifted a brow. "I wish that man lived on Nevis! Then we would not be seen as such pariahs!"

"Indeed. If only all planters were as benevolent as that man was. And as Gray is today. But sitting there in that meeting, my heart softened. As the speaker continued with his story, I was overcome. I wept for him. Wept for all he had suffered." He shook his head and rubbed his face. "I can only explain it as that—the Lord opened and softened my heart. And in that moment, I knew I wanted to work with slaves. Give them a reason to continue on and, hopefully, lead more than a few to the God who gives every one of us freedom in Christ, if not here in our earthly toil."

"So that was it? You took the next ship on which you could find passage?"

"No, I needed to save the funds for that passage first, as well as prepare."

"Your parents?"

"As I have said, once they heard I had been called, they could say little other than 'go.' 'Tis what they believe. That is not to say my mother was not tormented by fear of the illnesses that claim so many in the tropics. I am certain that it is due to her fervent prayers that I have not had a day abed in the months I have been here."

Selah nodded. "So many perish."

"'Tis a wonder that you and your sisters have escaped illness too."

"God be praised. We had yellow fever on the Double T our first year here. Lost people dear to us." She leaned against the rail too and paused, weighing her words. This felt good—the ability to have a conversation as friends. "'Twas brave of you, Jedediah. To sail to the West Indies. To go where God called you. I do not know if I could be as courageous."

He cocked his head. "But you are here on Nevis. That itself took some courage."

"Only because I refused to be separated from my sisters."

"You helped Akunta," he whispered, after a glance down the empty veranda. "That took courage."

"We had little choice. We could not stand by and see her killed."

"Be that as it may, it was still courageous," he said, crossing his arms. "Perhaps it is because of how God called *you*?"

"Indeed," Selah said. It surprised her a bit, to think of herself as called, let alone courageous. But it was true. She had followed her heart. Had God planted that there? Given her the idea of what to do? Was that a *calling*? Perhaps.

The first guests arrived at the top of the road, and the servants lining it raised their lanterns higher, murmuring their greetings as the guests passed by. It was Mr. and Mrs. Browning from Gingerland. 'Twas likely due to their agreement to attend that any of the others agreed as well. Well, that and the promise of some fine music. Entertainment was in short supply on-island. Last year, a troupe of actors had come to St. Kitts, and they were so wildly popular there was not a hope of purchasing tickets. That was the one thing Selah missed most of England—concerts, plays, and the like. Tonight, hearing Jed play would be a joy.

As Keturah and Gray exited the house to descend the stairs and greet the Brownings, another carriage arrived at the top of the hill. The Pimbertons.

"Would you do me a favor this eve, Selah?" Jedediah said, standing and straightening his coat.

"What is that?"

"Would you play a duet with me?"

"A duet? Why, no, I could not!" Jedediah had been practicing for days, and she had made a point of making herself scarce. "You yourself said I lack the skill. Why should I embarrass myself in front of our friends? We wish to win them over, not repel them," she said in a whisper.

"Please forgive me for teasing you," he said. "I should never have done so. I have heard you play the Minuet in G without fault, and that is what I wish to play with you. Given that you are a lady of the house, I think your friends would enjoy hearing you join me."

She considered him. "Why could you not have asked me earlier? So I could practice?"

"Come now. You know the piece by heart. I suspect that song is your favorite. And practice would have only made you nervous."

She frowned. Was it true? Was this better? But the thought of sitting down at the harpsichord in front of others made her heart hammer. She had never been one to play in front of a crowd, even before Jed had teased her so. Now, *now* he thought her worthy of taking the stage with him? When she had to play hostess half the night and spy the other?

"I shall consider it," she said. Then, with a brief nod of her head, she left him.

Verity appeared, looking glorious in a burgundy gown, and waved Selah closer. She clearly did not wish to be alone as the guests moved up the stairs to her but wanted her sister by her side to encourage pleasantries. Was everyone going to demand something of her this night?

"Goodness," Verity whispered, looking from Selah to Jedediah passing into the parlor. "Mind your expression, Sissy. You look like a tempest in a teapot."

"I have good reason. That man!" she whispered, gesturing with a quick, irked move toward the doorway.

"That man?" she asked, taking her arm.

"He . . . *unsettles* me so."

Verity gave her arm a squeeze, a sly smile tugging at her lips. "He unsettles you? Hmmm . . ."

"Cease your wayward thoughts, Ver. He has already made it quite clear that he thinks of me as but a friend. His heart is wholly captured by his ministry."

"Hmmm," Verity repeated, weaving her arm through her sister's. "Why do I doubt that?"

CHAPTER ELEVEN

It surprised Selah that they came, everyone who said they would. Some were formal and stiff, but after rum punch was served, and then champagne, formalities softened. Gray and Keturah spoke of their new crop to everyone who gave them opportunity. "I aim to assist my friends on-island," Gray said to Mr. Pimberton as he passed by, "by selling them seeds first. What with the price of corn now equal to what we can get for sugar, it only makes sense to devote a fair section of land to raise at least some of our own food."

"How do you keep your people so strong and plump, Mrs. Covington?" sniffed Mrs. Holland as she poked at Sansa's arm. "We have had to cut our slaves' rations in half."

Selah controlled her desire to slap the old lady's hand away from Sansa. The Double T needed as many allies as they could get. Especially if Gray was to slide the city councilman's seat out from under Angus Shubert. But she knew Mrs. Holland partially starved her people when she was clearly getting more than she needed herself. She moved away as Keturah gently informed her they were doing everything they could to provide ample food for their workers, believing it in the best interests of both the people and the plantation's production.

Guests filled the parlor, the veranda, and milled about the yard below. Servants stood at tables to refill either rum punch cups or champagne goblets. Others circulated with canapés. The mango tarts would be served after Jedediah began playing.

Verity was strolling with Captain Howard and Major Woodget. 'Twas good of the men to welcome her so while others gave her a broad berth. Perhaps seeing the soldiers converse with her would ease the tension with the other guests. As Selah approached, she saw Verity stumble and fall partially against Major Woodget. The captain took hold of her waist and set her to rights, asking after her welfare. He had always held a torch for Verity, even after he knew she had married a rebel smuggler.

"Are you quite well, Miss Verity?" the major asked, turning to face her as she smoothed her skirts.

"I am well, thank you. Forgive my bumbling! Perhaps I need not have the other half of my rum punch. 'Tis been some time since I imbibed."

"They do not have rum punch on Statia?" the captain asked.

"Oh, I think there is not an island without it," she said. "I simply find I am better off without it."

"Wise woman," said the major with a smile. "If only I was so stalwart. I suppose 'tis due to you that we also have champagne this night?"

"Why, Major! You know I cannot possibly confirm your suspicions."

He leaned toward her. "We have the capacity to look away when necessary. And in times like these, 'tis oft necessary. Supply the Double T as you see fit, Mrs. McKintrick. The captain and I have done all we can to do the same, but to little avail. We shall not impede your progress, especially when we benefit as well."

"That is most kind of you, Major." She nodded at both of them, took Selah's arm, and demurely moved away.

"I have it," she whispered.

"What?" Selah asked.

"The key!"

"What? How?" But then she remembered Verity's stumble into

113

the major. "Why, you sly thing! What is next? Your arrest as a pickpocket?"

"We must get to that box and return the key to him before he realizes 'tis gone. 'Tis more natural for you to be upstairs. And despite their magnanimous words, they plainly suspect me. If I were to be found near their rooms . . ."

Selah sighed. "Very well."

"You will do it?"

"I will. For the promise of provisions and the hope that it might aid the rebels in bringing this war to a swift end."

"Good girl," Verity said, sliding the key into her hand. "I shall provide a distraction if necessary."

"What? Now?" Already the tiny key seemed like a burning ember in her palm.

"As swiftly as possible."

Above them, Gray clinked a silver spoon against his glass and soon many others did too. "Friends, you have blessed us with your presence this evening," he said, looking about at the hundred or so guests beside him on the veranda and down below in the garden. "Thank you for the honor of your attendance. Whilst I sincerely wish that we could fit you all in our parlor, I doubt that would be comfortable. Therefore, we have opened the windows wide so that you can enjoy Reverend Reed's fine music, whether you are inside, on the veranda, or below in the garden. Feel free to dance as well."

On cue, the servants with lanterns moved to form a rectangle in the clearing below the veranda, beside Selah and Verity. Jedediah began playing, starting with Clementi's divine Sonatina in G Major, and everyone hushed and gathered close to the house or entered in order to hear.

"You shall make certain no one follows me upstairs?" she whispered to Verity.

"I shall. I am going to insist the soldiers help me encourage our guests to dance and tell them they all need to claim a dance with me. That will keep them here below. You shall have the span of four songs. Make haste, Sissy."

"Why do I not do the dancing and you go search the major's box?"

"As I said, too many suspect me. And that parlor is packed with people who will observe anyone going upstairs. The wife of a privateer for the Continentals should not be seen—"

"Very well," Selah interrupted in irritation. She could see the wisdom of it. She wanted to aid her people. But terror was flooding her heart, making a fine sheen of sweat cover her brow and lip and bosom. Was this God, warning her? Speaking to her? Or the devil, trying to dissuade her?

She forced herself to climb the veranda steps and enter the parlor as Jedediah finished his first selection. The room erupted in applause. Men nodded approvingly. Women tittered and whispered about the mysterious minister. "He simply showed up one day and asked for nothing more than what the slaves receive!" said Mrs. Jenner as Selah edged by.

"He's rather handsome, do you not think?" said the plump Miss Pinney to Miss Winsor, both of whom had recently come of age. Selah thought that intriguing; whilst Jed was not classically handsome, there was something about his demeanor that made him undeniably charismatic. It strangely agitated her to see others make note of it.

Jedediah began to play his next piece—Bach's Italian Concerto—and Selah neared the stairs. She had made it up the first when a hand gripped her wrist.

She turned back, fear making her heart pound in triple time.

But it was only Ket. "Selah. Are you well?" her sister whispered, her brow furrowing over Selah's odd reaction.

"Oh! Yes, but . . . uh, I am rather faint," she added. "I am going upstairs to lie down a moment."

"Probably the tight stays," Keturah said in her ear. "Shall I send Dolly to help you loosen them?"

"No, no. I shall simply rest for a moment and will be fine. 'Tis simply all the excitement."

Keturah reluctantly let her go. Jedediah was nearing the halfway point of his piece. Only two and a half songs left! But Selah forced herself to keep a steady, relaxed pace as if she hadn't a care in the world. As soon as she was out of view, she scurried down the hallway, lit a candle, glanced both ways to make certain she was alone, then edged into the major's room. She took a moment to lean her head against the door, wondering if she was really about to do what she thought she was, or if it was all but a dream.

The thunderous applause and cheers as Jed finished his second piece reminded her this was no dream.

She had a horrifying thought. What if the major came to fetch something from his room? But no, surely Verity had scheduled his dance last, to make certain he stayed within view. She simply needed to complete her task and make her escape.

Selah moved to the desk, sat down in the chair, and faced the correspondence box. Hearing Jedediah begin his third composition, she slipped the key from her pocket and inserted it into the lock. With a satisfying *click*, the box popped slightly open. She stared at the stack of correspondence, trying to memorize how it appeared so she might leave it in similar fashion. Then she hurriedly read page after page, looking for what Verity had described. There were missives on preparations that must be made by certain dates to ensure that any slave rebellion would be swiftly quelled. She resisted the urge to read those three, containing such detail it surprised her; she knew that was the primary reason for the soldiers to be stationed on-island. But to read about their preparations was rather eye-opening. There were other requests for reports to be filed, and what details they must reveal. Copies of letters and reports the major had written. She despaired that the letter Verity sought was not to be found when at last she came upon it.

She slid the page aside, marking where it belonged in the stack so she could return it. Hurriedly, she read the report, asking Major Woodget to be prepared to swiftly restock the three vessels, due to arrive somewhere in the next week to three weeks, depending on the weather. They would be in need of fresh water for a hundred souls per ship and perhaps some repairs after the voyage, and he was to ensure there was enough room for them to anchor at Finley Point, where they could most readily re-provision and be on their way. There was no manifest, no listing of what the vessels carried, but at the end, Admiral Marshall wrote, *"Be of good cheer, Major. If we can get these cannons and soldiers to the Loyalists, then we shall swiftly put an end to General Washington's ill-conceived plans. I thank you, in advance, for your assistance in seeing them onward."*

Selah slid the letter back into the stack just as Jedediah finished his third selection. When he began the fourth, she scanned the remaining pieces of correspondence in the stack but saw nothing else like what Verity had described. Satisfied that all was in order, she lowered the lid of the box, but it wouldn't close. Was something jamming it? She pulled the candle closer to examine it, yet she could see nothing.

She tried again, realizing she needed to turn the key in the lock to allow it to close in full. Relieved, she locked it and reached for the candle, but in her haste bumped it. It did not tip over, though a small puddle of wax spilled over the wooden desk.

Selah stared at it in stunned horror. The fastidious major would surely know someone had been here in his absence. Jedediah was already into his fourth piece! There was not time to let the wax harden and scrape it off. She hurriedly fished a lace-trimmed handkerchief out of her bodice and wiped off most of the hot wax. Now what remained would cool faster, and perhaps she'd have time to scrape it off completely. But with what? She opened the drawer and found nothing but pens and a pair of scissors. To the side of the bed was a shoehorn. That would have to do.

Selah began scraping off the wax edges that had dried, praying God would help her with a simple, repeated, desperate *please, please, please* . . .

Just as Jedediah finished the fourth piece, she got the last of it off. She quickly brushed the shavings into the ruined handkerchief, wiped the shoehorn free of debris on her skirts, and replaced the tool where she'd found it. Then she carefully lifted the candle, moved to the door, blew it out, and exited the room.

Where she almost ran into Keturah.

CHAPTER TWELVE

"Selah, wh-what were you doing in there?" Keturah whispered, her face a mixture of fear, surprise, and anger.

Selah felt the blood drain from her face, unable to think of a single thing to say.

Ket grabbed her wrist and pulled her down the hall to her room. Once inside, door closed, she turned to face Selah, arms crossed. "Out with it."

"I am assisting Verity," she whispered back miserably.

"By spying on the major?"

"By reading his correspondence."

Ket began pacing, hands on her cheeks. "Selah, they could send you to the gallows for that. Why did Verity have you do this? Why not do her own dirty work?"

"Because it would look less suspicious for me to come upstairs than her, unaccompanied. Especially given that all know where the McKintricks' loyalty lies." She moved to her own desk and placed the ruined handkerchief inside the drawer. She would dispose of it later.

"Oh, I could wring her neck! How dare she involve you!"

"Ket, I *wanted* to help her. If she is able to deliver the information she seeks, she will be paid in additional supplies. Supplies she intends to give to us on the Double T! 'Twill feed us all for another month!"

That gave Keturah pause, and Selah felt just a bit of softening from her. Then she resumed her pacing, shaking her head as she thought it through.

"Listen, Ket, I cannot remain here. I must get downstairs and give the key back to her. She will find a way to slip it back into the major's pocket."

"The major's *pocket*? You stole the key from him?"

"We *borrowed* it. And now we shall return it."

She moved to the door, but Ket stepped behind her and put a hand against it. "We shall discuss this in full after the party ends. All three of us, with Gray."

"Very well," Selah said, turning toward her and taking her hand in both of hers. "And you must resume your calm and lovely hostess demeanor in order to win back friends, yes? Put all of this out of your mind until we are free to discuss it. Please do not let it consume you, Ket. It shall be well. I promise."

She hoped she appeared as assured as she sounded. She and Verity would have to have compelling arguments when they met with Ket and Gray. Or the Covingtons might very well refuse to allow Verity to set foot on Nevis until this wretched war was over.

Her heart and mind in a riot of conflict, she turned the corner and began to descend the stairs. But as she did, Jedediah's piece by Domenico Scarlatti stilled her, as it had all in the room. Ket stopped behind her too. He played with such tenderness, attentiveness, it gave her pause. Slowed her heartbeat. Quieted her mind. His gift was truly mesmerizing. Somehow when he played, he became *part* of the music, an instrument himself, able to coax something out of the harpsichord that went beyond notes. This was a man who had the talent to have played in concert halls across Europe, to say nothing of churches. And he had given it all away to follow a calling from God.

Was that not what she too was doing? Going where God urged her? To protect and aid the people she loved? How could that be wrong? The thought of it settled her belly. Shoulders back, chin up, she descended the rest of the stairs.

He looked up as he moved into the last chorus and caught her eye, smiling a bit. She was doing her best to move through the crowd—which had become packed in the parlor—many of whom shouted "Bravo!" after Jed finished and rose. "Thank you, ladies and gentlemen. 'Tis a true pleasure to play for you tonight. And it is all due to Miss Selah Banning and our hosts, Mr. and Mrs. Gray Covington. In honor of them, I would like to invite Miss Banning to join me for a duet."

All eyes turned toward Selah. Horrified by the timing—and the fact that he truly expected her to do this—Selah froze. She needed to get the major's key back to Verity! And could she truly make it through the piece without making an utter fool of herself? Especially after Jed had just completed perhaps the most beautiful piece she had ever heard?

Keturah was behind her. She whispered in her ear, "Give it to me. I shall get it to Ver."

Numbly, she fished the key from her pocket and pressed it into Keturah's hand, hidden among her skirts. Once it was safely transferred, she forced a smile she did not feel and moved through the narrow path made for her to reach the harpsichord. Jedediah took her hand with a grin, faced the audience. He bowed as she curtsied, and all clapped in anticipation. Then he gestured toward the narrow bench, and once she was seated, stood beside her.

He leaned over her shoulder. "Selah, you have undoubtedly played this piece since childhood, yes?"

She nodded, looking into his eyes. While they were surrounded by people, there was something about this moment that somehow felt more intimate than the night he had kissed her. Somehow, he alone had her attention.

"I want you to trust me," he whispered. "Utterly trust me. No matter what I play, you concentrate on the piece you have known by heart and played perfectly since childhood."

"The *one* piece," she said with a slight smile.

"That is all we need," he said, smiling back. "Take the lead."

Selah's fingers trembled as they hovered over the upper, more narrow manual, especially as his long arms stretched out on either side of her on the lower manual. He wanted her to trust him. Had he not proven trustworthy? She thought about the night they had sailed to Saba. How this man worked in the fields every day with the people she loved. How fingers and hands that had once been meant to play fine instruments now were callused and scarred from using machetes and hoes and shovels. All because he was on the path that God called him to take. He was faithful and worthy. She knew it as she knew this house had a solid cornerstone—a cornerstone her father had chosen and used, and which Ket and Gray had used again as they rebuilt the grand old plantation house.

So with that, she began to play, the notes a comfort, a reminder of her childhood at Hartwick. She remembered how Father and Mother would clap for her when she was done, regardless of how many mistakes she made. How Keturah had once sat with her and the piano tutor and dutifully played a duet of this song with her.

But that duet had been perfunctory. Keturah was always more drawn to the gardens than the drawing room, and Verity to the stables. *This* duet . . .

What Jedediah began to weave around her basic core of notes was something ethereal. At times high, light, reminding her of feathers falling between and around her notes, and at others deep, dark, pounding, like thunder, giving her notes far more weight than she had ever imagined they could carry. His arms pressed in toward her shoulders and then out again as he played, trying to give her enough room to be courteous and yet reach the notes he needed.

By the time they were finished, Selah felt dazed, a bit disoriented, and yet . . . elated. Sharing something like that had been . . . magical. Again, the room erupted with glee. Jed took her hand in his and smiled into her eyes as she rose to join him. "That was quite brave of you, Selah."

"'Twas, wasn't it? But, Jed, what you did . . . that was otherworldly."

With one last grin, he led her to turn, and together they again expressed their gratitude to the audience with a curtsy and a bow. "I will return to play five more pieces for you," Jedediah said, one hand to her back. "But first I believe we could all use a bit of fresh air, do you not? Miss Banning and I shall lead the way."

The crowd murmured their agreement. It had become stifling in the parlor with all the bodies pressing in to hear him play. As Jedediah led her out by the hand, Selah heard whispers of admiration. Bits of questions asked and comments made. She could piece it all together. Some wondered if they were courting, others already fretting that they might not get to hear Jedediah play again. Some wanted to verify that this truly was the same man who worked in the fields with the slaves and freed people of the Double T, or if they had him confused with another.

As soon as they made it out from the press of people and to the stairs, Jedediah more properly offered his arm. She reluctantly took it. How good it had felt for him to hold her hand. To lead her, *claim* her in a way, even when they were not formally courting. It had sent delicious shivers up her arm and shoulder as they moved outside. Verity's "hmmm" and what they had just experienced together swirled in her mind. Surely it was not all simply her imagination. Surely he felt as drawn to her as she to him. Surely God was in this, this thing between them. Perhaps she simply had to help him see it too.

She wished that somehow the music could continue, so that he could take her in his arms and they could dance now.

"Do you know how to dance, Jedediah?" she asked.

"I do," he said, reaching for a cup of punch. He handed it to her and then took another for himself. "Although whilst I was in England, 'twas in a classroom or with the downstairs staff I danced. Most Methodists avoid the practice, but my music instructor insisted his students know every one of the modern and classical dances. He said if we could *feel* the joy of movement, it would help us infuse that joy into our notes as we played."

"Well, clearly his instruction was successful. Do you play other instruments?"

"My favorite is the piano. I itch to have one within reach. I am passable on the flute and fair on the mandolin."

"And you gave that all up to—"

"There you are! At last!"

Selah and Jedediah turned to see Theodore Kirk approach, looking more a man than ever in his finery.

"Teddy! Welcome!" she said.

"Thank you," he said, leaning in to kiss her hand. He held on to it. "I was hoping to secure a dance with you. That is, once Reverend Reed again takes to the harpsichord."

"'Twould be an honor," she said with a brief curtsy. She ignored what felt like a lingering stare from Jedediah. What was she to do? He was certainly not free to dance, and they owed the Kirks a great deal. 'Twas thanks to them that they could serve all the delicious mango tarts this eve, as well as bake more hardtack on the morrow.

"I caught the last of your duet," Teddy said. "I had no idea you were so accomplished on the harpsichord," he added, looking directly at her.

"I assure you I am not. 'Tis only Jedediah's fine ways with the keys that made my meager talent sound like more than it is."

"Oh?" He glanced at Jedediah. "Then I shall look forward to hearing you play on, sir. When do you anticipate returning to your task?"

"In a quarter hour," Jedediah said, a bit stiffly.

Teddy nodded. "I will return to your side then, Miss Selah, to claim that dance."

"Very well," she said, bobbing her head.

"Did you dance earlier?" Jedediah asked carefully, when they were again alone.

"No, I . . . I was talking with Verity and then had to retire upstairs for a bit. I felt a tad . . . dizzy." Which was true. What she had undertaken made her knees weak, even thinking about it. She searched for her sisters and the soldiers. They were all together, over by the stairs. The major had his coat on. Had Ket been successful in returning the key to his pocket? Or to Ver?

"But you are well now?" he asked, tucking just the pads of his fingertips beneath hers.

She looked up at him, the torchlight and lamplight dancing across his long face, highlighting fine cheekbones and a cleft on his long chin. No, he was not classically handsome—even dear Teddy was more so—but there *was* something irresistible about this man.

"Selah, if you would welcome it, I wish to speak to your brother-in-law this night. I *must* speak to him."

"Oh?" she said wanly.

"Yes," he said, moving to fully hold her hand in his again. "I spoke the truth before. I believe I am called to this ministry, and I am reluctant to subject you to the hardships of it. 'Tis why I believed I was to be a bachelor forever. But these last days . . ." He looked to the sea, misery etching lines in his face, then back to her. "I know I am not anything like you might have ever considered as a husband, but I know I must ask. May I court you? For Selah . . . I confess I feel as called to you as I was to the Indies," he said with a smile. "You are part of why I was supposed to come to this beautiful land and these people. I am certain of it. Might you welcome my courtship?"

She swallowed hard. In that moment, there truly was not anything she wished for more. She wanted to sink into the shadows to be alone, completely alone with him. To have him draw her into his arms and then kiss her, kiss her without any excuse but desire. She wanted to feel the music in him again, to see if they might be a duet themselves.

But . . . *Ket*.

Ket was enraged by what she had found Selah doing in the major's room, and for just cause. There would be consequences this night. Difficult conversations. Jedediah's request would be ill-timed, for many reasons.

"Selah?" he asked, moving a bit away from her to study her face. Despair turned the corners of his eyes downward. "I see I have placed you in a predicament," he said grimly. "You do not welcome my courtship."

"No, Jed. You do not—"

He leaned toward her, his brow furrowed in pain and confusion. "Is it that you cannot see yourself sharing my path in ministry? Or because you are drawn to young Teddy? Or . . . or is it . . . my lack of purse?"

"Jedediah!" Her face burned. "How can you ask such a thing?" Did he know so little about her? Could he not sense their shared passion for the people? Could he not see she was more drawn to him than to Teddy? That wealth mattered little to her? She shook her head in frustration. "You must trust me. This shall not be the night to approach Gray. We have other matters that must be addressed. But before we do, clearly you and I have more to discuss."

"Clearly," he said, folding his arms.

"Your audience awaits," she said curtly as the people on the veranda began clapping in unison, chanting his name. "Best assuage their demands." She brushed past him then, half eager to be away from him, half hoping he would call for her to return.

But he did not.

CHAPTER THIRTEEN

Theodore was a decent dance partner, but as he led her about the small clearing in a waltz, Selah's attention was more on the music that poured out of the open windows above them, as well as on the completely aggravating, passionate, irresistible man who played them.

She could barely look at Teddy, what with Jedediah's whispered words echoing in her mind. "*Are you drawn to young Teddy?*" Part of her wished she was. Their courtship would certainly be more straightforward than any she might share with Jedediah. Island gentility would not approve of Jed courting Selah, regardless of how they cheered for him now. Even Teddy was beneath her station, but as the son of a merchant, somewhat more tolerable than an itinerant preacher. And yet she found herself yearning for Jedediah. To set him straight on all he had wrong. To speak of courtship and how it might work, despite what was against them.

She tried to smile at Teddy, to appreciate his earnest ways. But he was not Jedediah. Not in how he held her hand or rested his hand at her lower back. Not the smell of him—more linen and starch than island soil and salty sweat. And the thought of Jed upstairs, playing while probably thinking about her . . . well, it left her feeling like an unfaithful fraud. The last note of the piece still hung in the air when she stepped away from her escort and curtsied. "Thank you very much. You are a fine friend to dance with me."

He straightened a bit. "A fine *friend*," he said slowly. "Is that all I am to you, then?"

"Oh, Teddy," she said sorrowfully, looking up at him. "I am afraid so. Might we still be so?"

"Of course," he said. But even in the lamp and torchlight, she could see his cheeks coloring. He had clearly come tonight hoping to begin something more. He gave her a curt nod, turned and took a cup of punch, gulping it down, then stalked up the hill.

"He will be all right in time," said a voice to her left. She turned and, with some surprise, noted it was Mr. Kirk.

"I fear I have hurt him," she said, wringing her hands.

Mr. Kirk pulled his head left and right. "Such is the way of young folk. You are drawn or pushed away until you find the one who welcomes you into their heart. And, unfortunately, sometimes again after that."

She smiled sadly. Everyone on-island knew Mrs. Kirk had left him, unable to tolerate life in such a foreign place. They had remained married but lived separate lives over the last fifteen years. It was commonplace to find men living alone on Nevis. And it was why many hired overseers and left their plantations; rarely was it managed as well as when the owner was on site, but most with families were better off in England.

"Teddy told me of your plans," Selah said. "You sail soon for England? To outfit your own ship?"

"'Tis my hope. I thought I might offer to take some of Gray's remaining sugar."

"That would be most welcome. We are but a couple months away from the next harvest."

"I never agreed with how the men in Charlestown colluded to lock him out. But until I sold out my supplies, I had difficulty standing against them. Might you forgive me for that?"

"Already done," she said. She took his arm and turned him toward the house. "And now you simply must have a mango tart,

Mr. Kirk. It was partially due to your kindness in sending us the flour," she whispered, "that we could bake them at all."

It was quite late when Jedediah quit playing, coaxed by their guests to continue time and time again. In the end he played songs more apt for the taverns than a gentleman's home. But this was the way of island soirees, and the dulling effects of the punch and champagne. While decorum fell away, the resulting camaraderie was welcomed, particularly by those of the Double T, who had felt little of it on-island over the past year.

The soldiers demanded he end with "God Save the King." Together with most of the guests who remained, they sang, "God save great George our king, God save our noble king, God save the king! Send him victorious, happy and glorious, long to reign over us, God save the king!"

Several guests looked pointedly at Verity as they finished, who now stood beside Selah near the kitchen door. Unperturbed, she stepped forward, applauding, until all looked her way. "You all sound so fine together," she said. "It has been a joy to see you gather in our home. But before you leave, I wish to make an announcement. In the coming weeks, I shall be auctioning off my black carriage and matched set of geldings."

Selah gasped. "Verity . . ." she whispered, but her sister ignored her.

"As you all know, I love those horses and that carriage, but I abide elsewhere now. And times are difficult enough without forcing my sister and her husband to find hay for animals in disuse."

"Verity," Gray said, stepping forward, but she held up a hand and gave him a wistful smile before clasping her hands before her.

"I shall sell them to the highest bidder. Funds may be paid in food staples or coin, which will go directly to Gray and Keturah, not me. You all are invited, because you have proven true friends to my beloved family. Gray and Keturah shall invite a select number of others. I want my team to go to a good home, where they shall be well cared for, not starved. If you are interested, please return. Gray, when might that suit you?"

He looked torn, glancing to Ket.

She was right to do this, Selah mused. Horses in town were looking as gaunt as many of the slaves. But for the most part, the people in attendance here appeared as if they kept their animals in decent supply, including the Covingtons, at great sacrifice. At least most of them did so. That Mrs. Holland—who had commented on how they'd needed to turn to half rations for their slaves—had arrived behind a team that fared less well. But she doubted she'd have the means to buy Verity's team. There were perhaps only two couples in attendance who could, given the times. Not that that would keep the rest away. They would return for the novelty of an auction.

Selah had to admire her sister as Gray shouted his invitation to return. She had effectively done four things: provided a means to attract even more Nevisians back to the Covingtons, gracefully allowed a way for Gray and Ket to escape the expense of feeding her team, promised to secure even further provisions for the Double T through the sale, and likely softened Keturah's fury over what had transpired upstairs.

Someone suggested a picnic that following Saturday, for which they all could pack baskets. Another suggested Jedediah play again for them, come evening, to which he nodded amiably. "Oh my," Selah murmured to her sister under her breath. "How we shall be the talk of Nevis."

"Indeed," Verity said.

"You are most clever," Selah said. "Even if you did get me in hot water with Ket."

"Oh?"

"Yes. She found me upstairs. She knows what I was after."

Verity took a long, deep breath. "I wondered how she came to be in possession of the key."

"Once everyone is gone, she and Gray will want to talk with us."

"Reverend Reed!" called Mrs. Beckford, a thin widow from an ailing plantation near Charlestown. "Oh, Reverend!"

He turned to look her way. "Yes?"

She looked up at him and smiled coquettishly. "I have a friend over on Saint Kitts who has a grand piano and an open-air theatre, complete with a fine grotto. It was he who hosted the acting troupe last summer—perhaps you heard of it? I know he would be most intrigued by your amazing talent. Would you consider playing for the Kittitians some evening?"

"Oh, no. I like to reserve my gift for friends and family alone. God called me away from both stage and cathedral, I fear."

"Are you certain? I believe he pays handsomely. It could aid you in your ministry here among the Negroes."

Jedediah considered her words, then glanced over at Selah. As if wondering what she thought of the idea? She only stared back at him in surprise. But Verity was not so slow. "You need not perform more than once. And would not a little extra coin be welcome?" She looked at Selah meaningfully.

Selah's cheeks burned. Was she aiding him in his desire to court Selah? If only she knew how their conversation had taken a dark turn . . .

Jedediah turned back to the lady. "I think it would be most kind of you to introduce me, Mrs. Beckford."

"I will send a note on tomorrow's ferry. Until next week?"

"Until next week," he said with a genteel bow.

In time, the rest of the guests followed suit, and the major and captain assisted the inebriated lieutenants upstairs to bed. Jedediah said a reluctant good-night and the servants concluded their cleaning. At last, only Ket, Gray, Verity, and Selah remained, and to make certain they were not overheard, they walked down the path to the beach.

"Can this not wait until morn?" Gray asked wearily as he sank down to the sand. The women followed suit, forming a circle. Moonlight danced on the curving gentle waves washing ashore, which would effectively cover their conversation.

"I think not," Ket said, looking to her sisters. "Tell us. Both of you. All of it. I shall have no more secrets between us."

"I shall begin," Verity said, leaning forward. "'Twas I who enlisted Selah's help in this bit of espionage. And she did so out of a desire to help feed the people of the Double T. Those supplies I brought tonight? Gray, I can bring even more in the next few days."

He took a deep breath. "You have my attention. But at what cost?"

"My French compatriots on Statia asked me to obtain information on three ships due to arrive in the coming weeks from England. They wished to know if they carried either weapons or supplies, and which contained which. They believed Major Woodget would have received warning of their impending arrival." She looked to Selah, eager to find out what she'd learned.

"Which he did," Selah said. "In a letter written to him, I—"

"Hold," Gray said, sitting up straighter and lifting a hand toward her. "*You* read the major's correspondence?"

"After Verity secreted away the *key* to his correspondence box," Keturah said, throwing up her own hands, "Selah stole into his room with it."

"I . . . see," Gray gritted out. "Go on."

"In the end," Selah continued carefully, glancing from one family member to the next, "the letter did not define which vessel carried what beyond a hundred souls per vessel. But they do intend to stop here for water and any repairs after the crossing, and there was a mention that they carried enough cannons that it might quell this revolution before it goes further."

Verity sucked in her breath. "Dates? Did it mention dates?"

"They are to be expected from next week forward."

"Were the vessels named?"

"The lead is the *Vitriola*, captained by a man named Turner. I do not remember the rest." She shook her head sorrowfully at Verity, but her sister gave her hand a squeeze.

"'Tis enough," she said.

"Enough for what?" Gray asked, rising and pacing a bit before turning, hands on hips. "What do they intend to do with this information? Attack? Attempt to capture them? Sink them?"

"I know not," Verity said. "Our job is often to obtain the information. At times we never know what comes of it."

"So hundreds of soldiers might die in defending what they carry?" Ket asked. "Right here, on our shores?"

"That is war, Keturah," Verity said. "A war that is strangling Nevisians, remember? Yes, hundreds of soldiers may die. But how many thousands more might die if they reach the States with those weapons?"

"And yet if they do, will this war be ended, as the admiral hopes?"

Verity shook her head. "The British are yet full of bravado, especially those who have not been to the American colonies. They do not know her people, her determination. Ian believes there shall be no swift end, and after being there, I concur."

"I understand your compassion for the colonists, Verity," Ket said. "Indeed, I feel solidarity with them as we suffer alongside them, unable to get food or wood or a bucket of nails, even as we are forced to house and feed soldiers. But I confess, what matters most to me at this point is that the war come to a rapid end. The longer it goes on, the longer we islanders shall suffer. Are there not yet Loyalists who remain in America, crying to their neighbors to remember their roots?"

"Most have been driven out. Ships are full of families fleeing to England. That said, yes, Loyalists remain. There are pockets and strongholds, and they shall move as the battle lines do. But, Keturah, I do not believe this is a war that England can win. Nor shall either side do so quickly. The Continental Congress is resolute. The people in America . . ." She sighed and rose, looking to the sea a moment, then glancing at them over her shoulder. "They are hardy. As hardy as we had to become when we moved here. Would you ever believe that Rose Kelly or Charlotte Littener might do as we did? Move here alone? Work this soil in our father's breeches?"

After a moment, Keturah slowly shook her head.

"Even the more stalwart, like Ruth Michaels? Or Jeannette Francis?"

Again, Keturah shook her head.

"Americans understand what we have learned," Verity said, tapping her chest. "That at times, hardship cannot be passed off to another. At times, we are who must suffer in order to obtain what we want." She began pacing. "For over a year now, women and men have worn rough homespun, refusing to buy the imported, expensive silks we ourselves wear this night. For over two years now, most have had nothing but daffodil or nettle tea, again refusing to purchase tea taxed at so high a rate."

She sank to her knees in front of Ket and took her hands. "I beg of you to believe me. This war shall not be a short one. England will not relinquish her hold without a fight. But the Patriots, Ket, the Patriots . . . they shall fight to the death to hold what they believe is divinely their own. And I stand with them. What right has England? To tax a land so far from her shores? To claim it as her own at all?"

"Well, 'tis they who settled her! Who sent pilgrims to create society where there was none."

"But how is it that any country might claim another? I understand land near your own. But across the sea?"

"Then what would follow is that Nevis herself should not be English soil!"

"Perhaps it should not," Verity said, lifting her hands. "She forces her citizens to quarter soldiers who do little but drink and eat their food, food they cannot supply from so far away!"

"And yet is it wrong to demand our loyalty? When they send ships to take our sugar and pay us a handsome sum in return?"

"Unless your neighbors turn against you," Selah said quietly.

All fell silent.

Gray inhaled slowly through his nose. "'Tis due to Ian and Verity that we are yet here, Ket."

"I realize that," she said quickly.

"'Tis due to Ian and Verity that we have food for the next month,

and perhaps the following," he went on. "It does not easily settle
with me, this path, but it has settled. Unless I win a seat on the
council, our very existence is in peril. What would be worse?
Throwing in with the rebels or finding ourselves in need of selling the Double T to Shubert?"

Keturah turned wide, horrified eyes toward him.

"Who else could afford to buy us out at this time?"

"Perhaps Mr. Browning," she tried. "Not that I wish to!"

"I doubt he could muster the funds." He paused. "Even Major
Woodget looked aside when the supplies arrived today, Ket. He
knows as well as I that if we do not accept them, we starve."

"So that is it?" she asked. "We are all now allies of the Patriots?
We turn our backs on our mother country?"

"Have they not done the same to us, Ket?" Selah asked. "In
leaving us to fend for ourselves? Even the staunchest of Loyalists
on-island suffer. If this drags on, many will die. And not because
of war, but by starvation and disease." She rose. "I know it disap-
points you. But I will aid Verity in any way I can. If it keeps us and
our people alive, I shall do anything."

"I believe England has overreached," Verity said. "Greece, Rome
. . . they were empires that fell. So shall Britain in time. We are
witnessing it, are we not? Her hold is weak. She shall fight. But
ultimately I do not believe she shall win."

"You have seen it for yourself," Gray said to Verity. "You believe,
with everything in you, that the rebels will prevail?"

She returned his long, steady look. "I *hope*, with everything in
me, they do. I have committed my life to it. Are you ready to do
so as well?"

Gray ran his hands through his hair, took another weary breath,
staring at the sea, then back to Verity. He reached out his fist.

Verity covered it with her hand.

Selah, after a moment, did the same.

And after a long, quiet moment, Ket did as well. But hers was
only the briefest of touches. A mere covering of Selah's hand.
Then she rose and trudged up the beach, her shoulders hunched.

Chapter Fourteen

At daybreak, as Matthew blew the conch shell to summon the workers of the Double T, Keturah rolled over and nestled close to Gray, resting her cheek on his chest.

He stroked her hair for a moment, then lifted his head to look at her. "You are thinking, beloved. As you have likely been thinking all night."

"You know me well, husband."

"That is the goal, yes?"

She sat up, folded her legs, and took his hand. "What if we are wrong, Gray?" she whispered, glancing toward the door. "What if by some chance you do secure Shubert's seat on the council? What does a Patriot sympathizer do then?"

"He keeps rather quiet," Gray said. "And if things pan out as Verity believes, then he speaks up more and more. If the Continentals are victorious, they shall be our future trading partners." He took her hand and kissed it, then covered it with his other hand. "Ket, my entire focus is on our best chances at survival here. Do you think I would gamble it away without thought?"

She looked to the window and brushed back some of her long brown hair that was an untamed mass before her right eye. Then she glanced back at him. "Was it not enough? What we faced already? Did the Lord truly need to bring this to our door as well?"

He kissed her free hand again. "And yet through it, did he not provide for us in our greatest need?" He sighed. "Let us make our way through, day by day. The best we can. Let us not be concerned about the future, but trust each day to the Lord's hands."

She shook her head and padded to the window. He did not understand. He did not know the depths of her concern. Running a hand across her belly, she looked back at him. "Gray, I am pregnant," she whispered.

He scrambled out of bed, staring at her. "So soon? Why, Madeleine is but little more than a year old!"

"Yes," she nodded miserably. "*Yes.*"

He rubbed his face, eyebrows high, clearly trying to take in the news. One baby had been a surprise, given her ill luck with her first husband. But two babies?

She stood there for several terrible seconds feeling entirely alone, but then he hastened over to her, wrapping her in his long, strong arms from behind. Touching her belly tenderly and kissing her cheek. "This is truly a gift," he said. "Madeleine will adore a baby brother or sister, as will I."

"But, Gray, now is hardly the best time . . ." she began.

"There is never an ill-timed baby," he assured her. "Even if they arrive in the midst of a war, is not the promise of new life the best gift?" Again he kissed her temple and wrapped his arms more firmly around her. "Thank you," he murmured. "Thank you for bearing my children."

She turned to him and cradled his cheek with one hand. "You thank me? I am utterly grateful for you, Gray, each and every morn. Each night, as I close my eyes. You and Madeleine are my greatest joys."

"As you are mine," he said, kissing her temple, cheek, and neck, making her giggle and shy a little away.

He caught her and drew her back into his arms. "You, Keturah," he said, stroking her cheek. "And Madeleine, and this babe now who yet grows within you," he added, running a hand across her belly. "Along with Selah, Verity, our people. You are all who matter to me." He took her hand and brought it to his lips, looking into her eyes. "We have fought hard here for the Double T. But if it comes down to *life*, for us, for those we love, I am with Selah. I shall choose *life*. For as many as we can save. No matter where England says our loyalty must remain. Are you with me in that?"

It was her turn to glance toward the window. She pulled away and went to it, running her hand along the seashell inlay her father had placed, a window frame she had saved and reset when they rebuilt the house. He came up behind her, running his hands along her hips and then interlocking them in front of her belly, peering over her shoulder.

"'Twould break my heart," she said at last, voice cracking. "To leave this place, Gray. Here, I have come to understand why my father so fiercely loved this island. And somehow it ties me to him again, and he to his grandchildren."

"Can we not trust God to make it right, if it comes to it?" he asked softly. "If we were to move, could he not awaken love for that place in you there as he has here? Can you not trust him in that?"

She frowned and turned toward him. "Do you wish to leave?"

"No, beloved. With everything in me, I want to stay."

"But you are so ready to trust the future to God's hands?"

After a moment, he chuckled softly and drew her closer. "Keturah. Whose hands do you think we have been cradled in all our days?"

Verity left at dawn. Selah and Keturah watched her go from the pier, holding hands.

"And she is off," Selah said, watching as George and Trisa lifted the ketch's second sail and the hired sailor pointed the boat toward Statia. "Why do I feel she carries our future with her?"

"She doesn't, dear one. Only the Lord holds our future. Gray made me think about that."

Ket gestured to the pier, and together they sat, legs dangling.

"And so . . . you have come to agree with Verity? With whom we must side?" Selah asked.

Keturah considered that. "To a degree. But 'tis tenuous yet. It grates on me, with an admiral as an ancestor, to become a turncoat."

"I understand."

Keturah pulled off her slippers and allowed her feet to slide into the crystalline waters. Below, they could see tiny fish pecking at fat coral. "Does it not give you pause, standing against the Crown? Given who our ancestor was?" Keturah asked.

Selah smiled. "I give him honor, for certain. He did as he was led." She looked up and out. "However, times change. People change. Societies change. 'Tis the way of history, is it not? Could this new way of the Patriots not be our own in the future?" She paused. "Why are you so reticent, Sissy? Surely 'tis not the pressures of our neighbors and not solely the pull of familial loyalties."

Keturah nodded, thinking for several moments, then looked up at the sky. "I am pregnant, Selah."

Selah glanced sharply at her. "You are certain of it?"

"Quite," she returned calmly.

Selah looked away again, to the climbing peaks of nearby St. Kitts, to the water beneath her toes. "I am most glad for you, Ket."

Keturah paused. "And now you understand my reticence at last."

"Indeed," Selah confirmed with a nod.

Ket brushed her toe back and forth in the water. "I yearn to be as venturous as you and Ver. I do. But life . . ." She sighed heavily. "Life makes you a bit more wary."

"And motherhood?" Selah asked.

"That quintuples my wariness," she said.

Selah smiled. "This explains much for me, Sissy."

"What? My wariness? My fear?"

"All."

Keturah frowned and reached for her hand. "Do not dismiss it. Understand it. Where you most likely venture, if you continue to aid Verity, are waters frequented by sharks and fathoms deep. Tarry not long there. Get in, but then get out. Promise me that?"

"As fast as I can, Ket," she said, kissing her sister's hand. They sat there in silence for a few moments.

"What of Jedediah?" Ket said at length. "Is he a rebel too?"

Selah laughed through her nose and smiled, brows lifting. She looked to her sister. "He is a rebel, I am sure of it. A rebel for the Lord. But where he stands on this battle with the colonies, I am uncertain."

Keturah cast a glance her way. "He is a fine musician."

"Indeed." She breathed deeply, knowing where this might lead. "But he is finer among his people."

"His people? Our people?" Ket asked mildly.

"All, Ket. All. You must hear him preach. How he brings the Word in such fervent passion. You have never come to the meeting-house. Can you come? 'Tis like nothing I've ever heard Vicar Michaels preach come Sunday at Saint Philips."

"And yet he is a *Methodist*," Ket said, sliding in that last word as if she might say *spy*.

Selah dragged her own toe through the water. "We have recently found ourselves surprised by the need to consider other points of view in regard to politics. Might we not open our hearts to other points of view in regard to religion?"

Keturah let out a scoffing laugh and lifted her hands. "I guess I cannot argue with that. But what of his interest in *you*?"

"In me?"

"Do not be coy. I was not the only one who saw how you looked at him after your duet. And he, you."

Selah lifted her hands to her face. "Was it truly so obvious? I could not help myself, Ket." She shook her head. "That is one thing I find most charming about Jedediah. He continuously surprises me. Challenges me. Sometimes frustrates me. And then makes it all right in the end."

"Well, you were always good at the Minuet in G."

"But you must admit, it never sounded like that."

"Well, no. But you only have two hands!"

"But what he does with *his* hands, Ket . . ." She shook her head again, feeling her face warm with a blush. "Whether he be in the field or at the harpsichord, whether he's waving them about as he preaches . . ."

"You admire him."

"Much."

"And he does you. That is plain too."

"He *admired* me," she said. "Until last night."

"Last night?"

"We had a disagreement. A misunderstanding, I suppose. But the fact that he misunderstood made me doubt him."

Ket gave her a sorrowful look. "I am sorry for that. But perhaps 'tis for the best."

"For the best?"

"He is penniless, Selah. Without a home. And he is a Methodist," she said. "Or have you *already* 'opened your mind to other points of view' in regard to that?"

Selah suppressed her irritation. Her sister's complaints about Jed were not unexpected. "I like how Jedediah preaches from the Bible. How he talks about God. He makes God sound more . . . approachable. And in regard to his station, I do not believe I require a husband who has means."

"'Tis easy to say that," Keturah said, "when you have a roof over your head and food to eat. Fine clothing. 'Tis another to find yourself in need of those things and have not the means to purchase them."

Selah nodded. 'Twas a fair point. "And yet here we are with the means, but threatened by the inability to purchase supplies. Wealth only grants so much security, Ket."

Her sister said nothing for a while. Then she rose. "Come. Let us go to town. I wish to buy some fish from the fishmonger for supper. And I want to stop by Penhurst to see if Mrs. Chandler would like to attend our auction and picnic."

Selah rose and walked up the path behind her, trying to forget the last time they had been in Charlestown and how Angus had so viciously attacked Jedediah. With luck, they would not run into him again. But someone at the party last night had mentioned how he favored staying at his northern Rose Hall Plantation just outside of Charlestown rather than at Downing, where his wife was reportedly on her deathbed. *A death he had likely hastened,* she thought, *keeping Eleanor in ready supply of laudanum.*

"You shall carry your sgian dubh?" Selah asked.

"Indeed. Surely Shubert will have learned of our soiree last night by now. I assume it shall make him more cantankerous. And I heard someone mention he's residing at Rose Hall most of the time."

"We shall bring Gideon and Primus with us."

"Is there a person on this island who truly likes the man?"

"Gray says that there are many who owe him. That is how he remains surrounded by 'friends.'"

"Do you think Gray truly might have a chance at unseating him on council?"

"We have a great deal of work to do if 'tis to happen. Shubert is not the only one who does not like how we run the plantation. He stirs up their fear. And fear often leads to defensiveness. If we could only get every family on-island to visit the Double T . . . to see that there is nothing to fear. That our workers are less apt to rise in rebellion than anyone's slaves, because they are treated as human beings."

"'Endowed by their Creator with certain unalienable rights, including life, liberty, and the pursuit of happiness?'" Selah quoted.

"You have gone back to reading the rebels' declaration, have you?"

"I cannot help myself. There is something irresistible about reading those words. But how can they all sign that document and yet not see the hypocrisy of owning slaves?" she whispered as they entered the house. "Surely they shall set all Negroes free once they win the war."

"Perhaps," Keturah said doubtfully. "*If* they win the war."

Selah sighed and scurried up the stairs to fetch her dirk and a parasol to shield her from the harsh sun. It always seemed much hotter in Charlestown, with all its stone buildings, than on the plantation. She tossed a guilty glance down the hallway toward the major's room. Had he seen any of the wax residue? Did he have a clue that someone had entered his room? It comforted her that he might assume a maid had spilled some wax but doubt anyone could get into his correspondence box.

It came to her then. The soldiers were the perfect emissaries to send about the island, touting the success of the Double T and testifying that there was little to fear about her people, or the minister who had come to preach to and teach them.

She would speak to Major Woodget at her first opportunity.

That opportunity to see the major came sooner than she thought it would, except there was no time to converse. When they neared the hot, sprawling area of Charlestown that hosted the slavers' despicable platforms, they saw soldiers galloping on horses and more running in the same direction.

"What is transpiring?" Ket asked.

They heard a woman scream. Another's pitiful cries. Another shrieking.

Gideon had pulled up to allow two soldiers to cross the road before them. "I do not know, Lady Ket, but I think 'tis best to get you safely away. Master Gray would not wish you to be involved in that."

Selah looked to her sister in horror. How could she hear those cries and not go to them? Was there something they could do? But memories of their waterside conversation—of Ket's renewed caution, given her pregnancy, was all the answer she needed. Ket needed to stay put. But she did not.

Before Gideon could urge the team forward, Selah had climbed out of the carriage.

"Selah! *Selah!*" Ket cried.

But she picked up her skirts and ran, ignoring her call.

The screams ahead of her were all she could truly hear. And they were growing louder as she neared the platform. A slaver named Titus was standing nose to nose with Angus Shubert, arguing vehemently. A whip dangled from Angus's hand, and on the platform three women cowered, the youngest already severely slashed.

"*Ejila ya! Ejila ya!*" they continued to cry out in what Selah thought might be Igbo. Selah had learned enough of the language to make out a few key words. *Do not take her. Sister.*

Tears rolled down their faces. The eldest was no older than eighteen. A Negro man, who had presumably come to their aid, was bleeding and unconscious beside them. Another family member? The slaver was angry, likely because Shubert had put down the male. But Selah could not look beyond the three girls. She thought of Akunta and how she had run from Shubert. And how enraged he would be with this one for causing a scene. How might he punish her?

Titus was demanding Shubert purchase the man he had knocked out. "Damaged goods," he called him. Shubert refused and wanted to be on his way. He headed for the girl, and the women closed in, shrieking. Snarling, he drew back and lifted the whip again and let it loose across all three of them. The Negro men near the girls lifted their chained wrists and shouted at Shubert in their native tongue, clearly demanding that he stop.

"Why are they doing nothing?" Selah gasped, seeing soldiers all about, but none taking action. She spotted Major Woodget, astride his horse, and pushed her way through the crowd. She heard the whip crack again and the women scream. "Major Woodget!" she shouted, reaching his side.

"Miss Selah! What are—?"

"Why are you not stopping this?" she asked, gesturing to the platform.

"We are here to quell any uprising, given the slaver's distraction. We cannot have fifty slaves go running amuck."

She gaped at him. "But Mr. Shubert! He abuses not only the slave he has purchased but also her sisters! Shall you not put a stop to it?" She winced as she heard the crack of the whip again, followed by Shubert's bellowing demands. She glanced back to see more slaves closing ranks around the girls. This would only enrage Shubert further. Might they revolt, forcing the soldiers to attack? How many would be injured?

"Miss Selah," the major said kindly, "surely you understand that we cannot interfere with the commerce of the island. Where is your sister? I shall see you safely to—"

Letting out another cry of utter frustration, Selah turned away and pushed between men to reach the platform stairs.

The major might be able to stand idly by while this travesty unfolded, but she could not.

The few women present cried out, seeing her climb the steps. Men shouted warnings. Angus spun, and his look of fury turned into scoffing rage. "Get off this platform, Miss Banning! You have no right to be here."

"You shall stop whipping these people at once!" she demanded, placing herself between him and the slaves. "They do not belong to you."

"One does!" he sneered. "And as soon as she comes along with me, this comes to an end."

"She is among her sisters!" Selah cried. "Surely you understand that if you bought all of them, this would not have transpired."

"I don't need three Negresses for Rose Hall. I need one. And I bought *her*," he said, pointing. "Now I shall have her."

Selah's skin crawled at the way he said those last words.

"I shall buy them," she said, striding over to the slaver, who held what looked like a broken hand in his other. "All three of them, plus the unconscious man who came to their defense. No money has exchanged hands with this man yet. Sell them to me."

"With what funds?" spat Shubert. "The Double T is rumored to only be surviving due to your sister's smuggled goods." He edged closer to her, and she slipped her dirk out of her waistband.

He huffed a laugh and shook his head. "You Banning girls and those cursed McKintrick daggers. 'Tis time someone taught you a lesson about standing against me." He turned away, took a few steps, and when he turned back he sent his whip flinging toward her.

Selah heard Keturah scream.

It was the only sound Selah heard. Not the crack of the whip. Not the cries of others.

All else faded as she watched the whip strike at her like a snake and wrap around her wrist.

It sliced through her kid glove as if it were but paper rather than cloth.

Red blood rose at once as the terrible, stinging pain finally registered in her brain. She dropped the dirk. Her whole hand now seemed to shriek in pain. She stared up at him.

But he was not finished.

CHAPTER FIFTEEN

She stumbled back, falling into the arms of the slaves behind her. One of the women tried to shield her, but the tip of the whip came hunting again, licking across her shoulder and cheek. Flaying her skin open. She felt hot, wet blood sliding down her cheek before she noticed the sharp sting of it, and as if in a dream she looked up to see Major Woodget tackle Shubert from the side.

Captain Howard fell atop of the man, helping to pin him. Lieutenant Angersoll kicked away his whip. And Keturah was running across the platform to her, face awash in horror. All at once, sound returned to her ears. Shouts of outrage. Cries of shock. Weeping.

"Oh, Selah, Selah," Keturah moaned, pulling a handkerchief from her waist sash and pressing it to her cheek. "Come. We must get you home and send for a physician."

Selah grabbed hold of the slave woman nearest her. "Not without them," she said. "I shall not leave these girls, Ket. Not without them."

"*Selah*," Ket said desperately. "As much as I wish to help, I have to think of all those already in our keep. We need not three more mouths to—"

"Ket, they are sisters. *Sisters*. I shall not leave them. And I shall not see this one go to Shubert." She shook her head vehemently, stubbornly. She felt wildly strong, distant from her injuries. She stood up and held her hand away from her skirts, watching as blood dripped to the platform. How much blood had been spilled on this platform over the decades? How many innocents bludgeoned into submission? She looked down the line of frightened and confused slaves, soldiers now pointing their muskets at them.

"Stop!" Selah said, pushing the nearest musket up in the air, then the next. "Stop! Can you not see? These are innocents! 'Tis Angus Shubert who is the monster!"

Gideon placed his own handkerchief across her shoulder wound. "Come, Miss Selah. We need to get you home." He put a warm, wide hand on her uninjured shoulder.

But she refused him. "Not without them," she insisted.

Shubert was yelling and demanding that the soldiers let him go. The slaver was talking to another captain and two more lieutenants. He spat in Shubert's direction, and the man tried to lunge at him. Two burly lieutenants grabbed Shubert's arms, only narrowly holding him back.

"Fetch the sheriff!" Shubert shouted. "Fetch him at once! I demand it as a councilman!"

"Yes, call the sheriff!" Keturah said, marching up to him. "For perhaps now you shall face justice, Angus Shubert. *Councilman*," she scoffed. "You are a disgrace to the title. What sort of councilman wounds a woman? What sort of monster attacks his *neighbor*?" she raged.

Shouts of agreement rose up around her.

"What sort of man so abuses his slaves before he has even taken proper ownership?" she went on. "What are we to believe you do to your poor people once they are on your plantation?"

"It is none of your business what I do with my property, and you know it!" Shubert yelled. He pulled at his captors' hold.

"Why? Because you fear your status as a councilman might be threatened if all knew how depraved you are?" she asked, hands on her hips. Watching her sister, Selah thought she never looked more beautiful. *A mighty warrioress . . .*

Gideon offered her his arm, as she was swaying a bit. "Come,

Miss Selah," he gently urged. "Let me get you to the carriage. Your wounds—"

"You and yours have crossed me for the last time, Keturah," Shubert said, looking like he wanted to strangle her. "You shall live to regret this final day you did not give me the respect due."

"I do not respect vermin like you," she said. She turned to the slaver. "We shall purchase the sisters, including the man. How much are the current bids?"

"Four hundred pounds," replied the man.

"You cannot sell the one!" Shubert cried. "I already purchased her!"

"You did not give me any coin for her yet," the slaver said, spitting at his feet. "And this woman did not break my wrist."

But Keturah had visibly paled, still struggling to take in the sum he named. "Why so much?"

He shrugged. "Prices are up, given the war in the American colonies disrupting trade. Ninety for the buck. Seventy each for the women."

"She doesn't have it!" Shubert crowed. "*I* shall take all four!"

Selah stepped forward, aware now that blood poured from her cheek, down her neck, drenching her bodice. She had to intervene; she knew Ket did not have a tenth of that coin. But she did. "I shall pay for them myself," she said, trying to say it as valiantly as Ket had but failing. She felt unaccountably weak . . . more than a bit dizzy, given the heat and blood loss. "Mr. Jacoby shall provide you funds by day's end out of my account."

The slaver looked doubtfully at Ket, while Ket could only gape at her. "Selah, that is part of your dowry."

"Yes," she said, becoming more resolute by the moment, even as her head began to spin. Was this what Jedediah had meant when he talked about his calling? Because this seemed utterly right. Almost . . . holy. An oddly still *centering* in the midst of what was becoming a tornado in her head. "Are we agreed?" Selah managed to ask the slaver.

"Aye, if the money is in my pocket this afternoon." He looked away from her wounds as if ashamed they had occurred on his platform. "Miss, you should truly sit down. You are a bloody mess."

"I shall in a moment. Rest assured, the money shall arrive in short order."

She looked down the line of captives again, shackles making their ankles and wrists raw, eyes wide as they stared at her, trying to understand what was happening. So far from home. So far from where God had meant them to be . . .

And in that moment she knew.

She would spend every last dollar of her dowry to free every one of them she could. Warmth flooded her chest, the sensation like drinking hot tea on a cold English day. Shivers ran down her neck, shoulders, and fingers.

And then she collapsed in a faint.

Jedediah set aside his machete as he spotted the carriage racing down the road below them. Gray and Matthew, alerted by his pause, followed his gaze.

Gray was the first to move, running for his hobbled horse, grabbing the gelding's reins and mounting with practiced ease. "Bring everyone in, Matthew!" he shouted as he whirled and galloped away.

Jedediah ran down the furrow behind him, his boots sinking six inches with every footfall, the damp soil threatening to drag him back.

He had seen the blood-soaked gown, the limp form in Keturah's arms, as Gray had.

Selah.

Selah. What had happened?

Oh, Lord, Lord, he begged silently. *Oh, help me get to her, Father. Protect her, surround her with your angels! Oh, Lord . . . !*

It seemed to take an eternity to reach the end of the furrow. Then he gained footing on the path at the edge that led downhill, this one tramped down by hundreds of bare soles day in and day out. He fairly flew down it, narrowly managing to keep his feet, concentrating only on the woman in his mind. What had befallen her in Charlestown? What could possibly have happened?

He reached Round Road, ran three hundred feet, then entered the drive of the Double T. He passed Gray's mount, still heaving from its exertion, and climbed the steps three at a time. But at the door, he paused, pulling off his hat. With one sidelong glance from Sansa, who raised a brow, he realized he'd left his shirt in the brush at the edge of the field. He blew out his breath and paced, trying to figure out what he could do. He saw servants scurrying up and down the stairs inside. Had they carried Selah to her room above?

Sansa reappeared around the corner and dolefully handed him a shirt. "'Tis an old one of Master Gray's," she said.

"What happened?" he asked, hurriedly pulling it on. "How badly is she injured?"

"It looks worse than it is," she said, crossing her arms. "Miss Selah got in between Angus Shubert and his newest slave. She refused to let him take her. That riled Master Shubert something fierce."

Jed took a deep breath, blinking rapidly. "And so he *struck* her?"

"He whipped her. Twice."

"*Whipped* her?" he repeated, trying to make sense of it. Rage flooded his mind. His fists clenched and unclenched. *How dare that man!*

Gray appeared at the top of the stairs and then thundered down them. Emotions that mirrored what Jedediah felt were seen clearly on the man's face. He passed Jed at the base of the stairs.

"Where are you going?" Jed asked, hand on the post to remind himself he must remain below.

"To town!"

"May I go with you?"

"No! Stay here!" Gray said, slamming the door behind him as he exited.

Jedediah looked up the long staircase. The last he had looked upon it, it was to see Selah demurely descending in her beautiful golden gown. Before she sat with him on the bench and they played their duet . . . before they had spoken last with its tortuous, confusing outcome.

He looked over at the instrument. It was forlorn in its disuse.

He looked back up the steps. Decorum would not allow him to climb them. It was impossible to find out more, until either Selah or her sister or a servant came to him.

So he would call to her from down below.

Selah looked to Ket as they heard the first notes from the harpsichord below. He had come to her, at least as close to her as he could. Mitilda was working on salving her wounds at the wrist, shoulder, neck and cheek, and Keturah was gently covering them with clean bandages. They had already washed her and put her in a fresh dressing gown.

"He does for you what he can," Ket said, giving her a gentle smile.

Selah winced as Ket laid another bandage across the cut the whip had created. There was a spreading bruise where her gown had protected her shoulder. A painful weal rose at her wrist where the whip had wrapped around it. Now that the glove was off, she could see it had protected all but the top side. But it was her neck and cheek that worried her the most now as she heard Jedediah playing for her.

"Shall it leave a terrible scar?" she whispered to Ket.

Ket met her eyes. "You are young, so it will heal well. But yes, Selah, I think it will scar."

Selah swallowed hard and looked to the window. "It should not matter so to me. What is beauty but fleeting? But will he . . . will everyone look upon me with pity now?"

Keturah took her good hand in both her own. "You will still be beautiful, dear one. And that man down in the parlor? Selah, I believe you could shave your head and he would still think you the most beautiful woman he has ever seen."

Selah let out a small laugh, then winced as the action tugged at the tender wound on her cheek.

"I am only thankful the whip did not take your eye. It came perilously close."

"I would say I am sorry for interceding, Ket, for putting you through such terror. But I am not. I am glad I saved that girl from Angus's hand. If he beat her so before he even left the platform, what would he have done to her on the plantation?"

Keturah did not respond for a moment. "You cannot save them all, Selah," she said sadly, adjusting one of her bandages.

"But I can save those God sets before me." She sat up straighter as Ket finished her ministrations and Mitilda left with her bowl of salve. "I must speak to Jedediah about that. Might he come and sit with me? If you were to remain?"

"Now? Speak to him of what?"

"Of how I wish to help as many slaves as possible to make their way to freedom," she said carefully, as if testing out the words. "I believe I may have been called by God to do so."

"By . . . God? You mean you heard him speak to you?"

"Not in actual words. But in that moment, Ket, I could do nothing other than what I did. 'Twas as if God was compelling me to act."

Ket frowned. "Or was it not simply the fact that they were three sisters—a fact that reminded you of us—that moved you to such rash action?"

Selah leaned back against the pillow, remembering. "When I realized they were sisters, it did affect me deeply," she admitted. "I believe God brought me to that platform, however, at that moment, and used the trio for me to truly consider what they suffer. Not only Angus's savage beating, but their separation. How would we have fought if someone tried to separate us? And what gives us the right to separate family after family? If they are fortunate enough to survive the passage, do they not, at the very least, deserve to stay together?"

She shook her head, feeling the anguish that seemed to rise as bitter incense from that platform again. The collective grief and disbelief and terror. She had thought she was doing all she could, here at the Double T, with those she could care for and protect on the premises. But did God want her to press out further?

"We cannot *feed* every soul you rescue, Selah," Keturah said, her expression sorrowful. "We have too many mouths to feed as it is. When Gray brings these three women and their man home, you must prepare four others to find their way in the world elsewhere." She rose and moved to the window, the trade winds blowing back damp tendrils of hair from her face. "Perhaps Verity can assist us in finding positions for them—as freed women. As cooks, lady's maids, or grooms."

"Perhaps," Selah said, looking away. What would Keturah think if she found out about Akunta and their perilous night voyage? "We can speak to her about it next week." She reached out and took Ket's hand. "The Lord will help me, I know he will. He did not lead me to this only to languish."

Keturah gave her a long, contemplative look. "The words from your mouth . . ." She glanced to the ceiling, took a deep breath and then looked her sister in the eye. "They are a woman's words, not a girl's. A woman determined. And God help us, Selah, because they frighten me."

Gray started out driving his team at breakneck speed in his haste to reach Charlestown. He wanted nothing more than to find Angus Shubert, snatch his whip from him, and give the man the lashing of his life. How dare he do such a thing to sweet Selah! How dare the man have done all he had to Keturah, to Verity, to Matthew . . .

It was over. *Over.* He had to be rid of Shubert. The island had to be rid of him. He was a cancer. A dark, rotting mold at every decent person's foundation.

Gray wanted to kill him.

But halfway there, after rounding a harrowing turn, he pulled up a bit on the reins, easing the team into a walk. Keturah had said the soldiers had taken him into custody and were awaiting the sheriff, who was apparently in Gingerland. Major Woodget would not turn a blind eye if Gray gave Shubert a sound beating—no matter how much he deserved it. Had not the soldiers gently informed him that if they had the opportunity to apprehend Ian McKintrick for the same crime, they would be compelled to do so, regardless of their sympathies?

So how might he best proceed?

Think, Gray told himself. *Think.*

'Twas the flesh that made him want to pound out his fury on the man who had so sorely abused people he loved. His own sense of justice begged him to make it right. But could he? He had not found a way to date.

Something Jedediah said in the fields the previous afternoon had given him pause. What had it been exactly? Something about God's timing was at times slower than a man liked, but it always proved to be perfect. *The trick is not to try and rush him.*

Gray would not be the only one enraged that Angus Shubert had dared to strike a woman. With a whip, no less. With collective might, they could demand he face a judge. What would be the ultimate punishment for a man who was arguably the most powerful person on-island?

The *loss* of power.

Like dominoes falling in a line, Gray could see it all collapsing. If he insisted Angus face a judge for his crime against Selah—the second she had endured—and if that judge ruled against him, surely Angus would lose his seat on the council. And if Gray could take his seat?

He sat back, thinking of the glory of that day. But then he checked himself. Even if it was a man he could respect, a man willing to listen to planters with alternative solutions on how to negotiate the challenging waters Nevis found herself surrounded by, that would be enough.

"Yes," he muttered. "'Twould be enough." But truth be told, he really, really wanted to take that seat himself. And see Angus Shubert's face as he did so.

The outskirts of town were oddly quiet, and as he drove in, he understood why. The chaos at the center of it had drawn in its inhabitants like a massive wave sucking in every bit of water possible as it built. At the center, people were shouting and lifting fist and sword, all surrounding the tiny building that housed the British garrison's offices. The sheriff was standing outside, brandishing his own sword, demanding everyone step back. Gray pulled his wagon team to a stop, tied them up, then ventured closer.

"Justice shall be served!" the sheriff shouted. "Settle down! Justice shall be served!"

"Hang 'im! String 'im up!" cried one, to which the crowd roared its approval.

"How dare he do that to a poor defenseless woman!" cried another.

Gray hid a smile. He knew Selah, though small, was far from defenseless. Still, if it furthered their cause . . .

"We've had enough!" shouted a man near the sheriff. "Shubert throws his weight around wherever he goes. And this time, it was in the wrong corner! We shall not stand idle after a gentlewoman like Miss Banning has found herself at the wrong end of Shubert's whip!"

Again the crowd bellowed their approval. Yet, as Gray looked about, it was not the nobility in company. It was those who might find themselves beholden to Shubert. Sharecroppers, servants at the tavern, tenants. No, the nobility remained on the outskirts, several men on horseback.

Gray eased closer to Mr. Hudson, who had been in attendance at the Double T the day before.

"Heavens, man!" Hudson said, spying him. He dismounted at once and took Gray's hand. "Is your sister-in-law gravely injured?"

"She shall survive, certainly," Gray said. "But the man sorely injured her. For the second time, I might add. You shall remember, three years past, he tried to take advantage of her. Only Verity's interference saved her. This time he dared to whip our sweet Selah. She has cuts to her shoulder, neck, and face that she shall live with all her life."

The big man drew back in dismay. "And she such a beauty! 'Tis a crime in itself!"

"Aye," Gray said, wincing inwardly at the man's assumption that Selah was no longer beautiful. "But foremost is that Shubert would dare to do it at all. No matter how much of this island he owns, he does not own *us*. Does he? We cannot allow him to do whatever he wishes."

"No," Carlson said, shaking his head solemnly. "We cannot."

Mr. Hall had dismounted and drawn closer too, hearing the bulk of their conversation. "Give our condolences to Miss Banning," said Mr. Hall.

"I would rather tell her that you are with me."

"With you?" he said, turning back.

"In unseating Angus Shubert. That would bring her the greatest comfort of all." He waved at the garrison hall. "The sheriff will see to the lout. A judge shall be summoned. Shubert shall stand before him." He leaned closer. "But you know as well as I that he will likely find a way to pay his way out of punishment."

Heads lifted, faces grim with unhappy assent. "The only way to see Angus Shubert put in his place is to take away his power," Gray pressed on. "To remove him from council. Is it not enough that he owns a quarter of the island? Surely we should not give him access to owning our future."

All heads bobbed in agreement.

"I hope I shall see you all for Verity's auction of her team and carriage. Bring your families and a picnic lunch at three, even if you do not intend to bid. You are more than welcome at the Double T."

He moved to converse with two more groups of men, doing the same as with the first.

Then, with a last lingering glance at the garrison hall—in which he knew thirty or more soldiers stood ready to defend Shubert—he swung toward the bank, where he was to secure Selah's funds from Mr. Jacoby and then bring home the four people that began this entire melee.

CHAPTER SIXTEEN

Jedediah had been playing for more than an hour when Keturah appeared, gently touching his shoulder. He had been so intent on his music that he did not hear or see her descend. All he could feel was the music and its message to Selah.

He stopped abruptly when she touched him and looked up, startled.

"Jedediah, Selah would like to see you."

"Sh-she would?"

"Yes. Come with me." Keturah gestured toward the staircase. He ambled off the bench and followed her up the stairs.

"I fear you missed your calling, Jedediah," she said to him.

"Pardon me?"

"Your calling. Clearly, the Lord speaks through your music as much as he does through your preaching."

"They are both callings, to be certain, Lady Ket," he said, deferring to the servants' use of her name, "but there was one I was to follow, and it brought me to your door."

"Indeed," she said, raising a brow as she paused by a bedroom. "As well as to our harpsichord."

"True," he said. But he had difficulty concentrating on the conversation. He was thinking only of Selah. What was this mercy that he might be allowed to come upstairs? To her bedchamber?

"She will be glad to see you," Keturah said. "You may enter."

Would she be glad? After all they had last said to each other?

He swallowed hard and then pressed upon the partially open door. Her room sprawled before him—a massive chamber with two windows on either side of a four-poster bed. He glanced at the Turkish rug. Silk curtains billowing in the wind streaming between them. An ornately carved armoire.

He cleared his throat. "Did you know the word *armoire* comes from the Latin *armarium*?'" he asked nervously. "It was a chest for strong armor. Do you have a suit of arms in there, Selah?"

She laughed under her breath. "Not at the moment."

He dared to look at her at last.

She was dressed in a silk dressing robe, embroidered with flowers, covered to the chest with her blanket. But all he saw were her wide, golden brown eyes, the bandages covering her cheek and neck. The blood spattered in her hair. The wrist bound and propped up on a pillow.

"Oh, Selah," he breathed, stepping forward, hands clasped, surprised at the sudden tears in his eyes. Who was this woman who so greatly moved him? Every trace of his fears from last night evaporated in the face of her injuries.

"Jedediah," she whispered, shaking her head. "'Twas so awful, what I witnessed. I could not stand apart. I could not stand against. I could only stand between. 'Twas a *calling*, Jed. I am certain of it. I had to stand up for those women. I believe . . . I believe I am to stand up for others too." Her eyes shifted to her sister as Ket took a seat on the other side of the bed, presumably to chaperone.

But he felt no remorse or hesitation as he stepped forward and gently took Selah's good hand in his. So overcome by emotion, he could not seem to stop himself. "You have been called, as I have?"

She nodded, and a tiny smile lit her eyes as they stared at each other.

"Gray has gone to town to fetch the four I was defending," she said. "Will you look after them? I will not be abed tomorrow, but my sister has insisted that I do so today."

"Of course," Jedediah said.

She glanced at Keturah. "My unplanned purchase has Ket worried, for more reasons than one. We need to encourage several people to go with Verity next week, to find work on Statia or elsewhere. Who do you think are most ready to leave Nevis and find employment? You have been working beside them."

Jedediah took the chair beside her bed, reluctantly letting go of her hand. Every single one of the people on the Double T had worked their way into his heart. Thinking of sending any of them away pained him.

"I can see on your face that you do not wish any of them to depart," she said.

He gave her a wistful smile. "I understand why we must send them, but yes. 'Tis a trial. Who wishes to send away friends?" He tapped his fingers together, thinking. "Frank and Junior have both expressed interest in a life at sea. Kuri's and Wednesday's skill with horses would make them excellent grooms. Miss Verity might have people in mind who would hire them on Statia or beyond. None would miss the fields." He thought about the others. "Salani would make a lovely lady's maid, as would Charelle."

"That is true. They are always braiding the others' hair. Do any of those four have romantic interests?"

"I do not believe so."

"Then will you ask them? If they do not wish to go, we shall not force them. We will find others who are willing."

Jedediah nodded. "Of course." The woman's care for her people moved him. "Selah, might you tell me—us—more of what you think this calling from God entails?"

She fiddled with her blanket, looked him in the eye, then glanced at her sister, then back to him. "Standing there on that platform, I knew I could not allow those girls to go home with Shubert. But it was more than that, Jedediah. For as long as I have lived on Nevis, I have done my best for the enslaved. The very first day we arrived on-island, I interfered in an auction and we bought a slave to save her. Another that Angus Shubert wanted. Perhaps 'twas then that he decided we were his enemies."

His pulse picked up at her words. She had dared to do this before?

"But I am ashamed to admit that I have become somewhat . . . *accustomed* to it." She shook her head. "Standing on that platform, seeing their desperate faces . . . all at once it was as if I could feel the first shock of it again. The anguish of the thousands upon thousands who had passed across that very platform. And I knew I was not only to save those three girls but any others I can as well."

"I shall say it again. You cannot save them all, Selah," Keturah said with a sigh.

"No," she said with irritation. "But I can save quite a few."

"You do not intend to use your entire dowry," Ket began.

"I do," Selah said. She smiled shyly over at Jedediah. "Something tells me that the man I wish to court me would not care that I come to the marriage with a light purse."

Jedediah had started to smile when she spoke of how God moved her heart and more so when she asked about her people's hearts. But what she said last made him grin. "Any man worthy of you would not care a whit," he said.

Keturah sighed and leaned back in her chair, rubbing her face. "I fear you are choosing a very challenging road."

"Undoubtedly," Selah said.

"'Twill be all right," Jedediah said. "The Lord takes care of those who take the challenging roads *he* sets before them." He bit his lip, staring at her. "Selah, I owe you a sincere apology. What I said last night . . . clearly, I misjudged you." He glanced around at the finery about her. "But are you truly ready to leave such luxury behind?" He dared to look to Ket, then back at Selah. "A courtship with me, and where I intend to go . . . we would be fortunate to have a house as big as this room."

Selah took a long breath and sat up a bit straighter. "Jedediah

Reed. For a man who sees the ways of God so readily, you are rather blind when it comes to women."

"I-I am?"

"Yes."

He smiled at her then, laughing internally. She was right. And was it not obvious, the passion of her calling, and how it dovetailed with his own? What more did she have to do to prove herself? She, now covered in ointment and bandages, after bearing a whip that had beaten slave after slave? Suffering a wound that would likely leave her scarred forever?

He leaned toward her and took her hand. "I told you I believe I was called to you as surely as I was called to the West Indies to minister to slaves," he said.

She stared back at him with those big brown eyes that oft filled his dreams. "And now?"

"Now I am more certain of it than ever."

"Well, here he is, the horse behind the cart," Gray said as Jedediah climbed the veranda steps that evening, hat in hand.

Jed gave him a sheepish smile.

Keturah gestured to a chair beside them, then poured him a cup of tea. More must have arrived with the supplies from Statia, because Jed had understood they were nearly out. "My husband teases, Jedediah, but judging from your exchange with my sister this afternoon, you are a tad late in speaking to us, are you not?"

"I am," he said, nodding. "Please forgive me for that. Truthfully, I had thought of speaking to you last night, but Selah and I had a misunderstanding. And she indicated that you had a more pressing matter at hand to discuss."

Gray set down his teacup and leaned back in his chair, waiting. Keturah had yet to take a sip of her own.

"So here I am at last, truly the cart behind the horse," he said, looking from one to the other, knowing it was imperative he obtain both their blessings. "A man with little to his name other than a willingness to work for his keep. But I confess that Selah has so thoroughly stolen my heart that I find it difficult to imagine my life without her. I am here to humbly ask your blessing upon our courtship."

"A courtship that is already well on its way, as far as I can tell," Keturah said, taking a sip at last from her china cup.

"I fear my heart was leading me before my mind could fully catch up."

"As was Selah's, truth be told," Keturah said.

Gray took Keturah's hand. "Was ours not an unconventional courtship as well?"

"'Twas different. We were friends."

"As Selah and Jed have become friends?"

Keturah's mouth pursed and she gently pulled her hand away. So Gray was already leaning toward approval, but she was the one he would need to win over, he surmised. "Jedediah, you heard yourself that Selah is considering giving away her entire dowry in order to aid more slaves in gaining their freedom."

"I did."

"And you approve of her plans?"

Jedediah considered the challenge in her tone. "I do. If Selah has been called to do as she said, she and the world are best served by seeing it through."

"And it does not alarm you? That you shall not have those funds at your disposal should the two of you wed?"

He smiled a little. "Lady Ket, I have not had much in terms of funds at my disposal in quite some time. And honestly, I thought I would be on this path as a single man, never considering I might need woo a bride. Particularly a bride of means and station."

"What of your own inheritance?" Gray put in.

"My parents are in good health, and there shall be little to leave me when they pass on to eternity."

Keturah sighed. "How is it that you do not fret about tomorrow, or the next, or the next?"

Jedediah smiled and leaned forward, considering her question. "Saint Paul has taught me the secret to avoiding fear and anxiety."

"And that is?" Keturah asked, setting down her cup.

"Gratitude. Rather than fretting about what I do not have, or what I might not have tomorrow, I consider all I have at this moment." He raised his hands. "What do I have today? A great deal. Food. Shelter. Friends." He grinned a little. "And hopefully, the love of a good woman."

Gray smiled with him while Keturah sat back in her chair and took another sip, blinking rapidly as if thinking over his words. "Did not the apostle Paul do what he could to make a living, here and there? Was he not a tentmaker?"

"He was," Jedediah said. "I suppose I am doing the same in working your fields for my keep."

"But would it not be wise to have a bit in reserve?" Keturah set down her cup. "It is one thing to live day to day as a single man. Quite another as a husband responsible for a wife. Or as a father with children."

Jedediah nodded. Lady Ket made a good point. He'd gone to bed hungry himself. But to look into sweet Selah's eyes and not have anything for her to eat? Or for their child? He closed his eyes and took a deep breath. He could only do what God had ordained him to do. Surely he would show him the way. Perhaps there would be some way for his music to help provide for them . . . Had not God already utilized that to help provide for the Double T? And there was the potential concert on St. Kitts. Suddenly it seemed more appealing than ever.

"What if we refuse your courtship?" Gray asked gently. "What then?"

"Then I shall be quite downcast," Jedediah admitted, trying to get his whirling thoughts to settle, even as Gray's words made his heart sink. His eyes shifted back to Gray's. "Rest assured, I would endeavor to change your minds."

"As would Selah, I wager." Gray said. "You are a gifted preacher. Why not return to England? Attend seminary? Become a proper pastor or vicar?"

Jedediah smiled with him. "Because I have not been called to be a proper pastor. I have been called to love and serve slaves in the West Indies, as has our Selah, it appears." He paused and leaned forward, turning his hat in his hands. "God has taken each of our paths and clearly made them one. Might I pursue her heart as well as her companionship along the road?"

Gray glanced at Keturah.

"You will remain here, with us? Serving the slaves?" she asked.

Jedediah hesitated, fully understanding what she truly inquired about. "For the foreseeable future. But I cannot promise forever, Lady Ket." He fought not to wince as he said the words, knowing it might be a breaking point for her. "I go where God sends me."

Keturah lifted her hand to her mouth, considering. "But you would consult with Selah? 'Twould have to be a call on her heart as well as your own?"

"Yes," Jedediah said slowly. "I believe that is how God speaks. One might hear the call louder than another, but it seems right for the partner to trust. That is what my father once told me."

"You truly are a most unusual minister, Jedediah," she said.

"I am only what my Lord made me."

"Well then," Keturah said, rising and glancing at Gray. The men rose with her. "I suppose that given so much of your relationship is tied to the Almighty, I am not one to stand in your way. Are you, Gray?"

He shook his head, smiling.

"We grant you our permission to court Selah," she said. "But know that I shall be praying fervently that God allows you to remain here by our side for years to come."

Jedediah grinned and reached for her hand. "Thank you!" he said, bowing over it. Then he reached to shake Gray's hand too before putting his hand to his heart. "My constant endeavor shall be only to love and serve your sister."

"See to it," Gray said, patting his shoulder, "and all will be well."

Chapter Seventeen

Selah grimaced as she rose from her bed the next morning. Her wrist and arm were painfully sore, and every move she made seemed to tug at her wounds. She went to her dressing table and sat down before the mirror but avoided her reflection. Instead, she lifted her hairbrush and worked her way through several clumps that had become knotted with dried blood. The task made her remember the terrible moment when the whip sailed toward her. How it had wrapped around her wrist with a searing pain. How the second strike had so easily sliced open her bare skin.

Hand trembling, she set down the brush and dared to look at herself. She reached up to pull aside the bandages Ket had plastered to her cheek, beginning at the top. As she pulled each bit away, revealing the red wound below, she thought of all the slaves who had suffered lashing after lashing. How there were workers in the Double T fields with backs crisscrossed with old scars. If her two lashes hurt this much, how much more would fifty?

The bandages peeled away easily. The bleeding had stopped, and Selah supposed the wounds would heal better uncovered. When she was done, she turned in her chair to see the whole red serpentine line of it, beginning near the corner of her eye and curving over her cheek and down her neck. There was a second cut across her shoulder about six inches long.

She had seen how her wounds had enraged Gray. How they had made Jedediah blanch. But she herself felt curiously distant from them. If anything, she felt almost *glad* for them. It was akin to what she felt when watching the workers in the field. She was glad that she and Ket and Verity had dug in that same soil themselves. Planting cane, weeding, harvesting that first year. She knew how difficult it was. How tired one became by the end of the day. She could empathize with them. Similarly, she was glad for these scars. In some small way, she understood a bit more of how her friends suffered.

Talking with Jedediah about who might leave the plantation made her eager to see them, as well as the four newcomers Gray had brought home last evening. It had planted an idea in her mind. What if they asked everyone what they liked doing most? Then trained them in that task, be it as a seamstress, cook, nanny, maid, or groom? That way, they could continue to welcome more freed people—or assist others in earning their emancipation. People who could serve in the fields as they learned to read and write and speak English, while she and Jed helped those ready to do so to move on.

She was so excited, she could barely wait for Dolly to arrive to lace up her stays. She went to call for her and found the young woman was right outside her door, a plate of food in hand. "Oh, there you are!" she said. "I was about to call for you!"

Yet her gladness quickly faded when she saw Dolly's face melt in sorrow. "Oh, Miss Selah," she moaned. "Oh, your beautiful skin. I am so sorry that this happened to you."

"Thank you," she managed, trying not to bristle in embarrassment. "Now come, lace me up. I cannot wait to properly meet our four newest arrivals."

Dolly followed her inside and set down her plate. Selah took a bite of mango as she turned to be laced up.

"How do they fare, Dolly?"

"Sansa and Mitilda saw to their wounds. Got them something to eat and drink and proper clothes. Then they fell asleep in one another's arms. The man is their cousin."

Selah nodded. Would she not do the same thing? After all they had suffered, experienced? Memories of the platform came flooding back. If anything, a night's sleep only seemed to strengthen her resolve to help every one of them she could. "Dolly, if you were to do any job on the plantation you wished, would you still be a lady's maid?"

Selah watched the woman's face in her mirror, saw the surprise lift her brows as she paused.

"No one has ever asked me that, Miss Selah." Her dark eyes met Selah's in the mirror.

"I am sorry for that. It would have been right for us to ask."

Dolly smiled shyly. "You folks are already the kindest in all the West Indies, as I hear tell it."

"Which is not to say we could not be kinder. So, what do you think? Is there something else you would rather be doing? If so, I shall speak to Keturah about it."

"You would do that for me?"

"I intend to do so for every person on this plantation."

She paused. "What if everyone wants to cook? Who shall work the fields?"

"My idea is this. Gray and Keturah already employ freed men and women to work the fields. But I imagine a fair number would prefer another task. After newcomers serve in the fields for several years, as the opportunity arrives, why not train them to be whatever they wish? Cook? Seamstress? Blacksmith? Silversmith? What have you . . ." she said, waving about her hand in excitement. "Then, if they wish to move on, we help them find a position. That would allow us to welcome others to the Double T."

Dolly smiled, showing the charming gap between her front teeth. "'Tis a grand idea. But would Master Gray approve?"

"If the system works, and the work gets done, Master Gray will be satisfied." She lifted her arms to slip into the bodice of the gown, her shoulder wound making her wince. She glanced down to see if it was bleeding again, but nothing appeared through the silk fabric. Then she stepped into her skirt, and Dolly laced that too. "So, Dolly, what would you like to do as a job once you leave this place?"

"Oh, I do not wish to go anywhere, Miss Selah." Dolly turned toward her. "The people of the Double T are all the family I have left."

Selah nodded. That would be true for many of them, something she had not thought enough about. She took Dolly's hand. "Could you do so if leaving meant we saved another soul from a far worse fate?"

Dolly considered her, visions of the slavers' platforms practically reflected in her dark eyes. "Perhaps," she said at last.

"Think about it for a while and then let us discuss it again. There has to be a way. Help me think it through."

"Very well, but . . ."

"But?"

"What if . . . what if a person was married?"

"Why, Dolly," Selah said with delight, "do you have a suitor? You do! Who is it?"

Dolly grinned. "No, but Tomas held my hand last night at the meetinghouse. And then he tried to steal a kiss!"

Selah laughed. "You did not allow him to?"

"No." She shook her head. "But then later, I wished I had," she confessed.

"Something tells me he might try again. A pretty girl like you. But in answer to your question, we would need to find couples positions together. We would not divide any family. So," she continued, taking Dolly's arm as they walked down the hall, "suppose you and your Tomas are heading to Saint Kitts to assume new positions. What would that position be?"

"I suppose I would stay a lady's maid. I like to see you ladies in your fine gowns with your hair done up. And Tomas? He seems content in the fields."

"Good then. You are content. But I wager there are a good number of people who would give their eyeteeth to do something else. It is time we find that out."

Mitilda told her that Keturah and Madeleine had gone off that morning to call upon Lady Pimberton, hoping to encourage her to come to their upcoming picnic and auction. The old woman had always had a soft spot for babies. Gray was up in the middle field, surveying the gardens. Philip had left for town to find out what was to become of Angus Shubert.

As Selah made her way up to the meetinghouse, she wondered if Angus would have to be in jail until the judge came to Nevis or if the rumor was true—that he would be confined to his plantation until the judge arrived on-island. Major Woodget had told Gray last night that this was his intention. "And given that the jail is already full," Gray went on, "the major said he wouldn't be surprised if the sheriff didn't agree. He thinks Mr. Shubert must be paying the man. 'Tis only because your whipping was such a public spectacle that they held him at all."

As Selah walked to the meetinghouse, she thought about how long it would take for the judge to arrive. He served six different islands and was only present every sixth week. And what then? Would Angus receive a fine? Jail time? For striking a woman who had interfered in his purchase of a slave? As horrific as his attack had been, she had likely done something unlawful herself. It would not take long for Angus to plead his case too.

She climbed the steps and entered through the open doorway. As she hoped, Jedediah was there with the three young women, gently talking to them along with the aid of Mary, who had been teaching Selah a bit of Igbo—spoken by perhaps a third of the slaves—in recent months. When the one who Shubert had wanted spied her, she jumped to her feet and let out an unearthly cry, running toward Selah. She fell at her feet, kissing her hand and crying, repeating "*Daalu*" over and over again. *Thank you.*

Her sisters fell at her feet too, echoing the first's actions, each of them kissing her hands, putting their foreheads to her knuckles in a frantic act of fealty. But Selah could only see how frightfully thin they all were—how the skin at their wrists was raw from the shackles they'd worn, how they all bore marks of Shubert's whip too. Selah sank to the floor. "No, my friends. It was not I who saved you. It was God." She looked through tear-laced lashes at Mary, overwhelmed by their emotion. "Tell them, would you?"

Mary did so, but the three young women only kept shaking their heads and crying, which made Selah cry harder. The man—their cousin—stood against the wall, arms crossed, warily watching them.

"What are your names?" she asked in Igbo.

Chully was the first. Her sisters were Abana and Dala.

"I am Selah," she said, touching her breast.

"No, no," said one, tears still streaming. "*Aha gi bumara mma.*"

"Your name is Beauty," Mary translated quietly.

"*Aha gi bu ihunanya,*" said the second one, the one Angus Shubert had meant to purchase.

"Your name is Love," Mary said, eyes bright as she glanced at Selah.

"*Aha gi bu ihunanya ebere,*" said the third, reaching up to gently trace her scar.

Selah looked over to Mary and saw the young woman had tears streaming down her face as well.

"What did she say?" Jedediah asked.

Mary smiled through her tears. "She says Miss Selah's name is *Mercy.*"

Which made Selah cry in earnest.

"I could not agree more," Jedediah said, offering her a handkerchief.

She took it gratefully, ignoring how his eyes were tracing her ugly red scar in consternation. Did he think it repulsive? She turned to smile at the threesome, wishing to concentrate on them instead. "Did I guess right? They are sisters?"

"Indeed," Jed said. "And that is their cousin, Turu."

"Oh, I am so pleased you are all here." Selah looked from one to the next as Mary translated for her. Selah noticed Turu had pushed off the wall, hands fisted, immediately on guard when two men came through the doorway. He was as brittle as she felt, jumping at odd, normal sounds such as a creaking floorboard. Undoubtedly the repercussions from their trial the day before. His cheek was swollen from where Angus had beaten him, his eye bloodshot. And he was clearly thin and frail from the voyage, just as his cousins were.

The women returned to their lessons with Mary, with Turu looking on.

"They have their own cabin?" Selah asked Jedediah as they walked outside.

"Yes, old James gave his to them. He moved in with Kuri and Wednesday."

"And they're getting plenty of food?"

"Rest assured, dear one, they are receiving good care. Matthew will not call them to the fields for a week yet. He wants them to gain their strength first."

"Have you told them? That we'll pursue emancipation papers soon?"

"I have."

"Will they return to Africa?"

"Just as soon as they can earn the money to do so. It will take a few years. By then, perhaps they shall choose to stay. The important part is that they get the opportunity to choose. Thanks to you." He faced her and took her hand in his. "You are so remarkable, Selah. You are aptly named. I find my mind continuously reflecting about you."

"Oh?"

"Your heart, your generosity . . . they are as breathtaking as your beauty."

She turned slightly away from him as if to hide her wound, but he held on to her hand. Selah dared to look at Jed, and his eyes were full of kindness and love. "Is it really quite horrible?" she asked. "Will you forever look upon me and be reminded of what transpired yesterday?"

"It is not horrible," he replied, covering her hand with his second. "It shall fade in time. But should I notice it, I shall re-member what those women you saved said. Your name is Beauty, Love, and Mercy. 'Tis those aspects of love and mercy that make you most beautiful, Selah." He looked about, and finding they were temporarily alone, pulled her closer and bent his head. "May I kiss you?" he whispered. "I have thought of nothing else since Gray and Keturah gave me permission to court you."

"What? Here?" she asked in surprise. One of the women or Turu might come outside. Her face burned.

"Here," he said, leaning closer. "May I?"

He wanted to kiss her, despite her wound. He didn't find her repulsive; he found her enticing. And that made her lift her lips to accept his. One of his hands cradled the unscarred half of her face. The other went to her lower back, easing her closer. His kiss was tender, reverent, feeling a bit like a wave building and building before it crested. But there was also a measure of caution in his kiss. He pulled back, his brows lowered in concern. "Does that hurt you at all, Selah?"

"A bit," she said, but then she gave him an impish smile. "But I believe 'tis worth it. Tell me, Reverend. Shall you someday kiss me with the passion you did that night we saw Akunta to freedom?"

He gave her his lopsided grin. "If our courtship progresses as I hope, I shall endeavor to try and kiss you, Miss Banning, any which way I might." He reached up and cradled her cheek again, smiling into her eyes, then pulled her against his chest. She settled in his arms, content to feel the long, lithe strength of him. And in that moment she found she did not care a whit who might see them. He was as drawn to her as she was to him.

Thank you, Lord, she prayed silently. *For this man. For this calling we share. How you are knitting us together. Be with us as we court, Father. Show us your way forward. Amen.*

Two days later, she was working on her Igbo, and the sisters their English, when Abe came running into the meetinghouse.

She lifted a finger, reminding him not to interrupt, and listened to Chully, Abana, and Dala all repeat the English word Mary had said in Igbo. *Window.* She did her best to ignore her fidgeting half brother as the sisters formed the word.

"Pardon me, Miss Selah," he said when they paused at last.

"Yes, Abe. What do you need?" she asked, speaking the words slowly so that the girls could easily hear. Selah was eager to resolve his trouble and return to getting to know the sisters.

Mary translated her words in Igbo.

"May I . . . I mean, might you . . . ?" He glanced around as if afraid someone might hear.

Selah sighed in frustration and led him outside. "What is it, Abe?" she asked, irritated now by his reticence to simply say what he must.

"I . . . well, you see . . ." He bit his lip and looked to the jungle.

"*Abraham.*"

"Yes'm?"

"Out with it," she said, folding her arms.

But he simply reached for her hand. "Please come."

She reluctantly allowed the boy to tug her forward and down the stairs, a niggling fear growing into full-blown angst in her gut.

He led her down the path and into the stables. He took a lit lantern from a peg and led her to the farthest stall. She followed silently, trepidation continuing to build in her mind and heart. "Abe . . ."

When they reached the stall, he lifted the lantern high. At first, all she saw was fresh straw mounded in the far corner.

"'Tis all right," Abe said quietly. "I brought a friend. Come out."

Selah held her breath, hoping this did not mean what she thought it might. But despite her hopes, two young girls rose from the straw as Lazarus might have from the tomb, strands sticking to their nubby hair and clothing.

"Miss Selah," Abe said tentatively, rubbing his hands together, "this is Sarah and Florence, slaves from Cold Spring."

Selah closed her eyes and brought a hand to her lips. Again from the property owned by Angus Shubert, just south of them.

They were likely twins, though not identical. Perhaps twelve or thirteen. One girl's lip was split and seeping. The other girl's eye was bruised and swollen shut. They held hands.

"They're sisters," Abe said. "Master Shubert got mad at Sarah for spilling his tea and hit her."

"Pardon me?" Selah said, lifting a hand to her head and spinning toward him. "Did you say Master *Shubert*? How could that be? He is in jail!"

"No, miss," said Florence. "He got out this morning. And came home spittin' mad."

Selah sank against the wall, her knees feeling wobbly.

Abe said, "When Florence stepped in, he hit her too. They knew they had to run. Master Shubert . . . he's been nosing around their quarters at night. He has his eye on them. One wouldn't go without the other. And when they ran, they ran here."

"Of course they did," she snapped in agitation, stepping away to pace. She pinched the bridge of her nose. Could they do it again? Aid more slaves in escaping? When Akunta was only but a few weeks gone? When she had just stolen a slave out from under Angus at the platform? She turned back to Abraham.

"We cannot do this again, Abe. We endanger everyone on the Double T! He will come here after them. You know that, right?" She paced back and forth, kneading her forehead, trying to think. Those poor sisters up in the meetinghouse . . . seeing Shubert might send them into hysteria.

"I know it, Miss Selah," he returned somberly. "But when they come askin' for help, what am I to do?"

Selah closed her eyes. She had no answer for that. If these girls had come to her, would she not have done exactly the same thing as Abe had? Their master was despicable. Claiming children just entering womanhood for his bed. What sort of vile creature—

She froze, hearing hoofbeats approach. Riders, and many of them, by the sound of it. "Covington!" a man bellowed in the clearing above the stables. "*Covington!*"

Her mouth went dry. *Shubert.*

CHAPTER EIGHTEEN

"Quickly, girls, come with me," Selah said, waving them forward, heart hammering in her chest. She went to the far wall and pulled aside a panel that melded with the rest of the stable wall. "Inside! Quickly!" They only barely fit, perching atop sacks of grain and corn.

Abraham stared in surprise. Gray had crafted it to hide supplies for emergencies, afraid that those in the storage shed might someday be stolen. Inside were ten sacks of grain and dried corn, enough to keep the people of the Double T fed for a week, on rations. They heard more men arrive outside. How many? Six? Eight?

"Spread out!" Shubert yelled. "I want those pickaninnies back in hand. *Now*."

"You shall stay in my sight at all times, Councilman Shubert!" yelled a man. Captain Howard?

Selah motioned the girls into the small space, where they sat down. "Grab the pitchfork, Abe," she said. "Act like you are doing nothing but mucking out stalls."

She had just set the panel back in place and was hanging a bit and reins on a hook when Shubert appeared in the doorway, a hulking silhouette against the waning evening light. "Miss Banning," he said. "You hiding from me?" He moved toward her, squinting. He lifted his arms and smiled a little. "I do not have a whip on me today."

Captain Howard appeared in the doorway and approached them. "That is close enough, Shubert. Ask her what you must, but you shall not antagonize Miss Banning."

"You are *with* him, Captain?" Selah asked in confusion.

"We are watching him. He is to have two guards at all times until the judge returns."

"Which suits me fine," laughed Shubert. "Especially on a day when I need extra men to find my runaways."

He stepped toward Abraham and wrenched the pitchfork from the boy's hands. "We are looking for two girls," he grit out, stabbing into the hay of the stall where the children had been hiding just moments before. Selah's mouth went dry at the thought of it. If Abe hadn't come to get her when he did . . .

Shubert moved a foot over and stabbed again, methodically checking the entire pile. "Sisters. Sound familiar?" He angled a glance at Selah. "I wager every slave on-island has their tongues wagging about the saintly Miss Selah Banning, savior of sisters."

"So now you assume every sister who escapes you shall come to me?"

"Wouldn't you?" he grunted. "They have only been gone an hour. They could not have run farther than here."

"Well, as you can see," she said, "just as before, you shall find no runaways on the Double T."

He turned toward her, his eyes tracing her red wound, and huffed a laugh. "Got you good, didn't I?"

"*Councilman!*" barked the captain.

Selah clenched her hands into fists, thinking for a moment that she ought to grab hold of the pitchfork and run the man through.

Shubert let out a dismissive sound and pushed past her, his eyes searching every corner of the stables. Every stall, every bin. Then he climbed up into the hayloft and searched it before returning to her. Captain Howard stood beside her, but Angus ignored him, staring only at Selah.

"You know where they are. I can smell the fear on you."

"That is not fear," she said. "'Tis *disgust*. Perhaps your slaves would not run from you if you did not abuse them so."

"How would you know that they were abused?"

"I assume they are. Because if you treat your neighbors as you have us, how much worse might you treat people you own?"

He leaned closer and gripped her arm. "Tell me where they are. You may have helped Alice escape. You may have stolen that slave I wanted yesterday. But you will *not* steal these girls from me."

"Mr. *Shubert*," the captain said, coming to stand between them, forcing Angus to release her. Shubert still stared at her, hands clenched.

"I did not steal from you before, Mr. Shubert," she said, willing herself to stand her ground. "Nor shall I in the future." *Because no person should own another,* she thought. "And I refuse to allow you to damage our reputation by spreading such lies. Go. Search for your slaves. But you shall soon find that they are *not here*."

He swore under his breath and spat into the corner, eyeing her from the side, clearly still suspicious. "You'd better hope we find those girls," he said, "or I will be back."

"Get away from her," Gray said, striding into the stables. "You dare to come and harass my sister-in-law after what you did to her on that platform?" He feinted and, when Shubert ducked, hit the man with his other fist.

Shubert took a half step back from the blow. He rubbed his jaw and sneered at him. "She deserved that and more. But I suppose if I was in your shoes, I would think that punch was deserved too. We'll call it even now."

"Even?" Gray said, edging closer to him, murder in his eyes. "I should beat you as bloody as Ian did last summer, and we still would not be even."

Selah reached for his arm. "Gray . . ."

"You should let go of your attachment to your sister-in-law, Covington. Because when I find out what she did with my slaves, I will see the judge sentences her to swing," Shubert pledged, pointing at Selah. "You might be gaining some friends back, but there isn't a planter on this island who can abide another who would steal his property. They'll stand with me, despite the fact that I lost my temper on the platform."

Jedediah arrived then, face alive with both fury and fear. "Selah?"

Selah hurried over to him, and he put his arm around her. "Are you well?"

"I am."

"Get off my property, Shubert," Gray said. "Your slaves are not here."

"What about him?" Shubert pointed at Jedediah. His eyes narrowed as he noted Jed's arm around Selah. "Did you hide away my slave girls?"

Jedediah lifted open palms and shook his head. "As God is my witness, I have seen none but the people of the Double T this day."

"Perhaps they hide among the trees," Gray said in exasperation, gesturing outward. "They are *not here*, Shubert. And you shall not intrude upon us every time you lose track of one of your slaves."

"We've been through this before. I will intrude as I wish in pursuit of my property," Shubert said, pushing past him. "The law is on my side on this, Covington. I can search every inch of the Double T!"

"Then get it done and get out," Gray growled, following him out. "We were about to take our noon meal."

"Oh, I would not want to intrude on your *meal*," Angus said sarcastically, turning to face him again in the yard. "Speaking of which . . . your people seem to continue to be in fair supply of food. I have it on good authority that you have not been able to purchase supplies for almost two months in Charlestown. Explain to me how you continue to feed your people, when most others struggle to do so."

Gray stepped forward, mere inches from Shubert's face. "Taking a neighborly interest in our needs, are you? Or leading the charge in trying to starve us out?"

"Cannot say," Shubert said with a hint of a smile. He didn't drop his gaze from Gray's.

"Fortunately for me, I planned ahead," Gray said. "Put up stores for such a time as this. And our gardens are proving a lifeline."

Shubert let out a disbelieving snort and turned to yell commands at his men. They spread out to search the slave cabins, and when they turned up empty-handed, demanded to search the main house. Gray stood on the stairs, refusing them.

"Do you have something to hide, Covington?" Angus asked, his eyes narrowing.

"Gray, let him do what he must," Selah said, climbing the stairs to stand beside her brother-in-law. She knew his infuriation might turn to stubborn resolve. She touched his arm. "The sooner he finishes his search, the sooner we see him leave."

"So be it," Gray grunted. He lifted a warning finger to Shubert. "But you make certain nothing is harmed."

Captain Howard and a lieutenant she had not met stepped forward. "We shall make certain they comply with that request," said the captain, crossing his arms.

Shubert lifted his chin. He turned to his men. "Spread out and search every corner of this house. Those girls have to be here. Somewhere. Find them."

Jed climbed the steps and stood beside Selah. "Come and sit," he said to her, gently urging her to a chair on the far end of the veranda.

It was only then that she realized how close her trembling knees were to giving out. Together, they sat in silence, listening as the men searched one room and then the other. Jed took her hand in his and gave her a long look, as if he meant to will confidence and peace back into her. Gray was inside with the two soldiers to keep watch on the men. In the corner, Mitilda bent and whispered to Abe, clearly finding out bits of the story where no one could overhear.

"They will be through in short order," promised the captain, nodding paternally at Selah. "'Tis a good thing, really," he added.

"There are those in town who pass along idle rumors and gossip about your family. We do our best to curtail it . . ."

"But perhaps the best defense is an eyewitness account from an enemy," Jedediah said. "Shubert's men shall not find what they seek in the Covingtons' good home, as much as they would like to."

In time, Shubert's men trickled out of the house, having pulled up rugs and searched both root cellar and attic. The frustration radiated from them. Shubert said nothing further to Selah, nor to the men who followed them out, only yelling at his own to mount up. They made a plan to search the narrow band of jungle that bordered their land, from sea to mountain, then thundered off.

Moments later, Keturah arrived in the carriage, looking wide-eyed as Gideon pulled up on the reins. "Was that Angus Shubert? How is it that he is out of jail?"

"He was after two more runaways from Cold Spring," Gray said, going down to take the baby from her and then assist her from the carriage. "Come in and we shall tell you of it. Sansa has our noon meal ready."

"Two more runaways," Ket said, shaking her head. "And of course he turns to us first." She went to Selah and took her hand. "I am so sorry you had to see him, and so soon, beloved."

Selah forced a smile. "We live on an island. 'Twas only a matter of time."

"Even so," Ket said. "I do so wish we could be rid of him once and for all."

"As do I," she said.

Ket's golden-green eyes followed the line of Selah's wound. Selah knew she would have to become accustomed to that—each person she met visually tracing her scar. Ket squeezed her hand. "'Twill heal well." Inside, Madeleine began to cry. "She's as hungry as her father, it seems."

"Go," Selah said, urging her onward.

Given a private moment at last, she hung back and looked meaningfully at Jedediah, and her wringing hands and wide eyes stilled him. He understood at once. His mouth set in a line. He lifted a brow and bent his head, silently asking if she knew where the girls were. Grimly, she gave him a single nod. He let out a long, slow breath.

It was only then that she noticed Ket inside the window, watching them. Her sister came back out at once. "Selah?"

Selah felt the heat of a blush rising up her neck, her cheeks. "Yes?" she asked, trying to sound as innocent as possible. But Ket reached out and grabbed her arm. "*Selah*. What has transpired?"

She knew she had to tell her. She glanced over her shoulder to make sure no one else was near.

"Do you know where those girls are?" Ket whispered frantically.

After their meal, Gray rose and strode to the window, anxiously studying the skies. It felt like storm weather, and Keturah knew that he feared what might come. They were a month away from harvest, the cane growing tall and fat. They needed every stalk's yield, this year in particular. Paying freed people to work made a plantation far from a handsomely profitable venture. But she had something more urgent to discuss with him.

Ket wrapped her arm through his and studied the swaying cane below. "Gray?"

"Hmm?" he said distractedly.

"I need to speak to you in private. Come," she whispered, pulling him out the door to the front porch. Before she closed the door, she glanced back at Selah, who paced back and forth, wringing her hands. *Wait there*, she demanded, silently forming the words. Where had her sister hidden away those girls? How on earth had Shubert not found them? As furious as she was at Selah for involving herself, she could only be glad Shubert had failed at finding the runaways. It was far better for them to stay out of his reach, as well as for those of the Double T who assisted them. Aiding a runaway was a capital offense. There were some on-island who would tar and feather Selah for such a crime. Others who would hang her. Shubert would tie the noose himself.

There was no easy way to say what she must. "Gray, Selah and Jedediah know where Shubert's runaways are," she whispered.

Gray's face paled and he dropped her hands. "What?"

"They *know*, Gray. And I would wager they knew where the first went too."

"Do not blame them, Lady Ket," said a small voice from the corner of the porch. Abe bit his lip and edged forward. "'Twas me. Me who needed help when I found 'em."

"Abraham!" Mitilda said, coming around the corner. "There you are! Did I not tell you to leave the missus and mister alone? You come along and—"

"No, Mitilda," Keturah said, lifting a hand. "Please. It is all right. But I fear we need a family meeting, immediately. Abe, go and fetch Reverend Reed. Then meet us, your mother, and Miss Selah here."

"Yes, Lady Ket," said the boy, running for the meetinghouse.

"Selah, join us please," Keturah said to her sister. Reluctantly, the girl did as she asked. Her dark blond curls bounced in the humid air, half of her bun having pulled loose of its pins.

"Philip, if you'd be so kind as to join us too?"

The man, reading a broadsheet from the colonies, looked up at her from the parlor. "But of course, Keturah."

Gray and Ket took a seat on a swing at the far end of the veranda, and Ket gestured to the chairs for Mitilda and Selah. Philip brought over another chair. Gray made small talk with Mitilda about the weather, asking if folks thought a hurricane was on the wind. She agreed that it had the makings of storm weather, all the while well aware that there was something more on the Covingtons' minds.

Jedediah and Abe joined them at last. Jed leaned against the porch rail while Abe moved to his mother's side. Sansa and Bessy were washing up dishes in the kitchen, chattering on together. In many ways, it felt to Keturah like an idyllic plantation afternoon, despite the heat. But she felt the coming storm in more ways than one.

She looked to Selah, Abraham, and then Jedediah. "You three have much to tell us, I believe. Out with it. Start from the beginning."

"What were we to do, Ket?" Selah asked, leaning forward, wringing her hands again. "What would you have done? You would not have turned those girls away. Not Alice when she came, and not these girls today."

"Start at the beginning," she insisted.

"It was me, Lady Ket. I found Alice," Abe said, biting his lip again. "Or I'd say Biri found her." He motioned to his pet monkey, now fully grown and never far from him. Even now the monkey raced along the porch rail and climbed up a post to the roof.

"And I discovered her in the root cellar," Selah said.

"The root cellar!" Mitilda cried.

"Shhhh," Ket urged, making a quieting motion and glancing over her shoulder to the kitchen.

"It was the only place I could think of," Abe said, glancing sideways at his furious mother.

"He only narrowly saved her from Shubert's clutches," Selah added.

"What did you do with her?" Gray asked, frowning.

"We helped her escape," said Jedediah a bit sheepishly.

"How?" Gray asked.

"Selah and I took the *Hartwick* and sailed that very night to Saba, just in time to get her to Ian and Verity."

"You sailed at night?" Gray cried, rising, face flushing. He cast Jedediah an accusing look.

"Do not be angry with him, Gray," Selah said. "I threatened to attempt it alone if Jedediah would not accompany me. In retrospect, I am certain I would have perished had he not. The winds at night—"

"Yes, the winds," Gray said, shaking his head and pacing, hand going to his neck. "All *three* of you could have perished."

"I know," Selah said wanly, guilt lining her face. "But we could not involve you, Gray. Nor Ket. We wanted you to be innocent if anyone was caught. To honestly be able to say you knew nothing about it. And now—"

"And now we have *two* fugitives on the premises and we *all* know," Gray said, still pacing. He rubbed his face with both hands, eyes darting back and forth as he tried to think through it all. "I assume you hid them in the stable with the supplies?"

Selah nodded. "They are still there, poor things. They need food and water."

"After dark we shall see to them. Not before. We dare not," Ket said. She lifted her eyes to the veranda ceiling, tracing the straight lines of the inlaid woodwork as if they might be a map toward the wisest course forward.

"And then what shall we do?" Selah asked.

Everyone was silent.

"We shall get them to Verity," Keturah said. "She figured out what to do with Akunta. Perhaps she has considered other options since then. Find them a safe master or a way to obtain freedom papers and employment."

Philip let out a low whistle. "That is a tall order. Shubert might send bounty hunters to go looking for them, even as far as Statia."

"Verity would need to see them safely away as soon as possible," Gray said. "But if we sail for Statia, perhaps we should take others who are willing to go? We keep trying to provide for the free folk who arrive at our gates, but I do not know how long we can feed them all."

Keturah and Selah exchanged a look. *To say nothing of those whom Selah hopes to welcome in the future . . .*

"There are many who wouldn't mind immigrating to the Americas," Gray went on. "Finding work as field hands."

Philip tapped the paper in his hands. "This broadsheet from the colonies mentions some states are turning to freed Negroes to fill their enlistment quotas. They are paid half as much as whites. But they are paid."

"'Twould be perilous," Jedediah said, "with the war on. But you're right. There are many who would rather take on that risk than stay here. Many ache to stretch their wings. See where God might lead them, beyond plantation work."

"If we could help those who are ready to leave the Double T find positions," Selah said, "it would allow us to take on others seeking a home and work."

"*Freed* slaves, not runaways," Keturah whispered. "This business with runaways is liable to get us all killed."

"How was it that these girls came to us?" Gray asked, glancing over his shoulder to the kitchen, which had grown quiet as the women finished with the dishes.

"They found Abe," Selah answered. "I had told him that if any runaways came to us again, he was to go straight to me or Jedediah."

"But how did they find *you*, Abe?" Gray asked.

"I was climbing the path and they called to me."

"By *name*?" he pressed.

"Yes, sir."

He sighed, resuming his pacing, hands on hips.

"Someone knows about Akunta," Philip guessed, understanding his concern. "Knew it was Abraham who helped her escape."

Gray nodded. "And word now spreads among the slaves."

"We need to get Abe away from Nevis too," Selah said, looking so worried she could cry. "If Angus finds out . . ."

Gray grimly agreed. "This very night," he said to Mitilda, who looked back at him, terror in her eyes. "'Tis all right, Mitilda. We shall get him and the girls safely away. Maybe he could sail with Ian. Serve as his cabin boy."

"But Captain Ian sails into danger, Master Gray," she said miserably, reaching out to pull the child to her lap. She bit her lip, her big brown eyes shifting back and forth as she thought it through. "And yet Abe cannot stay here either. I understand that too. If Master Shubert gains word of Abraham's involvement . . ."

"Verity will bring you word of him. He shall not be lost to you."

Mitilda took a deep breath and let it out slowly. She nodded at last.

Tears in his eyes, Abe turned and said, "Oh, Mama, I'm sorry. So sorry." He flung himself into her arms, and she rocked him back and forth as tears streamed down her face.

"I am not, son. You did right by those girls. You saved them. Right, Miss Selah?"

Selah nodded. "Yes. He was very brave. And those girls will never forget his fine deed."

"You protected the weak, Abraham," Jed said, leaning down to look him in the eye. "Saved those who could not save themselves. And faced down the prowling lion. Now the Lord is sending you on a new adventure. You shall never be alone, Abe. God will be by your side."

"Now come," Mitilda said, lifting a hand to the child. "Let us get you packed up."

"Might you accompany them, Philip?" Gray asked as mother and child walked down the steps. "We are asking much of Verity. I am certain that she would welcome your assistance in looking after Abe, the girls, and our people."

"Philip should stay here," Selah said, standing. "I am partially responsible for this, so I shall go. 'Twould be good for me anyway to discover how we might direct people who wish to move on from the Double T." She glanced at Jedediah.

"Then I shall go too," he said immediately. He looked to Gray. "There will be many scoundrels on Statia who would gladly sell our people right back into slavery, papers or not. I have met up with my share of such souls. I can help Verity and Selah avoid them."

Gray studied them, thinking.

"No," Keturah said, shaking her head, incredulous that Gray was even considering it. "Selah cannot possibly go."

Gray looked at her, disagreement in his eyes. "She will not be alone. Verity is there. And Jedediah shall attend them."

"Amongst a nest of vipers!" Ket said, throwing her hands in the air.

"Come now, Keturah. Statia is not as bad as all that, despite how the Nevisians and Kittitians deride them. And Verity will look after them—as well as see them home as soon as she can."

"And what are we to say to those who inquire about their absence?"

"Few shall ask, other than those on the Double T." He turned to Jed. "You shall get to Saint Kitts for the concert next week. And return here for Verity's auction. Those are the only occasions I do not think we could hide your absence." He gestured to Selah. "We can tell anyone else who comes to call that you are convalescing, caring for your wounds."

"You do not think that shall make her all the more identifiable on Statia?" Keturah asked.

"Ket," Selah said, taking her arm. "Please. A word?"

Keturah reluctantly tore her furious gaze from her husband and followed her sister to the corner of the porch. There, Selah turned to face her. Her wound was a serpentine red line. This was what happened when Selah faced the world on her own. What might happen to her on Statia?

Selah took her hand in both of hers. "Ket, you fear for me. I understand that. All my life you have endeavored to protect me, and the attack undoubtedly made it seem all the more important to do so." She gestured to her wound. "But, Keturah, I am a woman grown. I have already ventured into risky territory in aiding Akunta. In aiding Verity," she added in a whisper, referring to the major's correspondence. "Then with Chully, Abana, and Dala. And all of that occurred with my living within the safety of the Double T and you looking after me."

Keturah met her gaze. "None of it occurred with my blessing."

"I understand. But again, I am a woman grown, and I shall follow where my God leads me."

"Is that what you have learned from Jedediah?" Ket whispered back, gesturing toward the man at the end of the porch. "Perhaps this courtship is even more ill-advised than I had first thought."

Selah's lips set in a firm line as her brown eyes searched Ket's. "You speak out of love. Out of a desire to protect me. But you do not speak out of wisdom, Ket. I am going. And I shall aid whomever God leads me to aid. You may either support me or turn away."

Keturah swallowed hard, tears rising in her eyes. Selah was right. She was of age to make her own decisions, regardless of what Ket thought about it. All she could do was do her best to advise her. Nothing more. And she never wanted Selah to go away without the opportunity to urge her to swiftly return. Verity's absence was already keenly felt. What would it be like to be without them both? What if Madeleine and this new baby she carried never had the opportunity to know their aunties?

Ket gathered her sister in her arms. "Be wary, Selah. Careful. Promise me that. I fear you are wading into shark-filled waters."

"I shall," Selah said, clinging to her. "Thank you, Sissy." She pulled back and the two shared a long, tearful look. "This is not a forever farewell," Selah said.

"I shall hold you to that," Ket said, forcing a smile. "Now let us get you properly packed."

Plans were swiftly made. Philip would sail with them for Statia as soon as it was dark, with four more freed people willing to take their chances on a new path, and with Abraham and the twin girls hidden among them. With luck, they'd be out of sight before the moon rose. And as it sank, providing cover of darkness, Philip would return the ketch to the Double T's pier.

As Selah followed Jed down the path from the meetinghouse, he reached back to take her hand in his.

How good it felt to have him lead her. The day had been full of hasty plans and preparations and packing. Jed and she had spent hours in conversations with one freed man and woman after another, finding the right people to first go to Verity in order to seek paid positions. Selah felt elated with their success and flushed with excitement at the idea of aiding additional souls find their way toward freedom in the future. And yet it also was daunting, this plan, the responsibility feeling more and more onerous with each step she took back toward the main house. She looked out to sea, in the direction of Statia, and her heart pounded.

Jedediah's hand, so strong and sure, gave her just the confidence she needed. This was not her path alone. It was theirs, together. And God's. Jed had never wavered in believing her when she said she felt called in this. He had jumped right into helping her find the people who might first make the leap.

As they neared the house, they could hear Madeleine wailing, sounding as if she were in pain. "Probably her teeth again, the wicked little things," Selah said to him.

"'Tis awful," he said, leading her across the veranda to two rockers that sat side by side. He waited while she took her seat, then took his own. This time it was she who reached for his hand.

"So bold, my love," he teased her in a whisper, bringing her hand to his lips.

"Perhaps 'tis the effects of the afternoon," she said, smiling over his use of *my love*. He had not confessed his love to her. But even the hint of it sent a thrill down her neck. What was this wonder? These rapid turns in the course of her life that she had not foreseen?

"We are about to set a group of souls off on a new road," Jedediah said, settling back into his chair to rock a bit but not letting go of her hand.

"We are. I feel at once both victorious and terrified."

"How so?"

"Victorious in seeing them through to what I believe God planted in my heart and mind. Terrified that we have made a mistake. Either in choosing the wrong people or in timing."

Jedediah considered that for a bit. "The timing was somewhat chosen for us. The need to get the twins off-island precipitates it. And the chance to usher additional people on to their next steps as freed men and women . . . well, we could not truly send a partially full ketch to Statia, could we? When might we be able to do so again?" He brought her hand to his lips again. "No, Selah. You must trust that God shall hold all of us in his hands now. He has seen us this far; he shall see us through this too."

CHAPTER NINETEEN

Verity tucked Brutus into his cage after his early morning flight, closed the door, and then leaned heavily against the stable wall. She took a deep breath, realizing she had not been breathing well at all. Her tiny store—once full of goods she was able to secure because of the letter Selah uncovered in Nevis—was now empty, the goods sent on to the Double T with Philip. So that was not what weighed upon her. It was the fact that there were seven people asleep in her hayloft now . . . three children and four men and women for whom she had to find positions as quickly as possible.

The two little slave girls had to be placed first, lest Shubert come hunting. She thought they might be welcome in Madame Chantal's home, and she knew the Chantals were to sail to Paris within the week, but she had to obtain forged freedom papers for them in time. More worrisome was Abraham—she thought she could secure lodging for him with Monsieur Bieulieu in exchange for serving as his temporary groom. That way, if Shubert sent bounty hunters, he would be safely apart from her. Bieulieu had trapdoors in both his mercantile and stables, places where Abraham could hide at a moment's notice. And Bieulieu would not mind Biri accompanying the boy; he had already taken in an injured parrot as a pet. She *thought* so, anyway. What if he said no?

She lifted a hand to her pounding head.

"Mrs. McKintrick," Jedediah said from the other side of the stables, startling her. "Forgive me." He lifted a hand of supplication and came closer. "Are you unwell?"

"Please, call me Verity. If you are courting my sister, then we are practically family, yes?"

"Yes," he said, giving her a lopsided smile.

She blinked slowly. "Perhaps it is fortuitous that you are first up this morning," she said as they exited the stables and walked toward the house. "I find myself in need of counsel."

"Oh?"

"I am burdened. Concerned for our charges." She looked to the broad sweep of ocean below them, what had become habit for her. "And I am missing my husband. That is the only good thing about our new task," she said, gesturing back toward the stables where her company slept. "It keeps my mind off of his welfare."

"When do you hope to see him return?"

She rolled her eyes. "I would rather not guess at all. It could be tomorrow, or it could be months from now. 'Tis best for me to think he is months away so I do not end each day feeling quite forlorn."

He nodded. "Well, perhaps I can be of some aid in terms of our charges. That is why Selah and I are here, after all. Salani and Charelle would be suitable for positions as lady's maids or cooks. Charelle often helps Sansa and Bessy in the kitchen. And Salani has been training with Selah on the intricacies of being a lady's maid. And Frank and Junior are quite ready to sign on as shipmates. They are eager to expand their skills from soil to sail. But there does not seem to be any ships in your harbor at the moment."

"No, there does not," she said. "Wouldn't you know it? The harbor was rife with them four days ago."

"Rotten luck, that. Or God's hand," he added thoughtfully, hands behind his back. "Perhaps those captains would not have been the best for our friends."

"We may not have much of a choice. There is Montserrat . . ." Verity bit her lip. It still unsettled her to consider leaving Statia when Ian might return home for a brief visit.

"Montserrat?" Jedediah asked.

"A friend said she has three ships in harbor. At least she did as of yesterday. And he mentioned there are several families on-island seeking new house slaves."

"I see. Might they entertain employing paid servants instead?"

"I have no idea. He merely mentioned it. But I suggest we go and inquire, since I have no leads here on Statia."

"Might we sail for Montserrat this afternoon?"

"No time like the present."

As he turned to go into the house, Verity touched his elbow. "Jedediah, thank you for accompanying my sister."

"I confess 'twas rather self-serving," he said, then gave a bashful smile. "I would do anything for her, but I could not imagine seeing her sail off as you watch your husband do."

She nodded with understanding. "Still, 'tis brave and selfless, two attributes I know my sister appreciates in you."

"As I do in her," he said, opening the door for her. Inside, Trisa was frying up slabs of bacon and preparing to fry eggs, some of the cargo bounty Verity had reserved for her own house. It had been ages since she had had a proper piece of bacon.

Selah was waiting for them and rose as they entered. *Brave and selfless.* Her sister's wound was startling, and Verity tried not to let it show. Was not the wound evidence itself of her bravery? Her selflessness? "Good morning," Verity said cheerfully.

"Good morning," Selah said, smiling at her, but then quickly focusing all her attention on Jedediah alone.

Verity studied him as they greeted each other. He had known Selah's beauty before she was marred. Had her wounding diminished her attraction in his eyes? Verity could not detect a bit of that. Instead, the young man held nothing but adoration and devotion in his expression. It settled something deep within her; perhaps a long-held desire to protect her little sister and see her find love? She could only hope that Ket had seen a measure of the same.

After settling Abraham with Monsieur Bieulieu and introducing the twins to Madame Chantal for a day's trial to see if they could manage as house servants, they sailed for Montserrat just after noon. They arrived two hours later. Two ships were moored in the harbor, the *Valiant* and the *San Francisco*. "You said there was a third?" Jed asked Verity.

"Indeed. Perhaps she has already sailed." Disappointment laced her tone.

"'Tis all right. Surely, Frank and Junior can find positions on those two ships." Selah studied the lines of each sloop with their trimmed sails before smiling at the young men in the back of the boat. The ships appeared unharmed from their journey, only set upon re-provisioning. Again, she wished that Ian was sailing the *Inverness* into port, with perhaps a captured ship in tow. Verity said he would be in need of more hands aboard his ships. How much better it would be to send off Frank and Junior on one of his schooners rather than with one of these unknown captains, even if he was a privateer. She could only hope that she could inquire about the reputation of those in charge before encouraging the young men to sign on as shipmates.

Selah told herself she had to become accustomed to such unknowns and trust the fate of her friends to God's care. If others wished to leave the Double T, she would need to have men trained on how to tie every sailor's knot Gray could teach them, women trained by Sansa and Mitilda in the kitchen or Nellie in the nursery, with both men and women ready to serve as house servants—lady's maids, valets, chambermaids, and footmen. And once they were properly trained, she would have to find them suitable positions.

Her thoughts returned to Chully, Abana, and Dala. Right now, they served as field hands. But what might they like to do in the future? She had asked Gray to consult an attorney in drawing up freedom papers for each of them, as well as for their cousin Turu. For she would never own another. Never again. She had grown up with slaves as well as servants, but that day on the platform had changed everything. Her hand traced the rough scab of her long scar.

Changed everything. Truly everything. Except . . . She looked to Jedediah, who, sensing her gaze, glanced her way. His expression was tender and he gave her a tiny smile. *Except his devotion.* From the start, he seemed not to even notice her scar. It was as if he saw her so deeply that he could not even take in something so superficial. It made her love him all the more.

Love? she thought, startling as she caught herself.

Love, her heart affirmed. And then she gave him a broad grin that left him looking both gratified and puzzled.

Their hired captain brought the vessel expertly around, called for his mate to drop the front sail, then used the smaller back sail to maneuver toward the pier. She could see Frank and Junior taking in every move of the sailors, learning the nuances of rope and sail. At the last moment, the captain called for his mate to drop the remaining sail. As he did so, George stood and tossed a rope to a man on the pier, who caught it, wrapped it around an axle, and eased them to a stop.

They gradually bumped alongside the weathered wood with its familiar smells of salt and fish and tar. A gangplank was lowered into the vessel, and weathered hands reached for her on either side. Selah grabbed hold of both hands and scurried up the plank to the pier. She looked anxiously back at the others behind her. Jed had assured her the men knew how to swim—part of their preparation for a life at sea—but Selah was not anxious to see them test it.

When all eight of them were on the pier, Verity paid the captain, made certain he would wait for them to return to Statia, and then they set off for town. For all the intrigue of Statia, Verity had become accustomed to her rhythms, her moods. Montserrat felt distinctly different.

Even hours later, after she and Selah had found mistresses for both Charelle and Salani, interviewed them, verified both women were in good hands, and said their farewells, she found herself scanning every alleyway and every group of men that passed. What was it that agitated her so? 'Twas as if her skin crawled, so anxious was she.

"Verity?" Selah said, taking her arm. "What is it? You are as skittish as a street cat."

"I do not know," she said, glad that Jedediah and George strode before them, and burly Frank and Junior followed. "Do you feel it too? 'Tis some unspoken warning," she hissed. "Something I feel in my gut."

Her sister did not laugh at her—bless her. Instead, she seemed to become aware of one and all about them too. As the street opened up, Verity noticed that while they had been seeing to the women's placements, a third ship had arrived in harbor. She was fully at rest, her sails stowed, her decks mostly empty, which meant she had been there for some time.

Verity stopped abruptly. "Jedediah," she said, and he turned back toward her. "Is that . . . Jed, can you make out the name of that ship?"

"The *Juliana*," he said slowly, squinting. He glanced back and forth between the ship and her, hands on hips. "Why?"

"Oh, Lord, dear Lord," she said, her breath coming in sudden pants. *Santiago.* He was here? In Montserrat? How could it be?

A second later, she was chastising herself. How could it not be? He could be anywhere the British—and their sanctioned privateers—roamed.

"What is it?" Selah asked, pressing her around the corner and into an alley, out of the flow of pedestrians. "*Verity.*"

"The *Juliana*," she said, looking at her. "Do you not recognize the name? 'Tis captained by Ian's mortal enemy, Captain Santiago. The man whose mate killed Duncan. The man who chased us out of New York and only narrowly spared our lives. A privateer serving the Brits now."

Selah visibly paled and covered her face with her hands a moment. "Are you certain? Could there not be two vessels of the same name?"

She shook her head. "I would recognize that vessel anywhere."

Jed took a step away from her, biting his lip and rubbing the back of his neck, clearly trying to think it through. "Now what?" he asked, gesturing toward Frank and Junior. "We are to meet the captain of the *San Francisco* in that pub around the corner."

"Let us see it done and be off," Verity said, still warily watching the mouth of the alleyway as if she thought Santiago might turn the corner at any moment.

"I shall take you women to the ketch. George can see the men introduced to the captain of the *San Francisco* and be certain they're in good hands."

"No, Jed. Please. I want to be there," Selah said. "I have to be certain they have every opportunity to succeed. Santiago does not know me."

He shook his head gravely. "I promised Gray I would see to your safety. And I aim to do so." He glanced at Verity. "We must take precautions. This is but the first step for Frank and Junior on their own. After they leave us, every decision shall be up to them."

She glanced at them in concern.

"'Tis true, Miss Selah," Junior said, stepping forward. "You done your best for us. Now 'tis up to us to make it right."

"If you are safer on the ketch, we want you to go on," Frank said.

She touched one man's arm and then the other. "Be safe, my friends. Remember us."

"Always, Miss Selah," Junior said. "Always. Now get on so we know *you* will be safe."

They said their farewells to Jedediah, then disappeared with George around the corner, heading to the Steel & Sail.

Jed turned to Verity. "Let us go. Quickly." He took Selah's arm.

"Follow behind us, Verity," Selah said over her shoulder. "We shall do our best to shield you from passersby. All eyes shall likely be on me and my scar rather than you. We shall be back to the boat in minutes."

Jed led them out of the alley, and they strode down the board-walk at a leisurely pace, adopting the most settled and genteel look possible. After they passed the first block, Verity's heart ceased its frantic beat. After the second, she told herself she had imagined the threat. Santiago was likely in one of the taverns, already ordering victuals and ale. But halfway past the third, she sensed someone was trailing them. She glanced backward and saw two sea-hardened men just ten paces behind. "Jed," she whispered. "Selah. I believe there are men following us."

Jedediah immediately turned and came between the women and the men. "Run for the ketch," he growled over his shoulder. He spread his arms wide, and when the men who were following paused and looked at each other, Verity grabbed Selah's hand and started to run.

They were reaching the alley between the third and fourth blocks when a man casually strolled out and faced them. It was Santiago's first mate, the hulking black man with a gold earring. Verity pulled Selah to a swift stop.

She was reaching for the dirk at her waistband when a strong arm wrapped around Verity from behind, the second neatly grabbing the wrist that held her dirk. "Imagine my delight in discovering you here, señora," the man said, pulling her against his chest. "I cannot see you leave so soon."

She struggled for a moment, trying to take in that her worst fear was actually transpiring. Then she leaned forward and tried to ram her head into his nose, which he avoided by pulling his head to the side. Another man had grabbed Selah, covered her mouth, and was dragging her into an alley,

"Come now," he said, bringing her own knife blade to her throat. "Enough of that, yes? I only wish to talk." But as he said it, he dragged her farther down the alleyway. She glimpsed the other man pause, then look down at his leg. Selah had managed to hold on to her dirk and stab him! Selah turned and ran, but Verity glimpsed the mate gaining on her just as Santiago dragged her around the corner.

"Selah!" she screamed. Did she see her? See where Santiago carried her? Was she safe?

"Shh! Enough, enough, señora," Santiago said, covering her

mouth, muffling her cries. He dragged her through an open doorway, through a building and out to another alley, then into a second building. Would Jedediah and Selah ever be able to find her? Were they even alive? Had she led them all into a deathtrap?

Santiago hauled her upstairs, grunting when she fought him. "I only . . . wish to . . . speak to you!" he gritted out.

"This is not . . . the way . . . a gentleman . . . asks for . . . an audience!" Verity cried, her words interrupted by desperate grabs at the stairway railing, doorjambs, and other attempts to deal him a crippling blow. Did no one live in this building?

At last he tossed her into an empty room and slammed the door behind him, disheveled and panting. "It needed not be so challenging!" he said, lifting a warning finger at her as they circled each other, panting. She saw he had tucked her dirk into his waistband.

"You thought you could swarm us and I would *willingly* go with you?" Verity asked.

He drew himself up and straightened vest, coat, and neckcloth. Then he rolled his neck and stared at her. "I only wish to know where your husband is. And his mission. Tell me that and I shall happily see you on your way."

She laughed and folded her arms. "You think I would tell you how to hunt down my own husband?"

He paced back and forth, hands clenched behind his back, thinking. "If you shall not tell me where I can find him, I shall throw you and your sister into jail here and wait for him to come and pay ransom for you."

"Ransom? The Patriots shall not pay my way to freedom. And Ian has no money. We put everything we have toward this cause to bring our enemies down. Besides, I do not expect him for months yet." She cast him a saucy, defiant look, hands on her hips.

"Why do I assume you lie to me, Mrs. McKintrick? I know he is still among the Leeward Isles." He tapped his finger on his lips. "Even if he truly does not intend to return to you for months, perhaps I can gain funds to further outfit my ship. What of your family? The Nevisians? Surely they shall be most eager to see you returned to their arms."

"They have no funds. They await their next harvest."

"Then perhaps we wait for that," he said, lifting his hands, as if that were a perfectly viable solution. He shifted them as if weighing something in each hand. "That way I either get a bounty from the king for capturing your privateering husband or a ransom for you."

Screaming and heavy footsteps cut off their conversation. Santiago drew closer and grabbed her arm, waiting. In moments, his massive first mate with the gold earring came through the door and unceremoniously dropped Selah to the ground. She scrambled backward on hands and feet like a crab, even as he winced and looked to his shoulder, dripping blood. "The she-cat stabbed me!" he complained to Santiago. "Fredrick too! In the leg!"

The captain laughed and moved forward to grab Selah and roughly lift her to her feet.

"Be away from her!" Verity cried, shoving him aside and pulling the girl into her arms.

He stared at her in surprise, then huffed a laugh. "*Selah*, you called her. Another woman armed with a dirk. One of the famed sisters, I presume? Yes, yes. Miss *Selah* Banning." He swallowed his grin and gave her a gallant bow, even as Verity continued to back away with her sister. "I see it now," he said, cornering them. "Even with those blond curls and that terrible wound down her pretty face, I see the resemblance. Who hurt you, *mi dulce*?"

He reached out to touch her face, and Selah batted away his hand. "Get away from us this instant!"

Verity's heart sank. Now he had two of them. Thoughts of ransom had to be doubling in his mind.

He tapped his lips again and turned back to his mate. "What of the man?"

"Out cold in an alley," he grumbled as he wrapped his wound with a dirty kerchief.

"Jedediah?" Selah gasped.

"We have little interest in him or the others who accompanied you," Santiago said. "Only that they do not interfere. Verity was our quarry. But you are a welcome addition."

"Whilst I am a privateer's wife, my sister is loyal to the Crown," Verity said. "There are soldiers on Nevis who shall take issue with her kidnapping. Soldiers my family quarters."

Santiago let a slow smile slide across his face and crossed his arms as he stared at one, then the other. "I do not fear British soldiers. I fear my empty coffers. I confess I rather miss my privateering days. This business of working for the Crown is far less profitable."

Selah glanced at Verity. "Of what does he speak?"

"He either intends to trap Ian," Verity muttered, staring at him, "using us as bait, or rob our family through demanding ransom."

"Your husband has already captured one merchant's ship, and I wager he is after more. 'Tis unorthodox but not out of hand to keep you two for trade. Or I shall collect a sizable ransom so I can outfit my ship and *then* go after him." He lifted his hands and smiled. "A double bounty!"

"Our family has little means," Selah said. "This war starves the islands. Surely you have seen—"

"I shall wait for your ransom in the form of the coming harvest. I am a patient man." He put a hand to his chest and bowed.

"Patiently greedy," Verity said.

"And if our family cannot meet your demands?" Selah asked. "Or Ian does not return for some time? You would allow us to languish in a jail cell for months?"

"If necessary, yes," he said easily, picking a thread off his jacket sleeve. "Nobles languish in jail cells for months, if not years, all over the West Indies."

Verity stepped closer to him. "You intend to put *Ian Mc-Kintrick's* wife in a jail cell for months? The man who intended to kill you for killing his brother? Why reignite that particular line of powder? Surely you have other enemies of the Crown to hunt down."

He raised a brow. "It amuses me, the thought of capturing one of the first Continental privateers. The commander is most keen to see him on the gallows, lest he inspire others to join the cause." He leaned closer. "And if I can return that captured vessel, as well as her supplies? I would be duly rewarded by that merchant." He paused. "Now that I consider it further, perhaps I shall offer you both for ransom merely as a ruse. 'Tis best if I get Ian McKintrick in hand sooner rather than later."

Verity smiled. She was unable to hide her glee. Ian had done it! Captured his first ship! *As well as supplies*. Enough that it had made their enemy sit up and take notice.

Santiago stilled. "You think this a game, señora?" he sniffed.

"No. I am merely glad to know of my husband's success."

"Tread carefully," he said with narrowed eyes. "Those are treasonous words on this isle. More than enough to send you to jail, even before I make my claims against you."

"My husband shall kill you this time."

"You think so?"

"I know so. When he finds out you kidnapped me—"

"Kidnapped? Such a rash word, señora. I am only borrowing you." He began to circle her. "What is it about a woman that not only entrances one brother but two? What is it about you, Verity Banning McKintrick? What is it about all of the Banning sisters?"

She stilled as he neared Selah.

"Oh, yes," he said, reading the surprise on her face with a smug smile. "I know of your elder sister as well." He tapped his chin as if in thought. "Your cherubic little niece too. You are not the only one adept in espionage, my pretty adversary."

Eyes wide, nostrils flared, she faced him, hands clenched. In that moment, she thought that *she* might kill him, even if Ian would not. To threaten her sisters, even little Madeleine! "How dare you—!"

He caught her wrist as she reached to slap him, and then her second. With a swift move, he turned to bring her against his chest again, pinning her arms in front of her. Silently, Verity cursed herself for losing her dirk to him. She had not even managed to wound him, as Selah had her adversaries.

"Come now," he said in her ear. "As much as I enjoy having you in my arms, must we do this more than once?"

"You are despicable!" She tried to stamp on his foot, then twist away, but each time he anticipated her move.

"Tell me why you are here on Montserrat."

"No."

"Are you on your husband's errand?" he asked, twisting her arm behind her. A bolt of pain shot through it, up her shoulder and neck, and she cried out. He held it there, waiting as she gasped for breath, determined not to cry out again. "I have heard that you continue in his stead, on Statia. What are the French dogs up to?"

"Cease this at once!" Selah cried, grabbing his arm, trying to tug Verity loose. "We were merely seeking to secure positions for the freed men and women in our company!"

"Hmm." Again he abruptly released Verity.

She took a couple of steps before turning toward him, rubbing her aching shoulder. Verity was halfway to the door, Santiago ten steps from Selah. The first mate was still tending to his wound, obviously thinking Santiago could handle them. Without further pause, Verity grabbed Selah's hand and made a dash for the door. Pushing up on the crossbar, she yanked the door open and found herself face-to-face with a broad-shouldered, deeply tanned sailor posted outside. The man filled the door, arms crossed.

"You think me so foolish?" Santiago said, casually coming around and firmly closing the door. She turned away and pulled Selah back in her arms. "I am well aware that you are as intrepid as you are beautiful. After all, it was you who wore Mrs. Harrington's jewels at the ball, which likely funded a portion of their new start as rebel leaders. You who managed to get a note off to the rebels in the midst of that ball, a note we could not find on you, even when you were stripped to your stays. You are as deep into the rebel cause as your husband is."

She glanced over her shoulder, sensing him draw closer.

"So tell me, Verity. Tell me where your husband intends to hole up with that captured ship. I might consider that payment enough and release you. Or shall you and your sister spend the first night of many in a dirty jail cell?"

She shook her head slowly, fists clenching. She could do neither. Not tell him that she thought Ian might be arriving any day. Nor could she allow him to put Selah in jail with her. Not after she had been so grievously wounded. The girl could not bear such a strain. But then Selah was moving between her and Santiago.

"Keep *me* alone. I have a portion of my dowry left on Nevis," she said.

"*Selah*," Verity began, drawing back in surprise.

"But I shall not authorize you obtaining those funds unless my sister," Selah continued, "is allowed to leave Montserrat with Jedediah Reed and our man, George, this very night."

Santiago stepped toward her and gave her a curious look. "Intriguing. How much is your dowry, miss?"

After a moment's hesitation, she named the sum.

Santiago pursed his lips and lifted one brow. "A respectable amount, for certain. But hardly what I expected from a landed lady."

"We sold our estate in England and put everything we had into the Double T," she said. "This is what remains of my share. I have purchased the freedom of several slaves and intended to do so again with the rest. But necessity demands I choose my sister now," she said, glancing back at Verity.

"No." Verity shook her head. "Stop this, Selah."

Instead, Selah resolutely focused her gaze on Santiago. *When did she become so self-assured and determined?* Verity wondered.

Santiago reached out to touch Selah's chin with his knuckle, gently lifting it. "You are clearly a merciful sort, setting slaves free and finding them employment. And beautiful, despite your recent wounding. Surely there is a suitor on Nevis who would gladly up the ante for your freedom?"

"No, stop it!" Verity said. The first mate dragged her a step away when she tried to force the captain's hand from her sister.

Selah gave a humorless smile. "My suitor is the penniless

preacher your men waylaid on the streets behind us. He has nothing."

Santiago grunted. "Pity, that. So then, barring McKintrick's arrival, we shall wait for your brother-in-law's harvest, as well as the sack of coins from your Nevisian banker."

"That was not what I offered," Selah said, shaking her head. "You cannot have my inheritance as well as my brother-in-law's harvest. The people on our plantation shall starve!"

"'Tis desperate, these times of war. And 'tis what I demand now in exchange for your freedom."

Chapter Twenty

Santiago and his men ushered Selah and Verity down the street to the jail on the edge of town. Selah looked left and right, desperately hoping to catch a glimpse of Jedediah or George, or any sympathetic face to whom she might appeal for aid. But the people parted before them, careful to avert their eyes from what appeared to be trouble. The jail was a small volcanic-stone building that held but five cells, forming a U around a desk occupied by a sweating soldier.

Three of the sweltering cells were already occupied—two by sleeping occupants; the third stood, hands on the bars, dolefully watching their arrival with sweat running down his cheeks. He laughed maniacally when Selah met his wide unblinking gaze. She quickly looked away.

"I am Captain Santiago of the *Juliana*, loyal to the Crown," he said to the soldier. "These women are suspected spies and must be held overnight. They refuse to tell me what they must. Perhaps a night on your hard wooden cot shall change their minds." He looked at Verity the entire time with those wide, dark eyes.

"I have but two cells left, Captain," groused the officer. "I need them for the drunks come nightfall. Why not take them to your ship and lock them in the hold? 'Twould have the same effect."

"I cannot. You know as well as I that women as comely as this, locked away alone, might prove too much a temptation for some of my crew."

The soldier looked upon them with new and hungry eyes.

Santiago fished in his pocket and drew out a silver coin, which he placed on the soldier's desk. "Lock them in a cell together and pledge it upon your life that no one shall enter it this night, including you. They are to remain unmolested. Otherwise you shall answer to me," he said, leaning toward him.

Selah frowned. Could the soldier be trusted? Were they in any less danger here than on board the *Juliana*? At least it was only one man who might menace them here in the jail, rather than an entire crew. Her fingers itched for her sgian dubh.

"Give them no food or water," Santiago added as the man wearily rose and opened the cell door.

Santiago and the mate pushed them inside and pulled the iron door shut with a chilling *clang*. Selah stood in the center of the cell, Verity beside her. The two sisters faced their captors in silence.

"It is terribly hot in here, is it not?" the captain said. "I think that by morning, Verity may wish to tell me what I need to know."

"I think not," she said defiantly.

Selah fought not to look her way. Already, sweat trickled down her own temples, neck, and back. The jail was in the full sun, and there were still a few hours of daylight left.

"As brave as you are beautiful." Santiago gave a flourished bow. "Ian is a fortunate man. As is your penniless preacher, Miss Banning," he said, looking to her. "I have seen my share of wounds. Your own shall fade in time—"

"You shall suffer a far graver wound if Ian finds out what you have done to us," Verity interrupted, striding to the bars and wrapping her hands around them.

"Exactly what I wish," he said, grinning. "The mouse coming for his cheese. The trap has been set. How many days do you think you can manage to survive in this cell until your husband presents himself or you grant me what I seek?"

Verity resolutely turned away, silently fuming. Selah looked through the tiny window at the top of their cell. Too small to escape through but allowing the tiniest bit of breeze. She glanced over her shoulder as Santiago and his mate exited. Outside, they conferred with two other sailors. The soldier left the door open, presumably to allow in the greatest amount of airflow. With one last glance at Verity and Selah, Santiago disappeared from view.

The soldier in charge of the jail came over to their cell, and Verity took an involuntary step back. He wrapped dirty hands around the bars. "I took the captain's bribe to hold you here. But I would accept a bribe from you, pretty señoritas. Lift your skirts for me and I shall let you out. Tell the captain you escaped."

"Señora," Verity corrected. "I am the wife of Captain Ian Mc-Kintrick. And if he finds out you as much as touched me or my sister, he shall kill you. Slowly."

"I can bring you food and water," he said. "Keep that in mind."

The man across from their cell, who had watched it all transpire, let out his odd high-pitched laugh. Laughed and laughed. It made Selah shiver, despite the heat.

The soldier turned and went to the front step, sitting in the open doorway in order to gain the best breeze, staring out to sea. He bent to light a pipe. In time, the acrid, sweet-sour smell of the tobacco made its way inward.

Selah backed up to the corner of the cell and slowly lowered herself down to sit, forearms on her knees. "Oh, Verity," she said quietly, cradling her head in her hands. "What are we to do now?"

Jedediah paced back and forth in the alley, hands on his aching head. "How could I have let it happen? How?" he asked George for the third time, dabbing a handkerchief to his split lip.

"You could not have done more, sir," George said again. "You were outnumbered."

'Twas true, but Jedediah shook his head, feeling alternately defeated and enraged. Gray and Keturah had trusted him to protect Selah, to say nothing of Verity. Trusted him! He had failed Selah as well as her family. Completely failed them. Now they were gone. And to where?

Try as he might, he could not think of what to do next. He had searched every alleyway, calling Selah's name, then Verity's. Where had that scoundrel taken them? And for what reason? To hold them in order to trap Ian McKintrick? He knew some of what had unfolded between them. Selah had told him a bit of it. But clearly, this desire for retribution ran deep.

"I should never have volunteered to accompany the women as guardian," he muttered to George, pacing. "I am a pastor, not a soldier. I carry no weapons. I have neither brawn nor funds. How am I to protect her from scoundrels like this?"

George crossed his arms and studied him. "You did your best. Now we must find them."

Jed dabbed at his still-bleeding lip and resumed his pacing, shaking his head, trying to figure his way out of this. A way out for them all. "How? We have scoured the streets."

George shook his head, at a loss too.

"If I had not come with them, Philip would have been here."

"And he would have likely been similarly waylaid. One man cannot fight off five others, Jedediah."

Jed heard the words, yet inside all he could hear were his own recriminations. His mind swirled with one berating comment after another. *If I had not come to Nevis . . . not come to the Double T . . . not taken my mind off my mission . . . not begun to court Selah . . . not agreed to find placement for freed slaves elsewhere . . .*

"Reverend Jed."

Jed glanced at him, tried to cease his pacing but could not. "What is it?"

"You are like a lizard caught in a bucket, desperately searching for the quickest way back to his nest."

Jed huffed a laugh and waited for him to continue.

"The lizard is in the bucket, yes? He wants to get back home, yes? But he must first negotiate the water in the bucket. Find his way up and over the edge of the bucket so he can see in which direction his home lies."

"I must go to the *Juliana*," Jedediah said, trying to follow his logic. "Demand to speak to the captain."

"No, sir." George shook his head. "Santiago may choose to capture you, too. What good will you do Miss Selah and Mrs. Verity then? Remain in the waters of the bucket first. Are there other fish in the bucket with you?"

"Right," Jed said. "Of course. But then how are we to find them? What if he sails off with them?"

"He has not taken them to the *Juliana* yet," George said. "I have been keeping watch. He has returned to his ship alone."

Jed considered him, pausing to pray at last. Then he said, "Let us go to the taverns. There shall be talk of this. Or Santiago."

"Very good," George said.

The two set off, silently parting at the mouth of the alley to canvass taverns in either direction.

No one responded to the questions Jed called out in the first tavern, each consciously looking away from him, clearly not wishing to get involved. But at the second, the Steel & Sail, he came across a middle-aged Hispanic man yelling out his offer—ten pounds for any man who signed on as crew for the *San Francisco* by nightfall. Apparently they were in need of more men, even after signing on Frank and Junior.

While most ignored him, Jedediah turned toward him. "Are you the captain of the *San Francisco*?" he asked. Perhaps if he aided the captain in his need, the man would aid him as well.

"I am the first mate," replied the short broad-shouldered man. "Jauquin Juervo. You are?"

"The Reverend Jedediah Reed," he said, offering his hand.

After a moment's hesitation, the man took it, squinting at his wounded face. "You look like someone tried to shanghai you, Reverend."

"Undoubtedly. While my man was in here, helping Frank and

209

Junior sign on with your crew, I was attacked. Two women in my company were kidnapped. Have you heard anything of it?"

The shorter man's eyes narrowed and he glanced around. "I heard the captain of the *Juliana* carried two women to the town jail but an hour ago. He intends to hold them for ransom."

Jed's heart leapt. *They were still on-island! In the jail . . .*

"You were their guardian?"

"He overwhelmed us," Jedediah said, holding back the words *five to one* when he saw the man dismissively shake his head. Apparently no man had ever tried to kidnap a woman in his presence, and his judgment made Jed's face burn.

"Go and free your women," grunted Juervo, "regardless of the ransom's price. That jail is no place for a gentlewoman."

"Thank you," Jedediah choked out, feeling more a boy than a grown man, especially when he noted that all conversation had stopped and everyone's eyes were on him. He hurriedly left the tavern, then waited for George to appear back on the boardwalk. Hurriedly, he told him what he'd learned of the women.

George frowned. "He wants the ransom. Or to entice Captain McKintrick to come after them."

Jedediah's eyes opened wide. That made more sense than a simple ransom. *Think, man!* he chastised himself. *Were you not the one who told Gray you were aware of the ways of scoundrels?*

The man across from their cell continued to laugh for an hour, then faded to an occasional giggle. Clearly he was mad. The drunk next to them sobered enough to be released. The other kept on slumbering.

The only blessing of nightfall was the end of the sun's blazing heat, but the stones radiated warmth for hours after the sun had set. Selah's gown and underdress were drenched with sweat, tendrils of her hair sticking to her neck in the most cloying manner. Verity looked little better. Soon her head nodded forward as she gave in to sleep. Selah wearily swiped her hair off her damp neck, listening to the distant sounds of raucous men and a few laughing women. The soldier on guard was relieved by another. In undertones at the door, she assumed the first informed the second about who they had captured and what had gone on throughout the day.

The first man disappeared, and another Hispanic man came inside. He peeled off his jacket and tossed it on the desk. He circled the jail, pausing briefly to stare at the madman before continuing on to the drunk, still snoring away, then stopping outside their cell. Selah did not rise. His presence only made the infernal heat all the worse. She longed to be out of here. To be back home on Nevis, diving into the freshwater pool with her sisters . . . Dimly, she realized she was not thinking quite clearly. She had to pay attention! Learn what she could of this newest adversary if they were to remain unharmed.

"What is your name?" he asked in heavily accented English.

She drew herself up. "Miss Selah Banning."

Her words awakened Verity, who shook her head wearily and rose. "I am Mrs. Verity McKintrick, and Selah is my sister," she said. "I am the wife of Ian McKintrick, a fearsome sea captain. You should release us before he finds us here."

The soldier stared at her, his features indistinct in the faint light of a lone candle burning behind him on the desk.

"Perhaps he does not speak much English, Ver," Selah whispered.

"Or perhaps I do," he said, again with the heavy accent. He remained there looking at her a moment longer, then edged to the side as if to better see Selah. He was a thin, reedy man, taller than both Verity and Selah. When he turned, she could see he was licking his lips.

"If you harm me or my sister, my husband shall make you pay in equal measure," Verity warned, this time in halting Spanish.

"I do not wish to harm you." He pulled out the key to their cell, considering it. "I never harm the women I make love to."

"Captain Santiago made the other soldier promise not to molest us. He shall be back in the morning and I—"

"He made *him* promise, not me," said the man.

"He gave him a coin. By rights, half of that is yours," Verity said. "Leave us unharmed and you can collect it in the morning."

"Or by rights *half* of his promise stands," he returned. "So I might collect my half in a different manner." He slipped the key into the lock.

A knock sounded on the iron door to the jail. Frowning, the jailer turned, hand on the hilt of his sword, and centered himself in the room behind the desk. "Enter!" he called.

When the men stepped in, Selah gasped. She threw herself at the bars. "Jedediah! Oh, thank God you are all right!"

Jedediah, clearly suffering painful wounds beyond those on his face, stared at her in consternation, then at the guard. George was right behind him. "These women are my charges," Jed said in Spanish, pointing at them. "They must be released."

"They are Captain Santiago's captives, charged with espionage. They are to remain here until morning, when he returns to question them again."

Jedediah drew himself up, fished in his pocket, and placed a silver coin on the desk. Selah gaped. She knew he seldom carried such funds on his person. "Release them. Tell your compatriot you got drunk and you do not know how they escaped."

The man laughed and sat down in his chair. "It seems you do not know the wrath of a Spaniard like Santiago when disregarded."

Jedediah leaned over the desk. "And *you* do not know this woman's husband, a stubborn Scot with a fearsome temper. Release her or die!"

Selah's eyes widened in surprise. She had never heard Jed speak in such a manner.

The jailer bit his lip, considering him a moment before dismissing him. "The captain shall reward me, come morning, for declining your offer."

Jedediah straightened and picked up his coin. He turned to Selah, clasping her hand between the bars. He had cuts on his chin and lip, as well as a black eye. "Are you well, Selah? Verity?" he added, tearing his eyes away from Selah to look to her sister.

"We are as well as can be expected," Selah said.

"You cannot speak to the prisoners!" groused the guard, coming over and pushing him away.

Jedediah glanced at him. "These women have clearly had no water or food."

"Captain Santiago's orders. Now get out."

Jed fished for his coin again and tossed it in the air. The guard caught it. "That buys me ten minutes with them. Step outside. If you see nothing, you can report you saw nothing."

Behind him, the madman began cackling, laughing as if he'd heard another joke. But the guard, fingering the coin for a moment, pocketed it. "Five minutes," he said, making certain his keys were on his belt before exiting. The madman doubled over in his laughter.

Selah stared at Jed in wonder. "You are most commanding when you wish to be, Reverend."

He grimaced and ran a hand through his hair. "Selah . . . Verity. I am so sorry you were taken. I was a fool, bringing you with me. I should have had you remain on Statia."

"That was not your choice," Selah said slowly. He was blaming himself for this?

"You could not have anticipated Santiago here," Verity said. "None of us did."

"Be that as it may, you were in my care. And I failed you." He went to the desk, taking a ladle from the bucket of water but finding it almost empty. Carefully, he poured the rest into the ladle and brought it to them. Selah drank rapidly, forcing herself to reserve the remaining half for Verity. "We have to go for help," Jedediah said, looking torn. "George and I cannot free you on our own."

"I know," Selah said, miserable at the thought of being left behind.

"Monsieur Bieulieu may be able to help," Verity said to George. "Or François. They would attempt to intervene. For Ian's sake, if not for mine."

"I shall find someone and return tomorrow," he promised. "He has not hurt you? Santiago? Or that wretch outside?"

"No," Selah said. "Other than denying us food and water."

"Santiago wants information, Jedediah," Verity said. "About Ian. About anything I might know of his whereabouts. And tomorrow . . . my sense is that he shall not be as patient. And if he does not continue to pay off these guards . . ."

"They are like hungry lions at your door," Jedediah finished for her. He glanced back to Selah, brows knit in consternation.

"Go to Statia," she said. "Find Verity's people. But please, do not tarry long."

"I shall not," he pledged.

"What of Frank and Junior?" she asked as he turned to go.

"With luck, hired on by the first mate of the *San Francisco*. They shall set sail in the morning. They were most concerned about you two."

"Neither wished to go," George put in, "until they saw you freed."

"But that is not happening this night," Selah said with a heavy sigh. "I am glad you found them a position. That is something for which we can praise God this day."

Jedediah gave her a long, beleaguered look, then nodded once. She frowned. There was something else in him that gave her pause, something beyond their kidnapping. Try as she might, she could not put her finger on it.

"Santiago threatened to hold us for months!" Verity said. She shook her head in misery. "Until either Ian returns or our family comes to pay the ransom themselves."

"I will find a way," Jedediah returned. "Regardless of what I discover, I shall return to you here by nightfall tomorrow."

Despite the comfort she drew from his promise, two things troubled Selah as he departed. He had not looked to her again, and he was oddly distant. Was it merely a focus on helping free them? Or something more?

CHAPTER TWENTY-ONE

Ian hopped out onto the beach as soon as they scraped across Statia sand. The small ketch carried five of his men, five more on a second behind them, captained by Michael McKay. The rest remained with the newly captured ships, hidden among three tiny isles. A new mate, Frederick, long familiar with these waters, had helped him navigate past frightful sandbars, shoals, and banks of coral in order to hide the ships away from any British patrols or privateers.

It had taken them all day to sail their smaller vessels to Statia, but they had made it. At long last, Ian would see his bride. It had been weeks, and every day apart from her had been a sort of sweet torture. He could not wait to have her in his arms again, see her face when he told her of his success. His men laughed as he hit the sand and immediately began running for Eagle View, their cheers behind him making him smile as he ran, even as his land legs threatened to give way.

In five minutes he was at the edge of town, working his way through the meandering crowds, startling a maid with a flock of chickens, and a man fighting to keep his drunk feet on the road to home. In ten more minutes he was at the base of the hill and trudging up the winding road. Only the thought of Verity kept him running in his heavy boots, ignoring his heaving lungs. But when he reached the cottage, it was Trisa who came to greet him at the door. A young man he did not recognize came around from the stables Verity had built, already containing three mares prancing in a circle as if excited by his arrival.

"Captain!" Trisa said with glee. "Welcome home!"

But he could barely summon a mutter in return, so focused was he on Verity. "Verity!" he called. "Verity, where are ye, lass?"

"Captain," Trisa said sorrowfully, coming closer, nervously wiping her hands on her apron, though they did not appear wet. "Mrs. Verity sailed for Montserrat this morning, along with George, Reverend Reed, and Miss Selah."

He frowned. "Montserrat?"

"Yes, sir. They had their minds set on finding positions for four freed slaves from Nevis. Finding none for them here on Statia, Mrs. Verity thought she best try there."

"What? I don't understand . . ."

"Mrs. Verity heard there might be ships looking to hire on more mates," Trisa went on to explain. She eased his coat from his shoulders and turned to fetch him a cup of water.

He swallowed back his disappointment and pushed the hair from his damp forehead. "When are they due back?"

"Tonight, sir. They planned to be gone the day and that is all." She handed the cup to him.

"Ah, good. 'Twon't be long then." He sat in a chair and looked out the window, thinking of his wife and sister-in-law off to find their people placement. Verity never was one to stay in one place for long; it did not surprise him that she would do such a thing. He drank down the water and lifted the cup to Trisa for another. "Did Reverend Reed and Verity bring those freed slaves from Nevis?"

"Yes, sir." She glanced away and back, returning to kneading her apron.

"What is it?" he asked, trying to school his tone into something more comforting than anxious. "Come and sit, lass. Tell me what ye ken while we wait for the family to return."

Trisa took a seat on the edge of a nearby chair as she told him of Selah's wounding on the slave platform, the runaway twins, and the four souls whom Selah and Jedediah convinced to try to find work and so ease the burden on the Double T.

He sat back, fingers to his forehead, trying to comprehend Angus Shubert striking his sister-in-law with a whip, leaving her with a scar for the rest of her life! He ought to have killed him that fateful night last year. Why on earth had God seen fit to spare the vile man? He had brought nothing but misery to everyone he encountered. If Ian was to be banished from Nevis, never to return—forcing Verity to stay away for the most part too—why could the Lord not have kept his wife's loved ones from further harm?

"And Miss Selah saved that slave girl?"

Trisa nodded. "And her sisters—she was one of three. Their cousin also, a man who rose to their defense."

Ian lifted his chin in understanding. Selah had always had a heart for the enslaved, but finding sisters among them would have threatened to be her undoing. Trisa went on to tell him how the young minister was now courting Selah, and together they spoke of teaching, training, and sending out as many freed people as they could.

"All of which makes them far from popular on Nevis," he guessed.

"Yes, sir. And yet, just last week, they succeeded in bringing many former friends back to the Double T, all because of the young minister's talent on the harpsichord." She slowly shook her pretty head. "I haven't seen a party like that on the Double T for nigh on a year. And then . . ." She returned to wrinkling her apron in one fist.

"And then?"

"Mrs. Verity announced she was going to sell her matched geldings and carriage in an auction. Reverend Reed said he would play again, so many should be coming back 'round."

"She plans to . . . *sell* them?" he said, blinking.

Trisa licked her lips. "Yes, sir. You see, it remains hard for the Covingtons to feed all the mouths they have on the Double T, let alone the animals. Mrs. Verity is auctioning off the horses and carriage not for money but for supplies."

Ian took that in. "My wife is quite a woman." *Insightful. Caring. Thoughtful. Generous* . . . to the point of self-sacrifice.

"That she is, Captain."

He rose and went to the front windows, then on to the porch, willing dust to rise on the road below them, telling him she was on her way home. He paced as the sun set. And as it grew dark, he knew he could not remain there any longer. "You, young man! Come here!" he shouted, belatedly realizing he had summoned the man more as a sea captain than as a gentleman.

"Yes, sir?" the man said, turning from the doorway of the stables. He had Brutus on his arm, the falcon apparently having returned from his evening flight and now set upon obtaining his supper.

"What is your name?"

"Andrew, sir. Your new stableman."

"Good. I am Captain McKintrick. Saddle a horse for me, please. I dinnae ken why your mistress is not yet home. I aim to find her!"

"Straightaway, Captain!"

Trisa followed him as he strode to the kitchen, sliced himself a bit of bread, and drank several ladles of water. "You do not think Mrs. Verity has come to any harm, do you?" she asked.

"Surely not," he said. "But they should have returned by now. With luck I shall find your mistress in town and escort her home within the hour. She is probably down visiting Abraham, unaware that her husband has returned to her."

The woman nodded, but he sensed she did not really believe his words any more than he did.

As the sky gave way to an indigo blue, he almost ran past George and the young minister, Jedediah, on the boardwalk. George turned at the same time Ian did, Jedediah following. Crying out, the men rushed toward each other, clasping hands.

"God be praised," Jedediah said, voice filled with relief.

"We are so glad to see you, Captain," George added.

He stilled, sensing there was more they had to tell him, based on their pensive looks in the torchlight. Was the minister's eye swollen? Was that a cut on his lip?

"Captain," George said, "we ran into Captain Santiago on Montserrat. He has Mrs. Verity and Miss Selah locked up in a jail cell."

Ian reached out to a lamppost to steady himself, suddenly feeling as if he was yet to gain his land legs. "What is that ye say, man? *Santiago*? Here?"

George nodded his head.

"He is after you, Captain," Jedediah continued. "He wants you, or he wants Verity to tell him what your next target is. He claims he will hold them in that jail until he either receives information from her, you show up to claim your bride, or their family pays a hefty ransom."

Ian let out a guttural sound of dismay, drawing the attention of several passersby. He paced away, then quickly back. "Where is the jail?"

"'Tis on the western edge of town."

"But the women are all right?"

Jedediah paused, then shook his head. "I cannot say they are safe. That is why we are here. To seek help." Then, as Ian's nostrils flared, he raised a hand. "They are in a cell alone."

"But?"

"But there is a lecherous guard on duty."

Ian let out a growl, running his hands through his hair.

"We could do nothing but sail for help. We knew we could not face Santiago without it," Jedediah said, his face awash in shame and frustration.

"I understand, man," Ian said.

"But, Captain, there is more," George said. "Santiago demanded they receive no food or water. And that jail is sweltering. We need to get them out of there tomorrow. You know what the heatstroke can do."

Ian turned to him, so riled he fought the urge to take George's shirt in his fists. "What? What has he ordered?" he sputtered. He'd heard the man; it simply made no sense. People died of heatstroke. What good would Verity do for Santiago if she died? How would he collect a ransom then? Or did he merely intend to weaken them, so that Verity was forced to tell him what little she knew?

He put his hands on his hips and dropped his head a moment, then suddenly looked to the sea. That was it. If Santiago could not find him, he wanted Ian to come to him. Even if Verity died, Santiago knew Ian's resurrected vendetta would force him to seek him out. Ian had thought that after Santiago's explanation of Duncan's death, the man had a shred of decency in him. And while they had hardly parted as friends, only with a temporary ceasefire, each pledged to do as he must if they crossed paths again.

Ian stared at the water, nothing but dark until the crest of white appeared as waves crashed onto the beach.

Jedediah stepped up beside him. "What are you thinking?"

"I am thinking Captain Santiago believes I am some distance away yet, and tonight I have the element of surprise. Tell me, were there other ships at harbor on Montserrat?"

"Yes," Jed answered, "but they set sail today. Only the *Juliana* remains."

Ian nodded, excitement growing in his chest. "Help me canvass the taverns." He patted George on the back and glanced at Jed. "I need my men out here before they are too deep in their cups."

Without waiting, Ian headed toward the nearest tavern. Not seeing any of his men inside, he hurried to the third, knowing George and Jed had gone to the second. There he spied Michael. He casually walked over to him, not wishing to raise any suspicion or talk.

Michael was laughing with one of the crew and glanced up at him in surprise when he came into view. "Cap'n," Michael said, rising.

"Round up the men and meet me outside at once."

"Yes, sir," Michael said with a frown. Ian knew his men would hate that their shore leave was interrupted, but all would know the need urgent.

They found Jedediah and George outside with the other five. All circled up, waiting on him.

He paced back and forth, wondering if he could truly do what he thought he ought. They already had a skeleton crew on his ships. And if Ian lost any of these ten? What then?

What then? What did it matter if he lost Verity?

No, in this he had the chance not only to save Verity but also rob Santiago at the same time. Obtain a ship outfitted for battle—the *Juliana*—forming a small armada ready to do anything the rebels asked of him.

Michael had learned what he could from George. He stepped up beside Ian. "Tell me you are not considering what I think you are considering, Captain."

"I cannae do that."

Michael gestured toward the dark sea. "There is no moon to-night! We might sail right past Montserrat! Guadeloupe as well! We could be lost for days, weeks!"

"Keep your voice down, mate," Ian growled. The last thing he needed was fearful sailors. "There will be fires and torches on Montserrat. We know it typically takes two hours and that the currents fairly drop us on her shores."

"Ahh, Captain," Michael groaned, slowly shaking his head.

"If we reach her in the dead of the night, we are likely to find a skeleton crew aboard the *Juliana*, and I'd wager her guards shall be given to more napping than pacing the decks. Some of you could steal aboard and commandeer her. I shall take two others and free Verity and Selah. We shall set sail at sunup, our ketches dragging behind the *Juliana*." He turned to Michael and clasped his shoulders. "Think on it, Michael! We'd have four ships, all ready to serve the Continental Congress, however they dictate. And I'd have some satisfaction in regard to Santiago."

"Is that what is driving you most?" Michael challenged, still clearly not convinced.

"No. 'Tis Verity and her sister, of course." Ian leaned closer to him. "Santiago is keeping them from food and water, Michael.

They languish in a sweltering jail. Another day . . ." He shook his head, fighting off panic. "I must get to them. And I must not fail in freeing them. Tonight is my best opportunity to do so, regardless of what transpires with the *Juliana*."

Michael folded his arms and considered him for a long moment. Then he lifted his hands. "So be it. But let us pause long enough to gather several days' supply of hardtack and water before we do this, in case we are at sea longer than . . . *anticipated*."

CHAPTER TWENTY-TWO

Selah faded in and out of sleep on the wooden cot, her head throbbing, her stomach roiling, despite that it was empty. She felt hot and feverish. *Heatstroke,* she thought dimly. 'Twas something they worked hard to fight against on Nevis, offering their field workers water at the top of every hour. Reminding each other, even in the heat of the kitchen, to do the same.

She glanced over at Verity, who moaned in her sleep and moved her head in a way that made Selah assume her sister was feeling as wretched as she was. No sweat rolled down her face any longer, presumably because she was as dehydrated as Selah.

The lecherous guard had decided to leave them alone, perhaps thinking to spend Jed's silver coin on a tavern wench once he was relieved of duty. The man sat in the doorway, his profile outlined by the flickering torch outside. His head bobbed as he continuously fought off sleep. Selah struggled to stay awake, watching the guard, intent on waking Verity with alarm if he changed his mind and came after them.

It was nearly an hour later and still dark when Captain Santiago appeared, nudging the guard awake with a nudge of his boot. The man rolled inward and caught himself, looking back in dismay as Santiago and his first mate and another man entered the jail, carrying a tub between them. While Selah's heart pounded, she had to force herself to sit up. They had not expected him to return until daybreak.

"Verity," she whispered, her voice hoarse. She coughed. "*Verity*."

The first mate put a lantern on the desk. The guard went to the corner, hands on hips, clearly wondering what was transpiring. Across the jail, the madman giggled in his sleep. The drunk to their left groaned. Verity wearily pushed herself up to a sitting position and frowned.

"Open their door," Santiago demanded.

The guard did as he was told, and Santiago and the mate lifted the tub and placed it in the center of their cell, sloshing water. It was neither big enough to bathe in nor small enough to be a regular water vessel. Selah looked up at him. What was this?

"You are thirsty, Mrs. McKintrick?"

Verity remained still, obviously sensing a trap too.

Santiago looked to Selah. "What about you?"

After glancing at Verity, warning making her heart pound, she returned her gaze to the tub with all that enticing water sloshing about. She tried to swallow but failed, her tongue thick and dry in her mouth. All she could think of was cupping her hands into the water, splashing her face, swallowing handful after handful . . .

"No, Selah," Verity said hoarsely as she rose onto wobbly knees.

"Come now, Verity. Clearly your sister is in need."

"*Selah*," Verity said again, shaking her head. But all Selah could see was the water. Taste it already. Feel it washing away the grime and sweat and heat. Relinquishing the ache in her throat.

"Please, Miss Selah, drink!" he said, flashing her a grin. "I do not know why your sister tarries."

Dimly, she understood that Verity thought there might be some sort of threat here. But would they not be better able to fight off the threat if they were not suffering from heatstroke? Slowly she lowered herself to her knees, eyeing each of them warily.

"Go on, sate yourself," he languidly invited, squatting beside her.

She cupped her hand and lifted it to her dry, parched lips. It seemed to barely wet her tongue, its mass feeling like a dried prune, refusing to soak in anything. She took another, then another, until she turned to cup both hands, washing her face, feeling the water run down her cheeks and throat. Then she drank some more.

"Good, yes?"

She nodded, still feeling dizzy. She knew from experience that it might take days to recover. Heatstroke was rather like the fever, sapping one's strength.

He gestured to the man behind her.

"Selah!" Verity cried. The first mate shoved her back to her cot when she tried to rise.

Selah looked up in fear. "What? What is this?"

The other man moved behind her and wrenched her hands together, even as Santiago gathered a fistful of Selah's hair in his hand.

Her breaths came fast then, fear rising in her chest.

"Your man, the reverend? He was seen sailing off this evening with Verity's servant. Likely to Statia, correct?"

"I do not know."

"Come now, Miss Banning. Of course you know that much." He wrenched at her hair, shaking her a little.

"Yes. He went to Statia."

"To seek help."

"No," Selah lied. "To get word to our family. About the ransom."

He dunked her so fast, she had no time to take a breath.

He held her under, waiting five seconds, then ten. Even underwater, she could hear Verity screaming. It was perhaps fifteen or twenty seconds before he let Selah up.

"Tell me the truth," Santiago gritted out. But he spoke to Verity, not Selah. Water dripped down Selah's head, face, and neck, drenching her bodice as she sputtered for breath.

She knew then what this was about. Verity might refuse him. But in threatening her sister, he knew he exposed her one vulnerability. *And I walked right into his hands,* she thought with chagrin and shame. *Made it simple for him. All because I was weak in my need.*

"They went for help," Santiago said to Verity. "That is what my man heard them say. Who shall aid them? Who shall be coming to your supposed rescue tomorrow?"

"I do not know."

"I have it on good authority that your husband captured a second ship three days ago near Hispaniola. My commander shall be most cross if I do not waylay him shortly. Is it he they hoped to contact? Or another who might assist you? Some dirty spy you have cozied up to on Statia? French forces?"

She kept her mouth clamped shut.

He got a better grip on Selah's hair. "'Twould be best for me to find out what you know now, Mrs. McKintrick, before the reverend returns."

She remained silent. But she turned helpless, desperate eyes on Selah.

"Tell me where I can find your husband, Mrs. McKintrick."

"I do not *know*."

Selah was able to take half a breath before he dunked her again, though it was long gone before he let her up.

"I do not know!" Verity was screaming, now on her feet, struggling to get around the first mate, who held her easily. "By design! Ian knew that if I knew what he was to do, where he was going, it might make me more of a target!"

"There is a certain glamour in being a spy for the rebels, is there not, Mrs. McKintrick? But you see, there is a dark side to being a spy too. Especially when you fall into the hands of your enemies." Again, he thrust Selah's head underwater. Fifteen seconds? Twenty? Thirty? Selah could not be certain. Only that she was glad, so glad when he let her up, choking on water, coughing it out in great spurts, unable to take a deep breath, though her lungs screamed for it.

Verity was weeping now, but she refused to answer him.

"Do *you* know where he is hiding, Miss Banning?" Santiago said in her ear, his hand gathering more hair, preparing to dunk her again. She stared at the water in horror. Would he drown her? "What was his mission?"

226

"I shall tell you!" cried a man, rushing through the door and tackling Santiago to the ground.

Selah fell to her left hip, staring in disbelief. Ian? Here? It could not be. She was dreaming . . . the heatstroke making her imagine things. She had witnessed such hallucinations in others. But it looked so much like her brother-in-law that she gasped and felt tears prick her eyes.

Ian swore at Santiago in Gaelic, landing a punch before his enemy rolled him over, knife in hand. Ian grabbed hold of his wrist as he gradually wrestled it toward Ian's neck. Beyond them, Michael McKay was fighting with the giant who held Verity. The third man put a hand on Selah's shoulder, silently warning her not to move.

Verity edged away from them. Ian managed to roll Santiago over and, as he did so, tossed Verity a dagger. Santiago's first mate saw it and savagely punched her, sending her to the ground.

"Verity!" Selah cried, trying to move toward her, but her captor pulled her to her feet and backed out of the cell, using her as a shield.

Verity shook her head and then, using the bars, rose. She still had a grip on her dagger. She looked wildly from Selah to her husband, clearly wondering whom to try and help first. Then Verity's eyes widened and she turned to Santiago, again on top of Ian.

Santiago grinned, gaining the advantage. Ian's fingers dug savagely into his face, searching for his eyes, but still Santiago's knife came closer, now just an inch from Ian's jugular.

She chose him, Selah thought distantly, as if not inside her own mind. *Of course she did. She must.* The man dragging Selah backward abruptly stopped.

"Let her go!" Jedediah ground out.

The man's arms tightened in surprise and then he dropped them.

Selah let out a gasp and stumbled into Jed's arms, now certain she dreamed. George was pressing a pistol into her captor's neck. Selah turned just in time to see Verity let her dagger fly straight into Santiago's arm before fainting to the floor.

"Verity!" Selah cried.

"I will see to her. You stay right here." Jed gave her a stern look. He edged around McKay and the first mate, still scuffling, and lifted her hand. Verity did not rouse.

Ian and Santiago came to their feet as Santiago wrenched the dagger from his bicep. Ian let out a guttural yell and ran at Santiago, ramming him into the iron bars. His head hit; he blinked slowly, then slumped to the ground.

His burly first mate fell to the ground, after Jed tripped him and Michael delivered one final blow. Selah staggered over to the cell, watching as Ian dragged her sister into his arms.

"I've got ye, lass," Ian said to Verity, silently imploring her eyes to open. "Ye are safe with me."

But it was Jedediah's pause beside Ian, hearing his words—and his sudden look at Selah—that made her heart halt for a moment. His expression was so grim, so far from hope that she took a step backward. It made no sense.

"Jed, what is it?" she asked as he locked Santiago and the mate in the cell, taking the keys with him. "You should be jubilant! You have done it! Freed us!"

"They freed you," he said morosely. "I merely aided them."

She frowned and took his arm, following Ian, who carried his wife out of the jail. It mattered not, she decided. There was time enough to sort it out. For now, she had only one thought in her mind—to see to Verity and get off this island before Santiago rose to consciousness and raised the alarm.

Outside, Selah rushed forward to walk beside Ian. "Is it the heatstroke?"

"I assume," he grunted under Verity's weight. He glanced at her. "Do you suffer as well?"

"I was showing some signs," she said, "but perhaps Captain Santiago's torture saved me from succumbing." She wryly lifted a soaked coil of hair from her temple. "I swallowed a great deal."

"Ahh, Selah Banning. Always the silver lining with you, eh?" he said, the corner of his lips quirking in a smile.

Selah reached to touch her sister's cheek. She was cold and clammy.

"Has she had anything to drink since you were captured?" he asked.

"Only a bit. Not nearly enough to stave off sickness." They reached the harbor, where she saw six men waiting beside two rowboats, presumably Ian's men. She wished they could take her to the Double T. "Where shall we go?"

"We shall take the *Juliana* to Statia," he replied, settling Verity into the bottom of one of the rowboats, speaking as much to his men as Selah. Jedediah and George drew closer to hear. "We dare not stay more than the day there. If another ship arrives, Santiago shall convince them to pursue us. We must tend to Verity and then be on our way."

"You intend to take her with you?" Selah asked.

"I intend to take both of you to Nevis. Santiago is a threat to you as well as Verity now, but he shall not dare to approach you when you are surrounded by family and friends."

They shoved off from the beach, and the men hauled against long oars to get them quickly to the *Juliana*. Selah tended to Verity, trickling water into the corner of her mouth a tiny bit at a time as they rowed, then again as she tended her in Captain Santiago's cabin.

She let out a sigh of relief as she heard Ian call for the sailors to weigh anchor, and thanked God that there was not another ship in the harbor for Santiago to commandeer and give chase. While Verity's temperature steadily climbed, Selah sank into a chair, a bit delirious as she felt the rise and fall of the *Juliana* upon the waves. The hint of sunrise was visible through the cabin's porthole, a soft peach hue on the horizon. They had done it. Managed to find positions for all their people, as well as escape from Ian and Verity's most fearsome enemy.

She ached from head to toe with weariness and what she suspected was her own fair share of dehydration. Recognizing that she needed to keep her wits about her, she forced herself to drink more water, even after downing half the skin en route to the ship.

A knock sounded at the door, bringing Selah's head up. Wearily she went to the door and opened it.

"Jedediah," she said, glad to see him.

But he did not give her his customary lopsided grin. Her eyes fell to his long fingers, anxiously turning his hat around and around. "Jed?"

"You are well?" he blurted out, his eyes scanning her hair, likely a mass of unkempt curls as it dried without attention. "Did that man harm you, Selah?"

"In no way lasting," she said gently. Was this what was troubling him? "Come, sit," she said, gesturing to a settee on the far side of the bed. "Verity is resting. I must stay where I can keep an eye on her."

"Of course," he said, obediently going to where she pointed. "Is she showing any improvement?"

"I have managed to get some water down her throat," she said as she moved to her sister and placed a hand on her forehead again. "But her fever is rising. 'Tis the heatstroke." She moved around the bed and sat down beside Jedediah on the settee.

"I know this is an inopportune time, but it cannot wait." He met her gaze. "I failed you, Selah, as well as Gray and Keturah. I promised to keep watch over you. To keep you safe."

She shook her head in confusion. "Jed, no one could have kept us safe. No one expected for Santiago to be on Montserrat."

He was shaking his head too. "I could have done more. If I was more of a fighter." He turned helpless eyes on her. "But you . . . *Selah*. When Santiago and his man carried you and Verity away . . ." His face turned to the porthole, the sun now visibly rising. "'Twas one of the most awful moments of my life."

"Both our lives," she said, frowning.

He licked his lips and then bit the bottom one. "It has been made clear to me that I am not the right man for you. I cannot provide adequate protection. The West Indies is yet a wild place, given to bringing out the basest parts of man."

"But no man would have been able to protect us yesterday," she said, resting her hand atop his. "Not Gray. Not even Ian. They would have been overwhelmed, just as you were. Still, you came back and rescued us! You fought again, for me. And look!" She gestured about the cabin. "We managed to secure another ship for Ian in the bargain!"

Again he did not smile with her. "Gray or Ian may not have managed it. But they would have left you safely on Statia."

"Ian might have, but I am not so certain about Gray. Even so, it does not matter. I would have insisted with them, just as I would have with you."

"Regardless, I cannot forgive myself. If anything had happened to you . . . if anything happens to Verity . . ." He sighed heavily and looked over to her, still turning his hat in his hands but now at a more methodical rate. "Selah, here in the Indies, if a suitor cannot provide adequate protection, he must hire on others to do so. And as you know, I do not have such means. You deserve better."

She rose, anger causing her face to flush. She could feel the heat of it. "I am not a helpless woman, Jedediah. I have funds of my own."

He rose too, slowly. "Funds you said God called you to use in a far different manner. If you marry a man of means, you may do so. He can see to your protection."

She frowned. "You are ceasing our courtship?"

"I am. I beg your forgiveness."

"I see." She turned away, folding her arms, her eyes shifting across the heavy brocade linen that decorated the cabin walls as if it might yield an answer to this puzzle. She glanced over her shoulder at him. "So it matters not that God brought our hearts together?" She turned to face him again, reached out and put a hand on his arm. "That love even now grows between us? A love like I have never known?"

He dragged his eyes up from her hand to her face. Anguish lined his forehead. "'Tis for the best, Selah. For *your* best."

She swallowed hard, willing the tears that rose in her eyes to cease their climb. "So be it," she said. On wooden legs she moved back to Verity's side. Moments later, she heard the cabin door quietly open and then close behind him.

Only then did she let helpless, furious tears slide down her face.

CHAPTER TWENTY-THREE

Once on Statia, Ian turned to one of his sailors as they hailed a carriage on Front Street. "Go to Monsieur Bieulieu's shop. Tell him we are in need of some of his ice. I do not care what it costs. Tell him it is for Verity, that she ails from heatstroke. Abraham can bring it to the shop."

"Yes, Cap'n."

A driver pulled up in front of them, and Ian carefully climbed the tiny steps, then settled on the seat with Verity in his arms. Selah and George sat across from him. Selah leaned forward and took Verity's hand. "C'mon, Sissy. Wake up," she said, patting it. "Wake up, Sissy. You are back on Statia."

But Verity still did not respond. The driver set off for her shop, five blocks distant.

For the first time, Ian seemed to truly see her, as well as her scar. "Selah, what has been done to ye . . . both on Nevis and Montserrat. 'Twas reprehensible."

"Indeed. But please, let us concentrate on Verity's care now," she said, gesturing toward her sister. She could not bear his tenderness. It threatened to unravel her when she already felt tattered by Jedediah's admission.

Ian looked to his wife and then heaved a breath. "In times of war, men will do most anything."

Selah leaned back into her seat, thinking that through. Now she need fear not only Angus Shubert, but also this privateer who had threatened them? A shiver ran down her back. "Santiago will be enraged that you stole his ship."

Ian flashed her a small smile, the first she had seen from him. "Dinnae fash yourself over Santiago. He will think we took to the open sea in an effort to put as many leagues between us as possible. He will not believe that we traveled only as far as Statia. And he will have to wait for another vessel to arrive on Montserrat that he might commandeer to give chase. By that time, we shall have delivered ye to Nevis and be safely away."

They pulled up in front of Verity's shop. Ian tossed George a key—which he found still tied at her waist—to open the door. Then Ian carried her in and set her on the cot in the back of the shop.

Abraham arrived shortly afterward with a precious block of ice the size of two fists. He stared at Verity in obvious horror.

"She is not dead, Abe," Selah said, putting a gentle hand on his shoulder. "Thank you for the ice. Can you go and fetch us a pail of fresh water?"

The boy nodded, handed Ian the ice, then turned and ran out the door. Jedediah moved inside as he left, carefully looking only to Ian. "May I be of any assistance?"

"Chip this ice apart and wrap it in burlap," Ian said to him. "You should find a pick in the drawer under the front counter. The burlap is in the cabinet to the side."

Jedediah went to do as he was told. Selah sat beside Verity, stroking her hand and talking to her. She knew that slaves on other plantations frequently succumbed to heatstroke, either passing out as she did or becoming delirious before death came. It happened among the gentry as well, particularly those new to island heat.

"This is all my fault," she muttered, trying to get Verity to take a bit more water. "If I had not brought our people here to find positions, she would not have gone with me."

"Nay," Jedediah murmured, returning. "'Twas my fault too. I should have known better. Thought it through."

Selah said nothing. He was punishing himself for something he could not have controlled. Yet she had tried to tell him that and failed.

Ian glanced back and forth at them. "I ken this. A man—or woman—is best served thinking through his next steps, not punishing himself for previous steps he could not have guessed would have led him to trouble."

Selah again refused to look Jed's way. She reached for the bag of ice chips and settled it on Verity's chest, right at the base of her neck.

"As it happens, I can now employ as many men as you can muster," he said with a grin. "I am suddenly in need of many crewmen. We were a skeleton crew for three ships. We'd be but a ghost crew on four. Are there others on the Double T who would be willing to leave the soil to sail with me?"

"Perhaps," Selah said. "Where are the other ships?"

"Safely away," he said with a tender smile. Meaning he could not tell her. The fewer people who knew, the better. "We shall get you, Verity, and Jedediah to Nevis, and before the garrison in Charlestown gains wind we're on the leeward side, we shall haul sail and be off."

"Verity shall be most cross to be apart from you again."

"No more cross than I," he said, rubbing his cheek as he stared at his beloved wife. "I confess this is not the reunion I had imagined."

"And yet if you had not arrived when you did . . ." Selah began. Even the thought of it sent her heart to pattering. Would she have survived the interrogation? Would Verity have given up some piece of critical information in order to save her? Her heart surged for the rebels' cause. She had been moved before; this rough treatment by one of their own cemented her passion to assist.

"We must not speak of what *might* have happened, lass," Ian said, sounding a bit breathless at the thought.

One of his crewmen appeared in the doorway. "Orders, Cap'n?"

"Yes, get all these goods in the store loaded onto the *Juliana*. Keep them atop the deck. We shall off-load them at the Double T, along with anything in the hold that may be of use for my wife's family."

"Aye, Cap'n."

"She shall want to go with you," Selah said, squeezing Ian's hand. She glanced at Jedediah. What would it be like to be separated by miles and months? Would he now leave the Double T and Nevis?

"Ach, how I wish she could," Ian said as Jedediah looked away, as if sensing her unspoken questions. "But now that I command four vessels, I may well have the bulk of the Royal Navy in pursuit of me. We must get to America and do what we can on behalf of the Continentals. That shall likely lead to some bloody battles. I dinnae want my wife in the midst of them."

"You shall not lie in wait for the three vessels bringing weapons?" she asked, forcing her attention from the door through which Jed had just disappeared without a word.

He stilled. "Three vessels?"

She bit her lip. "Before you leave here, perhaps you should speak to your contacts. Verity and I learned of three vessels to come to Nevis en route to America. They each carry a hundred men, as well as enough weapons to possibly change the course of the war."

He stared hard at her a moment, as if imagining she had just said what she had. Then he blinked slowly. "Am I to understand that *you* engaged in a bit of espionage on behalf of the cause?"

"On behalf of my people," she corrected. "The people of the Double T. I was promised supplies—these supplies," she said, waving about at them, "if I assisted Verity. Which I did."

"I see." He turned back to his wife and took her hand. "Come, lass. Come back to us. Feel that cool ice?"

Verity did not respond.

"How is it that Monsieur Bieulieu has ice?" Selah asked, eager to concentrate on anything but her sister's unconscious form. With every passing hour, her terror grew. "I did not know anyone in the West Indies had it."

"He keeps a block of it in his cellar, deep below his shop," Ian said. "Few know he has it, because he might well be robbed if they did. 'Tis quite valuable. There used to be quite a few nobles who imported ice for their icehouses on-island. The blocks would have to arrive every two weeks, of course, given our heat. But that trade has died out with the war on. This is likely the last of what Bieulieu has."

"It was a brilliant thought," Selah said. After all, there was no better remedy for heatstroke than cooling the patient down and trying to get them to accept water as fast as possible. Selah touched the bag resting near Verity's throat. Tiny rivulets of melting ice ran down her chest and disappeared at the edges of her neckline.

"I have not even thought of ice for years," she said dreamily. Back home at Hartwick, her mother ordered massive blocks delivered in the autumn and spring. Men from the north imported it by sea, selling trunk-size chunks to the nobility to keep in their icehouses. But in the Indies? Such an idea seemed a folly. She sighed. "What I would not give to walk into the delicious cool of an icehouse again!"

"Aye," Ian said, sitting back on his heels. "Or gather a snowball in my hands." He glanced to the window. "I love the tropics. 'Tis become home to me, in many ways. But there is a part of me that wishes to wrap myself in plaid and walk the highlands again. To feel the cold north wind stinging my cheeks. To sit by the warmth of a fire afterward."

"Oh, a fire," Selah said with a tone of longing, resolutely putting Jed out of her mind. "It was so cozy to sit by a fire on a winter eve." Now all did what they could to be near the cooking fire or sugar melting pits for as little time as possible.

"Yet 'tis autumn now, and there are those in England likely yearning for the heat of the tropics penetrating their bones. The feel of escaping it beneath the sheltering branches of a tree or the fronds of a palm."

Selah nodded. "Have you ever sailed to a place you thought might be perfect? A bit of heat as well as a bit of cold?"

"The southern part of America is like that. 'Tis hot in the summer and cold in the winter, but neither too hot nor too cold."

"Hmmm," Selah said. "I would like to visit America someday. Help the Continentals bring this war to a swift close, will you not, brother? So that we might go there?"

He grinned. "I shall do what I can, lass, to oblige ye."

Verity shifted and moaned, then her lashes fluttered open. "Oh, my head . . ."

"Ah, there ye are, beloved," Ian said, stroking her cheek, his brogue deepening in his excitement. "Ye gave us a wee fright."

"Here," Selah said, coming behind her to help lift her up a bit as Ian handed her a tin cup. "Drink, please. You have the heatstroke."

"As well as a shiner," Ian said, gently turning her face to see it better.

Verity groaned but did as she was told, and Ian handed the cup to Abe to refill. When the boy brought it back, he opened up the burlap sack and set a chunk of ice in the water. "Please, lass. Drink some more."

With a wince, Verity managed half the cup. "Please, lay me back down," she said wearily, "or I might vomit up that water."

"Does your head pain you?" Selah asked.

"Only if you do not mind a blacksmith hammering out one's brain," she grumbled, making them laugh. Her eyes opened to stare at Ian, and she reached out to touch his cheek. "I thought I was dreaming. How . . . how did you find me? When I needed you the very most?"

He took her hand in his and kissed the palm. "Providence."

"He saved us from Santiago's torture," Selah said. "As well as from that awful jail cell."

"And you saved me," Ian said. "My bonny lass sent her dirk flying into the pirate's shoulder just as his own knife neared my throat."

"Once again, Duncan was proven right," Verity said, eyes closing, "in thinking every woman should always carry a sgian dubh."

"Agreed," Selah said. "Especially in the West Indies."

"More water, lass." Ian helped Verity to drink a little more. "We must be away to Nevis as quickly as possible. I want ye in your sisters' care as you recover from this ordeal."

"I shall not argue," Verity said, leaning back again, lifting a hand to her head.

"Abe?" Selah asked.

"Yes?" said the boy, moving to her side.

She took his hand in hers. "Is there anything you wish for us to tell your mother?"

"Tell her I am well. Monsieur Bieulieu is kind to me, and I love two of his mares and might come to love the third."

Selah laughed. "I shall. You stay out of sight, will you not? You remember your hiding places if bounty hunters come searching?"

"Yes, ma'am. I think Monsieur Bieulieu forgets where they are himself half the time."

"Good. Then run for Eagle View, please. Tell George and Trisa that Verity is going to Nevis for a time and to look after the cottage. Bring Brutus back with you. She'll want him with her."

"Yes'm." He set off through the back door.

In the front of the shop, they could hear the scraping and groaning sounds of men lifting and carrying the supplies outside.

"Ian, before we go, must you not visit our . . . contact?" Verity asked, frowning in confusion at him.

He nodded and knelt by her cot, taking her hand in his. "You will be well for a bit without me?"

"Go," she said. "I shall be well."

"Ye wish me to do *what*?" Ian repeated, having heard the Frenchman but fervently wishing the words would change as they left his mouth this time. "Are ye daft, man?"

"Leave three men on Nevis," François repeated calmly. "They shall gain positions with the re-provisioning yard via our contact and sneak aboard the three incoming ships as they undergo repairs. Whilst undergoing repairs, only a skeleton crew shall be aboard.

Most shall be in town, enjoying a bit of liberty. At the appointed time, our men shall light a fuse leading to the ships' own powder kegs, then run for their lives. If all goes well, they shall dive off the edge of each ship just as each explodes, sending those ships—and the cannons they carry—to the bottom of the sea."

Ian was pacing. He rubbed his mouth and then the back of his neck, thinking. "It cannae be more than a hundred feet deep off that point. That's what makes it good anchoring ground! They shall simply hire divers and bring the cannons back up in time."

"A hundred feet of water shall take them months to negotiate, to say nothing of bringing additional vessels to Nevis or repairing the ships. With luck, the salvage shall be all the more complicated given the wreckage of each ship. Between weight and water, I imagine the hulls shall descend to the deeps in chunks."

Ian frowned and shook his head. "What you are asking of those three men is suicide." He rubbed his temples, trying to imagine who would possibly volunteer. He was passionate about the cause, but this . . .

"We understand the gravity of the task," said François. "That is why each man who succeeds in bringing down their appointed ship shall earn a thousand pounds."

Ian gaped at him. A thousand pounds? 'Twas a veritable fortune. Enough to convince a man he need try. It made Ian himself consider it. At least for a moment.

"I do not have the men to spare," he said at last. "We are in sore need of additional hands for each of the ships I now command."

"We already have the men," said François. "We shall send them along with your wife and sister and the supplies on your ship. They shall appear as nothing more than additional sailors, ready to assist. Once the cargo is off-loaded at the Double T, they shall disappear, then find their way to Statia after the deed is done."

"What word have ye about British warships in the vicinity? Do I dare take the *Juliana* to Nevis?"

"She flies the Union Jack, yes? Word will not have spread yet that you captured her—if we move quickly. But even if it did, there are none but slavers currently in Charlestown or Balsterre. The nearest warships are off Barbuda. If you can weigh anchor within the hour, you shall be a half day ahead of any who wish to give chase. Once you have dropped our men, you sail on to Philadelphia and present your prizes to the Continental Congress. They shall direct you next."

Ian kept pacing. Was he placing Verity and her sisters in any danger? Would anyone find out that the interlopers had originated on a ship captained by Ian? Would Verity be held in the Nevisian jail cell this time, until he surrendered himself?

"Do you have an *alternative* method to bring these ships down, Captain?" asked François. "We do not have the manpower to capture them. Therefore, we must sink them when they are at their most vulnerable."

Ian thought about it. He had four ships to their three, but between their superior firepower and a hundred soldiers per ship, there was no way he could challenge them on the open sea.

"Captain?" asked François.

Ian shook his head. They were out of time. "I shall do it," he said gravely. "But pray for your men. They shall need it."

Ian carried Verity back to the carriage an hour later. It heartened Selah to see her sit this time, but as much as she appeared to be gaining physically, she clearly suffered over the fact that Ian must be away as fast as he had returned. Her eyes followed his every move as he told Michael to sail for the other vessels with the twelve new men they'd hired in Statia, and then meet him near Anguilla in three days' time. The two clasped hands, briefly embraced, and parted.

"We shall get you home," Selah said, taking Verity's hand as they set off for the harbor. "You shall not be as lonely there with Madeleine to hold."

Verity nodded, but she reached over to Ian, who took her hand. Selah stole a glance at Jed, longing for the comfort of his hand too.

Had he meant what he said? Their courtship was over? Would she be seeking as much comfort from her sisters and little Madeleine as Verity would?

"Selah," Ian said, clearly for the second time, leaning toward her.

"Y-yes?"

"Verity tells me that ye may have other freed men who might wish to sail with me."

"Others?" She shook her head. "None that I would deem ready. We found positions for all who were most ready to take to the sea."

"Might you convince a few more?" he pressed. "I am fairly well versed in forming seasoned sailors out of those who are green to a deck."

She bit her lip and glanced at Jedediah. Was this not exactly what she had dreamed of? An opportunity for employment for her people with a man she could trust? And yet were any others ready for a life at sea? Ready to leave the Double T behind? And what dangers might they face with a rebel privateer?

Verity threw her a weary glance. "Shall we not ask *them*, Selah? That is the way of freedom, yes? To be offered an opportunity, then given the chance to decide what to do about it."

Selah suggested two men to Jedediah, daring to address him. "They may be content with a life at sea. There is also Terell, Albert, and Titus. They are friends; perhaps they would consider this a venture they would like to take on together."

Ian tapped his lips with one finger. "Ye can trust me, lass, to be a good steward of them. There are those—"

"Those who would not grant them freedom at the end," Verity finished for him as the carriage pulled up. She touched Selah's knee. "Send them with Ian, Sissy, now when you have the chance."

"I do not know if Gray shall approve," she said, stepping out of the carriage and walking with her down the beach to the rowboats that would take them to the *Juliana*. "We are but a week or two away from harvest. It is the one time of the year when extra hands are most needed."

"I agree with Verity," Jedediah put in, turning toward her with folded arms. "This opportunity shall not come 'round again for some time. Send any who are willing to go. Then we shall hasten to get the word out that the Double T can hire other freed men and women willing to bring in the harvest." He cocked his head. "Word like that tends to spread fast. It'd be across to Saint Kitts and beyond within a few days."

She said nothing. But he had said *we*. Apparently, he was not anticipating leaving the Double T.

Yet.

Chapter Twenty-Four

Ian brought the *Juliana* 'round on the wind and neatly in front of the Double T as if he had been sailing the vessel for years. As miserable as Verity felt, with her head pounding and stomach still roiling from the heatstroke, she had to admire his deft ability, even if it was the reason that would take him away again. Keturah had tried to dissuade her from falling for a sea captain, not once but twice. But what was she to do? Her husband had embedded himself in her heart as thoroughly as the anchor now slowing the ship to a stop, lodged among the coral below.

Men immediately set to dropping the rowboat to the water, then lowering Selah down in the boatswain's chair. Supplies had already been placed in the vessel, and they did the same with a second and third.

"'Twill be enough to sustain you and the people of the Double T for some time," Ian said, kissing her hand.

"We will be well," she said. She wrapped her arms around his strong torso, closing her eyes, wanting to memorize this feeling of being in his arms. "Promise me you shall be too."

"I promise ye, lass. I shall take these ships to Philadelphia and return to ye as soon as possible."

"But that could be months. Even a year or more if General Washington has other ideas about how you might be of use."

"Aye," he said gravely. He put a knuckle under her chin and made her look into his eyes. "I promise to write often, Verity. If I do my job well, perhaps I can help bring this war to a swifter end than we fear."

She looked away, not wanting him to see the doubt in her eyes. How was he to do his job well when the Continental navy was outnumbered a hundred to one? *Please, Lord,* she begged God silently, staring at the sea. *Please, please, please make a way for Ian to return to me.*

"Your turn, lass," he said, taking her hand and leading her to the boatswain's chair. She wished he could go to shore with her. Spend at least one evening with her and her family before departing. But they both knew that if he set foot on Nevisian soil, he risked capture.

He made a knot in the rope that secured her in the seat. "Until we meet again, love."

"Until then," she returned. "I love you, Ian."

"No more than I love ye, lass." Then, staring into her eyes, he made a motion to take her up and over. In moments she was safely in the rowboat below, rolling on the waves, and shielded her eyes to watch him as two men at the oars began rowing them to shore. A third sat at the prow. The first vessel was already at the pier, where men began unloading her. The second was halfway there. Verity turned back to look at the *Juliana*, and at her rail, her husband.

She smiled. He truly was in his element aboard a ship. Someday, when the war was over, she would look forward to sailing with him again. Together they would reestablish her mercantile, on Nevis, or improve the new one on Statia, importing goods and horses to the West Indies. Someday there would be peace in her life. They only needed to get through this war to discover it.

Verity insisted they remain on the beach until the *Juliana* sailed away. Workers had already carried all the supplies from Statia up the hill, as well as Brutus in his cage. Eight men were hastily gathered from the fields and agreed to try their hand at sailing, then packed up and rowed to the ship within the hour. Keturah and Selah stayed with Verity on the beach, as did Gray and Philip. Jedediah had not returned with the men.

Major Woodget and Captain Howard rode down to them just as the ship disappeared beyond Saba. Selah shared a covert look of alarm with Verity. *Thank God they had not arrived a minute earlier!*

"Good day, friends," the major said. "A scout from the peak garrison sent word that there was a war ship anchored outside the Double T. We came to investigate and report back." In several places on the island, the soldiers had built wide platforms partway up the peak on which they had positioned cannons to defend the island in case of attack.

"Yes," Gray said. "That was the *Juliana*, a Spanish vessel but flying the Union Jack."

"Her captain has sworn fealty?"

"Her captain is a man named Santiago," Gray returned carefully. "And I understand that he is a privateer for the Royal Navy."

"And he agreed to trade with you? Is it from the *Juliana* all those supplies came?" he asked, waving up the hill.

"Yes, they came from the *Juliana*. Her captain was most generous."

"That is grand news," the major said. "I must say, you all are most resourceful in the midst of trying times."

"We do our best," Gray said.

"Well then, I shall report back," the major said. "Until this evening."

"Until then," Gray said.

The soldiers rode off.

"They shall not be pleased when they find out who *currently* captains the *Juliana*," Keturah said to him as they led Verity slowly up the hill.

"No, they shall not. And yet the major has turned a blind eye every time he has gained wind of how our ill-begotten goods come to us. Why shall he not this time?"

"But when he learns that Captain *McKintrick* dared to sail directly up to our shore . . ." Keturah said.

"Then he might be a wee bit cross," Gray said. "Until we feed him roast chicken," he added with a laugh.

Selah smiled and then paused to look back to where the *Juliana* had disappeared behind Saba. She tapped her lips, thinking. They had managed to send eight men off with Ian, men who would learn to become sailors. And while the men would be paid well for their toil, she knew that it was as dangerous an assignment for them as it was for Ian.

"You could die," she had said to Terell, taking his hand in hers. "You learn a trade, yes. A trade that could serve you for the rest of your life. And Ian is a fine captain. Stern but fair. But there may well be cannon fire, bullets, battle in your future. Do you understand that?" She had looked beyond him to Albert and Titus, as well as the others in their group. All had fallen silent.

"I could die here, Miss Selah," said Terell. "We all could. The pox. Malaria. The ague. An infection. At least this way, we have the opportunity to see a bit of the world. As free men. And as you say, we learn a trade. We can take wives. Have families. Build homes in some port."

That had made her smile with him, to see the hope in his eyes.

"We understand the risk, Miss Selah," Malik put in. "You made a way for us, and we are grateful." He turned to shake the hands of Gray and Matthew, then bowed toward Keturah and Selah. The other men followed suit.

Then they were rowed back out to the *Juliana*. For some of them, it was the very first time they had even been in a boat. There had been no time to train them or teach them to swim. Was that what was niggling at Selah? Fear for them? She did not think so. She trusted Ian and Michael. They would look after the men and train them well.

Her mind went back to the rowboats, bobbing across the waves. Two men at the oars, the eight men of the Double T distributed among the three vessels. What bothered her?

It came to her then. Each rowboat had come to shore with three sailors. Two at the oars, one at the prow. But they returned to the *Juliana* with three fewer men.

Her eyes flew to the trees and brush, as if expecting them to pop up at any moment. Had they become lost? Or abandoned their posts? Surely if that had happened, Ian would have remained at anchor and sent his men back to fetch them. He had not one spare man. Wasn't that what drove him to compel her to send men with him, green or not?

No, those men had been deliberately left behind. The question was, on what mission?

Selah leaned against the meetinghouse wall, watching as Jedediah drew his sermon on trust to a close. Many of the Double T's people were mourning, already missing the eight men who had sailed off that day, as well as those she'd taken to Statia and Montserrat. More were worried about them. She shifted in agitation. Half of her still wanted to leave, finding it rather torturous to be near Jedediah when he had just broken her heart; half of her wanted to stay, curious to see if she would see any cracks in his armor. Make him see her there, think about her. Force him to reconsider his rash withdrawal of his suit.

"What God calls us to do is trust in him," Jed said. "No matter what comes. We have talked about how Jesus was asleep in the boat when the disciples encountered a fearsome storm. Waves were coming across the edge, threatening to capsize them! They were so frightened, they awakened Jesus. Jesus immediately arose and calmed the waves and wind with a word. Do you know what he asked them?" Jed leaned down and smiled into a little boy's eyes. The child shook his head dolefully.

"'Why are you so afraid? Do you still have no faith?'"

"But, Reverend," called a young man named Trevon. "Those people were done drowning if they didn't wake him up!"

Jed smiled and nodded thoughtfully. "That is how it appears, does it not? It *appears* that our Lord is asleep as we suffer." His eyes shifted to meet hers for but a moment. "It *appears* that our Lord is asleep as we face death itself. But would Jesus have allowed them all to drown as he slept on? Certainly not. Even when it appears our Lord is sleeping, or ignoring us, he is not. He sees it all. He is aware of us and all we face."

He moved over to a young mother and waggled his fingers, silently asking if he could hold her baby. She handed him over. Jedediah smiled down at the child, and Selah's heart seemed to painfully squeeze. He never was more attractive to her than when he played with a child or sat beside an older man or woman, quietly talking. He lifted the babe, showing him off to the ninety souls surrounding him, seeming to look at everyone but her. "God was with us when we entered this world. He will be with us when we breathe our last. From our first moment here on earth to when we at last see our Savior in paradise, we are called to do one thing: trust. He sees us. He loves us. He is for us. And He shall never leave us."

With that, he handed the baby boy back to his mother and laid a brief hand on her shoulder. Selah knew she should leave with the others filing out of the meetinghouse in groups, but for the first time anger roiled in her mind and belly. This man talked of trust! But when it came to her, he trusted not! He had broken off his suit. Said what he felt he must. Now, well *now*, she would say what she must too.

She forced all thoughts of him from her mind as the three sisters—Chully, Abana, and Dala—shyly approached her.

"Good evening, Miss Selah," Abana said carefully in English. "Welcome home."

Selah smiled. "Good evening," she returned with a dip of her head, "Miss Abana. Miss Chully and Miss Dala."

Her use of "Miss" set the girls to giggling, all three of them covering their broad white teeth with their hands. Their unsmiling cousin, Turu, gave her a ceremonious nod. She sobered and answered in kind, which set the girls to giggling again.

Turu shooed them out the door and chastised them in the

calming, melodic sounds of Igbo. But Selah recognized it as family banter, no matter what he might be saying.

Moments later, the meetinghouse was empty but for Jedediah and Selah.

"Selah," he said, rubbing the back of his neck and sighing. "I did not expect you here tonight."

"No?" she replied. "I have spent more evenings here than you have. And I shall continue to do so after you leave."

He lifted pained eyes to her. "I only meant that I thought that after all you have been through, you might be resting at the house."

She waved him off. "I took my leisure all afternoon. I could not rest a moment longer. Besides, I was happy that I was present to take in your sermon."

"Oh?" he asked, raising a wary brow.

"Yes. Although I do find it rather puzzling."

He waited, silent.

"How could you say you trust your God to see you through anything, and yet you fear so much for my safety and well-being that you have ceased our courtship?"

He lifted his chin and stared down at her with mournful eyes. "I trust him to see *me* through anything. What we went through . . . " His eyes drifted to the window as if remembering it all. "It helped me see that it is not fair for me to ask you to do the same. Selah, my road . . . what lies ahead of me . . . "

"You do not think I have thought of the potential risks and dangers?" she asked, shaking her head. "You think me so thoughtless that I did not imagine where an itinerant pastor might be led?"

He bit his lip and continued to stare at her.

"You told me that you have suffered imprisonment and beatings." She stepped toward him and dared to put a hand on his chest. "Jedediah, I have thought about what it might be like to suffer those same things by your side. And I was willing. Because I would be with you."

His breath was coming fast, his heart pounding beneath her palm. Slowly, he lifted his hand and covered hers. "*You* imagined those things," he said, each word etched in pain. "But I did not. Not truly. Seeing you there, Selah . . ." His eyes begged her to understand. "Seeing that you had suffered so, and I could do nothing to abate it . . ."

"But then what transpired?" she insisted. "God saw us through the storm."

He shook his head, took hold of her hand, and gently slid it off his chest. "I cannot do it, Selah. I cannot go where I wish to go, following God's lead, and ask you to risk your well-being, even your very life, to accompany me."

She put her hands to her hips. "Missionary couples do so every single day. To the Orient! To the Sandwich Islands! Even among the tenements of London!"

He shook his head miserably. "I know that. But that was not my plan. My plan was to do so on my own. Until I met you, I never considered another option. But what happened on Montserrat . . . it awakened me, Selah. Your life might be in danger at times here, but I cannot be the source of that danger. If anything happened to you, especially if I was to blame . . . I do not know how I would recover."

She rolled her eyes and threw up her hands. "Do you know what that sounds like to me, Jed?"

He waited, watching her with hooded eyes.

"That sounds like *fear* to me. And who is adept at using fear? Satan. I heard a gifted Methodist preach about that once."

He did not acknowledge her statement, yet she could tell he was remembering when he spoke of it.

"Do you know what it does *not* sound like to me?"

After a long moment, he gave her a slow, tiny shake of his head.

"*Trust*," she whispered. And with that, she turned and walked out the door.

CHAPTER TWENTY-FIVE

Despite Ket's fussing over Verity, it took only one day for her to figure out that something had gone wrong between Selah and Jedediah. Selah was excusing herself from the dinner table when Ket said, "Oh, Selah. Would you mind joining me and Verity on the veranda for a bit? I thought we could take tea together, just the three of us."

Selah hesitated but then agreed, reluctantly following Verity out the door. They retreated to the far end of the veranda, away from the open windows. Verity and Ket sat together while Selah leaned against the porch rail, looking down toward the swaying green cane, dancing in the wind, and the soothing roll of wave after wave, a particular turquoise blue that one only saw at this time of the evening.

Mitilda brought a tray with the Danish blue porcelain pot and matching cups that Selah had always favored, then disappeared with none but a nod after Ket softly thanked her.

"What is it you wished to say, Ket?" Selah asked, turning around to face her sisters.

"Say?" she said innocently. "Can a woman not merely seek some time alone with her sisters?"

"A woman can," Verity said with a sly smile, "but that is rarely you. You love your sisters and want to spend time with us. But when we are summoned to tea, it usually means you have something to say."

"Very well," Keturah said, giving an irritated shake of the head. "I only wished to know if Selah was all right." She looked at Selah then. "I take it you and Jedediah are at odds?"

Selah took a deep breath and let it out slowly. Then she sank into a chair and told them all that had transpired. To their credit, neither of them said anything until she was done, other than to gasp, groan, or cover their mouth in surprise.

"Do you believe he loves you?" Verity asked.

"I do," she said, feeling the heat of a blush rise on her cheeks. "Though we have never spoken frankly of love."

"A woman knows," Verity said with a shrug.

"She does," Ket agreed. "So he has broken off your courtship because he fears he can neither provide for you nor adequately protect you once you leave the Double T."

"Yes," Selah said, "and because his path might further endanger me."

"Honestly, every man struggles with that," Verity said. She lifted her hands. "Which is why I am back on the Double T."

"But Ian brought you here," Selah said. "He did not divorce you."

"True," Verity said with a sigh.

"Has Jedediah ever been in love before?"

"I do not believe he has. He said he came to the West Indies having decided he would be single forever."

"Until you changed his mind."

Selah nodded. "Or as he says, until God placed us on the same path."

Keturah rose and paced back and forth, chin in hand. "He does not have immediate plans to leave? He has committed to that concert on Lord Bennett's plantation in a few days, correct? The invitation arrived from Saint Kitts last week. Shall he see that through?"

"And what of our auction the week after?" Verity asked. "He was going to play for our friends and neighbors here on the Double T again."

"I believe he shall attend both. After that . . ." She gave them a tiny, dejected shrug. "If God points him away from Nevis, he shall follow."

"Then there is only one thing to do," Ket said.

"And that is?" Verity asked.

"We shall pray that if this is right, if you two truly belong together, that God shall continue to point him toward not only Nevis but you too."

"As well as show him that your life is in the Lord's hands, not any man's," Verity put in.

Keturah cocked a saucy eyebrow. "And we shall begin forcing the good reverend to continue looking your way by making you the most stunning woman on Lord Bennett's plantation."

"With this scar?" Selah said. "What shall you do? Veil me?"

"Oh, Sissy." Verity took Selah's hand in hers. "Do you not know that that scar only makes you intriguing as well as beautiful? Every eligible man on Saint Kitts shall want to know what transpired. And when they hear how courageous you were, you shall be thronged with admirers."

"Or reviled for daring to intrude on a slaver's auction."

"True. There shall undoubtedly be some of those on-island as well," Keturah said. "But we Bannings are accustomed to a measure of ostracism wherever we go, are we not?"

"I thought our goal was to win friends and admirers, not repel them," Selah said.

"It is. And it shall be done," Verity said, assuredly rising. "Now, follow me. I have something wonderful to show you." They climbed the stairs together and went to Verity's room. Her surprise was piles of dresses mounded on her bed.

"Courtesy of Captain Santiago." Verity lifted one with delight. "We three shall pick out a few favorites and I shall sell the rest in my store."

"You could reopen your store in Charlestown!" Selah said, reaching for a deep rust-colored gown.

"That is a grand idea," Ket said.

Verity appeared to be mulling that over, though a smile began to form. "Would that not make Angus Shubert furious?"

Three days later, all three of them boarded the *Hartwick* and sailed for St. Kitts, along with Jedediah, Gray, and Philip. Selah did her best to ignore Jed, but she could not stop herself from sneaking a few glances. He looked quite handsome in a new navy jacket, crisp white shirt, and tan breeches, all secured from the *Juliana*'s hold, along with the dresses. His breeches were tucked into new black boots, which he might have purchased in Charlestown, because his feet were much larger than both Gray's and Philip's. It surprised her that he had bought such finery, and yet if these sorts of opportunities for him to play arose in the future, he would need them.

She turned her face to the wind and hoped that he might sneak his own peek at her. Her sisters had encouraged her to choose a beautiful brown silk gown with embroidered peach flowers lining the edge of the bodice as well as the voluminous skirt. It sat just on the edge of her shoulders, and the neckline scooped just below her clavicle. "But then everyone shall see the scar on my shoulder as well," she had said.

"No one shall be looking at your scars," Ket had returned. "At least they shall not for long. Because that shiny cocoa color makes your eyes the most vivid golden-brown I've ever seen."

Selah had stood before the mirror in her sister's room, considering it as Abana pinned it in a few places for some minor adjustments. The young woman was proving to be quite adept as a seamstress, after only a few lessons from Mitilda. Once finished, she stood back, hands clasped in admiration of her. "You are . . . beautiful, Miss Selah," she said in halting English.

"Thank you, Abana."

She clung to her words, as well as to her sisters', as they neared the much bigger neighboring isle. Keturah wore a beautiful teal gown, Verity an ivory gown with gold trim. All three of them had their hair down, with plans to see to hairdressing once they arrived at Lord Bennett's plantation. Given the wind and the spray off the waves, they knew any other plan was hopeless.

Being so close to Selah and yet not speaking to her was a sort of exquisite torture Jedediah had not experienced before. It had been hard enough on the Double T, but there, at least, she had largely avoided the meetinghouse, exiting each day as he made his way down the hill with the others. He had barely glimpsed her since their last conversation. Here, in the *Hartwick*, he could hardly avoid seeing her. Truthfully, he wanted to stare at her. With her curly blond hair dancing across her shoulders, her beautiful peach-hued skin . . . Again and again, he tore his hungry eyes away.

His stomach clenched. He knew he would not be the only man at this concert, and the party that followed, who would be entranced. There would be many a man eager to bring her a cup of punch or make her acquaintance. But he had no right to feel jealous. He had ended their courtship. He had seen the pain in her eyes when he had done it. Heard the anger in her tone when they had last spoken.

How he had missed her from that moment on! His longing to speak to her, to see her, to hold her haunted his every waking hour. He had taken to his knees, begging God to affirm his decision. But God remained stubbornly silent. Why? All Jed needed was some sign, some word to his heart that he had made the right choice. How could God not affirm him? Was he not the same God who had sent him here, the same who had first led Jedediah to read those verses and determine that his own ministry would be best served as a bachelor?

He had feared repercussions from Verity and Keturah, yet both sisters had virtually ignored him. The family had circled around Selah, as well they should. But after feeling so welcomed, even envisioning himself a part of their clan, it was an odd sensation to be fairly banished. Of the family, only Gray continued to speak to him, given that they interacted each day in the fields. Three days ago, Gray had confirmed that he still intended to see through the concert on St. Kitts, as well as the auction at the Double T afterward. It was he who had offered him the new jacket, shirt and breeches, then sent him to town on his own horse to purchase the boots. It had taken nearly everything he had, but he knew Lord Bennett intended to pay him handsomely. Through it all, Gray was gracious, clearly grateful for how Jed was helping the family through his music, but there was also a measure of frustration and fury just beneath the surface.

And Jedediah understood why. He had asked for their blessing on his courtship of Selah; they had risked in granting it. And his turning away from Selah must have felt like a slap to the face. He had considered speaking to Gray or Philip about his ongoing confusion and doubt, but never dared; he could feel their frustration with him. However, as they sailed into the bay and prepared to dock, his eyes went again to Selah, who sat with her back to him, leaning on the edge of the boat.

Did I make a mistake? Selah's challenging word to him about fearing rather than trusting had taken him aback, but he'd dismissed it. This was the very first time he'd allowed himself to ask the question he feared most. He thought about how much easier this evening would be with her by his side. She would know how to charm the guests. Men would have looked at him with immediate admiration, with a woman such as Selah on his arm. And when they discovered that she was so much more than a beauty, they would have admired him all the more.

Forgive me, Lord, he prayed silently. *Such vain thoughts! Such idle temptation!* He should not have agreed to play. This was what it led to . . . a reliance on the ways of men rather than God. Still, he could not avoid watching Selah accept Philip's hand, take her skirts in hand, and daintily clamber out of the boat. He stared at her small hand, remembering the feel of it in his own. He wished it was him helping her. Or him instead of Gray on the dock, ready to catch her. Which only reminded him of catching her on the dock that night they had seen Akunta to freedom. The night he had kissed her . . . which led him to remember saying he could think of hundreds of ways he wanted to kiss her . . .

"Jedediah!" Philip called, obviously not for the first time.

Jed started, looked up, and saw that the ladies were already partway down the dock.

"Stage fright, is it?" Philip asked as he passed.

"Something like that," Jed muttered.

Lord Bennett owned a sprawling plantation, and they saw where the concert was to be held as a carriage took them over the winding road up the mountain. They had terraced out several levels, forming an amphitheater with a stone grotto on the stage below in the shape of a clamshell. At the center of it stood a piano.

"Goodness, they can probably seat three hundred people," Ket said.

"Have you ever played for that many, Jed?" Philip asked.

"A few times, yes."

Selah guessed he was merely being modest. The churches in which he grew up playing could no doubt hold as many as a thousand on a Sunday. But if Bennett succeeded in filling every seat tonight, Jedediah would earn a small fortune. *What will he do with such a bounty,* she wondered, *now that he is no longer thinking of providing for a bride?* She swallowed hard.

The three women sat directly across from the men. Selah was grateful that her sisters had made certain she sat opposite Philip, not Jed. It was already uncomfortable enough, how he looked anywhere but her way. The others kept up a lively conversation, commenting on everything from the fine cobblestone road, to the flowering trees that bordered it, to the acres upon acres of thriving sugar cane waving in the wind.

Several minutes later, they entered through the main gates, greeted with nods from four servants dressed in livery. The main house was grand, surpassing even the finest on Nevis, with white granite columns, manicured gardens, and wide windows. They could see that although they were early, there were already a fair number of guests in attendance, perhaps also from neighboring islands. Valets reached up to assist them down from the carriage, and Lord Bennett—a tall, jovial, broad-shouldered man—strode down the walk to greet them. A maid at his side softly invited the women to a room where other ladies gathered to see to their grooming before the concert began.

"Is Lord Bennett a single man?" Verity asked the maid as they walked into the grand house.

"No, miss. But his wife prefers London to our Indies." She gestured toward a room halfway down the hall, where dozens of women sat around tables with mirrors, putting on blanc face powder or dabbing carmine to their lips while maids saw to their hair. It was nothing like what Verity had described in the American colonies, but for Selah it was the first time in a very long while that she had glimpsed proper society matrons and their daughters preparing for a party. In the corner, a seamstress was sewing her mistress's skirt, apparently after accidentally ripping it. Introductions were swiftly made. Selah could hear the whispers behind their backs as they passed. Many had apparently heard of the Banning sisters before today. More stared at her scar, then pretended not to notice it.

Selah wished they might simply ask her about it. Be honest in their curiosity. Their stares as she passed made her want to cover her cheek and shoulder with her hair, rather than pull it up. She had not missed this part of society—the subtle competition among women. She rubbed the bare, tanned skin of her arm, noting that many of these women clearly spent much more time in the shade or under a parasol. She stifled a sigh . . . as well as an urge to gather up her sisters and sail home.

Skilled lady's maids saw to Keturah's long sable hair, Verity's brown waves, then Selah's blond curls, combing, pinning, and curling with such adept hands that Selah wished she had brought a couple women from the Double T to watch and learn.

Three women at the nearest table were debating *mouches*—

beauty marks—and their meanings. Selah met Verity's sidelong glance when their conversation turned from proper placement to catch a potential lover's eye to marks that might denote rebel tendencies. She knew her sister hoped to learn something more here that might prove beneficial to the Continentals but doubted she would be privy to much. Her reputation as the bride of a rebel privateer would likely rapidly spread before her. But perhaps Selah might learn something she could pass on. At a function like this, she would be surprised if there were not quite a few high-ranking military men in attendance, as well as their wives. And if she occupied her mind with a bit of espionage, she would not be thinking about Jedediah.

Jerusha Miller entered then, and when she spotted the sisters, let out a little yelp of surprise and cast them all wide grins as she hurried over to hug and kiss them all. They responded in kind. It had been years since they had seen her, and she had been one of their favorite friends in England.

"What has brought you to the Indies?" Ket asked, face alight in wonder.

"My handsome husband," she whispered, leaning forward.

"Does he own a plantation?" Verity asked.

"He's a merchant with several ships, actually. We have a small home on Saint Kitts, but our manor is on Hispaniola."

As her sisters continued to catch up with their old friend, Selah slipped away, finding talk of husbands and married life rather like tiny arrows piercing her heart.

She left the house and began a tour of the gardens, stopping to admire fragrant jasmine bushes that filled the air with their heady fragrance. She paused at a small sign that said *Grotto* with an arrow pointing to the right, knowing that Jed was likely down there right now, practicing or perhaps tuning the piano. From here she could see Nevis across the channel and again felt a pang of longing. Could they not have sent Jedediah over here alone? Resolutely, she turned in the opposite direction, continuing her exploration.

Twenty minutes later, she was directly beneath the corner of the house's wide veranda, its expanse three times as big as the Double T's. More than a hundred guests now mingled, gathering in pods to talk and laugh, debate and exchange pleasantries. After so long apart from society—their own gathering only but breaking the ice—and not knowing as many people here on St. Kitts as she did on Nevis, Selah hung back, strolling along the banks of flowers. *I pretend as if I am as much a horticulturist as Keturah or Gray,* she thought, dismayed with herself. She thought back to the roomful of women. How she had longed for friends, as they once had had. And how she had become accustomed to their isolation on the Double T over the last year. She knew this was an opportunity to reach out again, but the idea of doing so left her feeling at odds.

"What is this?" said a voice behind her. "A flower among the flowers?"

She turned and tried to compose herself. It was none but a young man. He was dressed in silk finery, the cut of his jacket presumably the latest of Europe. It was distinctly different from what most of the men wore now among the West Indies. She turned partly away, belatedly remembering her wound again, the scabs still present in places. What would he think?

"Forgive me," he said with a courtly bow. He rose and tucked a blond strand of hair that had escaped his neat tie at the nape of his neck. "I am Ernest Holloway, recently of Liverpool, here to learn the intricacies of running a sugar plantation from my uncle, Lord Bennett."

"I see," she said. Hearing his name, and now knowing he was a part of their host's family, she decided to face him. He had a long patrician nose, square jaw, and green-blue eyes laced with blond lashes. He was perhaps two years her senior. "And I am Miss Selah Banning, of the Double T, a plantation on Nevis."

"N-Nevis," he said, momentarily distracted by her wound before forcing his gaze back to her eyes. "Do you oft visit Saint Kitts?"

"Surprisingly enough, no. Life on Nevis keeps me quite occupied."

"I see," he said, unable to keep his attention from returning to her scar.

She had put it out of her mind until she reached St. Kitts. On the Double T, most were growing accustomed to it. Their lack of reaction had made her forget it for hours at a time. In the last couple of days, she had not thought of it at all between the time she sat at her dressing table, come morning and night. She had been a fool not preparing herself for this. This Holloway was perhaps only the first man of a couple hundred who might gape at her. Only the fact that St. Kitts had three times as many men to women, like Nevis, likely kept him standing here.

"May I fetch you some punch, Miss Banning?"

"Certainly." Her throat suddenly felt parched.

He turned to a circulating footman in livery and took two etched-glass cups from the man's silver tray. "You seem quite young to be at a party unaccompanied, Miss Banning, despite your fearsome battle scar."

She almost spit out her punch. But she choked it down and laughed a bit as he smiled. "You know, you are the first person to so openly comment upon it," she said, lifting fingers to where it looped over her jaw. "I was thinking but an hour ago how I would prefer people asked about it rather than pretended they did not see it. 'Tis more honest, I believe."

He cocked his head, took a sip and perused her, squinting his eyes. "I am an artist. I enjoy unique, beautiful subjects. And I would very much like to sketch you, Miss Banning."

She laughed and looked away, embarrassed. "Surely there are much finer, unmarred women about for you to sketch, Mr. Holloway."

"Everyone has mars, Miss Banning," he said as he leaned slightly toward her from the waist. "Some are simply more apparent than others. I would very much like to know how you obtained that wound."

"Yes, well, perhaps I shall oblige you one day. But not this night."

"Ahh. A woman of intrigue, eh?"

"Not in particular," she said, looking away. "I am only reticent to share such a story with a man so soon met. And," she added, lifting a finger, "I am not all that young *nor* am I entirely unaccompanied. My sisters, my brother-in-law, and our friend are with me, as is another . . . *friend*, Reverend Jedediah Reed. The pianist for this evening?" she explained when Mr. Holloway frowned in confusion.

"I see," Mr. Holloway said. "So you are left to fend for yourself?"

She glanced about. "My family is somewhere about. But I am hardly a hothouse flower, Mr. Holloway." She paused to take a sip of her punch. "I have lived among these isles for more than three years. If you survive your first year in the Indies, you have proven you have mettle."

"And a strong constitution, able to beat back the pox and malaria."

"That too," she said with a gentle smile. She reached out to pluck a jasmine flower and lifted it to her nose. "Tell me. Did the ship that brought you carry supplies for our hungry islands? I am certain your uncle has told you how the war in America threatens to starve us."

"Indeed. Although she is largely a passenger ship, she brought barrel upon barrel of flour and corn to Saint Kitts. My uncle's storehouse shall be full by nightfall."

"How fortunate for him," Selah said. "Do you believe your uncle might pay our friend, Reverend Reed, partially in corn and flour instead of coin?"

Mr. Holloway pursed his lips. "Perhaps." Then a glint came to his eyes. "If I suggest it to him, would you allow me to sketch you?"

She scowled. What game was this? An attempt to capitalize on her mutilation? "Why? Because I am such a novelty? A lady with a scar?"

"No," he said, lifting his brows. "Because you are an extraordinarily beautiful lady with a scar." He leaned a bit closer. "It makes you, Miss Banning, quite . . . exotic."

She pulled back a bit. She was unaccustomed to such flattery.

Especially now. And yet he seemed quite frank in his manner, not at all like the dandy fellows Ket and Ver had warned her about. Simply as if he were stating facts. Selah ran her fingers along the embroidered flowers of her bodice, considering him.

"Why is it so important, Miss Banning, the supplies? Surely you are not so bad off as all that?"

"You might be surprised," she said, raising a brow. "And this?" she added, gesturing to her scar. "This is only a bit of evidence as to how we are treated at times."

His eyes narrowed, and one side of his smile went up. "Now you truly *must* tell me more. Not only are you exotic, you are mysterious too. You can tell me your tale as I draw you."

She laughed under her breath. "Take me to your uncle. Present my request. And then we shall go—someplace within eyesight and earshot of others—to where you may sketch me." As she spoke, she wondered at her sense of assurance. Her ease in making her way between gentle flirting and securing a deal that, if she succeeded, would benefit her people on the Double T. And a man like Mr. Holloway, nephew to Lord Bennett? Well, Verity would be quite proud of her for making inroads with one such as that.

Would she not?

Chapter Twenty-Six

Mr. Holloway secured his uncle's approval in paying the pianist in barrels of flour and corn. Lord Bennett turned to her. "My nephew is an accomplished artist," he said, "but he is not quick about his task. You may miss Reverend Reed's concert. Is that well with you?"

Selah nodded eagerly. All she could think about were the barrels of corn and flour she had succeeded in acquiring. And now she had an excuse not to be forced to sit and watch Jedediah play. "Let me seek out my sisters and inform them of our task. But it shall be well."

Soon she returned, and Mr. Holloway offered her his arm. Selah accompanied him to a side parlor in the grand house. "Sit there, if you would, Miss Banning," he said, gesturing to a chair. He went to light another candle and place it on the table beside her. He stepped back, his blue-green eyes tracing her, studying each inch of her as if he were already sketching. It was oddly intimate, yet at the same time not at all. She was but an artist's subject, was she not?

He moved to the side of the desk, and she saw he had an easel and canvas already there. He unscrewed the canvas and brought out a fresh one, which he placed on the easel. Then he set it about eight feet from her and put several pencils on the tray before it.

"Do you paint as well as sketch?"

"I do." He came over to her and studied her, chin in hand. "Will you please move your legs to the other side of the chair?"

"What? But then . . ."

"Yes, your scar shall be more visible. Is that all right?"

She thought about it. About her conflicting emotions. One day she considered the scar a blemish, a detractor. The next day she considered it a mark of courage, a bond with people she loved who had suffered in similar fashion. She moved her legs, remembering the girls' way of renaming her the day after the attack. *Beauty, Love, Mercy,* they had called her. She lifted her chin and stared steadily at Mr. Holloway.

"*Magnifico!*" He flashed her a grin, backing away. "Hold right there for as long as you can." With swift movements, he began his work, the scratching sound of lead on canvas making Selah imagine each stroke.

"Your uncle says you are an accomplished artist. As a painter, why not remain in England and make your living creating portraits?"

"Because I find it stifling. So many hothouse flowers, all the same, when there are beautiful, exotic flowers in the West Indies to be discovered."

Selah felt her cheeks warm at her own reference.

"So tell me how you ended up so far from home, Miss Banning. But do not move," he said, raising a finger of warning.

"My father died, and our sugar plantation was in disarray. My eldest sister, Keturah, elected to come and try to save it. My sister Verity and I could not allow her to do so alone." She shrugged, then caught herself. "Oh. Forgive me."

"'Tis all right." He paused, studying her. He came over, then touched her shoulders with light fingertips, gently reorienting her. It surprised Selah when his touch—none but an artist on task—sent a shiver down her back. "So you three came alone?"

She nodded. "Oh! Forgive me!"

He laughed, and this time he gently tipped her chin upward. "'Tis well. Only concentrate on answering my questions with your lips rather than your body." Mentioning her lips seemed to inspire him, and he went back to sketching. His focus remained on her mouth, and she could feel a slow blush warm her cheeks. "You were presumably successful with the plantation," he said. "But you have run into some trouble, given your scar, and your need for food supplies."

Trouble. Her mind cascaded through all that they had encountered, suffered, and struggled through over the last three years. "That is one word for it. There were many on Nevis who did not wish for us to be there. 'Tis uncommon for women to run a plantation on their own."

"And are you still on your own?"

"No," she said with a wistful smile, thinking of her sisters, Gray, and all the people she loved on the Double T. "My sister Keturah married a dear friend from England, Gray Covington, who owned the plantation next to us. Verity, next eldest, married Captain Ian McKintrick, who is a privateer for the Continental navy," she added in a whisper.

This again brought Mr. Holloway to a sudden stop. He eyed her briefly as he continued to sketch. "Truthfully?"

"Yes," she said, thinking it best to tell him rather than let him hear of it from the gossips.

Mr. Holloway paused and lifted his hand from the canvas. "'Twas not you and your sister who were the two Nevisians captured on Montserrat and held by a Spanish privateer?"

She lifted her brows in surprise and then frowned, thinking of the experience again. "'Twas, yes," she replied.

"How extraordinary. But no frowning, Miss Banning," he chided. "Give me that valiant look again. From what my uncle said, you were both quite courageous on Montserrat. From all accounts, that is a family hallmark."

Courageous, she echoed silently. She did not feel courageous. But at times . . . "We sometimes rise to the occasion," she said, lifting her chin.

"There you have it."

"So you intend to pursue your art as well as learn how to run a sugar plantation, Mr. Holloway? I must say, the two seem very different tasks."

He cocked a grin. "I am a Renaissance man." He went on sketching, pausing often to study her, then continue on. He turned to sharpen his lead. "I am my uncle's heir. Rather than learn how to run the plantation when he dies, as so many in England do, I thought it wise to come and learn from him before he advances further in age."

"That is most wise." What might have she and her sisters learned from their father had they arrived before his demise? Could they be a year ahead in their progress on the Double T? No, somehow she knew they were exactly where they ought to be. And even further in some ways than where they might be had Father still been alive, given Matthew's prowess and Gray's progressive ways. Surely, Father would not have allowed them to operate the plantation as they did now. Would he have argued to buy and keep slaves rather than hire free folk? Or would he have seen her passion, changed his mind and heart as Keturah and Gray had gradually done? Had he not set Mitilida and Abraham free? Did that not indicate a softening of the heart?

She sighed heavily, feeling a pang of sorrow. She had been but a little girl when Father last sailed for the West Indies. What would it be like to have a father present now? Or even an uncle, as this Mr. Holloway had?

"I have brought you sorrow," Mr. Holloway said.

"No," she returned. "Not really. Only a bit of melancholy, thinking about my father, who left us when I was quite young." Melancholy over her father's loss led her back to thinking of Jedediah and his own stubborn turn away from her. Father had died; Jedediah's decision to break off their courtship felt a bit like death too. Only he continued to walk and talk and work and now . . . play music for others.

"My own parents died when I was very young," Mr. Holloway said quietly. For a while he sketched on in silence. "Might you tell me how you received that scar?"

Selah bit her lip. What was the harm? Again she would rather he heard about it from her rather than from others. "I stood between a man with a whip and the slave he wished to purchase, but who refused to come without her sisters."

Mr. Holloway stopped, gaping at her. "You . . . *what*? Stood between a man with a whip and a . . . *slave*?"

"I did," she said. She shook her head, forgetting herself, feeling sudden tears well in her eyes. "I could not let him have her." Thinking back on that day, 'twas as if she remembered all that had befallen her in recent weeks. The slave platform, their imprisonment on Montserrat, Verity's terrible heatstroke, Jedediah's betrayal. "When I realized she was one of three sisters . . ." She smiled at Mr. Holloway, the tears cresting and falling down her cheeks. "What was I to do? I simply had to stand up for her. All I could think was what it might be like to be in her position. With my own sisters, about to be separated forever. And the man who attempted to buy her . . ." She shook her head. "He is a monster. I simply could not allow it to happen."

She choked back a sob. *If only I could stop other things from happening . . . Oh, Jedediah . . .*

Mr. Holloway's face softened, and he set his pencil down and went to her. He fished out a handkerchief from his jacket pocket and knelt before her, then took her hands in his. "Yes, what else could you have done? You brave, marvelous girl," he breathed, staring at her in amazement. He lifted her hand to his lips. "Please forgive me for bringing forth such a painful memory."

"*Selah*," Jedediah said from the open doorway, hands on either side of the doorjamb as if trying to hold himself up. His eyes were wide with disbelief, accusation. "The con-concert . . ." he stuttered, "it-it is about to begin."

She followed his gaze to her hand, clasped in Mr. Holloway's, and as if in a dream pulled it slowly away. "*Jedediah*. I . . . we . . ." she began, glancing toward Mr. Holloway, wondering how to explain. Then with a flash of anger, she wondered why she should.

But when she looked back to the doorway, he was gone.

"Jedediah," Selah said, pulling him to a stop on the path halfway down to the amphitheater. She tugged him into a small garden to the side, covered by a curved roof of wisteria vines with their conical purple flowers hanging prettily below.

"I must not tarry," he said, pulling away from her, his face a mask of anguish.

"You must for a moment! That," Selah said, gesturing over her shoulder, "was not what you are imagining."

"I knew it would not take you long to find a new admirer." He shook his head. "But to find you in some tryst—captivated by some dandy! I—"

"Tryst! That was no tryst! And Mr. Holloway . . . he is no dandy!"

"No?" Jedediah asked, leaning away from her. "It certainly looked that way to me, on both counts."

"You have no right, Jedediah," she whispered as a group of guests passed them. "You brought our courtship to an end, re-member?"

"Of course I remember!" he whispered back. "But to already have another suitor?" he said, pain now etching his tone.

"He is *not* a suitor," she insisted. "He is Lord Bennett's heir. His nephew, an artist." She took a deep breath, summoning calm. "Jedediah, I made a deal with him. If I allowed him to sketch me, he would convince his uncle to pay you partially in supplies for the Double T."

Jed put his hands on his hips and lifted his chin. He took a deep breath of his own, schooling his expression into something more dignified. "That is glad news, Selah. I am happy that you secured supplies for our people."

His use of *our people* gave her momentary hope. But his use of *glad news* brought no light to his face.

He looked aside, then to the ground, rubbing his neck. "And you are right. I have no right to respond in this way. I said it myself.

You would be safest if you found a rich suitor. And here he might be," he said, waving toward the house. "Forgive me. I was merely taken aback. I shall not stand in your way."

"*Jedediah*," she said, willing herself to remain calm, "if you would only allow me to explain—"

"What is there to explain, Selah?" he asked, his voice cracking. "I saw your hands, your tears, your shared passion. Did you know him, back in England?"

"No. We met only today."

He frowned in disbelief, ran his hands through his hair, and straightened his jacket. "I may be a simple man, but I am not simple-minded. There was much more between you two than is possible for a couple who only recently met." He pointed down the path toward the grotto. "I must go."

She folded her arms, dismay turning to fury. "Go, then."

He paused and his lips parted a moment. "You are not coming?" He pointed toward the house. "You intend to return to him?"

"'Tis not your affair. Go and play as you promised, Jedediah. Perhaps, come morning, you shall see how egregious your accusation has been."

With one last tumultuous glance, he pivoted in the gravel and stalked away.

She remained where she was for several minutes before Mr. Holloway appeared. He paused before approaching her and remained a few steps away, hat in hands. "Forgive me, Miss Banning. Apparently the good reverend leaped to an unfair conclusion. I was not aware he is your suitor."

"He is not my suitor," she muttered, stepping past him to the main path. In the distance, the sun was setting over the water, casting a broad swath of coral, tangerine, and pumpkin layers across the sky. The audience cheered as Jedediah took the small stage and sat at the piano.

He began with a stormy arrangement by Beethoven that she had never heard him play in practice, nor ever for that matter. He played it for her, she knew, just as she had known he played for her when she lay in her bed upstairs recovering at the Double T. Expressing his devotion, his care for her then. Now expressing what he thought to be a betrayal.

"Do you wish me to escort you to your seat, Miss Banning?" Mr. Holloway asked. "Or would you permit me to conclude my sketch?"

"The house," she said wanly. "Let us return."

Because, at that moment, the only good thing she could think about was the barrels of flour and corn they would take home to Nevis after this night was through.

CHAPTER TWENTY-SEVEN

Jedediah's anger seemed to ease as he played through one tumultuous selection after another, gradually moving to the more lighthearted pieces he had practiced to play on St. Kitts. By the time the concert was over, his fingers numb, his back aching, the audience cheering, he rose wearily, bowed perfunctorily, and then, despite his own internal warning, searched the audience for Selah.

She was not there.

Had she not come at all?

But could he truly blame her for not attending?

He shook hand after hand, accepting the congratulations of a job well done, praise for a fine evening spent, as if in a daze. Through it all he was searching for her, hoping to find her. *But what then?* he thought, wondering over their conversation. By the time his frustration was spent halfway through the concert, he admitted to himself that he might have unfairly accused her. That he might have happened upon them at an unusual moment. And again, that he had no right to feel jealous, regardless of what was—or was not—transpiring between them.

At last he was alone and he climbed the steep path of the hill, behind most of the guests who had attended, accompanied by Lord Bennett, who was already speaking of another concert to take place in a couple of weeks. Dimly, he thought he answered him, but he could not be sure. All he could think about was Selah.

How shocked she had seemed at his accusation. And how good it had felt to be alone with her again. Speaking to her. Hearing her speak to him. Even if they had been arguing.

Inwardly he groaned. If Lord Bennett caught wind of this, he would surely rescind his offer for Jedediah to return. And he had to admit that he enjoyed playing music for others. Moreover, he had to admit that he loved the idea of some coins in his pocket, coins he could use to help Selah in buying freedom papers for the people they loved—or earning supplies to aid the people of the Double T.

Or elsewhere? Might God lead him to leave Nevis? In some ways it would be ever so much easier. But even as he thought it, he did not know if he could bear leaving the Double T. All those people who had wound their way into his heart. Including Selah. Even watching her from afar was something. To never glimpse her again? Hear her encouraging Chully with her English lessons? Comforting a feverish toddler?

He made his excuses with Lord Bennett and paused in the flower-covered nook where he had left Selah. He shook his head. The idea of her beginning another relationship had unsettled him to the core. Where were his fine statements of faith now? Where was his trust in the Lord? And why did God remain stubbornly silent on this front?

He knew one thing. He owed Selah an apology.

He paced back and forth, trying to figure out what God was trying to tell him, but heard no words of guidance, felt no stirrings in his heart that might bring comfort. Knowing he would be expected at the party, he forced himself to head to the huge house just as Lord Bennett was entering the garden.

"You shall join the party on the veranda?" Lord Bennett asked pointedly when Jedediah turned toward the side parlor. He could see that candlelight still danced in there. Were the couple still present? Perhaps he could seek out a moment of private conversation with Selah.

"Of course. But I must have a word with Miss Banning before I join you all."

"Good man," he said, clapping him on the shoulder. "I am certain she will be eager to congratulate you on a rousing performance."

Jedediah only managed to nod, hands behind his back, as the older gentleman ambled off to join his guests. Tentatively, Jed turned and went to the side parlor. Seeing the door was halfway shut, he knocked.

"Enter," called a man, sounding distracted.

He pushed open the door. With some dismay he saw that Selah's chair was empty and that Mr. Holloway was alone. The artist stood at his canvas, continuing to sketch, although his subject had left. He gave Jed the briefest of glances. "May I be of assistance?" he asked stiffly.

He moved inward. "I am Jedediah Reed," he said, extending a hand.

The man shook it while showing no pleasure in the exchange. "Ernest Holloway."

"I fear I have proven myself a fool, Mr. Holloway," Jedediah said. "Please forgive my rash reaction."

"'Tis not I from whom you must seek forgiveness, but your lady," Mr. Holloway said, returning to his sketch. His hand stilled for a moment. "She truly is a remarkable woman, unworthy of such base assumptions."

"Agreed," Jed said slowly. He straightened. "However, she is not my lady."

Mr. Holloway cocked his head. "But your reaction . . ."

Jedediah lifted a brow and raised his hands. "We were once courting. But no longer."

"I see."

Was that the tiniest bit of victory lacing the edges of his eyes? Something told Jed that Holloway already knew there was no courtship. He simply was verifying that by his account, it truly had ended.

"Come," Mr. Holloway said after a moment, gesturing to his canvas.

Jedediah rounded the canvas and faced the work. He swallowed hard. The artist had created a perfect likeness of his Selah. Discovered and depicted her tenderness, as well as her tenacity. Her strength, as well as her wounding. Her beauty in spite of the scar.

"It . . ." he began, then cleared his throat. "'Tis nothing short of remarkable, Mr. Holloway. You have captured her."

"I would not mind capturing her heart as well."

Jed shot him a glance.

"I wager it is yet yours, however, given how she set after you."

Jed tried to swallow but found his mouth dry. What was this?

"I am one of the newest residents of Saint Kitts, Reed. I am here to stay, and my uncle believes it high time for me to find a bride. If you are not going to resume your courtship of Miss Banning, I very well might do my best to win her."

"I shall not resume my courtship of Selah," he said woodenly, watching as Holloway turned to shade in the hollow of her neck on the canvas. "I have not the resources she deserves and needs."

"Are you certain of that?" He paused and looked him in the eye. "When I go after a woman, I want her heart. Not part of it. I shall not pursue her until I know she no longer pines for you."

"She shall not pine for me for long." *My rash reaction this very eve might have ended any pining.* Jedediah sighed and walked away, then paused at the door and turned. "Tell me. Why was it that I found you kneeling before her, her hand in yours? Why did she have tears running down her cheeks?"

Mr. Holloway crossed his arms and gave him a disgusted look. "She was telling me of the day she was wounded. Explaining to me the passion that forced her to intervene with the three slave sisters. When she was overcome, I moved to comfort her. Not as a lover, you fool, but as any gentleman might when faced with a lady's distress."

His words were warranted, but still took him aback. Jedediah drew in a long, deep breath and turned away, hand on his chest.

Why did it feel as if his heart hurt? He looked to the ceiling, then over to the candle. "Has she rejoined the party?"

"She claimed a headache and elected to retire to her room for the night." Holloway returned to his shading. "Why do I assume you shall do naught but pace the floor of your own?"

The next day, there was little of the gaiety they had felt en route to St. Kitts, given the distance between Selah and Jedediah. She knew that they were casting a pall over the group aboard the *Hartwick*, but could not find a way to break the ice that seemed to surround her heart. It was as if she allowed it to crack, *she* might crack again, which was what had led her hands to be in Mr. Holloway's the night before, with tears flowing down her face.

The others did their best to keep up a conversation in the midst of their shared silence.

"Did you hear Major Tarone talking?" Verity asked Ket. "He said they have managed to push General Washington and his forces out of New York."

"Yes, by setting the city afire," Philip said, shaking his head in disgust.

"Could it have been the rebels themselves setting it afire?" Gray asked, trimming a sail. "'Tis common enough not to wish to leave spoils for the victors."

"I think not," Verity said. "Washington shall aim to recover the city as swiftly as he can."

"Fires can quickly spread in such tight quarters," Ket said, a hand to her burgeoning belly.

"True." Gray cast her a tender smile as he caught the gesture.

Their intimacy, their ongoing constant love, seemed to agitate Selah today rather than warm her. She refused to look to Jedediah. Refused to, no matter how her eyes itched to do so.

"I hope Ian is not in the midst of that battle," she managed to say, knowing that her silence punished her sisters as much as Jed.

"As do I," Verity said. She gave her a wry grin. "But knowing my husband, I doubt he is far from the fray. He would be quite pleased with you and Jedediah managing to secure more supplies for the Double T," she added. "With him leagues away, I know he shall be fretting over all of us."

"And yet we find ourselves in better stead than almost any other on-island," Gray said. "After our auction next week, I am certain we shall make it through the harvest."

"We are so very grateful to you, Jedediah, for lending your talents to the cause," Ket said.

"'Tis the least I could do, given your hospitality."

The group quieted, each likely wondering how much longer that hospitality might be required. In some ways, it would be easier if he moved on. And yet Selah could not imagine what that would be like. Despite her anger toward him, the hurt she felt, the idea of never seeing him again, serving alongside him in the meetinghouse . . . well, that felt utterly wrong as well. Might they find their way back to friendship in time?

She sighed and leaned over the edge of the boat, letting her hand drag in the water. She considered how some water in this channel washed ashore on Nevis, some on St. Kitts, and some of it joined the greater Atlantic. How easily could a life's course change? Jedediah had made a choice that changed the course for both of them. Was it right? God-led? Or born of his own fears and failures?

"Lord Bennett spoke of having you return, Jedediah," Gray said. "Shall you entertain that offer?"

"Perhaps," he said. "I . . . I am uncertain of how much longer I might abide on Nevis. It could be that the Lord is encouraging me onward."

"But not before you play at the auction next week," Verity said.

"I think not. But if so, perhaps Gray might step in. I have heard him play his violin. He is quite good."

Gray scowled. "I only play for my family and, on occasion, friends."

Keturah let out a scoffing laugh. "Was that not what Jedediah wished himself, until we pressed him into service? What leaves you free from serving in such a way? And if the two of you played together, we might draw people from Hispaniola!" She clapped her hands together. "Oh, Gray, 'twould be marvelous! Remember how it was to listen to Jed play with Selah?"

"And if he could do that with Selah," Verity jumped in with a sly wink in her direction before it became awkward, "imagine what 'twould be like to hear two accomplished musicians playing together."

Selah laughed under her breath and shook her head, accepting her sister's gentle teasing. But as the Double T came into view, she remembered how it had felt to play the harpsichord together that magical night. When everything had seemed possible, opportunity spreading before them in every direction.

On the dock, Philip and Gray assisted the ladies in disembarking, and Selah hurried down the wooden plank, eager to be away from Jedediah. She wanted to scurry to the meetinghouse, inquire about how they all had fared in their absence, fill her mind and heart with anything but Jedediah. But an hour later, he trudged up the steps, a barrel of flour in his arms. Glancing up in surprise, she rose from where she had been playing with a baby on the floor, the child doing his best to roll over. "Oh," she said, suddenly unable to think of a single thing to say. "Good day," she said to the young mother, casting her a half smile.

"Good day, Miss Selah," said the girl.

"Selah," Jed said quietly, setting down the barrel and reaching for her elbow as she passed. "May I have a word?"

She frowned, considering denying him even that. But then she swallowed and nodded. Rubbing her hands together, she went to the corner of the porch and turned to him.

"Selah, I behaved a fool last night," he began. "Can you please forgive me?"

"I-I suppose I might," she said. But why? Why did he care? Why not simply move along their separate shores?

"Do you believe we might continue our . . . ministry here together? In time?"

She stared at him. Their ministry? She believed it was possible. They did share the same hopes and dreams for all enslaved people. But was it all they would share? Forever?

"Per-perhaps," she said. "I would need to pray about that."

He nodded. "As would I. And I shall do my best not to . . . interfere between you and any other . . . gentlemen."

"Very well," she managed to say stiffly. Then she scurried past him and down the steps before he could see the tears welling in her eyes yet again.

For days, she continued to largely avoid him, but it became increasingly difficult when he arrived at the house each evening to practice on the harpsichord. Ket had convinced Gray to play at least a few songs with Jed, and so the two of them went through those pieces again and again. All the workers of the plantation took to bringing down blankets and spreading them out beneath the veranda so they could enjoy the music. As much as Selah wanted to be away from Jedediah, she wanted to be with her people, so she sat with them. She knew many of them wondered what had ended their courtship, but none asked. Still, she saw the shared sidelong glances around her, the concern in their eyes. To them, they thought their favorite preacher and the young mistress of the plantation were destined to be a couple.

If only it were that simple.

The morning of the auction, Selah watched Verity working with the geldings, reminding them of their manners so that they might show better come three o'clock.

People began to arrive as early as one o'clock, spreading out blankets and food and jugs of punch to share. It was with some surprise that the family saw five, then six, then seven ketches arrive from St. Kitts, word spreading from Lord Bennett of the fine auction to come. When Selah was up at the house, Sansa brought word that yet another had arrived, this one carrying Lord Bennett, Mr. Holloway, and two other men. Her pulse picked up at the news. Mr. Holloway had been charming the week before, but thinking about him only reminded her of Jedediah's sour reaction.

At least then she knew he cared, even if it was jealousy that drove him. He had promised not to interfere with any other courtship. Would he stick to that? Did she want him to do so?

She chose to wear another fine gown found in the *Juliana*, this one the creamy color of champagne and trimmed with Spanish lace at the neck and three-quarter sleeves. She sat down beside Ket to have Margaret and Ann—two lady's maids training with Sansa—see to their hair.

"Oh, why so glum, Sissy?" Keturah asked, patting her leg as she glimpsed her face in the mirror.

She stared back at her. *You know why.*

Ket gave her a sorrowful look. She looked beautiful in an ivory silk gown, her cheeks holding a bit more roundness these days, her eyes bright. Perhaps a gift of her advancing pregnancy? Or love? Love that did not fail as it had for Selah?

"Would it be easier if we asked him to move on?" Ket whispered.

"No. Well, yes. But that does not seem right either," Selah said.

"I hate to see you so miserable," Ket said. "This simply cannot continue."

"No," Selah agreed. But the idea of seeing Jed walk out of sight, never to return, made her want to bawl anew.

Downstairs, they heard Jedediah begin playing a joyful, jaunty tune on the harpsichord, a piece Selah had heard him practice for days. Four men had moved the harpsichord out to the veranda through the double doors so that more might hear the music better than the last time he performed at the Double T. "Give me but a moment, Margaret," Selah said to the maid. She moved to the windowsill and closed her eyes, feeling the delight of the trade winds on her face, as well as the dancing notes of the harpsichord in her ears.

"He truly has a gift," Keturah said, leaning against the other corner of the sill to listen.

"Indeed," Selah returned with a wistful smile. "One of many, I believe." She looked across the lawn. At least fifteen blankets had been spread already, with perhaps fifty guests milling about. One blond man stood, hand inside his jacket at the belly, another hand holding a cup of punch, looking her way. He smiled and raised his cup as if in a toast, and Selah smiled in return.

"Who is it?" Ket asked, seeking out who made her smile.

"'Tis Mr. Holloway, Lord Bennett's nephew." She hurried to sit on a stool, and Margaret continued to curl her hair. Her smile faded as she remembered that troublesome eve.

Ket crossed her arms and looked to her. "Clearly there is something more you must tell me."

With a sigh, Selah recounted what had transpired.

"So Jedediah found you in tears."

"And my hand in Mr. Holloway's too."

"Selah!"

She shook her head. "It was entirely innocent. But I am certain it did not appear that way. Jedediah was quite cross."

"I see." She returned to her dressing chair so Ann could finish her hair as well.

"He apologized the next day. Promised not to interfere with any further courtship from any man."

"Nor should he. He has relinquished the right!" She glanced at Selah. "But you still wish he had not."

Selah took a deep breath. "I think he regrets it."

"As well he should."

"I do too."

Keturah squeezed her hand. "Oh, Selah, I am sorry. But if it is meant to be, you two shall find your way together again."

"You believe so?"

"I do." She eyed her sister in the mirror. "But what about this Mr. Holloway? Was there something that intrigued you about him? Some reason you wished to spend more time with him? Was that why you agreed to allow him to sketch you?"

Selah sighed. She knew that Keturah would much rather she be courted by a wealthy heir than a penniless preacher. She could hear the hint of hope in her voice. As an older sister, her responsibility was to see Selah make as fine a match as possible. And no doubt she thought she had failed Selah, watching her weep over Jedediah.

"I confess it felt good to be admired by a gentleman, despite my scar."

"You know that you are still beautiful, Selah," Keturah said softly.

"I know. You say that. Jedediah has told me too. But to be admired by a stranger . . ."

"'Tis a thrill," Keturah said, lifting a triple strand of pearls to her neck. Ann fastened it behind her. "No matter how old or pregnant you might be, trust me, 'tis always a sweet reminder when it happens. The trick," she said, lifting a finger, "is to decide whom you wish to admire you most. And to not lead on the wrong gent." She rose, leaned over and kissed Selah's cheek, then met her gaze in the looking glass. "Tread carefully, Sissy. If you intend to recapture Jedediah's heart, then be very cautious around your Mr. Holloway. There is a reason they call jealousy the green-eyed monster."

Chapter Twenty-Eight

By three o'clock the Double T was filled with carriages, horses, picnic blankets and baskets—nearly three times as many as the week before. The mood was celebratory, with folks laughing and mingling as they had in better times. The weather was temperate, though Selah was glad for the shade of her parasol.

Selah looked to Ket as they strolled, greeting one friend after another. Nellie carried Madeleine on her hip, directly behind Ket. They stopped to greet neighbors and friends and acquaintances. "It seems as if the injunction against us has been lifted," Selah whispered, taking her arm.

"Oh, 'tis still there, just beneath the surface. But word has clearly spread about your Reverend Reed's musical talent. No one wants to miss his music, nor the spectacle of Verity's auction." They paused on a small hill, which allowed them to see from house to stables. Up on the veranda, Jedediah was playing, and the harpsichord was surrounded with people. Verity was down in the corral, working the team. Already she had drawn a crowd, and yet she remained entirely focused on the horses.

"'Tis truly a shame that she need sell them," Selah said. "I know it pains her."

Keturah nodded. "'Tis. But I have to admire her too. She understands the strain we are under. Between what she had been able to supply for us, and your own negotiation with Lord Bennett for Jedediah to earn his share in goods rather than coin, we stand a chance of making it until Mr. Kirk returns from England with his supply ship. He shall trade with us come harvest."

"We shall fare even better if the gardens begin producing next month," Selah said.

"They seem to be coming along quite nicely."

"Is that where Gray is?"

"Yes. He took about six men up with him, about an hour past. He could not wait to show them. But he should be back now," she said worriedly, glancing at the sun. "He is probably avoiding the house and his turn on the violin."

"Both the gardens and his playing shall win him more admirers, I wager."

"Especially if they want some seed of their own."

"Who would not? Most shall soon be harvesting sugar, as will we. Why not put in a few acres of corn and squash? It shall be perfect timing."

"I hope so."

Kuri and Wednesday, two grooms training with Gideon, hauled Verity's beautiful carriage to the front of the stables, then set to rubbing it to a beautiful shine with cloths. The men who had gone to visit the middle field arrived by horseback, smiling and speaking amiably. Their guests, appearing excited and invigorated, dismounted. Servants tied their mounts to posts before the house while Gray rode his gelding down to the stables. Verity's pair became excited at his approach and broke from her orderly lead, making her appear quite cross and, in turn, making Selah giggle.

"Selah," said Esmerelda Weland, catching her arm. Selah turned to face her, and the girl gasped, bringing a gloved hand to her mouth. "Oh, forgive me! I had heard about your wounding . . . but I had not thought 'twould be so . . ."

Selah swallowed hard. Esmerelda had always had the tact of a vervet monkey, and this only solidified her feelings. And yet it stung. She had seen several others react and turn away from her rather than be forced to find something to say.

"Yes, well, a whip is bound to leave a terrible mark, yes? Perhaps you can see to it that your overseer does not use one on the slaves at your plantation." She gave the girl a tight smile, waiting, unblinking, until the girl nodded eagerly. Then Selah parted from her.

"You handled that rather well," Keturah said, taking her arm again.

Selah sighed. "Women look upon me with sorrow, as if I have suffered something from which I shall never recover. Men look upon me with outrage, as if 'tis they who have been robbed. I find it difficult not to absorb their feelings." She shook her head. "Truly, 'tis only Jedediah, Mr. Holloway, our family and our people who have made me feel anything akin to normal since it occurred."

Those from the veranda began walking down the hill to get closer for the auction, and Selah and Keturah joined them.

"In time, the scar shall fade," Keturah said.

"In a way I wish it would not."

"What?" she said, pulling her to a stop.

"It creates a nice division for me. Those who see nothing but that which is on the surface, and those who see what truly matters."

"I suppose that is true."

"Ladies and gentlemen!" Gray called. "The auction for Verity's matched pair of geldings and her carriage shall commence in fifteen minutes. Please approach the corral now if you intend to bid and ask her any questions you may have!"

A low murmur at the back of the crowd made Selah turn. Her eyes rounded and she gasped, even as she reached for Ket's hand.

"What is it?" Keturah muttered, following her gaze. Philip stepped forward, taking Selah's elbow, while Ket strode ahead, obviously intent on intercepting the intruders.

Angus Shubert had made his way in uninvited. He and his men were followed by Major Woodget, Captain Howard, and the lieutenants who resided at the Double T, along with four other soldiers, all of them on horseback.

286

Jedediah caught her gaze and began to make his way over to her.

Selah fought for breath. She knew people were looking her way, curious as to how she might react, and she strived to regain her equilibrium. "'Tis all right, Selah," Jed said, turning his back to her, blocking her from Shubert's view. "Gray and Ket shall see to him," he whispered over his shoulder.

She nodded quickly, grateful that he understood. That he was there when it mattered most, even if he could not stand beside her the way she most wanted. Shielding her. From behind him, she could peek around to see what she wished but hide as well. All without it being apparent to others in the crowd.

Gray strode through the corral gate and up the hillside, coming alongside Keturah. The crowd fell silent. "This is a private event, Shubert. Find your way out," Gray said.

"You are about to hold an auction, are you not?"

"Yes. A *private* auction," Gray said.

Shubert reached inside his jacket and pulled out a paper. "Private auctions are not allowed. By public decree, dated 1 December 1713, our forefathers made certain that the resources relinquished by one should be accessible to all."

The crowd murmured their surprise and dismay. If Shubert was here to bid, surely no one could outbid him.

"My horses shall never be in your hands," Verity said. "I shall cancel the auction."

Mr. Holloway reached Selah and Jedediah, making Jed stiffen.

"Good day, Miss Banning," he said. "Reverend Reed," he added deferentially. "Tell me, why is that man unwelcome?"

"That is Angus Shubert, the wealthiest planter on Nevis. And the one who wounded me," she added wanly.

Mr. Holloway frowned and looked to Shubert and Gray, who were arguing, with Major Woodget attempting to intervene. "So your sister clearly does not wish Shubert to win her geldings and carriage. And Shubert is insisting the auction go on?"

"Presumably," Jedediah answered for her.

Mr. Holloway looked to Selah. "And your sister intends to sell

287

to the bidder who not only bids highest but also can pay his debt in supplies, yes? Not coin."

"Yes," Selah said, frowning in confusion.

Mr. Holloway pursed his lips and lifted a brow. "Well then, I would wager my uncle would have that in the bag. And rest assured, he is most keen on obtaining those horses and carriage. He brought the goods to prove it." He gestured toward their ketch, anchored below.

"Oh!" Selah breathed, eyes rounding in excitement. "I must go and tell them!" She touched his forearm in gratitude as she passed, ignoring when both men observed her action, giving it unfair import. She pressed through the crowd, reaching Verity and whispering the news in her ear. Then she moved over to Keturah as Verity hurried to Gray to inform him. She was as near to Angus Shubert as she was willing to get. Even from fifty paces, she could feel his eyes on her, the glee practically radiating off of him.

How he reveled in his power. Pressing his way into their private gathering by using a sixty-year-old decree to force his way in. Likely hoping to remind everyone here who controlled this island, no matter how they might be warming to the Covingtons again.

Gray and Ket walked off a few paces to talk. He did well in hiding his pleasure at her news. Instead, he turned back to the crowd, giving Shubert only a cursory glance. "My wife has asked me to lead the way in temperance and peace, something this man"—he pointed at Angus Shubert—"seldom does. Angus, you may remain on my property for the auction and then you shall depart directly afterward. Agreed?"

Shubert crossed his arms and narrowed his eyes, clearly aware something was afoot. "Agreed," he said.

"You may stand here, but you shall not move from this spot. I do not want you anywhere near any of the women of my family. Not my wife, not Verity, and certainly not Selah." He stepped closer to Shubert. "If you dare to approach any one of them, you shall find yourself on the wrong end of my pistol."

"You dare to threaten me?" Shubert said, huffing a laugh.

Gray stepped closer. "Most assuredly."

"Come now, gentlemen," Major Woodget said. "Be at peace. I shall keep an eye on Councilman Shubert. Gray, go about your business."

After a long, challenging look at Angus, Gray gestured to Verity. "Please. Proceed as you see fit."

"Gentlemen and ladies," Verity began, climbing atop a box so she could be easily seen and heard over the corral fence. She stood in the center of the corral, encouraging the geldings to continue to prance around the circle. "As you can see, we are offering my three-year-old geldings, purchased from an esteemed breeder in North Carolina. They are fifteen hands tall, in pristine health, and broken to both saddle and carriage yoke. In addition, we shall include my lovely carriage, one of the finest on all of Nevis. As advertised, we are offering these horses and carriage to the highest bidder in goods, not coin, given that our goal is to keep the good people of the Double T in supplies for as long as possible."

"What is the starting bid?" cried a man, sitting on a picnic blanket high on the hill.

"Ten hogsheads of corn, four of dried beef, and four of dried fish," Verity returned.

This set tongues to wagging. It was a fortune in foodstuffs, enough to keep them alive for a good month.

"Would you take it in sugar instead?" called another man.

This made everyone laugh, including Verity. "I fear not," she returned with a smile.

"I shall meet your opening bid!" Shubert intoned.

Verity's smile faded, and she barely managed to give him a nod.

"I will add a barrel of flour to that bid!" called Mr. Malone, a man with a large plantation on the southeast side of the island.

"And I would add two!" called Lord Browning, urged on by his wife.

"Fine," Shubert called with a dismissive wave of his hand. "I will add *three* barrels of flour." He smiled in satisfaction, as if that would certainly seal the deal.

Selah closed her eyes and groaned. What would his bid mean to the people on his plantations? How could he provide enough for them? Perhaps he had enough, but fear of seeing his slaves starve was yet another reason for him not to win this auction.

"I shall add a hogshead of corn!" cried Mr. Girard.

That surprised Selah. Perhaps his plantation was doing better than she had thought—or he had put aside significant stores.

Shubert lifted an arm. "I shall add a second! Let us be done with it."

A shiver of fear ran down Selah's back. It was a fortune in goods. Now enough to keep them supplied at the Double T for nearly two months. But what of his people?

"No, not yet," Lord Bennett called, rising to a standing position, cane in his hands before him. "I offer you double the opening bid, including those three additional barrels of flour, and two additional barrels of corn. With one caveat."

Shubert turned and gaped at the man. The entire crowd stilled, as if everyone were wondering if they had heard him right. It far exceeded the value of the horses and carriage, as lovely as they were. "My caveat is that I wish the young Reverend Reed to return to Saint Kitts each month for three months to play for us again. And if you, Mr. Covington, are as fine on the violin as I have heard tell, I would very much like you to accompany Mr. Reed. If we sell out each event, there shall be a bonus of a hogshead of dried beef each evening that occurs, as well as an additional stipend."

Gray's eyes rounded in surprise, yet his face was torn between pleasure and frustration. Selah's heart clenched. Would he say no to this potential bounty?

He eyed Jedediah. Jed grinned and lifted his brows and hands. He waved to Gray. "'Tis your decision. I shall serve you and this plantation if I may."

"Then so shall I," Gray said, shaking Lord Bennett's hand.

Jedediah turned in excitement toward Selah, reaching out to touch her hand. But then his face fell as soon as his fingers brushed hers. "Forgive me. I . . . forgot myself."

"There is nothing to forgive," she said softly. "This is such a blessing!"

"Indeed!"

"So the final bid is twenty-two hogsheads of corn," Verity called, "eight of beef, eight of fish, three of flour, all in exchange for my team, my carriage, and Jedediah and Gray's musical talents on three separate occasions. Would anyone care to outbid Lord Bennett?" Selah noted she did not dare to glance in Angus's direction. "Going once, twice, three times . . . sold!" she cried, grinning up at Lord Bennett.

The crowd erupted in applause and rose immediately to discuss it and shake their heads in wonder. Jedediah, as if not trusting himself, clasped his hands together and simply gave her a partial lopsided smile before turning away. Selah's eyes flew to Shubert. Gray stood before him, hands on his hips, waiting. "That concludes the auction, Shubert. Our party is a private event. You must leave now."

His mouth set in a thin line, Shubert gave Gray a long, silent look before putting on his hat and mounting his horse. Selah watched him ride up the road, not looking left or right, only forward. Major Woodget sent two soldiers with him but remained behind, turning to smile and shake Gray's hand. Selah moved away from the crowd, trying to accept the wondrous fact that they had just won such bounty that they need not fear rations, or worse, starvation, for quite some time.

"And again I find you among the flowers," Mr. Holloway said.

She spun around in surprise and then smiled, even as her hand was at her throat. "Mr. Holloway—"

"Ernest, if you would be so kind. 'Mr. Holloway' is so very formal, particularly among the islands, yes?"

"Ernest, then," she said. "And you must call me Selah. We are forever in your uncle's debt."

"'Tis he who shall be in debt to you," he said, offering his arm. "Rest assured my uncle is a clever businessman. He shall likely triple his investment, given the reverend's agreement to return to

Saint Kitts to play. The island is agog with talk of his last concert. My uncle shall have no difficulty filling the amphitheater on those occasions."

"Then all shall gain from our agreement." She tried to find Jedediah in the crowd ahead but did not see him. Perhaps he was already on his way to the veranda, intent on playing . . .

"I shall look forward to showing you the portrait I am painting of you," Ernest said, turning to take her hand in both of his. "I am halfway through a copy of it in oil."

"In oil!" she said, pulling her hand away. "Such an extravagance!"

He cocked his head and gave her a small smile. "I was dissatisfied with the charcoal. I wanted to capture the lovely golden tones of your skin."

"Oh!" she said, flushing.

"And seeing you tonight, I realize I need to add gold to your pretty brown eyes. Such a remarkable shade, they are. Halfway between amber and hazelnut." His own eyes seemed to cover her, searching every inch as if committing it to memory. "Perhaps you can sit for me again?"

"I am not certain that is wise, Ernest."

He followed her gaze up to the veranda, where Jed was playing. "Pardon me. I was under the impression the two of you were no longer courting."

"We are not," she said.

"But your heart has not caught up with what your mind has decided," he said gently.

She glanced at him in surprise. "Invite a sister along, then," Ernest said, lifting his hands and giving her an easy smile. "You shall see there is no seduction transpiring, only an artist seeking time with his muse."

Jedediah began playing, a light celebratory piece.

"Ahh, well, *perhaps*," she said, stepping around him. She was his *muse*? "Good day, Ernest. Please tell your uncle I am most sincerely grateful. We all are."

"I shall," he said, allowing her to escape. She was torn as she left his side. Glad to be free from what she could not quite pin down in terms of romantic intrigue, and yet at a loss too.

Down below, Verity was introducing Lord Bennett to his new team of horses while Brutus soared overhead. Selah was so very glad that it was he who had won them. She could not even begin to imagine what would have happened if Angus had somehow managed to offer the winning bid. There was a part of her that admired Angus the tiniest bit for riding away. Surely, he had the food in his storehouses to dominate had it been but pride that drove him. But he had showed a modicum of temperance and wisdom—care for the future and for his people. That was likely the driving force. Shubert knew, as they all did, that if his slaves were not fed, productivity would decline. And there was one thing Shubert wanted most: bragging rights for outproducing the Double T, acre for acre.

Keturah was grinning, showing off Madeleine to their neighbors. She caught Selah's eye and began making her way to her. Gray lifted a cup of punch in a toast with several others, and Jedediah moved on to a new piece, surrounded by admirers.

Selah reached for Madeleine, suddenly wanting the comforting weight of the chubby toddler in her arms. The babe was hot, but she loved how she nestled into her neck sleepily, then leaned back to look at her in utter delight. *She does not see my scars either.*

Verity climbed the hill toward them, a wistful smile on her face. "Well, that transpired about as well as I could have imagined it," she said, gesturing to the corral.

"Agreed," Keturah said.

"Indeed," Selah added.

Verity circled with her sisters. "Two months' worth of food! Surely this is of God," she said. "What with me unable to return to Statia at the moment. Do you sense it? God's provision and care?"

"Through every bit of it," Selah said, taking her hand. "Even to Angus attempting to take over and then having to turn tail."

Verity lifted a brow at Selah. "Might I come along with you to Saint Kitts for Jedediah's next concert?"

"That would be up to him," Selah said. Clearly her sister had intrigue on her mind. "I am not certain that I shall attend. But for now, might we only concentrate on the moment? The bounty and beauty of this moment? Here we are, three years after arrival, and look how God has blessed us." She blinked back tears. "I know it pains you, Ver, having Ian gone. But he is doing what he has been called to do, yes? And here, Keturah has given us this fine bonny lass of a niece," she added, trying her best at the Scottish brogue, "with another on the way. And now we have the hope of Mr. Kirk's arrival in a few months, and in the meantime a storehouse full of goods, thanks to your sweet sacrifice." She squeezed Verity's hand. "Thank you, Sissy, from the bottom of my heart. Thank you for providing for the people of the Double T."

"Of course," Verity said, eyes welling with tears. "This is how we do it, yes? We Bannings. We sacrifice for one another. We help each other to get through. We love one another through, in spite of, because of."

"And count every blessing," Ket said, turning to gaze upon the crowd around them.

Chapter Twenty-Nine

Selah put the slumbering Madeleine down in her bassinette as Gray played his last song with Jed. Nellie came into the room from the small adjacent room that served as her sleeping quarters, which was hardly wider than a single cot. "I will see to her, Miss Selah. You go on back to your party."

"Oh, that is all right," Selah said, moving instead to the window. She was glad for the excuse to be away from all who lingered yet below. The wagons and carriages were in line, people ready to be away and back to their own homes now that the party was over. She watched them as they clambered aboard and departed, glad for the renewed sense of camaraderie among the islanders, and yet also glad to see them go.

She leaned into the windowsill as Nellie saw to changing Madeleine's diaper and rocked her, crooning. She waited as more wagons and carriages pulled away, until only Keturah and Gray stood in the yard below, arm in arm and looking out to sea, stealing a kiss.

"'Twas a good day for us, Nellie," Selah said.

"A fine day, Miss Selah," the girl answered. But there was something amiss in her tone.

Selah paused, studying her. The girl was trying not to look her way. "Nellie?"

The girl, slight and yet strong, turned partially toward her,

Madeleine yet in her arms. The babe's eyes blinked heavily, and she reached up to touch the nursemaid's chin in contented, sleepy bliss. But Nellie's eyes dragged up to meet Selah's, clearly wrestling with something.

The girl lifted Madeleine up, kissed her forehead, then settled her beneath a light blanket in the cradle.

"You are alarming me, Nellie," Selah said. "What is it?" She took the girl's hand, silently urging her to unburden herself.

In the flickering light of the lamp, her hard swallow was all the more obvious. Selah faced her and took both of her hands. "What is it, my friend?"

Nellie's brows knit together. "Miss Selah, there is talk of insurrection," she whispered.

"Insurrection?" Selah repeated. "Here?"

"Not on the Double T," Nellie rushed on. "There are a few troublemakers yet here. But most see what you all are doing, how you aim to aid us, and are for you. 'Tis on the neighboring plantations, miss. Talk among the slave market come Sunday. Among some here this afternoon, accompanying their masters. There are many folks who are suffering, miss. Not getting enough to eat. Driven harder than ever before. And that . . ."

Selah's scalp tingled, but she forced herself to remain silent.

"There are some who are saying we should take over, Miss Selah," she confessed. "There are some who say we need to rise up and take what is ours."

Dread surged through Selah's mind. "Does Matthew know of this?" she managed to ask. "Jedediah?"

Nellie shook her head.

Selah frowned. "Is this a small group? More bravado than brawn?"

"No," Nellie said, fairly miserable as she shook her head, trying to pull away from Selah's handhold. "Only those most loyal to their masters, or those likely to stand against the idea of it, have been kept from it."

"Gideon? Primus? Have they known of it?"

The girl shook her head in misery. Then she lifted her eyes to meet Selah's. "You know they would never let it happen. None of us would. We would never let them hurt you. Or Madeleine. Or Master Gray or Lady Ket."

A chill ran down Selah's back. Not because of the girl's sweet assurance but because of what she was *not* saying. There were other families in peril, this very night. Some who had attended their auction and picnic.

Not that she could fault the starving slaves. She paced away, thinking, putting her hands to her face and rubbing, trying to will logic into this incredibly volatile situation. And yet if their roles were reversed—if she were in Nellie's shoes, and Nellie hers—would she not be thinking of radical options? Or if she and Ket and Ver had arrived on Nevis in chains, stripped to the waist for men to openly peruse, to pry open their jaws to examine the health of their teeth . . . if they'd been separated, would she be prepared to fight?

Yes, she thought. *Yes, yes, yes.* The thought did not bring her comfort, only a sick feeling in her belly. She reached out again to Nellie, taking her hand. "Thank you for telling me. I know that must have been difficult. But believe me, Nellie. All I want is the good for as many people on Nevis as possible, be they black or white." She turned to her, taking her other hand. "There might be some who think this effort shall be successful. And I understand the impulse to fight against those who oppress you." She thought of Angus Shubert, riding into the Double T that day as if he had every right, when all she wanted to do was drive him away.

"Please," she said, drawing the maid over to sit beside her on the bed. "Tell me everything you know."

"The slaves that belong to Master Shubert are sorely abused. Those at Cold Spring and Downing and Rose Hall fear he intends to allow them to starve to death, Miss Selah! And here he was this day, wagering some of their precious supplies!" She waved an indignant hand toward the window.

"I understand," Selah said. "How is this supposed to unfold?"

"The slaves on Cold Spring plan to sneak into the big house to-night and murder Master Shubert and any who stands up to them."

Selah forced herself to nod, urging her on.

"The call . . ." she began, then bit her lip. "The call is to murder every white master on-island after Shubert is dead. The soldiers too. If the slaves on Cold Spring succeed, they plan to blow the conch shell. Others on neighboring plantations will then do the same, when their masters fall."

"And what about the *families* of those plantation masters?" Selah managed.

"They are supposed to take them captive," Nellie said, looking to the window. "Hold them for ransom."

"I see." She rubbed her forehead, trying to think. Negroes outnumbered whites nine to one on Nevis, but the whites were surely better armed, and the soldiers garrisoned on-island had long trained against this very threat. Hadn't she seen missives about it herself? And yet it was one thing to prepare to meet a threat, another to actually face it in the dead of night.

"I must go to Jedediah," she said. "And Matthew."

Nellie nodded soberly. "Perhaps they can take this in hand."

"I hope to God they can."

In the meetinghouse, Jedediah was preaching about Joseph's brothers, coming to Egypt in their need, and tying it to their current need for food and how the Lord had provided this day. Selah considered his words and thought about Joseph. How sorely abused he had been by his brothers—sold into slavery. How he could have made his brothers suffer as restitution, denied them food to take home, allowing them to starve. There was a part of her—God help her—that wondered if the island might not be better off if Angus Shubert died this night.

They would. They *all* would.

But they could not be rid of him this way. It would only lead to more grief and heartache. Terrible repercussions for the insurrectionists. They had to intervene, and as fast as possible.

Selah waited in the corner and Jed finally caught her eye. He had no idea how much danger they were in. How much danger they were all in. Tonight, all of Nevis could be wailing, with loved ones dead or dying . . .

Jedediah finished speaking and strode over to her at last.

"I must speak to you, alone," she whispered.

He followed her outside as the mass behind him drew together. Did she imagine it or did some cast suspicious glances their way? Were others whispering behind hands?

"What is it, Selah?"

She turned to him. "Insurrection," she said, hugging herself when she had the mad impulse to rush into his arms. "Beginning on Shubert's plantation, then spreading outward. They think they shall win their freedom, Jed. But 'twill only end in much bloodshed, among all of us, black or white. And leave the slaves in a far more perilous situation."

"Here?" he breathed, glancing over his shoulder. "On the Double T? With our own?"

"No, I do not believe there are many who conspire here. Perhaps none. But elsewhere . . . Jed, there are slaves across the island who are prepared to take desperate action tonight."

Jedediah nodded, running his hand through his hair. "We must stop it. Without delay."

"Indeed. But . . ." Selah looked toward the sea. "If we intervene, how shall they look upon us afterward?"

"If we love these people, we must help them, even if that means standing against them." He looked at her, traced the long line of her scar about her cheek, neck, and shoulder with his eyes. "You were willing to do anything on that day in the market. Are you willing to do so again?"

"Yes," she said, finding strength in his reminders. There were many on-island who knew her and Jedediah and Matthew by sight. Many who might listen to them, if they could only reach them in time.

The trouble was, how might they speak to Angus Shubert's slaves without him discovering it?

When Matthew learned what Selah had heard, he set to pacing, rubbing his head, trying to figure out what they must do. They had invited Gideon and Primus into their circle too, knowing that the most trusted servants on the Double T must be warned of the imminent danger. They thought they were reasonably safe, but not all working among them were content, freed or not. Generations of abuse had produced a simmering cauldron that threatened to boil over at any time. And they all knew that mob rule oft made sane men mad.

Matthew turned to Cuffee. "Fetch Solomon for me," he whispered. "Quietly. Do not draw undue attention."

"Yes, Mr. Matthew." The young man ran off.

He turned back to the others. "Solomon has had his eye on Jenoa, a slave girl on Cold Spring. They've been courtin', each Sunday at the slave market in Charlestown, even though I told him they shouldn't." He shook his head. "That Shubert is never going to let Jenoa go. Lately, I think Solomon's taken to sneaking toward the border, giving her some of his food. I've been looking the other way, because . . ."

"Because you cannot put a stop to such a kindness," Jedediah finished for him.

"Do you think he's already been to see her this night?" Selah asked.

"No," he said. "Most nights he goes late. Probably because 'tis safer for Jenoa."

The man appeared at the corner of the meetinghouse and slowly walked toward them, nervously rubbing his hands together. "Mr. Matthew? You want'a see me?"

"Yes, Solomon." He urged him closer, into their circle. "We

have learned what is brewing tonight at Cold Spring. For Jenoa's safety, and for the safety of others, we want you to lead us to her."

Solomon's eyes widened, and he shook his head. "No. I can't do that. If Massa Shubert finds her with us, he'll take it out on her!"

"If you do not, she might die, Solomon. Unless they kill Shubert in his sleep, he will make every man, woman, and child in on this suffer terribly for even *thinking* of doing him harm." Selah reached out a hand to the man. "Listen to me. I clearly have reason to hate Shubert. To want him gone from this island forever. But this is not the way."

Solomon's glance fell to her scar. He turned partly away, hands on his hips and shaking his head.

"All you need to do is take us to her," Jedediah said. "Then we shall ask her to send us the leaders of this uprising. She can be safely away."

"What if they don' come?" Solomon asked.

"Then Matthew and I shall go to them," Jedediah said.

"As will I," Selah said.

Jedediah cast her a surprised look, already shaking his head.

"'Tis not only the people of the Double T who look to me. I see the slaves in town . . . Because of my scar, they know I would do anything to save them if I could. That might be the light we need this night to pierce the darkness they have planned."

Jedediah shook his head again. "Not this time, Selah. You cannot march directly into a known battle."

"If 'tis a battle to which I am called, then yes," she said resolutely. "And I will do anything to spare lives this night."

"I was to meet her shortly," Solomon admitted miserably, his tone so low they had to lean closer to hear him. "If we wanna catch her, we best leave now." He glanced between them, obviously uncomfortable by the tension between them. "Miss Selah . . . havin' her there might help, Mr. Jed. She, you and Mr. Matthew."

Jedediah took a deep breath, stepped away a moment and then turned back to stare at her, silently asking if she was certain about this. He hung his head for a moment, as if praying, listening, then

301

lifted it. "Very well, Solomon," Jedediah said, reluctantly turning from her and clapping him on the shoulder. "Thank you. You might help us to save many this night."

"Or I shall have many who wish me dead," Solomon said.

Selah frowned. She supposed he was right. There might be repercussions. "We shall not tell a soul."

Solomon surprised her by laughing softly. "Why, Miss Selah, you know as well as I do that there's not a secret kept on this whole island. I'd best be prayin', right, Mr. Jed? Tha's my only hope."

CHAPTER THIRTY

They walked along Round Road from the Double T southward, then Solomon took to a path through the trees and brush, so narrow that most would have passed it by. Selah noted the distinct Y-shape of the tree beside it, thinking that if she ever needed to return without a guide, it would be helpful to remember. She had changed into breeches, aware that their nighttime climb would be difficult in a skirt. She was only thankful that Keturah and Gray had retired for the night. Gideon and Primus had their instructions—they were to awaken them in half an hour. Long enough after their departure for Selah and Jedediah to reach Shubert's plantation and speak to his people, but early enough to prepare to defend the Double T if necessary.

They climbed without aid of a lamp, only by the moonlight skittering through the tree branches, occasionally illuminating the path. Selah almost tripped twice, but each time caught herself. Within twenty minutes, they had reached the border and, ten minutes later, a small outcropping where Solomon was to meet Jenoa. Jedediah gripped her hand, his touch welcome, warm and protective, even if it was but one of a friend, not a suitor.

Selah looked out to sea, where the moon shimmered on the water and white waves crested far below. It was a beautiful night—far too temperate and idyllic to consider that something so violent threatened to erupt. Together with Solomon and Matthew, they waited for the girl to arrive, trying not to hear imagined sounds among the crickets and tree frogs of the surrounding jungle. Selah's heart hammered in her chest; she knew that Ket would be furious with her for coming here, and yet what else could she do?

Jenoa appeared then, jumping down off a ledge between palm fronds before seeing that Solomon was not alone. She was a slight young woman with beautiful features—wide eyes, delicately arched brows, sculpted cheekbones, and full lips. Her eyes rounded and she turned immediately to run, but Solomon grabbed her hand. "No, Jenoa, 'tis all right."

She turned back, looking as if she might wrench her hand away, hurriedly glancing from one to the next, then finally back to Solomon. "What you done?" she whispered. "What you *done?*"

"They knew already, Jenoa," he said, folding his arms. "About it all. Somebody else tol' them. And they think it will only end up bad for black folk."

Matthew nodded and edged closer. "You need to bring the leaders to us. Have them talk to us before they do anything tonight."

She shook her head. "You are too late! 'Tis . . . 'Tis *already* happening." She hugged herself and looked over her shoulder toward the plantation. "I was goin' to ride it out here with you," she said to Solomon.

Selah stepped closer. "Can you yet reach even one of them? One of the leaders? We only want to speak with them."

Jenoa paused. Perhaps because Selah's hair was in a knot and she was in breeches, she hadn't known a woman was among them. Selah turned toward the moon so the girl could see her face.

"Miss . . . *Selah?*"

"Yes," she said. "'Tis me. Please. Can you find us someone to whom we could speak some sense?"

Jenoa shook her head miserably. "It too late, miss. Even now, they make their way to Massa Shubert's house."

Jedediah looked at Matthew, then her. "We must stop them,"

he said. "You wait here with Solomon and Jenoa, Selah. Matthew and I shall go."

"No!" Selah said, rushing to block them. "You need me. I think it shall take all three of us to bring them pause."

Jedediah shook his head. "I cannot do as you ask, Selah. 'Tis enough to bring you here to the border. To take you farther shall only invite your sister's—and Gray's—wrath. And for good reason."

"I will not make you choose then," she said. With that, she hopped to the small ledge from which Jenoa had emerged and ran as fast as she could along the path, praying she was going in the right direction.

She heard grunts and mutterings behind her, her name called softly on the wind, but mostly the slashing of greenery as she ran pell-mell toward Cold Spring. Selah knew that she had to get to the people before they did something that made every Negro man, woman, and child suffer for months to come. Did they think it was difficult now? That they had seen the worst of deprivation and abuse? They had not. This would unite the island's whites against them, bolster their worst fears, and convince them they would need to take the slaves even firmer in hand. There would be many who would be made examples . . .

No, she had to get there, and get there as fast as she could.

But when she at last reached the long, broad slope leading to Shubert's house, she stopped abruptly. From there she could see that it was surrounded—with perhaps forty men making their way upward, hunched over, crawling. Armed with what looked like hoes and machetes.

Above, in the house, she could hear men laughing, the flickering light and shadows that indicated a small gathering. The overseer? Shubert? Why were they attacking them before they were even asleep? It was madness.

Jedediah ran after her, but with her slighter form she caught fewer of the branches than he did. How could she be so audacious? So determined?

And yet her willingness to sacrifice all in order to protect others made his heart swell. He pressed it back as he ran. *Lord, she is so headstrong. So reckless!*

Born out of generosity. Love, came the answer.

She is impossible!

It is my own bold spirit she embodies.

No man could protect her!

She needs no protector greater than I. I am with her. Just as I am with you.

Jed stumbled with that last word. Matthew almost ran into him. "Are you hurt?"

"No," Jed said, resuming his run, desperate to catch up to Selah. He dared one last prayer before he reached Cold Spring's fields. *Save her this night, Father. Speak through her. Help us stop this insurrection.*

He refused to silently whisper his remaining words in prayer. But it mattered not; they repeated in his mind with every stride. *For I cannot imagine life without her.*

The others arrived then, on either side of her. Breathless. Before they could say anything or reach out to stop her, she rushed on, toward the man who drew closest to the porch of the house. A man to her right made a bird sound, and everyone looked up at her then. She did not hunch over or crawl, knowing she had not the time. Instead, she ran between two men and directly to the leader, turning and lifting her hands. "Please," she whispered in Igbo. "Please, please," she repeated in Swahili, wishing she knew every dialect they grew up speaking, wishing she could speak in the language of their mothers, their sisters, their daughters.

They had all frozen, as if she were but an apparition—a white woman where no white woman should be. "It be Miss Selah," said one in a hushed tone. "The one who took the whip."

More whispered, sharing the news as Matthew and Jedediah caught up with her again.

"My friends, this night shall end in bloodshed," she whispered. "You—"

"Be away!" returned the leader, realizing they were not going to sound an alarm. "Be away from here!"

"You might kill the monster who lives up there," she hissed, gesturing to the house, "but then many, many more of you shall die."

"We do not care," said a man to her left, looking anxiously from her to the house. "We die either way. The massa will starve us until we die in the fields, or we shall die as warriors this night."

"But what of your women? Your children?" she said in a hoarse whisper as the line moved forward. "Surely not all of you wish to die or suffer! That is where this leads. Because the planters shall defend themselves. The planters will wish to make an example of those who started it. Soldiers on this island shall hunt down every single person involved in this uprising and hang them in Charlestown."

"It will not matter," grunted a man to her right. "Because *he* will be dead first."

She shivered. She understood their hatred of Angus Shubert. "Even if Shubert dies this night, there will likely be some other to purchase his property and take his place. If you die, they will buy other slaves to replace you. Do you not see? You rise up tonight to put an end to this misery, *but it shall not end*. It is brutal; it is unfair; it is unrighteous. But this is not how you change the course."

The leader rose up, seemingly unafraid of being seen from above any longer. He was a good foot taller than Selah and carried a machete. "How then? How we change it?"

Selah swallowed hard. She had no true answer. "On the Double T, we do things differently."

"That is at the Double T," the man said, stepping toward her in anger. Jedediah eased between them, hands raised. "The Double T is but one plantation. There are three hundred more on this isle."

"But we are the most profitable," Matthew said. "Do you think that goes unnoticed by other planters?" He shook his head. "Greed forces them to pay attention."

"And my brother-in-law, Gray Covington, is trying to take Angus Shubert's council seat," Selah whispered. "If he is able to do that, then he has a greater chance of influencing how other planters run their plantations and how they treat their slaves."

"Will he try and set all slaves free?" asked a man, coming closer. He held a stick, sharpened to a point, in his fist.

"He will likely advocate for others to do as we are doing. To give all men hope." She licked her lips. At least she hoped he would. Was he not doing so already?

"When will that seat be up for the takin'?" grunted a man.

Selah swallowed hard. "Reviews are held each February."

"We will be long dead afore then, miss. There is not enough to eat," he said.

It came to her then. Food was driving them to this madness. Slow starvation not allowing them to think rationally, their desire to end the pain winning out over the desire to live beyond this day. She reached out and grabbed Matthew's hand. "The middle field gardens," she said.

His lips thinned, but he said nothing.

"Friends," she said. "If you come with me, I have enough corn and squash to ease your families' bellies for a week. Come and get what you need, and give us time to arrive at a solution."

She could sense the conflict within them. Some wanted to carry through. Some could think of nothing but food now that it had been promised. All doubted that they would not be in the same situation in a week's time. But if she could stave off this violence about to be unleashed across her island for a week or so? To have a chance to find a way that would help the Nevisians long term? It had to be a door that God himself was opening.

Men began arguing, pulling at others who turned to follow her. Others anxiously pointed up at the house, urging them to come along. Now that they were headed away, Selah resisted the impulse to run. To be on Shubert's property seemed equivalent to clambering into an angry bear's cave. She tucked her dirk in her waistband and waved them forward. Most were following them now, only a few remaining by the house, gesticulating angrily. There was no way they could storm the house with such few numbers.

She took a deep breath. It was working. With luck, there would be no conch shell blown this night. At plantation after plantation around them, hopefully those who were prepared to rise up would know it had not been successful here and return to their cabins. *Please, Lord,* she prayed silently, following Matthew through the jungle. *Protect us all this night.*

In the middle fields, Matthew gave them all firm direction, showing them how to take eight ears of corn—but only if it was mature—and leave the stalk to continue to mature additional ears. He cut the squash that was ready himself, handing each man three. When all had their supply, they gathered around. Some looked anxiously over their shoulders, aware now that if Shubert found them gone from their cabins, there would be repercussions.

"In a week's time, our seed squash and corn shall be ready," Matthew said. "We shall send seeds for all of you to plant your own, and in six weeks they shall be producing for you. Prepare small plots by your cabins so you are ready to plant."

Most nodded and moved off, the mood still one of defeat and acquiescence. "Thank you," grunted one of the last men present, shifting his heavy load in his arms. "For wha' you did this night. I didn' know what to do, other than go along with it."

"I understand," Matthew said, putting a hand on his shoulder. "But try and quash any future talk of uprising, will you? For every man's good?"

The man nodded, but there was something about the stoop of his shoulders that told Selah he was not hopeful he would be successful. They still hovered on the edge of disaster.

Together, the group took to the field path and returned to the big house, where Verity, Keturah, and Gray awaited them, anxiously pacing back and forth on the veranda. When they caught sight of them, the women rushed down to embrace Selah, alternately hugging her and shaking her in frustration. "Thank God!" Verity said.

"What were you thinking?" Keturah added, angrily shaking her head. "If Shubert had found you there—"

"I would have told him he owed me his life," Selah said with a small grin.

"If we had not gone, the entire island might be afire tonight," Matthew said.

Jedediah nodded soberly. "I did not want Selah to go. But if she had not been there, houses would have been burned. Men would have died, blacks and whites. Women and children would have been kidnapped. If Cold Spring had fallen, far more would have followed."

Keturah shivered and glanced up to the window where Madeleine slept. "How on earth did you stop them?"

"We . . . uhhh . . ." Selah looked nervously at Matthew, then Gray, kneading her hands. "We fed them. Gray, they were starving. That is part of what drives the madness of this insurrection. 'Tis enough to deal with the long, hard work. 'Tis another matter to deal with both abuse and starvation."

"You *fed* them," Gray said carefully, leaning against the veranda rail, arms crossed. "I see. Presumably from the middle field."

Selah bit her lip and nodded.

"You fed *Shubert's* people with *our* food?"

She nodded again. "We have enough now for months, thanks to Verity's auction."

"And we shall earn additional supplies, playing for Lord Bennett next month," Jedediah put in.

"And soon we shall be harvesting and Mr. Kirk shall return and we can trade for supplies with him," Selah added.

Gray was softening when Matthew added, "We promised them seeds in a week's time."

"Seeds!" Gray cried. "I have plans of my own for those! Just this afternoon I promised some to six other planters."

Keturah wrapped her arm through his. "Surely there shall be enough for all."

"We shall pray that God grant us a bounty of seeds," Jedediah said.

"See that you do, Reverend," Gray said. "I want those men firmly in my pocket when I go after Shubert's seat." He shook his head. "I have to say that it grates at me, thinking that I gave Shubert anything."

"You did not give Shubert anything," Keturah said. "You are keeping his people alive."

"And at peace," Verity said. "You need the island to be at peace to take that seat. If there are uprisings, Shubert shall use it as evidence that a tyrant's hand is necessary to run our plantations."

Gray put his chin in hand and nodded. "You are right." He lifted an arm to Selah, and she came under it. He kissed her head as he pulled her tight. "I am relieved you are well, Selah. And I believe you made an inspired decision tonight. But promise me one thing."

She glanced up at him.

"Next time, come to me and Ket. In the end, this is our plantation, and we have a right to be a part of such momentous decisions."

Selah nodded. "Forgive me. We were so alarmed, all we could think of was moving as quickly as possible."

"Had we not, we would have been too late," Matthew said.

"All right, then," Gray said, looking from one to the next. "Then at least send immediate word to us. We are in this together, friends. All of it."

After securing their agreement, and placing Matthew and Gideon on guard for the night—just in case an uprising still managed to take hold—he and Keturah climbed the stairs to bed, followed by Verity. But Selah, with the evening's excitement still roiling through her veins, found herself following Jedediah out to the veranda. He went down several stairs before turning to face her. She grabbed hold of a post.

"You were a marvel tonight," he said.

"Thank you. So were you," she said.

He ducked his head and scuffed the toe of his boot against the stair, thinking a moment. "Tonight I realized two things as we ran toward Cold Spring."

"Oh?"

He nodded and looked her in the eye. "I realized that I feared losing you. But I also realized you were running ahead of me."

"I couldn't wait, Jed. If I—"

"No," he said gently, cutting her off. "You could not wait. If you had, we might have been too late. And in my trying to protect you, I might have harmed you. I might have harmed all of us. I might have missed the chance that God gave us to stop this madness."

"What are you saying?"

"I am saying that perhaps I had it wrong. Any semblance of control is only that, a semblance. I can do my best to protect you, but I ought not to try and control you. As we ran . . . well, as we ran, the Lord reminded me that your safety, your very life, Selah, is in his hands, not mine. And as much as I do not wish to see you harmed, neither can I imagine my life without you. The only solution is trusting the Lord for every day he might grant us."

Her heart began to pound. *Us?*

He took a step up toward her again. "Selah, could you ever forgive me? You were right. I had given in to fear over trust. I might not be able to protect you from harm. I might not be able to always provide for you in more than the most simple of ways. But would you . . . ?"

She came down a step, placing them eye to eye. "Yes?"

"Could you learn to love a fool? Would you allow me to court you again?"

"Perhaps," she whispered with a small smile. "If that fool tries to learn from his mistakes."

"Oh, he will. He most assuredly will."

He leaned closer then, attempting to kiss her, but she squirmed away. "Not yet, Jed. Not yet. 'Tis been quite a night and I believe I shall retire now."

"Quite so," he said, backing away immediately. "There is no rush, Selah. I am only so happy," he said, grinning. "Thank you. Thank you for giving me another chance."

CHAPTER THIRTY-ONE

The next night, Major Woodget had no news of insurrection at supper—seemingly oblivious to the threat—but he had other news. "Three warships anchored at Finley Point this afternoon," he said, taking a big bite of fish stew. He cast a smug smile at Verity. "They are on their way to the American colonies."

Verity did not react. She merely took bite after bite of her conch chowder, demurely dabbing at her mouth with a napkin in between as conversation went on. Selah stirred her own chowder, thinking of the three men who had accompanied them from Statia and off the *Juliana*, but who did not return along with the rest of the crew. Where had they gone? What were they up to?

"How long are they to remain?" Gray asked.

"The *Norwich* has a broken mizzenmast. They shall get that repaired on the morrow," the major said. "Apparently, they endured a frightful storm en route."

"The *Drake* needs a new sail," put in Captain Howard.

"And all three hundred sailors are eager to lift a mug of ale or rum punch," Lieutenant Angersoll said. "Rum always tastes better on the islands than in Liverpool."

Lieutenant Cesley nudged his side. "All those weeks at sea makes a man thirsty."

The two lifted their goblets of water and toasted. Clearly they intended to join their red-coated comrades in the taverns after supper.

"How long were they granted shore leave?" Selah asked.

"Only a few days," Captain Howard answered. "All three captains are eager to get their supplies to the battlefront. With what those ships carry, General Howe's capture of New York shall be only the first of many victories."

"Hear, hear," the major said, eyeing Verity again.

"But none of them carried supplies for the islands," Gray said, setting down his spoon.

The major winced. "I fear not."

"Not even for the soldiers stationed here?"

"No," the major said regretfully. "I spoke with Captain Andrews of the *Drake*, for I had thought that since the supply ship did not arrive last month, perhaps these ships would carry some for soldiers quartered here. I am sorry to say that Andrews told me that England believes 'tis up to the islanders to care for our keep, since it is you who requested our presence for protection."

"Protection," Gray returned blandly. Selah held her breath. She dared not look to either of her sisters. "And how are we to care for those in our keep if islanders cannot obtain supplies? What do they believe? We are able to summon them from thin air?"

The major cast him a wry look and gestured over his empty bowl. "You have."

"You well know how that has come about. And whereas we shall make it through harvest, I have it on good authority that many others suffer. More than half the plantations have their slaves on reduced rations. You are here to curtail any insurrection as well as protect us from the rebels. What do you suppose might drive the slaves to rise up? Starvation, Major." He was careful not to meet the gaze of any of his family. "There is no greater threat than a man who believes he is about to die anyway."

The major grimaced and folded his arms. "I am quite aware, Gray. But what do you suggest I do?"

"Might you try to reach out to your superiors again?" Keturah asked. "Explain to them what you are witnessing? Express your concern?"

"I shall," he said, though his tone held little hope.

"There was another arrival today," Captain Howard said, his lips quivering with a hint of a smile.

"Oh?" Ket said, dipping her spoon into her bowl.

"Judge Albert Kensington, the Leeward Islands' newest judicial representative."

Selah set down her spoon. This was not the name of the man who had last presided over cases in Nevis, the one Angus Shubert had paid off. "Judge . . . Kensington?"

The captain smiled, his eyes a bit sad as they followed the line of her scar. "Yes. Your case shall be heard Thursday afternoon at four. What's more is that I hear tell this Kensington is rumored to be quite the level-headed and fair man."

Selah's pulse picked up with hope. Could it be? Might she see justice for herself and others?

"Angus Shubert and you are to be present at three o'clock," the major said. "And we shall attend you."

Jedediah was solicitous and careful over the next few days, not wishing to press Selah but anxious to spend any moment he could with her. She was understandably cautious, perhaps fearing he might withdraw his suit again. He had hurt her, likely angered her. But he was resolute, as determined to win her hand now as he had been to come to the West Indies to serve his Lord. He looked for reasons to go to the meetinghouse in the middle of the day, always ready to run a message down for Matthew or Philip, or from Gray to Keturah. For two nights, she did not return after supper to be with the people, as had been her custom. Then, on the third, she did.

Matthew had just asked him to speak about mercy, and Jed was turning the pages of his Bible, looking for the right Scriptures to form his response, when Selah caught his eye from the doorway.

She lifted a brow in silent invitation, asking him to join her on the porch.

He did not make her ask twice.

"I shall return," he said to Matthew, who gave Jedediah a sly look. But Jed ignored Matthew's wordless teasing, as he did the whispers as he passed by.

"Selah," he said, once they were outside, "I am glad to see you."

"I am glad to see you too." She reached for his hand. "Come. There is something I wish to show you."

Mesmerized that she had taken his hand, he followed her down the steps and up the road for a bit, then along a path. "Where are we going?" he asked.

"You will see." She cast him a flirtatious grin over her shoulder, so adorable that it took his breath away. They cut off onto a second path and moved deeper into the jungle. Minutes later, they arrived at the freshwater pool, surrounded by swaying palms, black against a violet sky. It was deliciously cool in the shade.

"Why, Selah! How could I not know this was here?" he asked in wonder.

"We are rather private about it," she said, leading him around the side to a rock ledge that jutted out over the water. "Come, sit. Let us dip our feet in."

She was already sliding off her slippers, and Jed had to force himself to look away from her tender pink flesh. He hurriedly did the same, then edged closer to her. Jed took her hand again as they let their feet dangle in the water. "How is it that everyone on the Double T is not here every night?" he moaned. "This feels wonderful."

"As I said, we are rather private about it. Perhaps 'tis greedy of us," she confessed. "'Tis where my father liked to bathe. My sisters and I come on occasion to do the same."

"I see. If everyone came, it would most definitely lose its sense of sanctuary."

"Yes, *sanctuary*," she said, looking about. "That is the perfect word for it. We have had many holy moments here, as well as very frank conversations. Here is where Keturah finally admitted to loving Gray. Where Verity confessed her feelings for Ian. And where I . . ." She nervously glanced down to her feet, dripping water as she lifted them. "Where I admitted I had feelings for you," she finished.

"Selah," he said, turning toward her, heart pounding. *Does she mean . . . Is she saying . . . ?* "Those feelings. Do you believe they might become love in time?"

She dragged her golden-brown eyes up to meet his. "They might have already," she whispered. "But I confess I am afraid, Jed. Afraid you shall break my heart again."

He lifted a hand to cradle her cheek. "Never. Never ever again, beloved," he promised, his heart soaring. She loved him! Him! "Because I love you too," he said, leaning in to kiss her searchingly. He lingered, his kiss deepening, and finding their side-by-side position awkward, drew back, stood, and pulled her to her feet.

She shyly came into his arms, but welcomed his careful kiss with her own. "Oh, Selah. How happy you have made me." In time, their kiss deepened, her small hands running across his back as he pulled her closer, thinking he could never have her close enough. "Oh, Selah, Selah," he groaned, pulling slightly away. "Is there any way you could forgive me for hurting you so? I cannot fathom that I almost let you go."

She smiled up at him, a question in her eyes. "There is one thing that might make it right," she said.

"Yes?" he said eagerly. "What is it?"

"Do you know how to swim?"

He frowned in confusion. She wanted to swim? Perhaps once they were married it would be all right, but now? And yet he was not eager to let this moment with her go. "Yes, I swim. Are you suggesting that we—?"

"No," she said. Then she leaned and, with all her might, shoved him backward.

Utterly surprised, he windmilled backward, teetered on the edge of the rock ledge a moment, but knew he was going in. He plunged into the pool, clothes and all, only glad that she'd found a way to spare his costly boots. His breath left him below the surface in a laugh. Would he spend a lifetime finding new ways that Selah could surprise him?

He emerged and swam over to the ledge, where she waited for him, her grin a streak of white in the gathering dark. "I deserved that," he said.

"Yes, you did."

"Is that the one thing that you thought would make it right?" he asked, treading water.

"'Tis."

"And did it make things right?"

"Yes. I believe it did."

"Excellent." He heaved himself up onto the ledge and went after her. She let out a little shriek and tried to get away, but he caught her by the waist. And then he firmly turned her around and kissed her thoroughly.

"Well, that was a new sort of kiss," she laughed, pulling back to look down at her damp dress. "One of the hundred versions you promised me?"

"It is likely the *wettest* you shall receive from me," he said, pulling her close again, finding her utterly irresistible, "until I kiss you in the rain. Or after a dip in the sea. Or when we swim together in this pool."

"I shall look forward to those kisses as well," she said, grinning up at him. "But now we ought to return. My sisters shall be wondering where I have gone."

"How am I to explain this?" He gestured to his wet clothes.

"You are the gifted orator, Reverend," she said. "I leave that to you."

The following afternoon they all loaded into the carriage, with Gray and Philip following behind on their horses. Selah worried they might run across Shubert on Round Road, yet they did not see another soul until they rounded the northern corner and spotted the three huge British ships anchored at Finley Point. In the distance, they could see men rowing supplies to the ships, others returning from them. It appeared as if the mizzenmast was going up on the *Norwich*.

Selah shared a conspiratorial glance with Verity. What had their information wrought? All appeared normal for the British. Selah wondered if all they'd done had been for naught. Verity said that often their duty was only to seek information, never to learn of what it meant to the cause, but that did not settle well with Selah. If she did something, she wanted to see the fruits of her labor, as she did with the people of the Double T. She did not have her sister's patience.

She glanced at Jedediah, sitting across from her. Sensing her gaze, he looked to her and gave her a small, encouraging smile. "Do you believe God will see Shubert to justice this day, Jedediah?"

He considered her a moment. "I believe God shall be with you, and I trust the outcome will be something he has foreseen. That allows me to trust in it, no matter what transpires."

Verity cocked her head. "You believe God knows what is ahead of us?"

"I do."

They hit a dip in the road, and everyone in the carriage swayed back and forth. "What of free will?" Keturah put in.

"What of it?" he returned.

"If we are free to make our own decisions, but God knows of it, is it truly free?"

His lips twitched, considering her question. "I believe that God allows us to make our own decisions, whether they be good or bad, but he knows all. I also believe that if we seek his counsel, he leads us to make the best decisions. 'Tis when we act as our own little gods that we tend to get into trouble. That is when fear overtakes trust," he added, eyeing Selah meaningfully.

She smiled back at him. *Little gods,* Selah mused. How often had she looked to her own counsel, or her sisters', before God?

"I hope Judge Kensington seeks the Lord's counsel this day," she said. "That he makes a wise decision on how to punish Angus Shubert for his actions."

Jed nodded. "As do I."

When they arrived at the town hall, they were surprised to see a crowd milling about. Apparently, word had spread that Shubert was to face justice today for his harming Selah. Many planters and their wives who had attended the gatherings at the Double T over the last weeks were in attendance, but there were more than a hundred others. There was no way they could all fit in the hall, built to seat a maximum of fifty people in the gallery.

Soldiers formed two lines, pressing the crowd away, only allowing Selah and her family entrance. When she arrived inside, she was chagrined to see Angus Shubert was already there, sitting with the overseer of Cold Spring. The gallery was already full to capacity. She wondered what would have happened if these two men had died four days prior, the night of the intended uprising. The slaver, Titus, arrived, along with a companion. His wrist was still splinted and bandaged, presumably broken as he had claimed that day a month ago.

"All rise," called an usher, entering from a side door. "The Honorable Judge Kensington is present."

Everyone stood, and then a tiny little man entered, appearing as wide as he was tall in his red robe, black scarf, and scarlet tippet. A pristine, curly white, freshly powdered wig covered his head, and he carried a Bible.

Shubert grinned at his companion and nudged him. Presumably he thought he had an edge over the judge simply because he outweighed him three to one. Selah reminded herself of Major Woodget's words as the judge paused to bow to the Royal Coat of Arms banner. He had called the man level-headed and fair. She would choose to trust and not fear.

The diminutive judge opened a packet of papers and perused them as the crowd settled. The door in back had been left open to allow others outside to hear the proceedings, as well as to welcome in an additional breeze. "We are present today to hear the case against Mr. Angus Shubert," the judge read, "accused of striking Miss Selah Banning with a whip, as well as the case against Miss Banning, for interfering in a lawful auction." His small eyes searched the courtroom and stopped on Selah. He took in the evidence of her scar with a doctor's detached air, then shifted his attention to Shubert for a moment, then back to the papers before him. "It appears as if we would be best served by hearing first from Major Woodget."

The major walked forward, tricorn tucked under his arm, swore an oath to tell the truth, then took a seat to the right of the judge, telling him how that day unfolded.

"And Miss Banning's goal, as best as you might ascertain?"

"To stop Angus Shubert from whipping the slaves."

"I see," said the judge, not showing any emotion.

"She said she wished to purchase the woman," the major continued. "Councilman Shubert had already purchased the girl and refused. Miss Banning went on to purchase all three of the women behind her, as well as the man who had been struck down. The slaver, given the opportunity to sell four versus one slave, agreed to her request."

"Which was why I took issue, Your Honor," Angus said, rising. "That Negress had been purchased already. Selah Banning stole her from me."

"Sit down, Councilman Shubert," said the judge with a sniff.

After a moment's hesitation, mouth partially open, Shubert did as he had been bid.

Next, Titus provided testimony, as did a lieutenant present the entire time of the incident. Then Angus himself.

The judge turned to Selah as Angus returned to his seat. "Miss Banning, please take the stand."

Angus turned to face him, mouth agape. "You cannot call a woman to the stand! She needs a man to speak for her!"

The judge looked at Shubert. "Sit down, Councilman. This is a civil case, not a criminal case. *As of yet.* Do you truly wish to move to high court proceedings?"

Shubert rubbed his chin, glanced around, and then shook his head.

"It seems prudent to me to hear from the woman you are accused of striking. Miss Banning, if you please," the judge said, gesturing to the chair on his right.

Red-faced, Shubert finally sat down. Selah rose on trembling legs. She too was surprised, having been prepared to defer to Major Woodget's account, either correcting or denying if he got anything wrong. Women and Negroes were seldom permitted to testify in West Indian courtrooms. But perhaps because she was the victim, this judge was allowing an exception.

The judge folded his hands and peered at her after she had been sworn in. His eyes traced her scars, now turning a light pink as they healed. "Miss Banning, why was it that you intervened that day on the platform?"

"Because I could do no other, Your Honor. He was whipping that girl, and she was huddled there between her sisters." She took a long, shaky breath. "I believe that was what moved me to act. In truth, it shames me to admit, but there were likely many other occasions when I looked away when slaves were being abused on the platforms. Whilst most on-island know I have a heart for the plight of Negroes, I confess that to a certain measure I had become accustomed to it. There was something in the woman's cries . . . and seeing her there . . . it awakened something in me, Your Honor. I knew I had to rise to her defense. And when I discovered Angus Shubert was the source of her torture, I knew it all the more."

The judge sat back in his chair and steepled his fingers. "You and Councilman Shubert have tangled in the past?"

"Yes." She looked to Shubert, who gave her a smug little smile. "Councilman Shubert once tried to rape me," she said.

The gallery erupted in gasps and whispers.

Angus frowned and rose. "A false charge!" he cried. "I was drunk and not myself. I never faced trial, because the judge threw out her charge."

"Due solely to the fact that he *bribed* said judge," Selah said evenly. She was calm now. Feeling an ethereal peace.

But the courtroom erupted at her words. Judge Kensington patiently waited, fingers still steepled before him, until at last all were silent again.

"Ask her if her sister pulled a knife on me!" Shubert blustered, waving back at her family. "Selah Banning's sister, Verity McKintrick, is a suspected spy for the Patriots. She should be on trial here for her attack on *me*. In addition, 'twas her husband, a privateer, who savagely beat me last year and in my own establishment. This family is not to be trusted!"

"Those who testified before you seem to disagree with you, Councilman," the judge said, casting him a baleful look. "And alas, the only ones who stand accused at this moment, Councilman Shubert, are you and Miss Banning."

Shubert stared at him, his face becoming a ruby red.

"Sit down, please, Councilman." He turned to Selah, refusing to watch as Shubert reluctantly took his seat. He tapped his fingers on the mahogany table. "I confess I am intrigued, Miss Banning. Indulge me, if you would. Your sister threatened the councilman with a knife?"

"She came to my defense when he attacked me," Selah explained. "'Twas how I was saved. And that was but one attack on us. Mr. Shubert is a neighbor, and over the years he has utilized every opportunity to torment us."

"Why?"

"He objected to our presence from the start. We were but three women, taking on a plantation. And we hired a black overseer."

"I see." The judge dipped a quill in an inkwell and scribbled some notes on a piece of parchment before him. He turned back to her. "Miss Banning, you are aware that you intruded upon a lawful sale?"

"I am," she returned. "If I had seen any other option, I would have taken it. But, Your Honor, Angus Shubert is not a rational or reasonable man. Action, *swift* action, was demanded. That girl would have been in dire straits in his hands."

"How so?"

Selah swallowed. "I have it on good authority that Angus Shubert chooses a Negress on each of his plantations—often little more than children—to indulge his own despicable pleasure."

Shubert rose, blustering. A flush rose up his neck. "What a man does with his own property is up to *him*!" He laughed and lifted his hands. "I am a man with an ailing wife. I am not the first—nor the last—to see to my own needs."

"No slave owner should subject their slaves to torture, starvation, and abuse," Selah returned, staring him down. "Common Christian decency demands that we feed, clothe, and shelter those in our care."

Shubert narrowed his eyes, stood and shook his finger at her. "Ask her, Judge! *Ask her* how she is so certain about my 'practices' on *my* plantation with *my* property. She has never visited Cold Spring or any of my other plantations."

"No need to ask," she said. "I have heard from the girls myself." She allowed a tiny smile of triumph to reach her eyes, enraging him further.

"Because . . ." He halted abruptly. He saw it then. While he longed to accuse her of aiding his runaways to escape, to do so would give credence to her testimony. That the girls had told her themselves. Shubert glowered at her. The usher forced him to sit back down.

"Miss Banning," the judge said, "do you believe Angus Shubert was aware that 'twas *you* who was between him and his slave? He is clearly a man ruled by his passions. Could it have been rage that blinded him?"

"No, Your Honor. Because Angus Shubert set his whip on me not once but twice. The first was to disarm me of my dirk. The second was simply out of spite. He let the whip fly, and it flayed open my shoulder, neck, and cheek. He might have struck me again had not Major Woodget and Captain Howard waylaid him."

"I see." He tapped his fingers together, thinking. "Miss Banning, had Mr. Shubert attacked you anywhere but that platform,

I would be considering a criminal case. But due to the fact that you interfered in a lawful sale—despite the repugnant manner in which Mr. Shubert conducted himself—I believe you hold a measure of culpability."

Selah's heart plummeted. Justice, of which she'd had but a taste, had been so sweet . . .

"Therefore, I do not believe I can sentence Mr. Shubert in the traditional manner."

She glanced at Angus, and he gave her a catlike smile, sitting back in his chair and crossing his knee with one booted foot as if he were in his tavern rather than a courtroom.

"That said, I believe his actions were reprehensible. To strike another—whether they be Negro or white—is the action of a brute. And you are a young woman in fine standing among your peers, given the support we see here today," he said, gesturing to the crowd. "Therefore, I ask you, Miss Banning. What is it that you require as recompense? What shall soften this grave blow to your tender visage? What might serve as justice for Mr. Shubert, if jail or fining is out of the question?"

She stared at him in surprise.

"Your Honor," Shubert sputtered, rising.

"*Sit down*, Mr. Shubert!" the judge growled, his voice a startling baritone in so small a man. He turned back to Selah, waiting.

Selah considered him. She thought of Jedediah's words. How God saw it all. That he had seen this day. That he had foreseen what she would say. *Please, Lord, help me to make a wise decision.*

It came to her then. She straightened in her chair and faced the judge. "Angus Shubert's slaves are some of the thinnest on-island, Your Honor. As supplies have become scarce, he has used the excuse to limit rations among them, despite having the storehouse to decently feed them. Recently, he offered quite a bit of his supplies in an auction for a pair of horses and a fine carriage."

"An auction that I quit because of supplies," Shubert bit out, half rising.

The judge ignored him, listening only to her.

"I ask that you force him to return to pre-war rations of two pounds of beans, one pound of dried beef or fish, and one pound of squash per slave per week on all his plantations."

"That is ridiculous!" Shubert cried. "Ask any planter here! We no longer have the supplies to do as she asks."

"Given your storehouses at present," returned the judge, "how long could you sustain your slaves on such rations?"

"Two, perhaps three weeks!"

The judge narrowed his gaze at him. "And upon pain of jail or fines or further repercussions, if I were to examine your storehouses this afternoon, would that truly be the extent of it, *Councilman* Shubert?"

Angus's mouth thinned. "Perhaps I spoke too hastily," he said reluctantly, as if each word must be pried from his mouth. "We could perhaps make it for as long as six or seven weeks."

"As I understand it, more supply ships are en route to the Indies," the judge said. "Intent upon trading for your coming harvest. When shall you be harvesting on most of your plantations, Mr. Shubert?"

"Next week and following."

"Well then," the judge said. "It sounds as if all shall work out splendidly. You shall return to feeding your people what they are due, and in turn they shall aid you in turning out a harvest with which you can purchase additional supplies. You shall do as Miss Banning has dictated."

He turned back to Selah. "Is that all you require, my dear?"

"All I require," she said, looking at Angus, "is that he set aside his brutish ways. That he behave as a civilized gentleman would every time he encounters me or my sisters. And that he discontinue his threatening mannerisms."

Angus let out a scoffing laugh, looking to his overseer for support. But the courtroom was silent, collective judgment raining down on him.

"This does not seem too much to ask of a gentleman subject to the Crown," the judge said pointedly. "I ask that you do as the lady has said. If you find it impossible, then I ask that you avoid

Miss Banning and her sisters, granting them a road-width of space any time you come into contact."

"This is an island, Judge," Shubert said, raising his hands. "We all encounter one another on a frequent basis."

"And now I have provided the means to keep the peace," returned the judge easily. "In addition, I find it necessary to remove you as councilman, Mr. Shubert, given your reprehensible behavior and inability to keep a level head. You do damage to the office."

Shubert bellowed in outrage, but the judge continued on. "I shall leave it up to your former fellow councilmen to elect an appropriate replacement. When I return in six weeks, you and Miss Banning shall return to my courtroom, and we shall review how these new rules have been observed. If they have *not* been observed, Mr. Shubert, there shall be further repercussions." He rose. "This court is adjourned."

Chapter Thirty-Two

They took to Round Road, Keturah already planning a celebratory supper, asking Gideon to stop at the butcher on the way out of town. "Would not a proper lamb roast be divine?"

Selah was considering that exorbitant expense, even as her mouth watered at the thought. Major Woodget and Captain Howard shared a gleeful grin.

But then they heard the first explosion, north of town.

The soldiers immediately urged their mounts into a gallop, leaning deeper into their saddles as they charged around the bend in the road, leaving them behind.

A second and third explosion resounded, spooking the team of geldings that drew their carriage. Gideon spoke in soothing tones to the horses, pulling hard on the reins until they settled. A plume of smoke rose over the hill. "Are we under attack?" Keturah cried, her hand going to her belly, clearly worried that they were there in town and Madeleine was back at the plantation.

Verity reached out a hand to cover hers. "*We* are not under attack," she whispered.

Selah straightened, belatedly realizing what was transpiring.

Gray, riding beside them again, frowned as Verity leaned back in her seat, a self-satisfied smile tugging at the corners of her lips.

"Carry on, Gideon," he said, looking forward. "Let us see what this is about."

"Yes, sir," said the groom, flicking the reins. The horses, skittish and eager, set off at a trot. More terrific booms resonated in the distance. Above the line of trees, they could see more plumes of smoke rising . . . from the water?

Selah had not heard such terrifying sounds since she was in Liverpool as a small girl and watched as a munitions building caught fire and one explosion after another occurred. Her father had picked her up and run away, but she had watched over his shoulder, mesmerized by the color and intensity, noise and smoke.

More explosions sounded, then still more. At last they rounded the corner of the road and could see down to Finley Point. Gideon pulled to the side of the road just as another contingent of soldiers from the lookout above charged by, telling them that there was indeed nothing to fear from the sea. Someone was attacking the ships harbored below, not the island herself.

From here they could see clearly. The re-provisioning yard below teemed with redcoats, yet there was little they could do. Two of the grand war frigates were on fire, one listing heavily. The third appeared to have been cut in half by the blasts, her hull already disappearing beneath the waves, the masts slowly receding with her. The second ship listed further, obviously taking on water at a rapid rate. Would she roll?

Men loaded into boats and rowed madly toward the ships but then paused, as though uncertain if they could do anything but risk their own skins. It was clear to Selah—even with her lack of sailing prowess—that they were better off away. The explosions had been effective, ripping holes and seams into vulnerable places belowdecks. The fires appeared to be setting off additional explosions. Even as they watched, a great blast went up from the ship in the best condition, sending splintered wood and goods high into the air. She even glimpsed several cannons that rose briefly before falling into the sea with great splashes.

Selah sucked in her breath and looked in wonder to Verity.

Verity squeezed her hand. Those who supported the American Patriots had found a way to stop the cannons from reaching the battlefront. And they had done so by sparing a great number of British lives. She knew most of the sailors had been on shore or working in the yard on land.

"We must go to them," Jedediah said to Gray. "There might be men injured and in need of care."

Gray frowned. "The women of this family cannot be seen any closer than Round Road," he said, glancing at Verity. "One in particular shall fall under suspicion. 'Tis our good fortune that the major and captain were with us when it occurred."

"Or Providence," Selah said.

"Or Providence," Gray agreed. "You go to them, Jedediah. Take my horse. Philip and Gideon, attend him. We shall send Primus back with the carriage to transport any wounded to the Double T." He gave Verity a hard look. "We shall care for as many as possible."

"Of course," Verity said. "This is war, brother. But that does not mean I have lost my heart."

The men set off, and Primus urged the horses to a trot, intent on preparing the house to serve as hospital, if necessary. Selah craned her neck for as long as she could to see the ships, believing she saw the second ship list to a deadly angle before the jungle trees impeded her view. She liked that it had been Jed who first realized there was a way to assist those hurting below. She wished she could be serving beside him, binding up wounds, giving the injured a comforting word or sip of water, and yet she saw the wisdom behind Gray's decision.

They could not be seen any closer. After all, it had been she who had reported what she'd seen in the major's correspondence. She who had told the resistance what they wanted to know. She leaned forward, head in hands, suddenly feeling the weight of responsibility. Had it been her fault? Were there men dead or dying whom she had doomed . . . all in an effort to aid her people on the Double T?

Selah paced that night on the veranda, arms around herself, her thoughts circling round and round again over all that had transpired. In the end, the soldiers had been able to save one of the ships, putting out the fire and hastily erecting a flood barrier that kept the grand ship afloat. She was listing heavily, but Major Woodget believed she could be repaired and set to rights within four to six weeks.

The other two ships were more than a hundred feet below the waves, their cargo of cannons strewn across the depths.

In total, twelve men had died, and thirty were injured. Four were in the Double T's parlor at this very moment, two with injuries to their faces, eyes, and necks, one with a broken arm and shoulder, the last with a frightful laceration to his belly that might very well take his life. A flying piece of wood had pierced him through. The soldiers had had to wrench it free. The amount of blood . . . even the memory of it threatened to send Selah into a dead faint.

She doubted he would live through the night, no matter how much she prayed.

Jedediah came out then, his hair in disarray, sweat lining his armpits and chest. He had worked tirelessly beside Gray, Philip, and the women to do all they could for the men. She fell into his arms, tears running down her cheeks. "Oh, Jedediah," she murmured, "I feel so utterly wretched."

"You, beloved?" he asked in confusion. "Why?"

She swallowed hard and led him to the far corner of the veranda, away from the parlor windows. "Jedediah," she said, stepping away from him and nervously rubbing her hands. "I must confess something to you."

He frowned. "What is it?"

"I . . . well, I aided Verity in obtaining a missive from the major," she whispered. "My goal was to simply aid Verity in earning additional supplies for the Double T."

He lifted his chin, slowly understanding. After a long moment he said wearily, "And tonight you understood that you had a hand in an act of war."

"Yes," she said miserably. She put one hand to her head, one to her belly, and paced to the rail. In time he joined her there.

"'Tis one thing to consider war from afar. Another to see it before you."

She nodded.

He put a comforting arm around her shoulder. "Do you regret aiding the Patriots?" he whispered. "I thought your heart was softening for Verity and Ian's cause."

She shook her head slowly, trying to get her thoughts in order. "I regret aiding death in any form."

He took a long, deep breath. "You did not set off those explosions on those ships."

"But I told people those ships would be present."

He considered that a moment. "From the Patriots' point of view, you likely saved many lives by keeping those cannons from reaching America's shore. Perhaps, without those cannons, fewer battles shall rage. Who knows how today shall affect the outcome? Perhaps you changed the course of one battle or ten. This is a burden, yes, love. But this is the reality of war."

"All I want is for peace to return," she said mournfully.

"All we can do is attempt to sow seeds of peace wherever we reside. As you do here on the Double T." He pulled her under his arm. "But perhaps you can leave further espionage to your sister?"

"Gladly. I do not ever want to leave your side, Jedediah," she said, snuggling closer. "The thought of saying farewell makes me want to weep."

"As it does with me." He held her for a long moment. "Say you shall never leave my side, Selah." Gently he pulled away and knelt before her. He held her hands and gazed into her eyes. "Please be my forever companion. My forever lover and friend. Please be my bride."

She stared down at him. "Jedediah . . ."

"Oh." He faltered and frowned. "This was ill-timed."

He began to rise, but she gently pressed him back with a soft laugh. Then she sat on his knee and took his face in her hands.

"You love me, though I am far from perfect. That is more than I could have imagined in a husband."

"Does this mean . . ." he began, his eyes widening in wonder. "Does this mean you accept my proposal?"

She leaned in and kissed him softly. "Yes, Jedediah. I shall be yours. Now and forevermore."

CHAPTER THIRTY-THREE

In the end, out of family and political necessity, Jedediah and Selah were married one sunny and breezy autumn afternoon at St. Philip's, under the doting eye of Vicar Hambry, and with twelve key families in attendance—those who had first drawn near to the Covingtons. All were friends who whispered of naming Gray the island's newest councilman.

But as soon as their evening guests were off to their own estates after dining at the Double T, Selah changed out of her grand gown from London—which Verity had obtained on Statia—and replaced it with a simple cream gown. This one was little more than soft cotton with a bit of lace around the top, which sat slightly off the shoulder. The bodice was tight, the skirt not the extravagant width of a traditional gown, nor with the bump at the rear. Instead, it fell in a rather sleek, slim skirt.

Selah looked at her reflection in the full-length mirror from St. Kitts, a wedding gift from Lord Bennett. In the simplicity, in the lack of folds and fabric, she found a sense of peace. She felt far more at ease, far more *her* than she had in the heavy, overwhelmingly luxurious silk gown.

Had she ever been a girl who felt at home in such grandiose gowns? Perhaps once when she was far younger.

Not now. Not here.

Outside, the sun had set. Torches had been lit. A pathway toward the meetinghouse was outlined in flame. As she glanced out the window her father had lined in shells and glimpsed the torches, she smiled.

What had come before was but a precursor of her wedding. An hors d'oeuvre. This, *this* was the feast that she and Jedediah had longed for.

A second wedding ceremony here at home on the Double T.

"Slippers, Miss Selah?" Dolly asked, leaning down to take hold of the embroidered shoes Selah had worn beneath her more elaborate gown.

Selah considered her. "I think not," she said with a slow shake of her head. She'd seen Dolly take Tomas's hand in marriage just a few nights before, and they had done so barefoot. She would come to Jedediah in the same way.

Dolly gave her a shy, conspiratorial smile and then straightened.

"Well, at least allow me to wrap this into your hair," Keturah said from a chair where she and Verity watched and waited. Ket held a long strand of beaded seashells, tiny, coiled Turbinellas in cream and peach. "Margaret strung these for you," she said. "She thought it might be pretty in your hair."

"Pretty?" Verity said, rising too. She took the brush from Dolly's hand. "It shall be perfect." With long, firm strokes, she brushed out Selah's blond waves, then began twisting a part of it. She took the strand from Keturah and began weaving it into a coil that she wound on top of Selah's head. Higher and higher it went, until Selah feared they would run out of the shells, but then it was done. With quick fingers, Verity pinned it in place and then stepped back. "'Tis perfect."

"Indeed," Ket said, stepping up beside her so Selah could see them both in the mirror behind her. Keturah put a hand on one shoulder, Verity the other.

"Selah, we are so glad for you," Ket said.

"More than we can say," Verity added.

Selah grinned and placed a hand on each of theirs. "Thank

you, sisters. For standing with me, beside me, behind me. I am so grateful for you both too."

"No more than we are for you," Keturah said.

A steady drumbeat began, slow and low, outside their window.

"So it begins," Verity said. She leaned closer to her ear. "Your *true* ceremony."

Selah smiled wider. What had come before had been required. What was to come was the ribbon on the gift.

The drumbeat picked up, beckoning her.

"You are ready?" Ket asked, offering Selah her hand. "This is it."

"I am ready," Selah answered, taking her hand and rising, suddenly more than anxious to be in the meetinghouse.

Outside her room, Gray and Philip awaited. Her sisters and Mitilda and Sansa rushed ahead so they could be present when she entered the small structure that would hold all whom she loved on the Double T. Even Abe had been secreted in along with the gown from Statia for a brief visit. The eight men who were drumming took the beat up a notch, alerting those ahead that she approached. Gray offered her his arm while Philip hung back, keeping watch, although this night, none but they were on the plantation.

Selah could feel it.

She was utterly surrounded by love and goodwill. Their earlier service had held a measure of the same, but nothing like this, being surrounded by those who knew and loved her and Jedediah best. As they left the house and took to the torchlit path, girls threw flower petals at her feet, filling the air with the heady, sweet scent of jasmine and the spice of fireclaw as her soles crushed the blossoms. The scent mingled with the salt of the sea and the verdant odors of the jungle, making her think that she had never smelled the island so thoroughly as she did that night. Flames danced around her as they passed the torches—planted at five-pace intervals—along the path.

And then they arrived at the foot of the stairs that led to the meetinghouse. The outside platform was full of people with wide grins, the inside full as well.

The drums picked up their beat, announcing they were present.

"Are you ready?" Gray asked, looking over to her as she paused, as she had not outside the doors of St. Philip's.

"I am ready," she said. "I only . . . Oh, Gray, is it terrible of me to want to pause and remember this moment?"

"No, dear one," he said, taking her hand and kissing it as a brother might, threatening to bring her to tears. "This is your moment. You should pause and remember. I wish I had. But I was in such an infernal rush to make your sister my bride, I did not even *think* of pausing."

She smiled and considered again the meetinghouse. The dear faces of all present. Bessy and Margaret. Nellie and Ann. Cuffee and Abana. Oriana and Kuri. All so hopeful. All so much *for* her and Jedediah.

And inside, he awaited her.

"Let us go," she said.

"As you wish," Gray said, leading her up the stairs. But then she held back.

Up until that point, she had not missed her father. She had had pangs of longing for her mother as she dressed, but her sisters stood in the gap. And what she remembered of her father, she supposed, was mostly from the eyes of Ket and Verity, given that she had been eight when he last left them. She had not missed him when they entered St. Philip's and Gray took her arm. But now, here, on the Double T—this plantation he had established and loved—waves of longing wafted through her.

Her father was not present, but her heavenly Father was, she reminded herself. Guiding her. Teaching her. Leading her, day by day.

"Selah?" Gray said, looking back at her with a measure of alarm, as if she might be having second thoughts.

She looked to him, *truly* looked to him.

How good it was of God to place Gray in our lives, she thought. *And Ian.* She glanced back at Philip. *And Philip too.* They were guardians, of a sort, coming alongside the Banning sisters. Not men likely to be mentioned in the histories of time, but good men, fine men. If Father could not be here, she was more than glad that they could. Fine men, showing her the way toward the fine man she would now call *husband*.

Making a way for her. For him.

She smiled and lifted her skirt, matching Gray's step again. Friendly, excited faces peeked out from around the corners of the doorway, anticipating their arrival. Mitilda and Abe. Gideon and Primus. Sansa and Matthew, surrounded by many more.

The drumbeat, now at a fever pitch, abruptly ended.

The meetinghouse was hot with the thick presence of humanity. But as Jedediah took her hands in his, as Matthew spoke the words of blessing in his warm Creole accent, as he wrapped their wrists in a thick, rough handwoven cloth . . . as their people laughed and cried out in praise, trilling and singing, Selah had only one thought.

I am surrounded by those I love, marrying the man I love most. How blessed am I?

Then Jedediah kissed her, kissed her in perhaps the tenth way of the hundred he had promised her.

And Selah considered with glee the other ninety to come.

Historical Notes

As is the case with most of my fiction, many things that transpire in the story were inspired by real historical events, but I revised and utilized them as best fit my story. For example, in Matthew Parker's excellent nonfiction book *The Sugar Barons*, many slave uprisings—and white fear of them—were well documented, and while there was one on Jamaica as recently as 1775, I never found one mentioned on Nevis.

Andrew Jackson O'Shaughnessy's book on warfare in the Caribbean during the Revolutionary War, *An Empire Divided*, documents that the British committed a heavy naval presence to protect their valuable assets among the sugar islands—from privateers and the threat of enemy invasion—and yet the three ships I depicted arriving at Nevis for re-provisioning and repairs was not a cited event. For decades, British ships en route to the Americas did stop at Nevis and other islands for fresh water and repairs, but I was unable to verify specifics about where and when and if they were still doing so in 1776. I know that a decade later, Horatio Nelson stopped at Nelson Spring to take on water, but I fictionalized "Finley Point" and the yard where repairs were being done.

Privateering was becoming lucrative and eventually included an impressive force of North American privateers. According to

Parker, by February 1777, they had taken more than 250 West Indian merchant ships, resulting in the collapse of four merchant companies in London (*The Sugar Barons*, p. 327). Things got worse for the Brits in 1778–1779, when the Spanish and French joined the war, and the British found it difficult to defend their interests in the Americas and the West Indies. Pressed, the defense of Jamaica was given priority even over the war in America. Suffice it to say that in 1773, "exports from Grenada alone were worth eight times those from Canada" (*The Sugar Barons*, p. 328). Money always talks, whether it is the eighteenth or twenty-first century, right?

As if it wasn't miserable enough for slaves, lack of supplies and the ensuing threat of starvation among those in the West Indies during the war was well documented. "In 1777, the Leeward Islands petitioned their governor for urgent relief to sustain them through the late summer and early autumn" (*An Empire Divided*, p. 161). There were fears of insurrection because of it, and many nobles begged for provisions. Still, in that year Nevis and St. Kitts each lost 300–400 slaves to malnutrition. Antigua lost over 1,000, and 1,200 died on Montserrat.

There were of course documented freed people throughout the age of slavery, and planters often hired them as well as signed on indentured servants, although that practice with whites largely died out in the latter 1600s. (White indentured servants had a harrowing survival rate, often falling ill to the tropical plagues of yellow fever and malaria, illnesses that Africans had a greater immunity against.) However, the Covington/Banning plan to eventually employ an entirely freed work force is sadly not anything I discovered in my research. That said, planters often freed beloved slaves upon their deaths and, in addition, occasionally left them inheritances.

John Wesley, a prominent Church of England evangelist and leader in a revival movement called Methodism, published the tract *Thoughts on Slavery* in 1774. He wrote that it'd be better for the British islands to be "altogether sunk in the depth of the seas than that they should be cultivated at so high a price as the violation of justice, mercy and truth" (p. 31). Despite enormous obstacles—

given the wealth of sugar traders and politicians who lobbied on their behalf—British abolitionists gradually gained traction, their message largely spread by Quakers and some Methodists. By 1807, it was illegal to buy or sell slaves in the British Empire, and by 1833 it became illegal to own them, thirty-two years before the same happened in the USA. So in crafting this novel, I decided it was a plausible premise for a progressive clan, led by conscience and faith, to try and treat those who labored in their fields and homes with some semblance of dignity and grace.

ACKNOWLEDGMENTS

Many thanks to my Bethany editorial team, Raela Schoenherr, Luke Hinrichs, and Kate Deppe, as well as to my fantastic marketing/ PR team, led by Noelle Chew and Amy Green. In addition, a great group of beta readers reread *Keturah* and *Verity*, then a draft of *Selah*, to make sure I kept things straight through the series (and saved me from a number of embarrassing errors). I am grateful to them all, but especially to Jennifer Kracht, Betsy Hildebrand, Carrie Davis, Mindy Houng, Maria Clara Martino, Kelly Hodgkins, Amanda Lamb, Melanie Stroud, and Amie Loader, who went the extra mile.

Lisa T. Bergren has published more than sixty books with combined sales exceeding three million copies. A recipient of the RT Lifetime Achievement Award, she's also the author of the Christy Award–winning *Waterfall*, RITA-finalist *Firestorm*, bestselling *God Gave Us You*, as well as several historical series such as HOMEWARD and GRAND TOUR. Lisa lives in Colorado with her husband and three big kids—one of whom is newly married—and a fluffy white terrier who makes her walk once in a while rather than just sit around and write. Visit her at www.lisatbergren.com, on Facebook.com/LisaTawnBergren, and on Instagram and Twitter @LisaTBergren.

Sign Up for Lisa's Newsletter!

Keep up to date with Lisa's latest news on book releases and events by signing up for her email list at lisatbergren.com.

More from Lisa T. Bergren!

In 1773, Lady Keturah Banning Tomlinson and her sisters inherit their father's estates and travel to the West Indies to see what is left of their legacy. On the island of Nevis, every man seems to be trying to win Keturah's hand and, with it, the ownership of her plantation. Set on saving their heritage, can she trust God with her future—and her heart?

Keturah
THE SUGAR BARON'S DAUGHTERS #1

✸ BETHANYHOUSE

Stay up to date on your favorite books and authors with our free e-newsletters. Sign up today at bethanyhouse.com.

facebook.com/bethanyhousepublishers

@bethanyhousefiction

Free exclusive resources for your book group at bethanyhouseopenbook.com

You May Also Like . . .

Arabella Lawrence fled on a bride ship wearing the scars of past mistakes. Now in British Columbia, two men vying for her hand disagree on how the natives should be treated during a smallpox outbreak. Intent on helping a girl abandoned by her tribe, will Arabella have the wisdom to make the right decision or will seeking what's right cost her everything?

The Runaway Bride by Jody Hedlund
THE BRIDE SHIPS #2
jodyhedlund.com

Determined to keep his family together, Quinten travels to Canada to find his siblings and track down his employer's niece, who ran off with a Canadian soldier. When Quinten rescues her from a bad situation, Julia is compelled to repay him by helping him find his sister—but soon after, she receives devastating news that changes everything.

The Brightest of Dreams by Susan Anne Mason
CANADIAN CROSSINGS #3
susanannemason.net

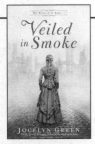

As Chicago's Great Fire steals away their bookshop, Meg and Sylvie Townsend make a harrowing escape from the flames with the help of reporter Nate Pierce. But the trouble doesn't end there—their father is committed to an asylum after being accused of murder, and they must prove his innocence before the asylum truly drives him mad.

Veiled in Smoke by Jocelyn Green
THE WINDY CITY SAGA #1
jocelyngreen.com

BETHANYHOUSE